THE NEXT GENERATION

First published 2024

Copyright © Bill Carmen 2024

The right of Bill Carmen to be identified as the author of this work has been asserted in accordance with the Copyright, Designs & Patents Act 1988.

All rights reserved. No part of this book may be reproduced, stored in a retrieval system, or transmitted in any form or by any means, digital, electronic, electrostatic, magnetic tape, mechanical, photocopying, recording or otherwise, without the written permission of the copyright holder.

Published under licence by Brown Dog Books and
The Self-Publishing Partnership Ltd, 10b Greenway Farm, Bath Rd,
Wick, nr. Bath BS30 5RL, UK

www.selfpublishingpartnership.co.uk

ISBN printed book: 978-1-83952-804-0
ISBN e-book: 978-1-83952-805-7

Cover design by Kevin Rylands
Internal design by Andrew Easton

Printed and bound in the UK

This book is printed on FSC® certified paper

Book three in the *Love in Store* saga

THE NEXT GENERATION

The Young Step Up

BILL CARMEN

BROWN DOG BOOKS

Thanks to all who have contacted me regarding the date of publishing Book 3. The wait is over.

I must thank Clare my wife for her patience when I give her yet something else to read. My IT skills are poor nowadays. It would not happen without your help my love.

Thanks to Yvonne, Julia and Sarah who are my beta readers and point out my errors. Thanks also to my daughter Sarah for her help with the publicity. Thanks to the people at SPP for making a great job of publishing my books.

Thanks to all my readers for your support.

CHAPTER 1

'Declan, wake up, I can smell smoke,' shouted Daisy, panicking. He mumbled something indiscernible then turned over, pulling the blankets up around his neck as he did so. Daisy resorted to shaking and slapping him. She knew he slept very deeply. Turning the bedside light on she saw tendrils of thick smoke coming under the door.

Declan and Daisy were young shop workers, he southern Irish, she a Londoner, who lived together in a flat above their place of work, which was owned by Tim Cooper, their boss.

'Declan, the shop is on fire.' The growing panic in her voice was obvious. Moving towards the bedroom door she was about to open it when Declan shouted.

'Daisy, don't do that, come over here.' This said in a commanding tone of voice that brooked no argument. Now he was approaching the door himself. When he reached it, he tapped the brass doorknob. It was warm but not hot. Kneeling down he opened the door just enough to see out. Hot black smoke billowed into the room.

Shutting the door, he said, 'Daisy, someone has torched the shop. There is a fire alight on the front door mat. The stench of petrol is really strong.' The flames were leaping up the glass. His Irish accent was now clearly discernible, providing proof of his fear and his concern for their lives.

'Get on the floor, we will have to go out the back door.'

Daisy grabbed her handbag, opened a drawer and emptied the contents into it.

'There's no time for that, woman, we will have to go down the stairs backwards on our hands and knees. I will go first, you must stay right behind me. Take a deep breath and hold it for as long as you can. Do you understand? When we get down there, I will point you towards the back door.'

Daisy, now obviously terrified, nodded. Declan started down the stairs. He was in his blue striped pyjamas and she in a long flimsy pink nightie. He could feel the heat building second by second.

Reaching the bottom he lay face down on the floor, pulling Daisy down beside him. There was about ten inches of clear air at floor level, above that there was an impenetrable pall of hot choking black smoke.

Now shouting in Daisy's ear above the roar of the fire he asked her, 'Can you see the door?' He was pointing as he spoke. She nodded at him. He could tell by the look on her face that she was terrified.

'I'm going for the key; I will get us out of here I promise.' He did not know whether she believed him or not. She did, however, start crawling in the right direction. He remained still for a moment, his fear blocking his memory as to the location of the back door key.

'It's in the till,' he said aloud. Turning round he began to make his way towards the heart of the fire, still creeping along on his belly. When he reached the till the heat was almost unbearable. He could not see the machine through the smoke, but he knew he was in the right place, he recognised the bottom of the wooden counter that the till sat on, he had swept round it countless times. Reaching up into the fire and smoke he found and pressed the drawer release. Nothing happened. He tried again, still nothing. When he retrieved his hand the arm of his pyjamas was alight. He spent a few seconds beating it out. He was now in so much pain he had to clutch his badly burnt hand to his chest for a minute while he gathered himself. He began to panic. His breath was shuddering in and out of his body. He could hear someone crying, he didn't realise it was him.

'I can't save her, I can't.'

Then he heard his father's firm voice, 'Declan you can do this, try again,' speaking as he had done all those years before when as a child he occasionally lacked the courage to do what was required.

This time he bunched his fist, took a deep breath, shut his eyes, and sat up. Feeling for the drawer release with his left hand and finding it he started down with his right hand, using it as a club, aiming for his left that was on the drawer release then snatching the lower hand away at the last moment. The draw flew open, for a few seconds he could not remember which compartment the key was in, then he saw in his mind's eye the key sitting in the rear left of the drawer. He scrabbled around for a moment unable to find it, his panic was building. Suppose it was no longer here? Then his fingers closed over it. I must not drop it he said to himself. He removed the key from the drawer and enclosed it in his left hand, his right did not seem to be working very well. Again, he had to smother the flames that had reappeared on his sleeve.

Now down on the floor again he started back towards Daisy, shouting, 'I've got the key, I've got the key.' He realised she could not hear him, and his coughing was getting worse, so he stopped calling out. The journey to the back of the shop that normally took a few seconds now felt like miles and was taking forever as he shuffled along on his belly. The pain on the back of his head and shoulders was growing. He was unaware but as he crawled he was now emitting a high keening sound that was being forced from him by the terrible pain on his back where his pyjamas were on fire. When he reached Daisy he discovered she was motionless, her eyes tight shut. He did not know whether she was alive or dead. Whatever, he was not leaving her here to burn. He had fallen in love with her at first sight, she was the most precious thing in his world. He would get them out of here or die trying.

He dragged her to one side of the door so he could open it. Now he adopted the same technique he had used on the till, a deep breath then sitting up he found the door handle with his left hand and attempted to put the key in the lock with his right and dropped it.

He was shouting, 'No! No! No!' followed by an outpouring of profanity he rarely used. Now he was plain bloody angry. Continuing to shout, he said, 'WE ARE NOT GOING TO DIE HERE.' He was at the same time scrabbling around with his left hand knowing he would find the key; he had felt it bounce off the inside of his knee, so it was trapped between his legs. His right hand was next to useless. He found the key quickly using his left hand. Sliding the key in extremely carefully he turned it, and the door was unlocked. Reaching out for Daisy he could not find her. Now he was frightened. She should be right here, had she crawled away? Then feeling around with his better hand he found her. Pulling the door fully open and grabbing her arm he began to haul her from the building. He was shouting at her, 'Daisy we are not going to die in here. Can you hear me? Hold on, just hold on.'

There was no response. There were lots of bright lights out there, some of them flashing blue. The last thing he saw was two firefighters running towards him.

Police officers and firemen saw a man staggering out through a wall of flame that curled around him, seeming intent on dragging him back into the fire's terrible embrace. He was hauling an apparently dead woman behind him. He stumbled and pitched forward onto his face just clear of the reach of the hungry flames.

* * * * *

Declan had come to in a hospital bed. He was lying on his face staring through a hole in the bedding that allowed him to see the floor and more importantly to breathe. He was trying to work out where he was when he was overwhelmed by the pain in his back and head and his right hand, so painful he had cried out.

He had spent many weeks in hospital, much of it heavily sedated, a lot of that time in great pain. Now discharged, a nurse had arrived every morning at Declan's aunt's house where the young couple lived to change his dressings. This week Daisy, who had been trained to do so, had taken over his care. Every morning and every night Daisy bathed his tortured black claw of a hand with the medication supplied and changed the dressings on his back, his head and legs as required. When he cried out because of the pain of her ministrations her tears fell afresh. He always apologised.

* * * * *

Shop Number One was a burnt-out shell. There were long discussions as to its future. No one was certain what should be done with it. Tim, the owner, was really too upset to discuss it. Now all he had as a memento of his godfather was his small black bible, which contained no proof of its former owner.

Tom Cooper, Tim's father, dressed in his usual mid-brown suit, said, 'Son, you and I both know who owned it. Why not put a few words in there. Something along the lines of the date of his death, his wartime experience and so on.' Tim, wearing his usual navy trousers and pale blue shirt, decided to include the newspaper cutting that contained details of his funeral and of his war service.

* * * * *

Jessica, an attractive, smart young mum in her work apparel, a mid-grey skirt and jacket, was Tim and Sophie's PA,. she was extremely concerned; she had a nasty feeling her ex-husband may have had something to do with the attack on the shop. After the fire he had disappeared. She did not believe he would attempt murder.

No, she thought, he would not know anyone was living there. It was an attack on Tim. On more than one occasion Tim had criticised Gerry's drunken behaviour to his face and had threatened him with the police when he had attacked Jessica and caused her real pain from a damaged eye and an injury to her cheek that required stitches. She would carry the scar for the rest of her life.

CHAPTER 2

Tim sat on the stern of his houseboat the *Sea Maiden*. It was his, Sophie's and their two children's home. It was moored in a boat yard opposite the town of Kingston on Thames next to the river bridge that carried the road over the river.

He had woken early; the cry of the town fox had drawn him from his bed. The grey predawn light and a faint mist off the river clothed the town across the water, the other boats and the grove of trees away to his right in a hazy shroud. The fox, peering out from the woodland's edge held Tim with a fixed gaze. A tug sliding by sounded its horn to warn others of its intention to navigate the central span of the bridge. Tim glanced at the craft with its line of rusty-sided empty barges then snapped his eyes back to the trees; the fox had gone. A few minutes later he heard its bark from some distance away. It was barely audible. Tim was sure the animal was calling goodbye, from one early riser to another.

Now he could hear the whump, whump, whump of swan wings as a vee of the majestic white birds flew from his right under the central span of the bridge, past him and on down the river into the distance.

Tim felt the boat roll slightly. Turning his head he saw Sophie, his wife, was making her way carefully down the narrow deck on the side of the boat, clad in pink pyjamas and a matching warm dressing gown carrying two large mugs of steaming tea. Looking at Tim's threadbare old navy dressing gown she made a mental note to replace it.

She sat down carefully, cross legged, intent on not spilling the contents of the mugs. Tim kissed her good morning and thanked her for the drink.

Tim had just taken a sip of the scalding hot tea. There was an appreciative 'Mmm' as he cuddled the cup with both hands.

'I do not know how you can drink it this hot,' she observed.

'I can't abide cold tea,' he replied.

'I heard our fox, Tim.'

'He was in those trees,' he said, pointing away down the bank to his right.

'What woke you?' she asked.

'I came to realising its thirty-five years since my mum died. It feels like so long ago, so much has changed. I was a grubby thirteen-year-old schoolboy when mum died of the flu. I started work part time on our market stall. I skipped school to do it. Mum's death had made Dad incapable, he went into a terrible depression. Mum had been the rock that the family was built on. She was so strong. She was extremely active in the women's suffrage movement. When she was handing out her leaflets and standing on her box doing her speeches about women's rights on Hyde Park Corner. She got into a lot of arguments with men who believed women should know their place.'

Sophie had heard the story numerous times, but she never said anything. It was Tim's way of understanding his life and reminding himself of the detail.

'I was thinking about this myself a while back. I believe your mum's death was the trigger for everything you have achieved since,' said Sophie.

'How do you mean?'

'Well if she had not passed away who knows what you would have done. I suspect you may still be working on your father's market stall. The trauma and your dad's collapse as a result of her demise, and your anger when he made you homeless, was, I believe, the catalyst to make you achieve. You were an extremely driven young man when I met you on the train, but now you are—'

Tim interrupted her to say, 'I know what's coming, now I am an extremely driven old man.'

Sophie corrected him, 'No, now you are a very driven middle-aged man.'

Tim kissed her on the ear, something she professed she disliked.

She slapped him on the arm. 'Look at what you have achieved, Tim,' she continued. 'Two delicatessens, the food hall selling the widest range of continental food in all of London. The restaurant, the staff you have given jobs to. The Longstaff Charitable Trust in memory of your great aunt that supports poorer families to allow their children to go on to further education.'

'Sophie love, there is no way I can take all the credit for everything you have mentioned, you have been an enormous support to me. We would not be where we are now without your input and that of the staff. I know Jessica does a lot of hours at home for the Longstaff Trust that she doesn't charge us for. She calls it her charity work. And the others all walk the extra mile to do their jobs as well as possible.'

The young couple were both silent for a while, then Sophie said, 'I remember how close we came to not finding each other again as that woman you employed lied to me about your relationship. She made it sound as though you were all but married. How surprised was I a year later when I found your shop with my name over the door.'

'I remember the image of you standing in the shop doorway bathed in light, wearing your cream outfit. You looked as though you had captured the sun itself,' recalled Tim.

'When you saw me I was so embarrassed—'

Interrupting her Tim said, 'You took flight. Thank God I could run faster than you.'

'I am glad you can run faster than me.' She was smiling as she bumped shoulders with him.

The young couple sat in a comfortable silence for a while watching the river.

Sophie shivered, saying, 'I am cold now, Tim, would you like a fresh cup of tea?' Tim, nodded, then followed her along the side of the boat as they went down to breakfast.

* * * * *

As Tim pushed his plate away he was looking at his watch, he said, 'Nanny's late today, is she ill?'

'No,' replied Sophie, 'her family are down from the north, so she is having a few days off. She did say she would come in if we needed her. I have a light week so I think we will be ok. I hope I am not tempting fate by saying that.'

Sophie held down two jobs, the first was as partner and financial director for Sophie's, the chain of shops and the restaurant that Tim was the chairman of. She also was the financial director of another large store in the high street. Privately she was proud of the fact that the owner of the store, Mr Wells, had head-hunted her. It was a job she knew she had got on merit, unlike the Sophie's job that people could say was hers because she was family.

Nanny was an essential member of the team. Initially she had been taken on as her title suggested to look after the children. She was a fully trained graduate from the Westminster Nursery service and still wore her uniform, a mid-green skirt blouse and jacket. There had been an unpleasant experience with a new housekeeper, who on her first day had started decluttering the kitchen, known as the galley on the boat. She then smacked Charlotte, known as Charley, their young daughter for bringing the items that had been discarded, the saucepans and one set of cutlery amongst them, back on board.

When the woman explained this to Sophie, adding it wouldn't take her long to sort the rest of the boat, Sophie's Italian temper burst into flames. As Tim said, it didn't end well, with the lady concerned running from the boat yard picking up her belongings that Sophie had thrown after her as she went.

After a short discussion Nanny had suggested herself for the post. Agreement was reached unanimously. She had been an essential cog in the wheel ever since and was much loved.

CHAPTER 3

Declan and Daisy were sitting around his aunt's breakfast table discussing the fire and their future.

Declan's Aunt Megan, dressed in her usual full-length dress, this one a dark red, broke into the conversation saying, 'You can live here as long as you like,' Megan was now laughing quietly, 'as long as you keep paying the rent.' She was teasing Daisy, who had insisted they paid a proper rent rather than the miniscule amount the older woman had proposed.

Declan's health continued to improve. He was waiting for Daisy to come home from work. His thoughts drifted back to his recovery in the hospital. The memory most uppermost in his mind was the pain that often persisted, even with the most powerful painkillers they were able to give him. He had spent a long time lying on his face while the burns on his back and head healed. His hand had been the worst. Taking the dressings on and off was a terrible experience. The pain together with the appearance was horrific. His right hand was in the beginning a black claw. To him it appeared to be something out of a horror movie. How could Daisy ever love him now? He had been warned that the hair on the back of his head may not regrow. His left hand was nowhere near as bad, although there would always be scar tissue. The sites around his body where the skin had been taken for the skin grafts had been sore as well. In the days after the surgery he was often unaware of people's presence at his hospital bed side.

For some time he was ignorant of Daisy sitting by his bed reading every evening when she was not working.

Slowly he had become more conscious of people around him and that she was always sitting there, her presence lending him support. He had not known what to say to her. How could any woman be expected to still love someone as grotesque as he was now, or would be, even after the healing.

One evening he had decided he needed to tell her they could not get married. He had been able to put his head on one side for the last few days so he could read her face. She was as ever wrapped up in a book.

'Hallo,' he'd croaked, 'we need to talk.'

Daisy's face had lit up, her smile was a mile wide, he remembered, her face was sunshine and rain as her emotions overcame her. Standing up she had leant in and kissed his cheek, the only part of him she could reach because of the dressings. He saw she was wearing the pale blue frock he loved, and he could smell her perfume. It was an indicator that some of the damage he had sustained in the fire was repairing itself.

'We can't get married,' he'd said.

Daisy had responded as though he had hit her as she flinched away from him. 'What do you mean? Why not?' she'd asked.

'You haven't seen what I look like under these bandages,' he'd replied. 'I look like something out of a horror film, I have a claw rather than a hand, the left one is not much better. My head and back's all burnt to hell, so it is.' All this had been said with Declan fighting back the tears.

A young nurse was going to enter the room. A senior nurse had stopped her and closed the door quietly, then she'd said, 'Leave them be, they need to sort this out. It's her courage they need now.'

Daisy had lost her temper and had said, 'Now another man is making decisions about my life without consulting me.' The couple both knew she was referring to her father, who had beaten both her and her mother and had tried to rape Daisy. 'The only reason I am standing here,' she had reminded him, 'is because you saved me. The time it would've taken for them to find me I'd have died, the firemen told me that. We don't need to get married, Mr O' Connor,' she had said, 'but there's one thing I promises you, for the rest of your life every time you turns around I'll be there, married or not.' She could see the tears running down his face. He was mumbling something she could not hear. She had leant closer.

'I can't do it, Daisy,' he had explained. 'The pain and everything. It's all just too hard. When I gets out of here I don't know if I'll be able to work, its hopeless. I– I won't be able to support you, lass,' he'd stammered.

Declan would always remember every word of her response, talking through her own tears and no longer speaking with the horrid rasp that the smoke and the heat had left her with. She had said, 'Declan darlin', you won't be doin' nuffin alone ever again, we'll be doin' it together, and as for your appearance I will always see the hero who saved my life. I loves you and always will. We'll manage, I promise.'

Her reply had given him the strength to continue. The doctors reported a continuing improvement in their patient from then on.

CHAPTER 4

There was a brisk conversation underway in the office. All the staff had gone home, only board members, plus Oliver and Jessica were present. The couple both wearing the company pale grey.

Tim had just proposed that Daisy be offered the job of manager of the food hall.

'I don't think she'll take it,' said Tom, 'she gets very nervous sometimes.'

Harry broke in, 'You're wrong, Tom, she and I have had a number of conversations about the changes she would make. She's completely at home on the shop floor talking to the customers. We had this discussion when we asked her to manage shop Number Two. I will have a small bet with you, I think she will jump at the chance, you wait and see.'

'We haven't agreed to offer it to her yet,' Tim reminded them. 'The alternative is to bring in a stranger. Also, I have to admit I am unable to give it the time it needs. In my opinion she has all the skills required. I would rather promote one of our own. Now there's a thought, how about you doing it, Dad, or you, Harry? You two definitely have all the experience. Why didn't I think of this earlier?'

'You can forget that, son, the hours will be horrendous. I am too bally old, no thank you,' said his father.

'That leaves you then, Harry, when can you start?'

Harry folded his arms across the front of his navy jumper that matched his trousers and said, 'If the girls were not here I would tell you what you can do with your job. I am thinking about retiring. Going home to Italy to sit in the sun.' He knew Sara, his wife, would never agree, they had discussed it a while back. She had said, 'This is our home here, Harry, everyone we knew in Italy will have passed away or moved. No, we are staying here. I do not want to talk about it any more, the subject is closed.'

Harry continued. 'I am though quite sure of our Daisy, she will snatch your arm off, you wait and see. She has a host of things she would like to try.'

Sophie said, 'I think she will take the job, but I would like to spread her salary increase over a year. This way if the job does get too much for her in the early days the drop in income will not be so painful for her.'

'Can I say something?' asked Oliver. Tim nodded. 'I understand what Sophie is saying but I think the increase needs to be substantial in the beginning to carry her through the early days when it will be extremely hard work for her. Too small an amount and the effort will not feel worth it.'

Sophie looked across at Oliver and was silent for a moment or two then said, 'You have a point, Oliver, the salary needs to be big enough to hold her in the job when she realises it's dark outside and she has been there for twelve hours already.'

'Ok, can we vote please?' asked Tim.

The decision was a unanimous yes. It was obvious to all that Tom had not voted yes immediately. He had a good look around the table to see what the others thought and then he had obviously decided he could not be the only one who voted no so he put his hand up.

CHAPTER 5

Daisy was walking to the company office. A day ago she had received a phone call asking her to attend a meeting at 9 am to contribute to a discussion about upcoming changes. She was a little nervous. As usual she had checked her memory but could think of nothing she had done wrong.

Early that morning Declan had said, 'I can tell you're nervous; just remember you are damn good at what you do so you are. Say it out loud now.'

'Don't be silly, I'm not going to say that. I'll feel right daft.' Strangely enough she had felt better after she had done as he asked. Looking around as she walked she established that no one was in earshot and said, 'I am damn good at what I do.' It did work. She sensed she was standing more upright.

Declan had also advised on her clothing, suggesting her black skirt and white blouse with a thin foldup plastic mack in her bag.

As she strode up the path towards the front door of the house that contained the offices it was opened by Tim with a welcoming smile on his face.

Tim said, 'Good morning, Daisy, come on in.' He noticed that as usual she was five minutes early.

Stepping into the meeting room she saw that Sophie, Harry, Tom, Jessica and Oliver were already seated. Coffee was being poured and nibbles were making their way around the table. They were all smiling and saying good morning.

Sophie asked, 'Are you well?'

Daisy, reaching for a biscuit and not knowing why she was there said, 'I saw somethin' on the telly last week that I've just remembered. "The condemned man ate a hearty meal."'

Everybody roared with laughter.

Sophie reached over and held Daisy's hand. 'This not a lynching,' she said, still laughing. 'We know you have some ideas for the food hall, we would like you to share them with us.'

Daisy saw Jessica open her note pad.

'Ok. Wooden sign posts pointing to the various stalls, sayin' what they are and where. If you're not very tall on busy days you can't see where everything is. Signs on the stalls themselves. Café to have a drinks licence, just beer and wine. More bushes around the edges where there's enough light. Uniforms for the staff, they are using their own clothes at the moment and that can be expensive. Also with us all wearing our street clothes you can't tell us from the public, that needs to happen now. Music. Other people's stalls, this will make more people come in to our shop. Do you want me to go on?' One way-out idea she'd had was to give the walkways between the stalls street names so that the sign posts made more sense. Perhaps something for the future she thought.

There was a long silence. Clearly everybody was stunned by Daisy's vision of what was needed. There were raised eyebrows and shaking of heads.

Sophie knew what had prompted Daisy to give it this much thought, she always behaved as though the shops were hers. She was sure the young woman had said to herself if this shop were mine I would do this that and the other. Turning to Daisy she asked, 'Is there more?'

As Daisy began to reply, already nodding her head, Sophie stopped her, saying, 'We will put you together with Jessica to get the rest.'

Daisy sat back in her chair relaxed now that her part was over. She was quite pleased with herself at the way she had handled it. Checking off the remainder of her list in her mind so as not to forget anything later she almost missed the mention of her name and then Tim's question.

'So what do you think, Daisy, would you like to do it?' Tim asked.

'Sorry, do what? I didn't hear, I was going through the rest of my list so that I didn't miss nothin.'

Tim smiled. She's just like me he thought, always working. 'We would like you to take on the manager's job for the food hall.'

Daisy was shocked, she almost instinctively said no. Suddenly her mind flashed back to the day her mother found the newspaper in the wastepaper basket in the offices they were cleaning at 1 am. Her mother had insisted she go to the interview. She had got the job with Sophie's. She could feel her mother standing beside her now, saying, "You can do this, girl; don't you dare say no."

Sitting up straight, she said, 'Yes please, I would.' There were a couple of shocked faces around the table, Tom's the most obvious.

Tim welcomed her into her new job, 'I am sure you will be fantastic at it, well done. Perhaps now I can have Sundays off.'

There was a lot of hugging from the women and handshaking from the men.

Daisy's only thought was, 'Wait till I tells me mum.'

The meeting was nearing its end when Tim called for any other business. Daisy waited to the end, then said, 'Can we talk about the uniforms please?'

Tim said, 'Can you do some research and let us have some figures? We will discuss it.'

'I'm quite happy to bring Daisy's stuff to the board if everyone agrees,' said Harry, looking at Daisy as he said it. She nodded.

At the end of the meeting Tim asked, 'Can you stay behind, Daisy, and tell Jessica what the basics are that you would like to introduce. Is that ok, Jessica?'

'Yes, I can type up the minutes later.' The two women walked into the other room, discussing Daisy's ideas.

Bonny, the second member of the admin team working directly for Jessica, came through from the kitchen and hugged her. 'Well done, you will be brilliant at it.' Bonny had suffered with polio as a child. This had left her with a shortened leg that meant her wearing a built-up shoe and matching navy trousers. Everyone loved her for her courage and disposition. She was well named.

Making her way home an hour later Daisy remembered nothing of the journey, in her mind she was in the food hall stepping out the distances to try and visualise how her changes would look and work.

* * * * *

She would go home and check up on Declan before she went to walk around the food hall. Some days were better for him than others. She knew they would both have died that day if it had not been for him and his courage to withstand the terrible burns the fire had inflicted on him.

He wore a soft black leather glove to protect his hand and hide the awful scars. Those on his head and back he hid with a grey cap and a matching jacket.

He will not believe that I have been offered it. He won't believe me when I tell him I have accepted it, she thought. Reaching Declan's aunt's house where they had been lodging since the fire, she found her husband and his Aunt Megan sat around the kitchen table with tea and biscuits.

'Come on then, tell us what Tim wanted,' said Declan's aunt.

'You'll never believe this: he wanted me to take over the running of the food hall.'

'What did you say?' asked Declan, surprise and pride writ large on his face.

'I said no of course, I'd make a real dog's breakfast of it.'

'Opportunities like this come along so rarely, you have to grab hold of them with both hands when they turn up,' said Aunt Megan. 'Never mind it's too late now.'

Declan was silent, shaking his head, then he said, 'We need the money. I will have to go back full time.' Declan had a part-time job at the food hall keeping the litter under control.

'No you won't, I took the job, and apparently I will earn a lot more money eventually.'

Declan climbed from his chair slowly. Some of the scars still pulled a little when he changed position. Wrapping her into his arms he whispered, 'Thank you.'

When Declan had resumed his seat Megan asked, 'Why eventually will the money be good, why not now?'

'Because there is a lot to learn, but the starting money's good.' She told them how much it was and then added, 'It will go up considerably in the future.'

'Oh wow,' said Declan's aunt. 'We shall have to call you Miss Daisy.' Daisy was not sure why Megan had called her that, or what she meant.

Declan reached out with his good hand and squeezed hers, saying, 'I am so proud of you.'

Later in bed that night he was holding her to him with his good arm. Immediately after the fire he would not let her see his injuries. Now he had mended enough for Daisy to do all his dressings. She had been firm with him. 'I would have died if it were not for you. The least I can do is help look after you. Now just lie still while I change this.'

They talked long into the night, one of the subjects was children.

'If you are going to work some very tough hours how do we fit children into our lives?' asked Declan.

'I have been thinking about that. I notice every time the pain grips you.'

'I do try not to let you see.'

'I know, but I have been thinking, how do you feel about becoming a house husband? I work you look after the children. If you felt ok you could walk the baby to the food hall, we could have lunch together, often.'

'Let me think about it. Now tell me about the meeting, what did they say?'

Daisy spent the next twenty minutes relaying all that had been said. 'One or two of them was right surprised when I accepted the job, Tom especially. I began to have some second thoughts on the way home, but I said what you made me say earlier. Tim explained that if I have staffing problems Oliver will step in and help. I don't think I will, there are no nasty people there, and by the way, if I makes a go of it the money will be twice what I'm earnin' now.'

Declan lay awake a long time that night. He was surprised by his wife's suggestion; he was always sure it would be him who was the wage earner. How would other people treat him, would

they think he was lazy? He knew many were quick to make judgements about others. Could he spend all day nursing babies? He would have to find a hobby. How hard can it be, he asked himself?

* * * * *

The following morning at lunch time Daisy walked down the road and registered at the local library, something she had never done before. She'd realised overnight she had no qualifications for her new job, maybe a couple of books on the whys and wherefores might help, that would at least let her sound as though she had a grip on the job. She made a determined effort to try to understand the content, there were words that tripped her up. Declan was an avid reader and never minded answering her questions.

One evening he slid a brown paper parcel across the table towards her but kept his hand on it.

'Now, Daisy, I don't want you thinking this present means I'm not going to help you anymore. This is for when I'm out or whatever.'

When she stripped the wrapping from it and discovered it was a dictionary, a new one, the tears started falling. The old Daisy could never imagine needing a dictionary,

'Look inside the front cover,' said Declan. Before she did as he had asked she fondled the book, lifting it to her nose and sniffing it. She read both the front and back cover and roamed through the pages. For her this was such a big day in her life. Anybody who knew her when she was cleaning would never have believed the young office cleaner Daisy Green would need a library card or own a dictionary. Eventually she did as Declan had asked and found the inside page, where it said: "To my clever wife, Daisy, with all my love, Declan."

CHAPTER 6

At 4.30 am she accepted the fact that she was not going to get any more sleep that night. She had lain awake through the small hours, going through all of the problems that she might face in the day ahead. Having given everything careful thought she decided that much to her surprise she was ready.

Declan rolled over carefully and asked, 'Are you looking forward to the big day?'

She did not answer straight away. Having checked her state of mind one more time she said, 'I am.'

Declan raised an eyebrow, silently questioning what she had just said.

'I am ready, I really am. You won't believe me but I'm looking forward to it. I've got so many plans for the food hall, just you wait and see. I'm getting up now, do you want a cuppa?'

Declan took her arm and said, 'I don't doubt you, Daisy love, but you've changed so you have. When we met you were a mouse, an extremely lovable one but a mouse, now you are a tough business lady.' Daisy went to interrupt, Declan raised a hand to stop her. 'Just remember back to when your mum got you to apply for a job here at Sophie's, you tried to cancel the appointment didn't you? Then when you were offered the manager's job at shop Number Two you tried to refuse. You only took the job because Sophie would not take your no for an answer. Now you have been offered the manager's job in the food hall, the toughest of them all, and you snatched their arm off, so you did. I am so proud of you; I know you will make a wonderful job of it.' Daisy did not let on that the same memory of her mother's words had occurred to her. As Daisy arrived at the large, varnished heavy oak doors to the food hall a London church bell began ringing the time. Six o'clock. To her surprise the door opened as she went to put her key in.

'Good morning, Daisy,' said Enzo. 'Another early riser.'

'How did you know I was here?' she asked.

'I saw you walking in,' he replied. 'I'm looking forward to working with you, it will be easier having just one person to liaise with. Tim and Sophie are so busy these days.'

'Hopefully I'll be able to take some of the load off them,' said Daisy. 'I know Sophie worries about Tim since he had his ticker trouble.'

'Daisy, you and I should be able to solve most of the problems between us. I hope all we will need is a yes or no from either of them.' Daisy nodded in agreement.

She followed Enzo into the food hall. He looked back and called, 'Good luck,' and waved as he began to run up the stairs to the restaurant.

Daisy walked into the middle of the large space, put her hands on her hips and slowly turned around through a full circle. It was pretty good. There was a half-full box of pasta on the floor stowed behind a stall. She decided to address that later on when everyone had got used to her. She picked the box up and placed it on the counter. Half an hour later Enzo called down, 'Daisy, have you time for a coffee?'

'Yes please,' she replied as she made her way towards the stairs. After, she and Enzo had chatted for a while. He was making a wonderful bechamel sauce and allowed her to lick the spoon. She finished her drink and started downstairs. Halfway down she stopped and looked out over the food hall and a huge feeling of pride overwhelmed her. Little Daisy the urchin from the slums was trusted to be in charge of all this. She muttered, 'Thanks,

Mum,' before she continued down to start her day.

As the staff began to arrive Daisy was standing by the open door greeting them, shaking their hands and exchanging names, and apologising in advance in case she forgot their names or got them wrong in the future.

When 8.30 arrived she asked Enzo to close the doors while she introduced herself.

'Can everyone come over here so I can have a few words please?' Once they had moved in and settled she said, 'I expect some of you have concerns as to what sort of boss I am going to be. I share your concern. At four am this morning I nearly phoned in sick.' There was a variation in the response, from smiles to belly laughs. She let them quieten down then she said, 'Some of you will have heard the tales about my family, the Greens. Some will be the truth; some will be fiction. I am going to tell you the truth, so you know who you are dealing with. You will be told my father is in prison, this is correct. He's in there for stealing money from Shop Number One. That's the one that used to be Mr Woodman's hardware store that got burnt down. It was the first Sophie's Delicatessen. My father is in there for attacking mum and me and a policeman, plus other minor thefts. I'm not tellin' you to gain your sympathy, I just want us to be straight from the beginning, when people say you know she's a Green you can say, "Yeh she told us".

'A few easy rules. Don't try and cover up your mistakes, we all make 'em, and I will find out. Next, never, never lie to me, it's the one thing guaranteed to make me lose my temper,' then smiling she added, 'and that ain't a pretty sight.' That met with a mixed reaction. 'I have one thing I think you'll be pleased about. I am hoping the company will agree to us having a uniform. This'll save your own clothes and make us more obvious to our customers. Finally, my name is Daisy, not Mrs O' Connor, Miss or Mrs, just Daisy.' Putting a hand on Enzo's shoulder she said, 'Last but not least, as most of you know this is Enzo. He is our master chef who is in charge of the first Sophie's restaurant that you can find upstairs.' She said this pointing towards the ceiling. 'Can you open the door please, Enzo?'

Before he went to do as she asked he whispered, 'Thank you for the promotion, but chef will do ta.'

As the staff began to make their way to their workstations Daisy called out, 'Good luck to you all.'

* * * * *

The first customers entered the building, all chattering, some laughing, some with eyes wide open and mouths agape as they saw the size of the food hall.

Enzo leant in close to her as he started on his way up to his restaurant and said, 'Well done.' She smiled in reply. She never did tell anyone that she had spent hours reading out loud the script her husband had written out for her after they had cooperated on the wording. For Daisy the day passed all too quickly. All her qualms about doing the job fell away. She left work that evening tired but extremely happy. An even bigger plus was that when she arrived home Declan had put a celebratory meal together. It was one of her favourites, egg, bacon, chips and beans. Megan confirmed that Declan had cooked the whole meal. The first time since his injuries.

* * * * *

A month later Tim and Enzo were sharing a late-night drink in the now empty restaurant. Enzo still had his apron and chef's hat on.

They were sitting on the slightly raised section in the far corner. There was a window that looked down into the food hall.

Tim asked Enzo, 'Why is there never anyone sitting here, and who is it reserved for?' While he was speaking he was pushing the dark varnished reserved sign with the gold writing about with his finger.

'You, Tim, it's reserved for you and the family, whenever you want to use it.'

'Who decided that then, Enzo?'

'The staff, Tim. One night we were extremely busy, all the tables were full, and somebody said what do we do if the family wants to eat here. Nobody was happy with that, I can tell you. So your table, this table, remains reserved.'

'How about we agree that if this table is the only one left and one of our high-spending regular customers arrives you sit them here?'

'If that's what you want, Tim, so be it. I can tell you now the staff will not be best pleased. They all have a great regard for you and the family.' He knew that this time Tim's directive was almost certainly going to be ignored. 'One other thing, Tim, I think we need to make it clear that our regular patrons will have to book their tables.'

'Really, Enzo?'

'Yes, and while we are talking I would like to discuss my wages in the near future, please.'

'That's fine, can you have a word with Jessica and ask her to book us a time? I owe you an apology. I should have done something about it before. Sorry.'

* * * * *

'So how do you think she is doing, Enzo?' asked Tim.

'Do you mean Daisy?' he asked.

Tim nodded. 'She is doing very well; she has the job by the throat, as we used to say back home. I think Daisy has given everything a great deal of thought, not just this shop but I suspect since she started working for you. I was talking to Harry about her the other day. He told me she is constantly working out how to improve the appearance, the sales figures and so on.

She is extremely good with the staff, always happy to help, whether its business or personal.'

'Thank you, Enzo. I will talk to Sophie and see if we can't increase her salary a bit.'

Daisy's next pay slip was a surprise, there was more in it than there should be. She rang Sophie in her tea break. When she queried the amount Sophie confirmed they thought her start had been very good and that needed recognising.

Daisy was staggered. She stammered a thank you and rang off. When she told Declan and his aunt over dinner that evening they were both thrilled for her.

Declan, laughing, said, 'That means I can have two beers down the pub on a Friday night.' Daisy just shook her head and rolled her eyes.

* * * * *

Tim had just arrived at his office when there was a tap on the open door with Jessica standing in the entrance waiting to talk to him. She was her usual immaculate self, a smart pale grey suit with a pencil skirt, a tailored jacket and black heels. Her dark hair was attractively cut into a bob.

'Morning,' said Tim.

'Good morning, Tim,' was the response. 'I'm sorry. I owe you an apology, I forgot to remind you about Enzo's salary increase.'

'Not to worry,' he replied. 'We can deal with it in the near future.'

'No Tim, I think we need to deal with it now. Some friends invited me out to lunch on Saturday to a nice restaurant across town, I forget the name. When I arrived Enzo was disappearing into the kitchen following the resident chef. I don't think he saw me.'

'Hmm,' was Tim's response. He thought for a moment then said, 'Have you got time to research what kind of money good chefs earn these days?'

'I am up to my neck in work, Tim.'

'I can do it Tim,' said Bonny as she walked through the open door. 'I know Jessica is snowed under.'

'I will get back to it, Tim, if that is ok,' said Jessica as she turned for the door.

'Thanks, Jessica,' replied Tim as she left. 'Take a seat, Bonny, while we work this out. We need to find out what the going rate is for someone of Enzo's skills. Ring Sophie, she is at her day job.' Bonny knew Tim referring to Sophie's job like this was his idea of a joke. In fact, her job as accountant, financial adviser and board member with a large rival store was an indicator of her education and financial skills. She was rightly proud of the fact that Mr Wells, the owner, had head-hunted her.

'Bonny,' said Tim as he stood up and walked over and shut the door. 'How are you two coping with the workload?' As Bonny went to reply he cut her short, saying, 'I don't want any flannel, Bonny, just tell me the truth.'

Bonny was silent for a moment then said, 'I don't want to say anything behind Jessica's back, Tim.'

Tim stood up walked to the door, opened it and called to Jessica to join them. As she entered he closed the door, pulled up another chair and indicated she should be seated.

Walking round his desk to his seat he said, 'I'm not apportioning blame here, if anyone is in the wrong it's me. I have put more and more work on your shoulders without questioning whether you can cope.' Jessica went to speak. He cut her off, saying, 'Jessica, your forgetting Enzo's salary increase is a clear indicator you are overworked. You never forget. That's my fault and no one else's. I am carrying the blame. What do you need to put it right?'

The two women looked at each other, then Bonny said, 'A girl Friday to handle the basics.' Jessica nodded.

Tim, noticing Jessica's frown, said to her, 'None of this will cross your desk.'

'Bonny, do you think you can handle this? If there is overtime you will charge me for it.' This was said as he looked at her with a query on his face. There was no initial response from the younger women, he could see the wheels going round. He was impressed that she was giving it thought. Now she was nodding, 'Can I ask Jessica for advice now and then?'

Tim nodded then said, 'Yes, but you have to do the work. Jessica your role in this is minimal. Bonny you can work with Sophie if necessary. I will warn her you will be in touch.' Looking at both women he asked, 'Is that ok?' Both agreed and went back to work.

Two weeks later he was introduced to an extremely young woman who was clearly terribly shy and embarrassed at meeting the big boss. Her face was flame red. She was wearing a pale blue blouse and matching smart trousers. Her name was Lynda. He had been assured she was good at what she was doing, filing etc.

'She is fresh out of college and has brought some clever ideas with her,' said Bonny.

CHAPTER 7

He heard Sophie's scream coming from up on the deck above him.

'Tim,' she shouted, 'Martyn has fallen in the water.' He could hear the panic and fear in her voice, running from the rear cabin through the lounge towards the bow, slamming the dining table out of his way as he ran, a small glass vase of daffodils fell and broke. Vaulting a low stool he rushed on. Sophie was crying out again, 'Tim, Tim, please help, I cannot reach him.'

Tim took in the scene at a glance, Sophie was holding onto the deck rail reaching down to try and help her son.

'Stand back,' he shouted as he leapt from the deck, vaulting the rail into the water, landing beside the boy. Martyn was hanging on to a rope dangling from a ring on the neighbouring boat. The water was only about four feet deep, but too deep for Martyn.

Grabbing hold of the terrified child he said, 'Hold on to me. Whatever happens don't let go.' In an instant the child was floating beside him holding Tim's shirt with both hands. The boy's knuckles were white, displaying the strength of his grip. Tim braced his back against the *Sea Maiden*, then moving one leg at a time he walked up the side of the other boat that was moored beside them and pushed it away a little. He knew he was strong enough under normal river conditions to stop the two boats coming together. Martyn on his own, however, could have been crushed or swept away in the current, or both.

Another figure strode into the water to arrive beside Tim. He was stripping his shirt off as he did so. He was tall and strongly built and spoke with an Irish accent. He threw his shirt up onto the deck of the *Sea Maiden*.

'Let me have him, Tim. I'll walk him out.'

'Thanks, Paddy,' said Tim as he lifted his son up and placed him in his neighbour's arms. 'How did you know we needed help?'

'I heard Sophie cry out. She sounded very scared, quite rightly with the boy in the water.'

No sooner had he handed the boy to the Irishman than a wash from a passing boat travelling much too fast began to force the two craft together. As hard as he tried Tim was losing the battle, now he was in danger of being injured himself. Paddy handed the boy up to Sophie on the deck then turned around and adopted the same stance as Tim, his legs braced against one boat, his back against the other. The combined weight of the two boats was measured in tonnes and the power of the waves had both men grunting out loud to avoid themselves being crushed. It took all of their combined strength to hold them apart. After a while, the wash subsided, and the two men walked ashore.

'I am going to have a drink, Paddy, when I have changed, I hope you will join me?'

'I will, thank you.'

I'll get the table out.' Entering the boat he found Sophie was clearing up the broken shards of the pretty glass vase that was a victim of the drama.

'Are you all right?' he asked her as he stripped off his wet clothing and wrapped himself in his dressing gown. He cuddled her to him. He could feel her silently sobbing into his chest. He was about to ask her where the boy was when he heard the bath stop filling.

Fighting to regain control, she said, 'Lately I have been having a recurring nightmare, only in it we are not as lucky as we were today, and that family that have just moved away, they will never get over the loss of their daughter. Tim, I know we both love it on here, but it is too dangerous for the children.'

Too dangerous for Martyn, he thought. His daughter Charley always moved around as though she were part of the boat. She was perfectly in tune with the movement, even in rough weather she walked around always in full control, a handhold in exactly the right place. She had perfect balance. She was the best of all of them. His son, however? He loved the boy of course but he could not work out how the child was so accident prone and timid. So far he could see no special skills in the boy. He was in nearly every regard a polar opposite of the rest of the family.

As the warm evening sun went down the other boaters joined Paddy, Tim and family on the hard standing in front of the boats. They brought their own tables and chairs and food and drink. All were shared. There was a discussion about the events that had just occurred. It was pointed out that Sophie's were the only babies on the boatyard.

Charley turned to her mother saying, 'I am not a baby, Mother.'

This made everyone laugh and lightened the mood. The only one who didn't think it was funny was Charley, who pulled a face.

Tim lay in bed that night trying to think of a way of making the boat safer. Bigger fenders may help. I'll do some research he promised himself.

Before Sophie slept she said a prayer for her son. One memory she would hold onto was when Paddy had stripped his shirt off and strode into the water. He was a perfect figure of a man. Tall, broad chested, a perfect six pack, narrow waist and in soaking wet trousers there was little hidden. She felt herself blushing.

CHAPTER 8

Tim and Sophie's clever daughter Charley was sitting in one of her favourite classes, mathematics, at the local grammar school. She was wearing her black with white stripes uniform. There had been discussion in the household as to whether she should attend a private girls' school. Tim was for it, Sophie against it.

'Tim, I believe she will receive a broader education at a mixed grammar, I know I am her mother and therefore biased, but I will be surprised if she is not able to pick the university of her choice later. She will bring that laser sharp intellect to it and shine.'

'I hope you're right; it will be a great shame if she only receives a mediocre education.' There was an extended silence while both of them digested what had been said.

'One thing I am sure of, Tim, is that if she feels it is not satisfactory she will let us know.'

'On reflection I think you're right. She has no problem explaining to me why she is right, and I am wrong. Lately it has been about thirty-love to her.'

At dinner one evening a few weeks later Charley asked, 'Mummy, can I attend evening classes? A girl in my class goes to mathematics classes twice a week after school. I would like to go with her. She said it is great fun.'

Tim had never heard mathematics described as great fun.

'Where are the courses held?' asked Sophie.

'At my school.'

'How will you get there?' asked Tim.

'Jane thinks her mummy will call for me. At lunch today she showed me some of the stuff she is doing. Let me get a note pad.'

Twenty minutes later Sophie and Charley were deep into whatever it was that Charley was showing them. Tim had been lost after the first few minutes. He had been able to tell by the questions Sophie was asking that she grasped the idea if not the detail.

'Do you see, Daddy?' asked his daughter.

There was a pause, then he said, 'To be honest, my darling, no I don't, but I am glad you get so much from it.'

Sophie reached over and took Tim's hand, 'Charley my love, your father left school not much older than you are now because his mummy died. Her death made Grandpa Tom very ill, so your father had to leave school and try to earn a living for both of them. All that we have is because your father worked incredibly long hours so that we are now comfortably off. Imagine if next year you had to leave school and stand out in all weathers ten, eleven hours a day and earn very little to begin with.'

Tim said, 'Harry was a great help and Mr Woodman was always there when I needed him, they both were. And your mother has helped ever since we met, Charley.' There followed a long silence, Tim was lost in his memories. He remembered how hard he had to work, how he sat up at nights going over the paperwork, in the winter rising when it was still dark to open the stall for the early birds, as he called them, those who did similar long hours to him. Spending hours on his feet.

He remembered recently being told how lucky he was, his reply had been something he had heard years before: 'Do you know what? You're right, "the harder I work the luckier I get."' He remembered on one occasion when he had lived in digs with a lovely little old lady, Mrs Clarke. He always thought of her as a little sparrow, always busy. He had woken up early one morning, his head on his arms, fully dressed and still sat at the table in his room. His meal from the night before untouched. It had become a greasy congealed mess, the glass of red wine was almost full.

* * * * *

Unknowingly he drifted off to sleep. Sophie and Charley let him rest.

He came awake to find himself alone. He could hear quiet conversation from the galley.

Walking through he interrupted the discussion about the transport to and from school. Tim was a little concerned when he heard that Charley was to wait at the entrance to the boatyard, in the dark.

Sophie said, 'Tim, I am sure she will be perfectly safe.'

Tim was a long way short of convinced. 'What time will they pick you up?' he asked.

'Just before six. Jane said her mummy is a little late sometimes, but she always arrives.' Charley remembered that on one occasion her friend's mother had not turned up and a teacher had run Jane home. She was not about to disclose that piece of information. Her father held her eyes in a steady stare, he saw the slight rise of colour in her cheeks.

'Right, that's not going to happen. Mr Graham will pick you up as usual here at the boat.' Both Sophie and Charley began to remonstrate with him.

'Has Jane's mother ever missed picking her up?' he asked, knowing that his daughter had fibbed. There was a long silence, Tim held the stare.

'Tim, why are you being so hard on her?'

He held up his hand with his forefinger raised, asking her not to interrupt. 'Did you lie to me?'

Now the tears were falling fast, these accompanied by a mumbled, 'Yes.'

Charley went to go to her bedroom.

Her father said, 'Wait. I'll always know when you lie to me. Do you understand?' Charley nodded. 'Now go to your room,' said her father.

Sophie was hurting for her daughter, but she knew Tim was right.

'Sorry if I seemed hard but we can't have her lying, and it sounds as though Jane's mum is unreliable. Also, think what Mr Graham would say if he found out Charley was standing around in the dark. No, I am more than happy for her to go to night school and meet Jane there. Mr Graham will as usual take Charley door to door and back again.'

Sophie thought for a while, then said, 'I will go in and tell her she can go.' She knew when Tim had reached a sticking point and that it was useless to argue with him. A moment later she was holding Charley while the child cried. 'Your father has agreed that you can go to night school. Mr Graham will take you and bring you home, is that ok?'

'Thank you, Mummy.'

'You are welcome. Now go and say sorry and thank you to your father.'

Standing in front of him and fiddling with a button on her blouse she said, 'I am sorry I told a fib, Daddy, and thank you for letting me go to night school.' What Tim wanted to do was gather his daughter up in his arms and cuddle her until the tears stopped.

'Right, we will put it behind us, but don't tell me fibs any more. As I said I will always know if you are lying, ok? Mr Graham will ferry you backwards and forwards because you mean too much to me to put you at risk, now come and give me a hug.'

A week later Charley returned from night school quite excited. Sitting down to her supper she said, 'You will never guess who I met tonight at school.' Both of her parents shook their heads.

Martyn, her brother, said, 'Jane.'

Charley loved her brother and always supported him. 'Yes,' she said, 'but there was someone else there, you remember that boy I met at the Number

Two shop, and I showed him the fairies, Daddy?'

'Yes I do remember, you showed the boy the well while his mother went shopping. He wore a hand-knitted dark green jumper with very long arms.'

'He goes to the college, I met him this evening. His name is Markus. He has been back to the well, but he has not seen any more fairies. I told him I think we are too old.'

'I can still see them,' whispered Martyn, worried he might not be believed.

'You might not be able to when you're older,' said Charley, gently.

'I hope I still can,' he replied almost silently. The conversation moved on.

CHAPTER 9

Tim was talking to his father about Mr Woodman's hardware store that had become the original Sophie's Delicatessen, known as Number One. Someone had torched the shop by pouring petrol through the letter box. They had almost killed Daisy and her husband, Declan. Tim and his father, Tom Cooper, had spent many hours over a pint since the fire discussing whether to rebuild it. The argument flowed back and forth, costs versus time, sell the ruin or rebuild it?

Eventually Tom Cooper asked the inevitable question, "What would Mr Woodman say?"

Almost in unison both men said, 'Rebuild it.'

Since Tim's godfather's demise, the expression, 'What would Mr Woodman say?' had become a mantra. It always presumed that the much respected elderly man would always have decided to do the positive thing, however, hard it was.

Tim spent a lot of time in his less busy moments thinking about Number One. One of the ideas he had was to tear down the ruin and make it a small garden, part of it glassed over allowing people to sit in the dry, perhaps with a café. He could dedicate one of the seats to Mr Woodman. He was not sure if the man himself would approve. On reflection the plot appeared too small. Tim finally decided to do nothing until he had made up his mind.

Charlie, their builder, put up a tall fence with a locked door. It was to remain like that for some time.

CHAPTER 10

Jessica, fully dressed, was sitting on her bed upstairs in her flat above the offices reading an article in a women's magazine about childcare. She heard the front door open and close. She realised it would be Tim or Oliver. Looking at her watch she saw whoever it was they were early. Having meant to finish this article twice before but having been interrupted, she decided to continue, there was only a page and a half. She heard whoever it was climbing the stairs. Her bedroom door was only just open. A mirror on her bedroom wall gave a view into the shower room.

Oliver must have assumed he had the place to himself; he was stripping his running gear off as he came into view. He was already naked from the waist up. Bare footed, he was sliding his underpants and his shorts down his bottom, then his legs.

Jessica could not look away. She knew he ran the three miles to work every morning and he occasionally discussed his evenings at the gym, and it showed in his body. The only male she had known intimately was her ex-husband's saggy flesh and beer belly.

She could not look away; words came into her head. Beautiful was one of them, a strange description for the male form but in this case correct. He was unaware of her gaze that was locked onto his every move. Her face and her body were aflame. Now completely aroused, her heart was hammering in her chest, her breath coming short. He walked across the shower room towards the towel rail and out of sight. She quietly eased her door further open.

As he left the shower he looked up and saw her looking at him, placing the towel around his waist he smiled at her. It contained everything a woman would hope to see in a man's face, love, affection, desire. Without conscious thought, answering an ancient need, she rose from the bed, walked into the shower room, and kissed him hard, pressing the full length of her body against him. Both of them were lost.

Whatever was going to happen was ended when Tim's 'Hallo' floated up the stairs.

Releasing him and moving away she said, 'Dinner here tonight.' It was not an invitation; it was a command.

He said, 'Yes please,' before walking away. Standing at the printer a little later she was amazed and embarrassed at what she had done. It was his smile that promised so much that had done it. She felt better shortly afterwards when he kissed the back of her head as he walked behind her after looking around to check no one was watching.

* * * * *

Later that day Tim asked, 'Jessica, can you do an extra hour or two this evening,? I need to get these details in the post to our German supplier please. It is important.'

'Sorry, Tim, I have made a promise to someone that I would be with them tonight that I cannot break. I will do them first thing in the morning.'

Tim was surprised, Jessica had always agreed to work late in the past. Never mind, tomorrow would do.

The day was difficult for both of them, each fully aware of what the other wanted, but unable to do anything about it. There were secret touches, unnecessary bodily contact as they passed each other. The second time he walked behind her, and the palm of his hand slid gently across her bottom she followed him into the other room.

Noisily opening and closing draws in the filing cabinets she whispered, 'Can we agree to stop the physical contact at work? I cannot concentrate. I have had to retype three pieces of work already this morning.'

Realising she was genuinely cross he said, 'Oops sorry.'

She kissed him hard, then pulling a pretty white lace hanky from her sleeve she reached up and wiped the lipstick from his mouth and went back to her desk.

* * * * *

Later at home Jessica was making their tea; Polly was explaining that she had been the bowler when they played rounders.

'Shall we go in the garden, and you can show me how you do it?' asked Oliver. Jessica smiled at him and had to stop herself kissing him, as he passed her on their way outside.

'I am going to freshen up,' she called to their retreating backs.

Oliver turned around and smiled at her. Her heart did funny things again as it had been doing all day.

When the man and the child returned to the kitchen Jessica was wearing a black, knee-length cocktail dress, gathered at the waist but full around her knees.

As they took their places at the dinner table Polly said, 'Mummy, you look lovely and why have we got the best dinner service and the best cutlery?'

Jessica's face flamed bright crimson.

Before she could speak Oliver said, 'It's in recognition of your skill at rounders. You are a very important person.'

'No it's not, it's because you are here,' said the child

Jessica said, 'You just wait until you bring a boyfriend home, am I going to get my own back.'

'Sorry, Mummy,' murmured the child.

Smiling at her daughter she said, 'Do not worry, I am only teasing you.'

Jessica had served the chicken stew while the debate had been taking place. Oliver, taking his first mouthful, said, 'Oh wow this is superb.'

Jessica watched him as he worked at sorting out the ingredients. 'Garlic, red peppers, sour cream, tomatoes, parsley. There is a herb I can't place.'

'Paprika, it's a spice I use a lot,' supplied Jessica. 'You did well though to get the rest. I can give you the recipe if you like?'

'I love cooking, always have,' he responded. 'Mother loves to cook. How did you manage to put this together so fast?'

'I didn't, I cook on Sundays and then freeze it. There is a big chest freezer that I brought from home that Tim has let me put in the outhouse that I keep full. I love cooking so it's no hardship.'

Changing the subject, he asked, 'How is the new girl doing?'

'Lynda. She has settled in really well and brought lots of good ideas with her regarding the filing. We have all got to get into line and follow the new system.'

'How do you feel about that?' he asked.

'Having seen the new system in action and now getting used to it I am really impressed. It's so simple but it really works.'

'That's good, as long as it reduces your workload.'

'Mummy can I go to bed? I am exhausted,' interrupted Polly.

While she was tucking her daughter in she heard the shower start. Polly said, 'Oliver is a nice man, isn't he, Mummy?'

'Do you think so?' she asked.

'Oh yes, he is much nicer than, Daddy.'

That would not be difficult, she thought. 'Yes, he is lovely,' she replied.

* * * * *

Having locked all the doors and closed all the windows she made her way upstairs, now a little unsure. He may not be what he appears to be she thought.

Reaching the bedroom, she found Oliver sitting on the corner of her bed wearing a Beatles T-shirt and a clean pair of washed pale blue jeans and bare feet.

As she reached the bed and bent down to kiss him he slid his hand up the back of her leg. Pulling her down and rolling her on to her back he discovered she was naked under her dress. His head moved down; he began kissing the inside of her knee.

Now she was fighting him off. 'No, no, I need you now.' jumping from the bed he stripped naked and moved onto the bed, lifting himself above her as he did so. She took a short breath in as he entered her.

As she started to respond to his rhythm and he slowly moved further into her she thought there is more man here than I have had before. All her emotions were overwhelming her, the whole of her body was one nerve ending. The explosion when it came blew her away. Breathing was difficult, she was elsewhere and only semi-conscious. He collapsed on top of her. His rapid breathing was blowing a hot gale against her neck. She held him to her while they returned to the everyday world. She could feel him beginning to move from her. Now they were both laughing.

* * * * *

Oliver had gone to sleep; she lay still trying to remember how long it had been since a man had made love to her. Sex with her husband had been perfunctory and had often for her ended far too soon.

Later in the shower they received and exchanged pleasure.

They spent the night exploring each other's bodies and learning each other's preferences, exchanging information and relating interesting events in their lives. One thing that made her laugh was that he had disclosed that he was scared of spiders.

In the dawn's early light, she admitted that she was ticklish. He had promised not to use whatever it was she was about to reveal against her; now of course he broke the promise. It was her screams of laughter that woke Polly, who appeared at the bedroom door rubbing the sleep from her eyes. She seemed unsurprised to find them in bed together.

Climbing into the bed on her mummy's side she leant around Jessica and asked him, 'Are you now my uncle? A girl at school has an uncle?'

'No, I am Mummy's boyfriend,' this said with an audible query in it. Unsure of its validity.

'Is that right, Mummy? I hope so.'

'We will see, my darling. Now back to bed it is still early.'

The couple chatted for a while, then Jessica rolled across to Oliver and slid her leg and her arm around him so that there was as much flesh on flesh as possible. Propped on her left elbow, her face above his, she began kissing him.

'You know this is going to get me started again,' he warned.

'Oh really? I hope so, otherwise I am wasting my time. We must be quiet.'

Rolling her onto her back and now having difficulty talking as they began, he reminded her that it was her who woke Polly up, not him. 'You have not said if I can be your boyfriend.'

'While you can make me feel like this you will always be my boyfriend,' this said between hurried breaths. As she climaxed, she drew his bottom lip into her mouth and bit down on it. Now it was him shouting.

* * * * *

Shortly after Bonny arrived for work, she drew Jessica into the kitchen. 'Have you slept with Oliver?' she asked.

'How did you know?'

'When you are near each other there are zillions of amps flying around. I keep expecting to see lightning strikes. Anybody who sees you two together is going to know. Was it good?'

Jessica, now bright pink and highly embarrassed, said, in a rather prim voice, 'Yes, thank you, it was better than that.'

Bonny gathered her into an embrace and hugged her, saying, 'I'm so glad, you deserve to be happy.'

Jessica reminded Bonny of a rose bud, so plain, ordinary and self-contained for so long because of her divorce and her ex-husband's assault on her. Now an amazing metamorphosis had taken place. Like a rose she had blossomed into this incredibly beautiful woman who had been hidden for ages.

CHAPTER 11

Marco returned from the cold store to tell Enzo the frozen steaks he had been sent for were not there. This was the second time this had happened in the last two weeks.

Enzo, becoming cross, asked, 'Have you moved everything? They will be under something.'

'Shall I have another look?' offered Marco.

'No thanks, I'll get it,' said Enzo as he marched away, his tone of voice conveying his annoyance with Marco's incompetence.

Standing in the cold store he began moving bags and boxes, hoping to reveal the meat. He persisted until he was certain the steaks were not there. Enzo kept a loose running total of the food generally; he knew approximately what there was in the kitchen. He was certain there should be about two dozen steaks left, now there were none. He returned to the kitchen and said, 'I owe you an apology, they are not there. If people order a steak, guys,' said Enzo loudly so they could all hear, 'and if they are upset, offer a free dessert or soup.'

Later that night Tim and Enzo discussed on the phone what had occurred.

'Enzo,' said Tim, 'you are obviously very sure the meat has disappeared, so it has been stolen. Worse than that in some ways, we have to assume the thief is a member of staff.'

Tim heard the young man take a long breath in before he responded. 'I guess you are right. What it means is that I have given a thief a job,' this said in a tone of voice that was heavy with self-blame.

'No, no that's not true, Enzo, how can you spot a thief? You can't. One of the things I am sure of is that you always do everything to the best of your ability, so don't berate yourself. We will just have to keep our eyes open and try and catch them.'

Unknown to the other, they both lost a lot of sleep that night trying to guess who the guilty party was.

In the small hours Tim finally fell asleep, having accomplished little. He still had no idea who the thief might be.

He received a phone call early the next morning from Enzo, who was obviously very downcast, in a sombre voice he said, 'Tim, I think I know who the culprit is.'

'How can you know that? There are no new workers, so who do you think it is?'

'Tim, if you examine the facts, it has only happened in the last few weeks. That may mean it is a new member of staff. How many staff members have started working for us in the last couple of months? Are there new workers in the shops or the café or the restaurant?' Enzo's tone of voice made it clear that he knew who it was and was very depressed by it. There was a long pause then Enzo replied, 'I think it is my cousin Silvio.'

'Surely not, he's family,' said Tim.

'There was a rumour at home in Italy that he was a gambler. When I interviewed him I asked him about it. He was adamant that he had seen the error of his ways and had given up the gambling. We cannot accuse him without proof. I will keep an eye on him and the stock. I will keep count.'

* * * * *

THE NEXT GENERATION

One morning some weeks later Tim was sitting outside the food store café enjoying his first coffee of the day, a flat white, strong and hot, when Enzo ran past him calling, 'Tim, Tim,' as he sprinted towards the entrance, dodging around surprised customers as he ran.,

Jumping from his chair and running after Enzo, he was fairly sure what the emergency was. He noticed some customers were becoming concerned. He called out, telling them not to worry. He cut the corner to the pavement, running across the grass and vaulting the low hedge that surrounded the square. As he joined Enzo at the edge of the pavement a small green van was accelerating away, its engine roaring. Silvio was on the floor holding a bleeding nose and clutching a fistful of money. Three frozen steaks lay on the pavement, spilled as the van driver snatched the large bag from the boy's hand before driving off. A very angry Enzo was leaning over the lad shouting in Italian. A small crowd began to gather, a thin brown dog with his ribs showing ran in, grabbed a steak and raced away. Tim pushed the meat up against the low wall that surrounded the square.

'We may as well let the dogs have them. Bring him in, we'll use the lift.'

Enzo spoke to Silvio in Italian, the boy looking extremely frightened and nodded emphatically, clearly agreeing with what Enzo had said.

Minutes later the three of them were in Enzo's kitchen, Tim seated on a stool, the boy standing opposite him. Enzo stood with his back to the door blocking the exit. Every so often the boy glanced behind him to check where his boss was.

Tim leant forward; his hands clasped under his chin. There was a long pause while he held his gaze on the boy's face. Then he said, 'Let me explain what is going to happen here. You are going to tell us everything. If I find you are lying I will march you down to the police station and let them deal with you. Now tell us how you got into this mess.'

The lad spent the next ten minutes explaining what he had done. He admitted he was virtually broke when he arrived in England. One of the men in the digs he was in offered to give him a loan. It turned out he was a loan shark and the interest on the money was exorbitant. He fell back into his old ways. To pay off the loan he had started gambling and lost again. He revealed that he would be thrown out of his accommodation next week because he had no money for the rent, that's why he stole the meat.

Tim had listened in silence; the occasional shake of the head was the only indicator of his disbelief.

Enzo, still at the door said, 'Why did you not talk to us? We are family.'

The lad admitted he was terribly embarrassed; he had hoped that somehow it would be put right.

There was a long silence. Tim sat staring at the boy. Finally he said, 'Firstly I'm not going to fire you, hopefully you have learnt your lesson. In future when you have a problem you come to Enzo or me, straight away, you do not let it fester. Do you understand?'

'Yes sir,' was the reply.

'Are you sure?' growled Tim. 'If this happens again I will march you down to the police station and press charges.' The boy was white faced and nodding.

'I'm going to pay off your debts. Now these are the terms. You will, never ever gamble again. Clearly you are lousy at it. Every day you are rostered to work you will always do overtime. The money you would have earnt will be put to paying off the money you will owe me. Now where will I find this loan shark?'

The youngster explained where he was staying.

'Tim, I will put the boy up at the flat I am renting. Once he has cleared your debt he can pay me some rent. Listen, lad, if you break your word to Tim I will put you on a plane home myself and Giorgio will meet you at the other end.'

Silvio flinched. Later that evening, after dark, the lad had packed his bag and left his digs, leaving a note to say he was moving on. Now he stood with

Tim and Enzo in the deep shadow of a large oak tree.

Eventually the boy said quietly, 'Here he is,' nodding at a short, thin, grubby weasel of a man in a dirty gaberdine raincoat topped off with a battered brown cap. As the man drew level with them Tim stepped out in front of him, Enzo stepped behind him.

The man turned to run and bumped into Enzo, who took his arm. 'Steady sir,' said the young chef, tightening his grip on the man.

'This young man owes you some money. How much did he borrow?'

The loan shark mentioned a much inflated sum. Tim knew this was wrong, looking at the youngster who was shaking his head. Enzo further tightened his grip on the man's arm who tried to pull it free with no effect. 'You're 'urting me.'

'How much was it?' asked Tim, repeating his question. The man offered a lower figure, it was still more than the original loan.

'I am getting fed up with your lying. I tell you what, I will pay you here and now the original amount plus five percent. That is a very good rate of return. The alternative is I pay you nothing and we walk you to the police station.'

'I– I'll take your offer. I don't want no trouble,' stammered the loan shark.

Tim handed over a brown envelope. 'You can trust me, the money is all there.'

Before Enzo let the man go he whispered in his ear. He never did tell anyone what it was he said. Tim often wondered if Enzo had mentioned the rumour about the Vieris and the mafia.

CHAPTER 12

Jessica was lying staring at the bedroom ceiling, comparing this new man lying beside her to her ex-husband. In bed her ex would take what he wanted then roll over and go to sleep. Often leaving her unsatisfied. They never held hands. He never was loving towards her. Jessica recognised he saw her as a housekeeper. In the last year of their marriage, he had never made love to her. She discovered he was seeing someone else. When she faced him with the evidence, an expensive set of black lace underwear in with his dirty washing, he lost his temper and hit her. The damage to her eye and face required stitches. She still carried a scar under her eye as witness to his violence.

It was a different world with Oliver, who was now cuddling her while he slept with his arm round her waist holding her to him. She loved the way he smelt. Now her head had moved to his chest, his dark chest hair gently tickling her cheek. When they were out, she saw other women's jealous looks as he and she walked by holding hands.

Oliver held doors open for her to step through first. When she was married, her ex went through doors in front of her, uncaring whether it swung back and hit her.

She did not understand why she had put up with her ex-husband's ill-mannered behaviour for so long. If she was honest, the reason was her fear of being broke, homeless and with a child to house and feed. There was one positive: a lot of women suffered far worse than she had, Daisy and her mum for a start. Jessica had great respect for Daisy. She had pulled herself up by her boot straps to leave poverty and abuse behind and to make her way in the world, and Declan her partner was lovely with his gentle Irish charm.

The alarm clock pinged; she had set it when she agreed to let him take her to bed in the middle of the afternoon.

Oliver sat bolt upright in bed, looked at the clock and said, 'Good evening, madam, would you like to shower first or share it with me?'

'We do not have time to shower separately, we will have to use it together.'

'Oh goody,' was his response.

'We do not have time for any shenanigans, or we will be late.'

'Certainly, madam, I understand, madam.'

As they stepped into the shower, he wound his arms around her waist and began to caress her.

Trying to push him away, she said, 'We do not have time, leave me alone, you madman.'

His kisses travelled down her body, minutes later she stopped fighting him. Now Jessica had a firm grip on his shoulders so she could remain standing as her world blew away.

In the next half hour, he found erogenous zones she did not know she had. Eventually he allowed her the further release he had denied her until now.

Putting both hands to his face, she, now soft mouthed, kissed him, saying, 'Oh my God, I do love you.' There was a long tense silence, the only sound was the click of the shower as it cooled down. Their eyes were locked together, she terribly embarrassed not knowing how to undo what she had said. She offered up a silent prayer. Please God do not let him walk out.

Now she was shaking her head, 'I am sorry, I have ...'

Interrupting her, he said, 'If you mean it say it again, please.' The concern in his voice was very apparent. Once again Jessica was trying to read what was in his eyes. Although she had blurted it out, she realised it was true. She did love him. 'I love you.'

Oliver let out a great roar and crushed her to him. 'I have known I love you for months; I didn't say anything because I assumed you would have had enough of men.'

There was a lot of kissing and hugging.

Finally, Jessica, landing on mother earth again, began panicking. 'Whatever is the time, we must be late. This is going to be so embarrassing.'

'It won't be, I shall simply tell them you would not let me out of the shower until you had finished with me.'

Now alarmed that he might just do it, she said, 'I forbid you to say anything like that.' He nodded. Jessica made a quick phone call to Sophie telling her they were on their way. Neither of them were properly dry as they dressed.

Jessica, shaking her head as she stepped into the little black dress she was wearing earlier, was still concerned he might do as he said; she knew he was crazy enough to do or say anything.

The taxi whisked them down to the river at Kingston where Tim and Sophie's houseboat, the *Sea Maiden*, was moored.

Jessica, still worried, said, 'The boat and the river are beautiful. You wait and see.'

There were hugs and handshakes when they arrived. Then Jessica started to explain why they were late …

'She is lying,' interrupted Oliver, 'she was having her wicked way with me, and we forgot the time.'

Jessica stunned that he would do what he had said would. She went bright red and put both hands up to her face, then she punched his shoulder hard.

Tim and Sophie were laughing their heads off, Tim holding the back of an armchair to stop himself falling over.

Sophie, now in hysterics, stepped forward and drew a thoroughly embarrassed Jessica into a hug.

Oliver was rubbing a sore shoulder. Tim could not stop laughing, eventually he said, 'Do we want a drink or coffee?'

Drinks were a unanimous decision. They were taken on the small rear deck. Oliver was enthralled by the river, the boats and the lights.

Tim was explaining the different types of river craft to him. Oliver did not like to say he knew most of what Tim was telling him.

Sophie said, 'I will finish getting the meal ready. Will you give me a hand please, Jessica?'

Both men knew this was code so that the girls could talk about what had occurred this evening.

Once downstairs Sophie said, 'Ok girl, tell me all about it.'

'Well, I am not going to tell you all about it, but what I will say is he makes me feel young again. I laugh all the time, I never laughed when I was with you know who. Oliver is kind and thoughtful and puts me first, but as you saw tonight, he can be dreadfully embarrassing. If he thinks it's funny, he will say it. Sometimes people are not amused.'

'You should not worry; I expect those people will find nothing funny. It is not a side of him we have seen at work, but we think he is lovely, and you appear extremely content.'

'Oh! you are right there; I have never been this content.' Both women laughed at what was implied in her response.

The evening passed quickly and was enjoyed by all concerned. The young couples quickly became firm friends.

On the way home Jessica wondered if her mother knew or hoped today would happen when she offered to have Polly to sleep over.

CHAPTER 13

Sophie sat waiting for her husband Tim in a quiet restaurant opposite the local London tube station. The attractive small brass lanterns hanging above each table in the restaurant had just come on, driving back the gathering dusk. Wiping the steam from the window next to her she sat watching the flow of humanity in and out of the station entrance now also lit. An older man stood flapping his arms across his chest trying to warm himself. He was well dressed, wearing an expensive heavy dark navy overcoat with a dark trilby. A red scarf was wound round his neck. His shoes were black brogues, they looked handmade. On reflection, she was not sure why she thought that. It seemed likely given the rest of his apparel, which appeared expensive. Watching him she saw him push back the left cuff of his overcoat and check the time on his watch. Five minutes later her gaze returned to the scene outside to see the man beginning to take quick steps into the station. A woman in a full-length fur coat and a matching fur hat was walking purposely towards him. Sophie guessed she was in her early fifties. They shook hands and started a conversation. The man led her away holding her upper arm. He was now carrying her overnight bag. They walked just far enough to leave the bustle and the bright lights behind, then he guided her into a poorly lit corner and enclosed her in an embrace. There was not the inferno of a young couple's desire, but it was not the polite greeting of a husband and wife. She broke the kiss and spoke. There was no way Sophie could know what she said or the content of his reply. It was she who leant back in and resumed the kiss. As she did so her hand reached around the back of his head and slid her fingers into his hair to prolong the intimacy. Stepping away from him a short while later she cast her eyes up and down the street, it was a nervous searching.

Tim arrived seconds later and leant across the table to kiss her. When she looked back through the window the older couple had gone. The brief meeting stayed in Sophie's mind for years. The memory returned occasionally. She would have loved to know more. She found herself weaving possible scenarios for the couple's behaviour. They were clearly lovers, not husband and wife, not a married couple. She felt sure they were both married to others. This was a clandestine meeting, unable to resist the attraction one had for the other, both had extensive families, too many people to hurt if these two followed their hearts' desire. She was overwhelmed with a brief sadness for the couple.

CHAPTER 14

The *Sea Maiden* was full of people. Tim and Sophie had invited Oliver and Jessica around for an evening meal. Jessica's daughter Polly was deep in conversation with Charley, both of them sitting cross legged on the floor. Barely audible music was playing in the background. The two women had laughed as the couple had arrived. They were both in a little black dress and the men wore blue denim.

Oliver was listening hard. 'Celine Dion singing "When I Fall in Love",' he declared.

'Yes, you're right,' confirmed Tim.

Oliver pulled Jessica into an embrace and started dancing.

'Oliver, there is not enough room,' she complained, dancing anyway. He kissed her and let her go. 'My boyfriend is completely mad,' she said, kissing him back.

'It looks like fun though,' said Sophie.

'That's one way of putting it,' laughed Jessica.

'Who is hungry?' asked Sophie, taking some cling film off the plates of food that were laid out on the table and the top of the sideboard.

'How did you get all this ready in such a short time?' queried Jessica. 'Don't tell me, it is the wonderful Nanny Bridget.'

'You are right,' confirmed Sophie.

'Mummy says she is a magic fairy,' added Charley from the floor.

'It would appear so,' observed Oliver.

'She makes it all possible,' confirmed Tim.

The two couples spent an extremely pleasant evening swapping yarns and stories about their younger years and their upbringing. Tim mentioned his new interest in sailing.

Oliver said, 'I love sailing. Until about five years ago my father had a yacht in Plymouth sound, near the naval base. He sold it because he was not using it very much.'

Tim went on to explain that Sophie had rowed at Oxford University in the women's eight and that now she rowed at the local club. She went on to explain that Tim was learning to sail.

'I am very much the beginner at the moment,' Tim added. 'But I do enjoy it.'

'How do you find living on board?' asked Oliver.

'We love it.'

'Tim's right,' said Sophie, confirming what her husband had just said. 'I dread that we may have to move ashore.'

'That's because Martyn doesn't like it because he fell in,' revealed Charley. 'I like it when there is a storm. The boat rocks and rolls, it is great fun.' The child they were discussing was at a sleepover with one of his friends.

'The two of them couldn't be more different,' said Tim. 'Still, never mind. Where have you sailed?' he asked Oliver.

'Our preferred trip was across to France, but we didn't always have the time, or the forecast was poor.'

'How did you learn?' asked Jessica. 'Did your father teach you?'

'He taught me the basics, but I did a proper course to get my qualification. If you are going to sea and want insurance you need the paperwork.'

'So Jessica, you are living with a sailor,' laughed Sophie. All manner of things were implied in her statement.

Jessica, frowning at Sophie, unsure of what it was her friend was trying to say, said, 'This is the first I have heard of it.'

Sophie was now extremely embarrassed and sorry she had opened her mouth without thinking. She was referring to the old saying that sailors had a woman in every port. Jessica's husband had played away and wrecked their marriage. She would not explain and hoped that her friend would not grasp her meaning.

'Perhaps we could come to the club one Sunday?' said Oliver.

'I am sure they would be happy to see you,' replied Tim.

'Anyone want a coffee?' asked Sophie. There were universal affirmatives.

'I will come and help,' offered Jessica.

CHAPTER 15

One afternoon at the Vieris', Sophie was chatting to Angela about her aunt's French partner, Alain. During a break in the conversation the two women could hear music coming from the extension. A phrase played slowly, followed by a repeat, hesitant but accurate. Angela was the first to rise, followed by Sophie, making their way to the music room. When they got there it was to find Martyn sitting on his grandfather Victor's lap seated at the grand piano. Mr Vieri had received a considerable amount of leg pulling when the grand had arrived. His response was, 'Why should I not buy the best?' The amusement had diminished when he sat down and after a few false starts began to play most competently.

Victor said, 'Earlier this afternoon I found Martyn kneeling on the piano stool tapping the keys with two fingers, it could not be called music, but it was musical. I sat down, hoisted him onto my lap and picked out three notes. Martyn had got it wrong the first couple of times but then it came right. Before you came in he could repeat seven notes accurately.' Victor could see the disbelief on his daughter's face. 'Right,' said Victor, leaning forward to talk quietly into his grandson's ear, 'shall we show them how it's done?'

Martyn was nodding. Victor played three descending notes, saying as he finished, 'Now it's your turn.'

The child played them slowly at first, then he began to speed up.

'Martyn try this,' said his grandfather, adding two notes to the list.

The child got the fifth note wrong; Victor went to correct him. The boy shook his head saying. 'No, no.' Tipping his head on one side the boy played five notes again, this time listening as much as looking, still it was wrong. His grandfather did nothing. The boy started again.

'Can you help him?' asked Sophie.

Victor shook his head as Martyn played the sequence again, this time playing it correctly. His face was wreathed in smiles as he banged the last note four times.

'I am sorry to end this, but Tim will want his tea.'

Martyn played the five notes twice more before Sophie scooped the boy from her father's lap and plonked him down on the floor.

Angela, on the way out, said, 'I think that's quite clever; I don't think I could do that.'

Relating Martyn's prowess to her husband later that night he was singularly unimpressed. 'I think you will find anybody could do that.'

'Not a child so young,' she argued. She was worried about her husband's lack of a close relationship with the boy. She knew he adored his daughter, but he appeared to have nothing in common with his son.

Later that evening her father phoned her on the boat. 'I have been thinking about what Martyn did today, it did not appear to be anything special but in a child so young it is. I would like to get my old music teacher to see him. Would you mind?'

'No, I see no problem with that. Will you be there?'

'Yes he will come to the house, I will let you know when. Is everyone well at your end? Can you let Tim know I need a chat when he has a moment?'

The goodbyes were said, Sophie said nothing about their son and the music teacher to Tim or Martyn. She did relay her father's message about a chat.

CHAPTER 16

Sophie arrived at her father's house with Martyn ready for the first piano lesson one Saturday afternoon. The teacher was a tall elderly man with a shock of white hair, a thin body and face. Sophie noticed he was a little stooped. His appearance dated him with his bow tie, closely trimmed white beard and a brown three-piece suit.

He shook Sophie's hand and said, 'Hallo, Mother, my name is Leo Carpenter. An extraordinary name for a musician I agree, but there we are. It was not of my choosing, my family were simple folk who knew no better.' All this said in a cultivated, quick, clipped, condescending manner.

* * * * *

Sophie and Martyn followed Leo and her father into the music room.

Sophie was making herself comfortable on an armchair when Leo Carpenter said, 'Sorry, Mother, but you cannot stay, you will interfere and give advice on a subject that you know nothing about. You will be certain that your son is another Mozart or similar. No, I am adamant you may not stay.'

'I have arranged for Mr Graham to run him home when we are done,' said her father. 'I will sit in on all the lessons.' He sensed his daughter's growing annoyance with this abrupt and rude man who was here to teach her son, and who was going to get paid well for being so unpleasant and abusive.

'Can we speak outside, Sophia?' asked her father in a firm voice that brooked no refusal, leaving the room as he spoke.

Outside Sophie was seething. 'How dare he speak to me like that, and why are you apparently protecting him? I am going back in that room and taking my son home.'

'If you do that I believe you will regret it for the rest of your life. I may be wrong, but I am fairly sure Martyn has a gift, the method he used to solve that problem the last time he was here was not what most children would have done. He was not remembering the position of the piano key, he was holding the sound of the note in his mind, did you see how certain he was when he found it? I explained to Leo what had taken place and he agreed to come and see for himself. Will you do one thing for me?'

'What?' snapped Sophie. Normally using this tone of voice and rude manner when addressing her father would ensure she receive a stern rebuke.

This time he ignored it and said, 'Please allow Leo Carpenter to do his assessment of young Martyn and then decide. To repeat myself, I do think the boy is gifted.'

Sophie drove home, slowly becoming less angry. She had not noticed any musical gift in her son. She felt sure she would soon see the back of the loathsome Mr Leo Carpenter.

In years to come Sophie would be annoyed that she had not made a note of the date Martyn played the five notes. Martyn's piano lessons became a regular part of the boy's life. When asked if the lessons had gone well he would shrug his shoulders and say, 'It's alright?' and go to his room.

CHAPTER 17

Months later Sophie heard music coming from the children's cabin, tapping and opening the door at the same time she saw Martyn hide something under the covers on the unmade bed. 'Was that you playing?'
Martyn, now bright red, said, 'Yes.'

'Why are you so embarrassed?'

'Because I was playing the wrong music.'

His mother, now with a confused frown on her face, asked, 'What do you mean the wrong music?'

'Because it's not classical. Grandfather and Mr Carpenter have both said I should only play classical music. They have said the blues are not music.' He shrugged, then said, 'Mr Lawrence, the music teacher at school, asked me what sort of music I liked to listen to when I was on my own.'

'What did you say?'

'The blues, that's what I love. He asked me why I was playing classical music when I loved the blues?'

'So?'

'I told him that was what the family wanted me to learn.'

'Play something for me,' said his mother, pointing to his record player by his bed. The child pulled a clarinet from under the covers.

Taken aback, she asked, 'Where did you get that from?'

'Mr Lawrence has let me use it since I said about blues music.'

He began to play a classical piece he had been practicing for his private lessons at Mr Vieri's.

'No, no, no,' said his mother, 'play the blues.' The child looked at his mother, his face showing his surprise.

Sophie nodded at him and then said encouragingly, 'Go on then.' The child began to play a blues tune his mother did not know. A few minutes in and the boy was lost in the music, eyes closed, gone.

This was not the practised mechanical sounds he produced from the piano, this was from the heart. All the pain of being a young under-confident, bullied, shy youngster was in the music. Sophie stood in tears, this child of hers with no obvious skills. She had worried that he had no confidence, no apparent abilities. How wrong she was. This music pouring from him was a gift, something he had been born with. How tragic would it have been if it had not been discovered. The music slowly died. Her son, who had been playing with his eyes shut, opened them and was shocked to see his mother so moved.

Extremely concerned, he asked, 'Why are you crying?'

Sophie dropped to her knees and hugged her child. Choosing her words carefully she said, 'I was worried you did not seem to have any interests. What was that song?'

'It was something I made up a while ago,' he replied. 'It just came to me, I did mess it around a bit at the end.'

Still holding him, she said, 'Martyn, you have been given a gift. Take no notice of what anyone says, you must keep playing the clarinet.'

'Do I need to keep having the piano lessons?' His voice was now downcast. 'It feels as though I have been doing them for ever.'

'I think the technical stuff will help you in the future.'

'Mr Carpenter is quite rude sometimes,' said the boy

'While he is useful you need to keep on with him. I want you to talk to your music teacher and ask him which clarinet we should buy for you.'

'No, please don't do that. I tried two others at school, I got along best with this one.'

'It looks a bit shabby,' she observed.

Down the years the instrument slowly changed in appearance. The black woodwork developed a patina that only time, constant use and polishing could impart. The keys always shone. On one or two the constant use had worn the chrome away to the metal underneath. He never did replace it.

'Mum, I don't care, it's the sound that matters, and I'm polishing it. I have swapped to a harder reed this week,' said the boy, pointing to the thin sliver of reed secured at the mouthpiece of the instrument. 'My embouchure is stronger so the sound will improve.'

He began to explain what the word meant. His mother interrupted him, saying, 'I know what it means, it is your mouth and jaw, et cetera.'

The child nodded. The kettle in the kitchen began whistling, she hurried to quieten it using a red and white striped drying up cloth to protect her hand from the kettle's heat. Filling the tea pot and replacing its lid she moved the towel to her face to stifle the sound of her sobbing. How close her husband and others had come to writing Martyn off. Even she had started to believe he was without any gifts or special skills. Thank God, she thought, that this amazing ability he possessed had been discovered.

Tapping on his bedroom door then opening it she said, 'In future, Martyn, play with the door open. Share your music with us all.'

The following morning Mr Graham arrived to deliver Nanny and then take the children to school. Sophie gave him a letter to take with him. 'Can you hand it in at reception please, Mr Graham?' The elderly man nodded. The children kissed her and arguing over goodness knows what made their way to the car. She and Nanny stood waving as the car disappeared out of the boat yard.

'There is not much to do, Nanny. I did some things last night.'

'I want to have a go at the fridge if that's ok. And one or two other jobs.'

'Help yourself, Nanny. You can put your feet up if you want.'

'Oh no, my mum God bless her said you have to keep keeping on, otherwise you die before your time. She never stopped until she went to bed.'

'I am having a cup of tea before I go. Will you share it with me?'

'Yes please, it will save me making one later.'

'I think you should make another one anyway, Nanny.'

The two women enjoyed a cuppa and a chat. Most of it was about Martyn and how surprised Sophie had been when the boy had begun playing the clarinet.

'I would never have known.' Sophie gathered her coat, briefcase and handbag, saying. 'I will leave you to it, I am at the day job if you need me, Nanny.'

'Don't work too hard, Sophie. I will see you tonight.'

'Mr Graham is late getting back,' said Sophie to herself, looking at her watch as she went through the door onto the ramp on the bow of the boat. Then she spotted him. He was talking to Tabby Johnson, the middle-aged boat yard owner, he of the enormous beard. Taking a second look she decided it was bigger and whiter than ever.

Blowing out clouds of tobacco smoke he removed his pipe to speak to her.

'Long time no see. Are you well?' asked Tabby as she approached.

'Oh you know how it is, all work and no play, Tabby,' was her response, smiling as she spoke.

'Well let's hope you're being paid well. How's the family?'

'We are all good thanks, Tabby, and you?'

'Fine ta. See you soon.'

Sophie waved from the car window as she and Mr Graham pulled away

* * * * *

The day was a long one. No sooner had she solved one query than someone else had a problem. At four o'clock her phone rang, it was Mr Lawrence. After the pleasantries had been exchanged he said, 'I was going to talk to you about your son and his music, his piano playing is improving. He says he has lessons; I don't think he is enjoying it.'

'I know his teacher is quite severe with him.'

'That's not doing him any good at all, he is too unsure of himself,' replied Mr Lawrence.

'I would like him to continue because of the technical stuff,' she responded.

'He can do that with me,' he replied.

Over the next few weeks Martyn became ever more reluctant to go to piano lessons with Mr Carpenter. Explaining to Tim, she said, 'As it gets nearer the time for him to go to his class he goes all droopy.'

Tim could visualise exactly what Sophie meant. Martyn's head would hang forward and his shoulders slump, he even walked differently. He looked like a puppy expecting a whipping.

Sophie tried to persuade her father to allow Martyn to quit the piano to no avail. His response was clear. He said, 'You need to stop this nonsense with the jazz, it is not music. There is only one avenue for him, the classical piano.'

Sophie did not know what to do. As a child she had learnt not to oppose her father. His anger when he had caught her disobeying him was extremely frightening.

CHAPTER 18

It was a filthy night. The rain was hammering against the windows; the wind was blowing down the chimney making the flames flicker and dance in the fireplace. He heard the clatter of a dustbin lid rolling down the road. To add to the noise someone began banging on Tom's front door.

Beth started barking, Tom and the boy looked at each other. This was unusual, the last time she had reacted like this was a long time ago now. Tom remembered, it was the day after he had brought Beth home from the rehoming centre and the RSPCA man had called to check the home was suitable for a pet. Beth had started barking and would not stop. She had forced herself between the arm of the couch and Tom. Usually her output was one bark accompanied by a single flick of her tail. Not this time. When he opened the front door a scruffy, dripping woman stood there. She looked like a tramp to Tom. She offered no introduction, only a single statement.

'I've come fer my boy.'

'What do you mean you've come for your boy?'

'My Sammy,' she said pointing into the living room.

Turning round Sammy was standing transfixed, struggling with Beth, who now was a terrifying sight, gums rolled back, long, curved white canines fully exposed, she was jumping forward trying to break Sammy's hold on her collar. It was blindingly obvious Beth wanted to tear this women apart.

THE NEXT GENERATION

How the dog knew that the woman was such a threat to the household he would never know.

'Wait there,' he commanded as he took a step back and shut the door to the living room behind him. A split second later he heard and felt Beth slam into the door. The woman took a quick step back. Tom could hear Beth's claws tearing the paint from the other side.

'Sammy has told me of the sort of life he has had with you, deserting him when you had another customer on board. Allowing the boy to go days without food. Him having to run from some sick beggars, sleeping under bridges. Condemning him to go to the child centre where he went hungry again because the big boys stole his food, and he was beaten and bullied by the staff and the boys. That dog in there is more of a mother to him than you ever were or will be. I will share one thing with you, sometimes Beth jumps the back gate when we have let her out. She always finds Sammy wherever he is. If by some means you manage to steal him away you know what will happen. The dog will come looking for you. Now I have said enough, I'm going to count to ten, then I will open this door.' His hand rested on the brass handle.

'One.' The women began a stream of foul language.

'Two.' She began to back away down the path, still swearing at him.

'Three.' Turning, she struggled to open the gate.

'Four.' The gate came open.

'Five.' Tom's neighbour came out to see what the shouting and swearing was all about.

'Six.' She began to run, swearing at the man as she passed him.

'Seven.' She disappeared around a corner. He could hear her heels clicking on the paving. At the top of his lungs Tom blasted out. 'Eight, nine, ten.'

'What's all that about, Tom?' asked the neighbour.

'That's Sammy's birth mother, she wanted to take the boy back. I told her

I would set the dog on her if she didn't go away. She turfs him off the boat, so he has to live rough when she gets a punter on board.'

'She's a what's a name then?'

Tom nodded.

'Poor little beggar,' said his neighbour as he shut the front door.

Back indoors Sammy was sitting on the floor cuddling Beth, struggling to control himself.

'Can she make me leave 'ere and live wiv her?'

'Over my dead body, lad.' Two days later Tom was sitting in the snug of a pub downtown having a pint with a local bobby he had known for years.

Addressing the policeman he said, 'Teddy, can we talk off the record?'

'Is this about, Sammy?' asked the policeman.

'Yes, how did you know?'

'I can't think of anything else you would want to talk about. That boy is a nice lad now he doesn't have to thieve to eat anymore. He's got a good name with the dockers, doing a bit of shopping for them. You can tell what they think of him, they nearly killed that drunken docker that beat Sammy to pulp for the boy's bit of savings. He's extended his errand-running service to some of the local elderly, by the way.'

'Thank you, I didn't know that about the old folks,' Tom admitted.

'So what's the problem then, Tom?'

'Sammy's mother turned up the other night and wanted the boy back.'

'You're joking,' said Teddy.

Tom shook his head. 'I had to threaten to set the dog on her if she didn't go away.'

'I never heard that, Tom. How old is he?'

'I don't know. He won't say.'

'Oh he's eighteen, you say. There is nothing she can do then. We will have a word with her.'

It took Tom a moment to realise what had just happened.

THE NEXT GENERATION

'One for the road, Teddy?'
The policeman smiled and nodded.

CHAPTER 19

Daisy was talking to a regular customer who was upset. She had been unable to buy her husband's favourite smoked cheese.

'I'm sorry we let you down,' said Daisy. Pulling a small note pad from her pocket, she asked the woman how much it would have been; Daisy wrote a credit note for the amount then looked over to the cheese barrow, waving the credit note in the air as she did so. The girl serving on there was watching for Daisy's signal and lifted her hand in response.

She explained to the customer that she could choose an alternative and use this credit note. The lady thanked her and moved away.

Daisy became aware of someone standing behind her waiting for her to finish. Looking over her shoulder her mum and her aunty were standing behind her. She could hardly believe her eyes. The number of times she had invited her mum to come and visit her at work and see what she did. Now she was here. Bereft of words she wrapped her mum up in her arms, then she hugged her aunty.

'Why didn't you say you were coming?'

'We only decided this mornin',' said her mother. 'It's a lot bigger than I'd thought it'd be.'

'What part are you in charge of?' asked her aunt, looking around.

Daisy realised that all she had told her mum was that she had a new job in the food hall. 'All of it, all of downstairs. Enzo the chef is in charge upstairs. He's very nice, we work well together.'

'Oh right, nice try,' said her aunt laughing, obviously disbelieving her.

A member of staff was standing at Daisy's elbow. Looking at her Daisy asked, 'What can I do for you, Kathy?'

'There's a bread delivery. It's not what we ordered.'

'Give me five minutes, I will be right there. If he tries to leave it, don't let 'im, and don't sign for it.' The girl nodded and moved away. A tall gentleman in a dark suit and holding a briefcase was standing waiting to talk to her.

'Hallo, sir,' said Daisy, 'how can I help you?'

'I have an appointment with Mr Tim Cooper this morning. My name is Tomlinson.'

'Tim is expecting you, Mr Tomlinson, his office is upstairs at the far end of the corridor. There is a lift just around the corner,' she said, pointing as she spoke. He took a look at the height of the staircase, said 'Thank you,' and made his way to the lift.

Turning back to her mum she said, 'How about a sit down, a cuppa and somethin' to eat?' Both of them nodded at her. She led them to a café table and made them comfy.

A young waitress appeared and said, 'Good morning, Daisy,'

'Good morning, Maria, this is my mum and aunty. They are to have whatever they want and it's on me. Mum have a look at the cakes in the café before you order.'

'This looks a bit expensive,' observed her mum.

Leaning down and whispering in her ear she said, 'Mum I can afford it, have whatever you two want.' Now in her normal voice she said, 'Right, you two, I must get on. I will check up on you now and then. I must sort this delivery out.' Saying, 'I will see you later,' she strode away.

The two women made themselves comfortable, ordered cheese on toast and selected a big slice each of cream cake from the display, all washed down with a large pot of tea. They watched as Daisy dealt with the rude, loud delivery man. Later she walked across to check that her mum and aunty had all they needed. Pulling up a chair she sat down at their table. A waitress walked over and asked, 'Do you want your usual, Daisy?'

'Yes please,' and looking at the crumbs on her mum's plate she said, 'and I will have a slice of whatever that was, Maria.'

'Can I talk to you soon about my holidays please, Daisy?'

'I suggest you have a word with Oliver, he is handling all that now. You can say I asked you too. He has agreed to take some of the load off me.'

'What was the problem wiv the bread, Daisy?' asked her mum.

'I reckon he has given our order to another customer and was trying to bully me into covering up his mistake. I have rung the baker and sorted it out. He's putting a new order together and his son is going to deliver it for us. The driver who was so rude, it's his first day. By the sound of things it will be his last. The baker was very apologetic.'

'Doesn't it worry yur 'avin' to deal wiv people like that?'

'No Mum, it's just part of the job.'

'I couldn't do it,'

'Nor me,' echoed her aunt, realising how wrong she had been laughing at Daisy when she thought the young woman was bragging.

Later Daisy caught up with them browsing the different stalls. 'We was just saying, Daisy, how nice the stalls are. They're like the costermonger's barrows you see down the east end wiv the big wheels and the canvas tops. The colours are nice, the blue and white stripes.'

'That's right, this is all Tim's idea. He knew what he wanted it to look like the minute he walked in.'

'I likes the trees. Are they real?'

Daisy nodded. Once again Daisy was needed elsewhere.

Tim had walked Mr Tomlinson down the stairs and said goodbye. Walking across to Daisy Tim arrived at her side at the same time as her

THE NEXT GENERATION

mother and her aunt. Daisy introduced her relatives. Tim was as always extremely polite and sang Daisy's praises.

'It looks like very hard work,' said her mother.

'She only does twelve-hour days,' said Tim, laughing.

'It's easier than cleaning offices till two in the morning,' observed Daisy. 'When you're so tired you can hardly stand up. Besides that I love the job, the buzz, getting to know the customers, working with the staff. It's great.'

Her mother nodded in agreement, saying, 'We're off now, Daisy love. It's been lovely. Goodbye, Mr Cooper.'

'It's Tim, Mrs Green. It's been nice to meet you, all the best. Daisy, I need a word about Mr Tomlinson please.'

Daisy kissed her mum and aunt goodbye and walked away listening to her boss. The two older women were quiet going home on the train. Eventually Mrs Green said, 'That ain't my Daisy, she's got right tough. My daughter would 'ave been shakin' in her boots when that rude b– started in on her.'

'She's right clever,' agreed Daisy's aunt. 'Who would have thought it?'

Daisy's mum never said anything about the new Daisy, as she now called her. She was certain her friends would not believe her. They would think she was making it up.

Daisy had a secret that she would never disclose. When someone started on her as the baker's delivery driver had, she imagined it was her father bullying her as he had done so many times in the past. There was one certainty, they would never win when they were in the wrong.

CHAPTER 20

Gerald staggered out of the pub. He was almost unrecognisable; his appearance was little better than that of a tramp. He was unshaven, his hair was long to his shoulders and filthy dirty, as was his clothing. Anyone who got too close to him stepped rapidly away.

Much to his surprise he saw his ex-wife and daughter disappearing down a side street on the other side of the road.

A deep, fierce anger filled his entire body, this together with the considerable intake of beer over the last hour robbed him of coherent thought. She was, in his mind, the instrument of his decline, the loss of his job that had him flying around the world first class was her fault. He was now working in the docks labouring. Heavy work that had him going to bed each night on his own aching everywhere. His secretary had dumped him when he had been fired.

He believed misguidedly that Jessica putting the work for Tim's company ahead of their marriage was the reason he was now living in scruffy digs in a rough part of London. With no clear thought in his head as to what he was intending he marched after her. He was now angrier than he had ever been before. He nearly fell as he misjudged the height of the kerb on the far side of the street. He thrust out a hand to hold the wall to stop himself falling. He was now moving as quickly as he could towards her. Her pace was faster. She would have escaped him had she not stopped to look in a shop window. He arrived as she started to walk away. He grabbed at her cloak, unbalancing her. Pulling her towards him he was spitting as he spoke.

'I need some of that money you stole from me you, you scheming cow,' saying this as he slammed her against the glass. Her face was pressed painfully up against the wooden dark navy surround of the shop window and held there.

Jessica said, 'We split the money fifty-fifty. In fact, you did better than me because you kept the car, you drunken idiot, now let go of me.'

'You owe me, what have you got in your handbag?'

'Very little and you are not having it,' she said, holding her bag away from him.

Polly was kicking him in the ankle as hard as she could, at the same time screaming her head off. He back-handed the child, knocking her off her feet. She almost rolled into the road, her screaming resumed, unbelievably louder than before.

Now Jessica was a wildcat protecting her young. As he moved in to snatch her bag, her hand without conscious thought shaped itself into a claw. Her nails were her pride and joy, one of the few things she made a fuss of. They were long, strong, sharp and varnished a deep plum. She now put them to use in the way mother nature had intended, to be used as a defence system. As his face and eyes came into range, using all her strength she lacerated the left side of his face, from the forehead downwards. The amount of alcohol in his system slowed his reaction times to a crawl. She then attacked the other side of his face with equal ferocity, aiming for the other eye. A lady from the shop came out wielding a heavy broom then proceeded to thump him with it. The last blow was with the heavy end of the broom that drew more blood. Now his head was ringing. Sirens were heard approaching, getting nearer by the second. Now scared, he let Jessica loose and at a shambling run hampered by his drunken state he made off down the street. Jessica was feeling extremely unsteady, she leant against the shop window to stop herself falling down.

The police car had entered the street from the other end and was already halfway towards him. Now her ex-husband was in a panic, scared that if the police caught him his first attack on his wife would become known. Also he realised there was a witness this time, the woman in the shop.

Blinded by the blood in his eyes and therefore unseeing, he rushed into the road. He was nearly across when the bus hit him. He had been aware of the scream of tyres. The nearside wheel was the last thing he saw before it crushed him.

Jessica, aware of what was about to happen, had gathered Polly up and wrapped her daughter's face into her red cloak, a present from her mother. This ensured that the child would not see the carnage as it took place. Jessica would hold the image of the bus driver in her head forever. The poor man was almost standing on the brake pedal. At the same time he was hauling on the steering wheel trying to miss the body in the road by sheer force of will, knowing his task was impossible.

The shop owner guided them into the shop and sat them down in a back room.

'I'll make us all a cup of tea, how's that? Is there anybody I should ring?'

'No, I will manage thank you.' As soon as she said it she realised it was not true. Changing her mind she asked, 'Could you ring my boss, please, and tell him where I am? His name is Tim Cooper.' She had to think hard to remember the number. The shock of what had just occurred had driven everything from her mind. Holding her head with the fingers of her left hand, she said, 'Sorry I can't think.'

The shopkeeper said, 'I'm not surprised, love, take your time. It'll come.' Moments later Jessica remembered and gave the woman a number.

'I will serve this customer, then I will ring him for you, sit tight.' Five minutes later she realised it had been Mr Graham's number she had remembered.

A short while later she heard the shop owner talking to Mr Graham on the phone. After a brief conversation the shopkeeper joined them in the back room saying, 'The car is on its way, you could pour the tea if you don't mind.' Another customer arrived; the shop owner went to serve her. Minutes later the three of them were sipping a restorative cup. Even Polly enjoyed tea if it was warm and sweet.

Mr Graham in his usual all-grey apparel arrived with the car at the same time as the policeman walked through the door of the shop.

Polly asked a question, 'Is Daddy dead, Mummy?'

'We will talk about it later, darling.'

Looking up at the policeman, she asked, 'Have you come to talk about my ex-husband?' The policeman nodded. Jessica realised that was a daft question. Why else would he be here? 'One minute, please. Mr Graham, will you take Polly and put her in the car and make her safe?'

'I will,' he responded.

The child took the chauffeur's hand as they left the shop.

The officer asked the usual questions. 'Did she know her ex-husband's address?' The answer was no. 'Where did he work?'

'I am sorry,' she replied, 'I have no idea.' Jessica furnished the officer with her own details.

When the policeman had asked all his questions Jessica was allowed to leave. Thanking the shop owner then walking the few yards to the car she approached three elderly women, each wearing a raincoat, a small hat and a shopping bag hung over their arms. Staring down the street they were watching the accident and blocking the pavement. Jessica, not wanting to push through them, came to a halt.

One said, 'It reminds me of the war when our street got bombed. The poor devils in that bus never stood a chance.'

'This is not quite the same, Mavis; this poor devil is under the bus.'

'I know that, but the passengers that saw it are going to be pretty shook up ain't they?'

'And the pedestrians. Some of them were right there,' said the third woman, as they moved away. The journey home was conducted in silence.

'Can we have cocoa and biscuits?' asked Polly.

Jessica nodded and hugged her child. That evening Jessica and her daughter sat in front of the fire and talked over the events of the day. 'Are you sad, Mummy?' asked the child.

'I am. He was not always a drunkard. When we first met he was nice to me. Things went wrong when I went out to work. His idea of a wife was to have me at home all day looking after you and him. In those early days I was reasonably happy doing that, but then I wanted more, a job, friends of my own, something to occupy me rather than just housework. Your father believed a wife's place was in the home. He would not compromise.'

'I'm sad, Mummy. I am sorry he was horrid to you, but I don't have a daddy now.'

'I am sorry, darling. How about you come into my bed tonight and we cuddle each other to sleep.'

Tim rang later, saying, 'I expect you will need some time to get over this. Take some time off until you feel better.'

'Thanks, Tim, can I take it one day at a time? I am mostly worried about the press finding me, or worse still finding Polly.'

Sleep evaded her for a long time. The terrible pictures kept replaying in her mind, this complete with the scream of brakes and the horrific sounds as the bus drove over him.

The following morning she rang the school to tell them what had happened. The school secretary was extremely kind and understanding and wished mother and child well. The following morning a reporter from the local paper found her and asked lots of questions. She was answering them until he started talking about the divorce, then she apologised, saying she did not want to talk about that and shut the door. As she went to bed that night she was missing Oliver, who was sailing with friends. He had warned her there might not be any contact for a few days. She shed a few tears before sleep claimed her.

CHAPTER 21

Jessica was not really aware of the progress of her husband's funeral service, her mind roamed over some of the details of their marriage. She was unclear why he had slept with his secretary. When she questioned him during the divorce he was unable to give her an answer. Sophie had said she thought he was intimidated by Jessica, because of the complexity of her job and how good she was at it. When she and Gerald had met she had disclosed that she worked for her father, a GP. He'd asked in what role. She had described herself as a competent filing clerk. Now with her doing overtime in the evenings at home in her new job with Tim and Sophie and talking to him about what she was doing clearly indicated what a clever woman his wife was.

She was brought back to the present at the end of the service by her ex-mother-in-law standing in the aisle screaming at her from the end of the pew. The woman, like Jessica, was in all black and appeared wild eyed.

'You killed my boy with your fancy ways and so-called posh job. You never had no time for him after you started working for that stuck up Sophia Vieri and her husband. You've got above yourself, you have. My boy's dead because of you. I hope what you've done haunts you for the rest of your days.' Jessica was searching for an escape route. The other end of her pew butted against the grey stone wall of the church. There was no way she was going to climb over the back of the pew. Her ex-father-in-law was now attempting to restrain his wife by holding her upper arm. She slapped him, hard, twice.

'Come away, Gladys, come away. You don't know what you're saying.'

'Let me go, you stupid man, this woman is a murderer.'

Now the vicar arrived and helped her husband ease the demented woman away from Jessica and towards the side room. Jessica almost ran from the church. One thing was for sure; she would never visit it again.

Over the coming months the dreadful sight of her ex-husband running into the road and then being knocked down and disappearing under the bus ran in her head like a ghastly video, often waking her in the night. She was left running with sweat and panting in fear. As the years went by the dream visited her less often.

CHAPTER 22

Martyn was enjoying playing with the other three in the evenings after school. He had slowly got used to the growing group of students who stayed behind to watch and listen. Most of the time all the songs were played as written but usually later in the evening Martyn let go and began to improvise. The small crowd always clapped and cheered as the group went who knew where with the music.

It had been agreed that they would put on a short session for everyone after school at some time in the future. For Martyn, he saw the approaching performance as a yawning abyss, a terrifying obstacle. He was trying to put it out of his head. It had somehow become a major talking point at dinner. This evening the discussion had been about Mr Carpenter and how he bullied Martyn and told the boy he was wasting the time with the clarinet.

'He said it was a misuse of my time messing about with this fixation on jazz. He said it's interfering with what I should be concentrating on, the classical piano. He told me I was an extremely spoilt young man. He went on to remind me that Grandfather had provided a beautiful instrument for me to learn on, and that he pays my fees, they are not inconsiderable,' he'd added. 'Mum, I don't want to do it any more. I know Grandfather will be cross, but I hate the piano and I hate Mr Carpenter.'

THE NEXT GENERATION

'Son,' said Tim, 'I've heard you play the piano. I have never heard you play the clarinet, so?'

'So, so what? Do you mean for him to play now in the middle of dinner?' asked Sophie.

'I do.' His family looked at Tim in disbelief. 'Well, can you play it or not?'

Sophie could hear her husband's lack of belief in the boy in the way he was speaking. So could Martyn.

Martyn stood transfixed, staring at his father. He then rushed from the room towards his cabin.

Sophie was losing her temper; she was so angry with her unfeeling brute of a husband. She spat out, 'Tim, you heartless ...' she never got to say any more. Martyn walked back into the room carrying his clarinet and began to play 'Don't Go Changing' by Billy Joel.

Tim sat and listened in silence, his face a picture of complete disbelief. He was shaking his head. This was his wimp of a son making music, on his own, from memory, eyes shut. The amazing sounds were just flowing out of him. Then the boy started to improvise. Tim was blown away. When his son finished, Tim rose from the table and walked over and wrapped Martyn in a giant bear hug.

When he could speak again he crouched down so that he could look his son in the eye and said, 'Son, I owe you a huge apology.' Martyn noticed the moisture in his father's eyes but said nothing. 'Can you play anything else?' his father asked.

'You name a song. I will see if I know it,' said Martyn.

'Play "Sultans of Swing",' said Charley. She had heard him practicing it.

The boy thought for a moment, then raising the clarinet to his mouth he began to play. This time there was no improvising. The amount of emotion the boy could put into it was unbelievable.

When it was done his father said, 'Finish your dinner. We will go for a walk.'

Father and son walked for an hour along the riverbank undoing the nasty knots that had formed in their relationship, there were apologies exchanged. After a while they walked in a companionable silence. The pale green-leaved trees were playing with the sunlight. They were arranging and rearranging the dancing golden patterns on the narrow path.

'One thing I do know, Martyn, is that if you can do this you do not need to be able to do anything else. When did you find out you could play music?'

'I don't know really. I have always heard music in my head ever since I can remember. I thought everyone could. I think playing at Grandfather's triggered something.'

'Can we keep that to ourselves? Otherwise he will insist you keep playing the piano with the nice Mr Carpenter for the rest of your life.'

'I don't think so,' declared the boy. His tone of voice clearly indicating that was never going to happen.

Back at home the discussion about the piano lessons continued. Martyn said, 'I will put a stop to them.'

'He will make a heck of a fuss,' said Sophie.

Tim waived a hand, brushing the problem aside, saying, 'They are the past tense. I will call round and tell him.'

'Tim, can I tell him?' asked Sophie. 'If you do it you will be butting heads. It will be open warfare again like it was when told him you were going to marry me whatever he said.'

The youngsters were listening to all this with dropped jaws.

'Ok, but there will be no compromises. It's done.'

'I do understand.' She was a little miffed about being lectured.

The rest of the evening was about Martyn and his music. Charley realised there had been a shift in the pecking order. Martyn, it would appear, was going to stand front and centre beside her in the family hierarchy in future. She loved her brother, but this was a complete surprise.

CHAPTER 23

Tim thought, I could try boxing. The training would get me fit, skipping, running and so on. He had boxed at school, it was compulsory. That was all right. He remembered he was always nervous before a fight. One year he was drawn against one of his close friends, whose nickname was Weedy. In school you boxed for three three-minute rounds.

On this occasion at the end of the middle round, his second, Mr Craddock the PE instructor, told him, 'At the moment, Mr Cooper, you are going to lose, I don't know how you will live that down, friend or not. You have not laid a glove on him. Just go out there and box.'

Mr Craddock always called you 'Mr' whenever he wanted to make a point.

The bell rang and as Tim walked towards his friend, he apologised, saying, 'Sorry, Weedy.' His friend knew what was coming. Tim delivered a fusillade of shots, none of them particularly painful but hard enough to score.

In his last year at school Tim and six friends won through to the county competition where they were to meet the Yanks, as everybody called them. It was a night to remember, all of his friends lost. The simple truth was the Americans were faster, harder and fitter.

Tim was in the last bout because he was the heaviest. Mr Craddock,

Tim's corner man, said, 'I think you stand a chance in this one, Tim. You have a longer reach. Stay on your toes, don't get involved inside. Keep your distance.' The first round was very even. Both boys took some heavy blows. At the end of the round the American hit him as the bell stopped ringing. Making a dramatic apology as he walked away, he winked when nobody else could see. The second was close, but Mr Craddock seemed to think Tim had shaved it.

'Right, lad, pick your moment then clobber him. I have noticed when he moves his head to avoid the blow, he takes his eyes off you. When you see that use that big right hand.'

The third round was the toughest fight Tim had ever been in. Towards the end both boys were bruised and carrying small cuts.

Then it happened, Tim pushed out his left hand and his opponents head swung away, and he shut his eyes. A heavy right cross slamming into the side of his face had knocked the young American down and sideways. Both knees and both gloves were on the floor, with him shaking his head trying to recover. Tim stepped back, dropping his hands. At the same time as the American referee arrived at Tim's side the American boy pushed one foot forward and leapt up, his impetus assisting the crashing uppercut to Tim's chin. Tim had come to being walked up and down in the venue's car park by Mr Craddock and another man.

He recalled hearing the two men talking. 'Mr Craddock,' said the stranger, 'I have never seen such a disgusting exhibition of bad sportsmanship in my life. Also I have never heard booing at an amateur event before. Tim here won that hands down, sorry for the pun.'

Tim rolled his head trying to dislodge the headache, saying, 'I didn't win then?'

'No, lad, you didn't. But you should have.'

The small team had been made to stand up in assembly the following morning with not a win between them. They were, he remembered, all

THE NEXT GENERATION

rather embarrassed. Every boy carried evidence of their endeavours, sporting bruises, bandages and plasters.

Tim knew the rules of boxing stated that when a boxer's gloves went on the floor the fight was paused while the gloves were cleaned. Grit on the glove from the floor could blind you. He also remembered another boxing instruction. Be prepared to defend yourself at all times: a maxim he would obey for the rest of his life. He never really minded losing. His academic success had been poor mainly because of his mother's early demise and his father's decline into ill health.

As a result, he was not there for most of the exams. His prowess in the ring and on the playing field had won him his school colours and laurel leaves, which had on occasion proved useful later in life.

CHAPTER 24

Tim was sat in the offices that were located in his now deceased great aunt's house mulling over the conversation he'd had yesterday evening with his dad, who had pointed out that Tim was getting no income from this house but had a large space unused above the food hall opposite the restaurant. Tim knew it was a petty wish, but he fancied an office like his father-in-law, Victor Vieri. On the opposite side of the building to the restaurant the windows overlooked a small park with its trees, grass and flowers. There was plenty of room up there. He would find out who wanted what in the way of an office and then decide.

He already knew where his office was going to be, at the far end of the corridor in the corner with two windows at ninety degrees to each other. This would make it considerably larger than any of the others. He wanted lots of light and good views. What sort of offices – open plan, separate, glass sided, doors or wood? He was unsure. Rising from his chair Tim walked through to the front office where the women were working. Arriving he plonked himself down in his usual chair, saying, 'Are you very busy?'

'Not too bad,' replied Jessica. 'What can we do for you?'

Before he could answer Bonny asked, 'Coffee, boss?'

Tim nodded and said, 'Can you give Jessica and me five minutes, Bonny, please?'

'Yeah, sure I'll make the drinks.'

THE NEXT GENERATION

'This is a bit worrying, Tim,' observed Jessica. 'Am I going to be fired?'

'Firing you, Jessica, would be the equivalent of chopping off my right arm. I am having to tread carefully now. It looks as though you and Oliver are an item. Is that true or am I jumping the gun?'

'The question you are asking, Tim, is does Oliver live here now. The answer is yes most of the time. Do you want us, him, me to move out?'

'No, no, no, none of the above,' he replied. 'I am going to have some offices built on the top floor of the food hall opposite the restaurant to accommodate all of us.'

'That will be nice, so what are you saying?'

'It would be nice if you could pay the running costs, electric, gas etc. here. I know that sounds mean but I could charge a lot of rent for the house.'

'Can I have a chat with Oliver tonight and see what he says?'

'Of course, I am not trying to force you out. Just trying to put things on a better footing.'

'Can I come out now please?' called Bonny, carrying a tray of steaming cups and a plate of ginger biscuits. She continued, 'Have you fired her? Am I going to get her job?'

'Not this week, Bonny,' laughed Jessica.

'Right I must go,' said Tim, swallowing his hot coffee as he stood up and made for the door. 'Let me know what you come up with.'

'Will do,' was the reply.

'Is it unwelcome news?' asked Bonny.

'No, Tim wanted to know what I want to do about living here. I must admit I have thought about it now and then, but I have been putting it off.'

'And now there is the delicious Oliver,' laughed Bonny.

'Thank you, Bonny,' was Jessica's stern reply. 'Shall we try and get some work done?'

'Yes, boss,' was Bonny's contrite response.

*****

On the *Sea Maiden* that night Sophie was voicing her disapproval at Tim's actions. 'It has not been six months since her husband's death, only a little more than that since the sale of the house. Before that the violence and the divorce. No wonder she has not done anything about it. I would still be sitting in a corner crying my eyes out if I were her.'

'Should I ring her and tell her to forget it for now?'

'No, you have done it now. I wish you had asked me first; I could have talked to her privately and found out what was happening with Oliver.'

Tim, feeling a little aggrieved at Sophie's reaction, said, 'All I was trying to do was get my ducks in a row before I talked to the board about building the offices on the top floor of the food hall.'

'How long has that been on the agenda?' she asked.

'A couple of weeks,' was the reply.

*****

At the house in question the atmosphere was far friendlier. Polly was sitting on Oliver's lap drawing.

Oliver asked, 'Is that your headmaster?' pointing to the figure the child had just drawn. 'Where is his beard and moustache?'

'He has shaved it off, everyone says he looks really odd,' replied Jessica. She was really impressed; Oliver had only taken Polly into school twice.

'He has a scar on his cheek, which was hidden by his beard. It looks nasty, it must have been very painful, poor man,' observed Jessica.

'Can we talk about where we live, Oliver?' said Jessica.

Before he could reply Polly butted in and said, 'Can he live here please, Mummy? He feels like my real daddy.'

THE NEXT GENERATION

Oliver squeezed Polly and said, 'Thank you very much. I would love to be your daddy.'

'He can stay now can't he, Mummy?'

'It's bed time for you, young lady. This is a decision for adults to make, not children. Off you go, madam.'

Polly kissed his cheek and said, 'Goodnight, Oliver.' Much to his surprise this choked him up.

Jessica followed her daughter upstairs, the child chattering away as she climbed.

Having snuggled her daughter down to sleep and kissed her goodnight she walked into the master bedroom and sat on the end of the bed.

Now she had a real problem, it was quite obvious Polly had fallen in love with Oliver and that she saw him as a father figure. To lose Oliver would cause her daughter enormous pain and who knew how much psychological damage. The child may never trust a man again. So much for her child, how about herself? She had made up her mind not to have any more men in her life. But Oliver was very kind and thoughtful, and good company, he was gentle in bed. She felt her skin warm as she recalled what had occurred the night before. Shaking herself she thought enough of that, what irritates me about him? He does not seem to take things as seriously as me. He is certainly not a worrier. The demon inside her said, 'He looks best naked.' That does not necessarily make a happy marriage, she thought. She immediately downgraded that to a happy partnership.

Looking back to her first marriage, her husband had been nice in the beginning. It had been when she got her good job as Tim and Sophie's PA it had come undone. He was jealous, and when he had been asked to do some chores around the house her husband had lost his temper. He had told her that it was her job to look after him and their child.

Oliver and Jessica lay in bed that night talking. They agreed to pay Tim a proper rent for the house. They both felt this would be a good test to see if they could live together or not. As she fell asleep that night she felt not so alone. Now there were two of them to overcome the everyday problems. Later in the week the three of them had agreed a figure for the rental, as Tim had explained he was not going to rip people off.

Sophie was surprised that they had agreed to pay as much as they had. She raised this over dinner, asking, 'Are you sure they can afford that much?'

Tim replied testily 'It was Oliver who came up with the original figure, he had done some research. It was too high, I reduced it. We are all happy. It won't start until we have moved the offices above the food hall.'

Checking in estate agents' windows over the next few days Sophie recognised Tim had been quite generous.

CHAPTER 25

Tim rang Charlie to start the ball rolling. A week later the two men, accompanied by young Tommy, Charlie's son, were walking around the space upstairs.

'Goodness me, Tommy, you've grown,' said Tim. The lad smiled.

'He should have,' said Charlie, 'he's eating us out of house and home.' Continuing, he said, 'There's plenty of room up here for,' he was walking, talking, and counting as he went, 'five I reckon, along here by these windows on the left, maybe six.'

'I'm going to spoil myself,' said Tim. 'I have taken extraordinarily little out of this business so far. I want a big office.' He had walked down to the far corner where there were windows on both walls. 'I want it here so when you walk down this corridor my office door is facing you at the end.'

'Sorry, Mr Cooper, I don't understand,' said Tommy.

'I'll explain it to you later, son,' said Charlie.

'That's ok, Tommy, walk with me.' The three walked back to the top of the stairs that were opposite the reception for the restaurant.

'So, Tommy, as you can see with the stairs behind us we are facing the reception for the restaurant.' Tommy nodded. Continuing, Tim said, 'There will be a corridor here running down beside the restaurant with a row of offices on the left lit by these tall windows.'

'My office will be wider than the others because it includes the width of the corridor. Got it?'

Tommy nodded, then said, 'That'll be right posh won't it?'

Tim laughed and Charlie told his son off.

Tim put his hand on the boy's shoulder and whispered in his ear, 'You're right, lad, it will be right posh. I'm going to have a big chair and a big desk, and you can come and sit in it when all the works done.'

Tommy was smiling at him again.

Charlie was busy making notes. Looking up he said, 'It shouldn't take too long. Basically, we just need to make some lightweight dividers and doors. I need to check up on clearances et cetera.' Tim looked perplexed. 'Things like wheelchair access and so on.'

Tim nodded and then said, 'Before I forget I want a fire escape by the stairs. How Declan and Daisy got out of Shop Number One I shall never know; I get the shivers just thinking about it.'

'He's brave that's fer sure,' agreed Charlie with Tommy nodding. 'I'll get a specialist company in to erect the fire escape,' added Charlie.

* * * * *

Early one Monday morning a month later Tim arrived to discuss a menu change with Enzo. Reaching the top of the stairs he discovered Charlie and Tommy moving wood and glass partitions around on the far corner that was going to be Tim's large office. Enzo was holding one end of a panel that was positioned at ninety degrees to the wall while Charlie and Tommy secured it to the brickwork.

Charlie began talking quietly to his son Tommy. It was barely audible. He was saying, 'Now listen, lad, there's a lesson here fer you. As you go through life, make sure you're the big boss. Then you get to stand and watch while people like you and me do the real work, the straining and sweating.'

THE NEXT GENERATION

Smiling, Tim removed his jacket and draped it over a chair in the restaurant. As he walked back he was rolling up his shirt sleeves. 'Ok, where do you want me?'

The men worked hard for nearly an hour; Enzo had retired earlier to his kitchen to start his days' work.

'So, Tim, what do you think?' asked Charlie, looking around inside the space that was to become his office.

'It's bigger than I thought it would be,' Tim replied.

'It'll shrink when you brings your desk and whatever in,' observed Tommy.

Over the next few days Tim became ever more impatient. When talking to Charlie there was always something else to install, the lighting, the radiators, the phone lines, the list appeared endless. There had been a lot of discussion as to whether there should be interconnecting doors between the offices, how much glass there should be in the side walls and the doors.

Finally it was agreed that the doors would be panelled glass with blinds. The occupants could place the internal furniture wherever they felt most comfortable. The three women wanted to work together so another office was double in size. There were not to be any interconnecting doors in any of them. Sophie's office was the first in the row. Permission was obtained to install the fire escape near the restaurant entrance by converting the lower part of one of the floor-to-ceiling windows.

* * * * *

Tim, walking down the length of the corridor to his new office, was, he discovered, really excited. He'd not had any time to visit the fitting out of the offices. He gave the other rooms a cursory glance as he passed them. He wanted to see if his ideas for the space he was going to spend so much time in looked as good as he hoped it would. Entering the room to his surprise it was dark. Fumbling for the light switch he realised it was a small panel of dimmer switches that threw independent pools of light onto various parts of the room. He was very impressed, a play with the switches proved he could alter the atmosphere of the space in all kinds of extremely attractive ways. He could choose to have only his beautiful, large, honey-coloured oak desk sitting in a single pool of light or have other areas lit gently and individually. Stepping across the room he drew the heavy, dark curtains aside, flooding the room with early morning sunlight. Now he could see the finished effect of the colour scheme he had chosen. The walls were a warm pale grey, the same colour as the restaurant. A pale polished wood floor was a wonderful foil for the navy furniture and the gleaming chrome coffee table. His desk was at an angle in a corner near the door, looking down his office to the view of the people strolling in the park. A waterfall of lights were hanging from the tall ceiling. A large picture of a field and a gate painted by a local artist hung on the wall behind his desk. While mulling over the office design he decided he wanted a wow factor, something to catch people's interest. He was looking at it now. A long tapering navy arrow started at its widest from the skirting board in the corner by his desk and streaked across and up the otherwise blank wall towards the windows. It finished in a point in the corner at the ceiling. The centre of the arrow carried a thin chrome strip along its length. He was never sure why but when he noticed the arrow he usually laughed. A large family photo hung on the wall to his right. In it Martyn was standing looking up at his mother. Tim had his arm around his wife's waist, Charley was holding his hand looking confidently at the camera.

Jessica entered the room and stood spellbound. Tim had informed the office staff that the offices were complete, and they were to come and look. 'Oh wow, Tim, this is amazing.' She was pivoting her head trying to see it all at once. Like him she laughed when she turned around and saw the navy and silver arrow.

THE NEXT GENERATION

'What is that!?' she shouted, pointing at the design on the wall.

Tim pretended to fire an arrow into the sky, saying as he did so, 'Onward and upward. Who's in your office?' he asked.

'Bonny and Oliver,' she replied.

'Fetch them in,' he responded, 'so they can see it.' Part of the reason for them seeing it was to gauge whether they liked his design or not.

The crowd arrived. This included Enzo, who had followed them to see what was so interesting. Bonny was soon playing with the box of controls for the lights and the curtains. There were numerous discussions as to who preferred which arrangement. Tim got Bonny to make a note of the switch combinations he preferred. The curtains fully open in daylight was everyone's first choice. Tim noticed Lynda had joined them.

Enzo started the exodus when he looked at his watch and said, 'Whoops, I must get on. Shall we see you for lunch, Tim?'

'Yes, Jessica and I have about half an hour's work, then I will come round.'

'You're not eating in here then?'

'No, Sophie has forbidden me to work through my lunch hour.'

'It's only because she is concerned for you. Have you had any recurrence of the ticker trouble, Tim?' asked Jessica. He shook his head. A friend of his had suffered a heart attack, it was his first and last one. He left a wife and three children behind. Before she left, Bonny did something with the lighting that Tim was never able to duplicate. He was too embarrassed to admit he could not replicate the effect.

CHAPTER 26

Tim was descending a long, steep escalator on the underground.

His head as usual was elsewhere when a young man on the up side who had drawn level with him called, 'Mr Cooper, Tim, I am Mr Woodman's grandson, hallo.' He was smartly dressed in a dark business suit.

Tim taken aback and frowning, looked away, thinking to himself, Mr Woodman didn't have any children, let alone a grandchild. Assuming it was a setup he did not reply. Further down the long escalator Tim did look back. The young man was smiling and then he waved. A train was arriving as Tim reached the platform. Intent on ensuring he could not be found he worked his way through the compartments to the front.

* * * * *

Tim and the young man were sitting at a table outside the café in the food hall. The youngster had written a letter to Tim explaining he was in London on a one-month course, and he only contacted Tim to learn more about Mr Woodman, his grandfather.

Tim said, 'I know your first name, Theo, from your letter. What is your surname?'

'Leventis, Theo Leventis.'

THE NEXT GENERATION

'So how did you find us, Theo?'

'It was surprisingly easy; I asked the elderly taxi driver who collected me from the station to take me to Mr Woodman's shop. He told me that he knew it from when my grandfather owned it. I told him I was looking for you. He explained my grandfather closed his store and in partnership with you had opened it as a delicatessen. He dropped me outside the shop. I asked inside and they told me I could find you here.'

'So, how do I know you are Mr Woodman's grandson?' asked Tim. Then he thought to himself, having seen the pictures in an old copy of a newspaper of his godfather when he came home from the war, this young man and Mr Woodman could have been twins. Theo had his grandfather's looks, a kind face, intelligent eyes and a shock of dark hair. Tim guessed he was about six foot tall with an upright stance. Yes he was definitely Mr Woodman's kin.

Theo said, 'Mother has three old photos of my grandmother and Mr Woodman.' He was searching through his wallet as he was speaking. Tim's mind went back to a recent evening when Sophie had asked him if he had a first-class stamp. Searching through his wallet without removing anything he was struggling to find the stamps; he knew he had two on a piece of card. Eventually he had to give in and pull everything out and sort it on the table. Sophie watched the growing number of different piles.

Sitting down she said, 'Let me help. You men take the mickey out of us women and our handbags.' Waving her hand at the items now lying on the table she said, 'This is the same in miniature.' The stamps were discovered in a small compartment that he never used, or thought he didn't.

After a couple of minutes Theo found the photos. On the back of the first one Tim read 'Barry and me'. She was dressed in a nurse's outfit; Mr Woodman was dressed in a dark coat and trousers. She was obviously a very attractive young woman.

'She didn't know his real name ever, I don't think. The shock of his being torpedoed, and all his injuries caused him total amnesia. They chose Barry because they had to call him something.'

'Is your grandmother still alive?' asked Tim.

'No, she was killed in a bombing raid on Crete shortly after my mother was born. The family cared for her daughter.'

'I gather your mother's still alive?'

'Oh yes. She is very well and still living on the island. She is married with two more children, both girls.'

'How did you find me initially?'

'Now that was interesting,' said Theo. 'There was a local nurse over here, a friend of my mother's, doing some special course or other at one of the big London hospitals. She was lodging not far away. When she saw the newspaper pictures of him in the paper covering his funeral she saw the wartime pictures of him they had added and recognised him straight away. She sent the papers home. Mother was sad that she had not found him before but as he had passed away there was nothing she could do. When the firm posted me over here for a month I decided to do a bit of a search to see what I could find out. The old folk round here remember him very well. They guided me here to this shop; they were very friendly. They've told me lots about him. He sounds like he was a good man.'

'He was very kind to me down the years,' said Tim. 'I'm his godson. I miss him a lot. if I had a problem I always went to him. You know he left the shop to me, is that difficult for you?'

'No, I don't think so. I know nothing about running a shop. Apparently he found his wife had died while he was away fighting.'

'Yes,' replied Tim, 'everyone thinks she died of a broken heart.'

'Poor man,' responded Theo. 'I understand he never did remarry.'

Shaking his head Tim said, 'No, sadly not. I did ask him on one occasion why he'd not. His response was that he was sure he would never find anyone who could replace her.'

The two men were quiet for a moment, then Tim asked, 'How long are you here for?'

'Another week, but I will be in Scotland from tomorrow on, then back home.' Looking at the big clock at the back of the food hall he asked, 'Is that clock right?' now checking his watch.

Tim confirmed that it was.

'I must be gone,' he said, standing and holding his hand out as he spoke.

Tim stood up, shook it and said, 'Please look in if you are ever over here again.'

'Will do,' was the response. Tim watched him walk away, thinking how sad it was that he had not found his grandfather sooner. Mind you, that could have had an enormous influence on his own current situation. Tim realised that if Shop Number One had been left to Theo and not himself and his father the two of them would very likely still be running the family stall in the market. It doesn't bear thinking about, he supposed, putting it out of his head.

CHAPTER 27

Tim arrived at the Vieri's in the Bentley to take Olivia, 'Sophie's mother', out in the car. This was now a regular occurrence. Mr Graham, Tim's chauffeur, would drive them to interesting places. Their destination usually depended on the time of year. Walks in the park in the spring and summer, slow cruises past famous buildings with Tim pointing them out to her in the colder weather. She often managed to add some further information to what he had said, often describing the war damage to the beautiful architecture that was now so carefully restored you could not see the difference between the original and the new. Her choice of clothing was always similar. A quiet dress with a dark fox fur over it. Depending on the weather it was either open or in the cold tightly wrapped around her with the strap tied in place. The café choices had now become regular. All dictated by Mrs Vieri. Tim often tried to talk her out of some choices. She was adamant that once she had settled in the car, arranged the cover over her lap and taken Tim's hand in hers then she would voice her decision for that day. She would brook no variation. He could discern no pattern, but it was clear hers was not a random choice. The cake choice was weather dependent. Light sponge cake in the warm weather, buttered crumpets in the snow and ice. Tim would always have the buttered crumpet if he could have his own way. Like tonight, Mrs Vieri would gently fall asleep on the way home, her head resting on his shoulder. When the car came to a halt she would look up at him, then lifting his hand to her lips she would kiss it. This while wearing a gentle smile of thanks. Today they had walked hand in hand beside the round pond in Kensington Gardens. A group of men were racing their model yachts. Mrs Vieri stopped to watch. As the leading boat crossed between two orange buoys at the other end of the lake a group of bystanders began clapping. Mrs Vieri was happy to stand and watch the racing for quite some time. Tim, who was being taught to sail in a small dingy by Gordon, the skipper of a local sailing club, recognised all the same sail setting and manoeuvres were identical on the model yachts as the full-sized dinghy he was learning on.

A couple of weeks later the two of them were waiting to cross a main road from the café back to the car. Mrs Vieri went to step into the road, not seeing a car exiting a side road on her right-hand side. Tim stopped her progress by holding her arm. Pointing out the car to her said gently, 'We can't go yet, this chap is turning this way.'

A young man and his girl walking arm in arm who had been standing beside them stepped out in front of them. He, in a loud mickey-taking voice, said, 'We can't go yet, this chap is turning this way.' They were braying with laughter as they walked away.

When they got to the other side of the road Mrs Vieri stopped and turned into him. He could feel her desperate cries. A tall, strong-looking African stopped at Tim's shoulder and said, 'I heard what they said, mate. Do you want me to go and sort them out?'

'No, please don't, you will get into trouble.'

On the way home Mrs Vieri was wrapped in her misery, silent tears ran down her face. She fully understood what the young man had said. For a proud woman like her it was so wounding. Tim held her. She would never agree to going out again. Tim replaced this by staying in and reading to her. He wondered if in fifty years' time either of the young people would remember this incident, when the rigours of old age had reduced them to enduring continual pain, loss of memory, or sight, or both. He doubted it.

CHAPTER 28

Tim's phone rang, he was finishing his discussion with Bonny. Now paying attention to the phone call he said, 'Hallo, sorry to keep you. How may I help?'

'Tim it is me, Sophie, my mother is mumbling your name and is quite distressed. Can you find the time to come and see her please?'

'Hold tight a moment, Sophie love.' Now addressing Bonny and Jessica he asked, 'Is there anything I need to sign or whatever? Sophie needs me.'

The two women looked at each other and shook their heads.

'Right, I shall be at Mrs Vieri's.'

* * * * *

Sitting in the back of the Bentley driving across town Tim began to feel really guilty. The evening visits to read to Olivia had petered out as the workload had grown heavier and heavier. Currently he was doing twelve-hour days.

As the car pulled up outside the Vieris' house Tim said, 'I don't know when I shall be done.'

'Usual drill, Tim, just ring.'

'Thanks, Mr Graham, I do think we take advantage of you rather.'

'With respect, Tim, that's tosh. Thanks to your family's generosity with the house and wages, Mrs Graham and I have lived very well. It should be us who are thanking you.'

'That's kind of you to say so, Mr Graham. I suppose I had better go and see what the problem is. Bye for now.'

'See you later, Tim,' was the response.

As he drove away Mr Graham thought to himself, 'This young man was supposed to slow down as a result of his health scare a while back. I don't think he has.'

Tim knocked on the door, it was opened promptly by Sophie. Shutting the door behind him she said, 'Mother is very weak. She has not had anything to eat or drink for the last three days. The nurse had advised Martha to stop feeding because Mrs Vieri was inhaling the food.' Then footsteps sounded as a nurse walked towards them.

Sophie did the introductions, saying, 'This is my husband, Tim.'

The nurse replied, 'Hallo, Tim, I'm Sandra. Nurse Gloria is doing the night shift at present.'

'I have a question, Sandra,' said Tim. 'Why are you withholding food and water?'

'That's a good question. It sounds as though we are being cruel, however, this could not be further from the truth. I have seen a patient choke to death just once. The look of terror on the man's face was horrific. I pray I never see it again. By the way, we never discuss the patient's condition within the patient's hearing.' The three of them moved to Mrs Vieri's bedroom.

Tim walked towards her bed, saying, 'Hallo, Olivia, how are you?' The elderly woman opened her eyes looked up at Tim and gave him a delighted smile. She slid her hand across the bedclothes towards him. He took her fingers gently in his then leant over and kissed her forehead. She closed her eyes and took her hand back, tucking it under the eiderdown.

The nurse watched her for a few minutes, then said, 'She seems far more settled. Thank you for coming.' Tim was shaking his head; he was unsure of what had happened.

'She is sound asleep now. We can leave her for a while. I'll moisten her lips.' Mrs Vieri did not stir while the damp sponge was applied. 'You two may as well go home. She will not wake for some time.'

CHAPTER 29

Early the following morning Sophie received a phone call. Still half asleep she mumbled, 'Hallo.'

'Is that Sophia Cooper?'

Sophie nodded, and then realised whoever it was could not see down the phone. Shaking her head at her own silly behaviour she said, 'Yes.'

'This is Gloria, the night nurse here; I am sorry to tell you your mother passed away in the night.'

Sophie collapsed and was now sitting cross legged on the floor in floods of tears.

Tim appeared, sat down beside her and took the phone away from her and said, 'Hallo, Tim here.'

The nurse repeated what she had just told his wife. 'Do you know what to do?' she said.

'Yes,' he replied, 'I will get on with it his morning. Thank you both for looking after her so well. Does Mr Vieri know?'

'Yes, but he has gone out.'

'Oh … ok,' said Tim, surprised, then he realised where he had run to – Sally's. Tim heard Charley approaching, dragging her eiderdown behind her. Martyn was following, more asleep than awake.

'Tea?' he asked, Sophie nodded. Now looking a little more composed.

Tim guided his wife and the two children into the main bedroom and into bed. Minutes later he reappeared with the tea tray, tucking a fresh hot water bottle in with them.

'Thank you, Tim. How did you know I was cold?'

'It was one of the things we were taught at scouts. When the body goes into shock the person's temperature plummets, I don't know why. You should be more comfortable now.'

Charley was busy making sure her mummy was properly tucked in. 'The tea needs to brew; I will ring round and tell people what's happened,' he said as he left the room.

'No, I need to get up and work, Tim.'

'Not today.'

'But–'

'Sophie, I am putting my foot down. Today is about us and your mother. There are lots of things to do. We will do them one at a time. You can talk or cry as you choose, I will be here,' he said as he left the room, carrying a handful of his clothes.

Sophie realised he was using a tone of voice that meant he would brook no argument. Returning to the main cabin now dressed, he found his wife and daughter cuddling, the blankets pulled up around their chins. Martyn was already sound asleep. Charley drifted off to sleep shortly afterwards. The tapping on the door announced Nanny's arrival. Tim went to let her in. Sophie could hear Tim explaining about her mother. Tim's head appeared around the door.

'Nanny wants to know if she can come in.'

'Of course she can. I might cry all over her but never mind.'

Nanny entered and reached for Sophie's hand. 'I am so sorry to hear your news. I didn't realise she was that poorly.'

Sophie said, 'Nor did I.' She was palming the tears from her eyes as she spoke. 'please do not be nice to me, Nanny, or I will be in tears again.'

Tim sat on the bed on the far side.

Sophie continued, 'I do feel a little guilty. It must be a week since I saw her. She seemed much the same.'

It was longer than that, thought Tim. He didn't correct her; they had both been terribly busy.

'Tim, I was thinking in the night. You will be sure I am going crazy; I think she was hanging on because she wanted to say goodbye to you.'

'What happened then, Sophie?' asked Nanny.

'We had a phone call from one of mother's nurses. Apparently she was becoming quite distressed and was calling for Tim.' Sophie went on to talk about the hand holding and the little smile from her mother for Tim. 'I do think she wanted to say goodbye to you, Tim. She was so much calmer after she saw you. I really do think she was holding on until you arrived.'

'I'm not sure of that,' was Tim's response. 'I think that's a bit farfetched.'

'The more I think about it the more certain I become,' responded Sophie. 'Tim, when she was with you over these last months she was a girl again. You made her laugh, you paid her attention. As hard as it is to believe, in spite of the terrible way she treated you at the beginning I think she had become extremely fond of you.'

In the future when Tim thought back he could never be as sure as Sophie was about her mother's reasons for wanting him to visit her.

CHAPTER 30

Sophie struggled through the funeral arrangements. Two of her mother's close Italian relatives had, on hearing the news, got on a plane and flown to the UK. With Sophie's permission they took over the arrangements as soon as they landed. A large marquee was erected on the sizeable lawn at the back of the family home. There were flowers everywhere, mostly white lilies. The coffin was open so that people could say goodbye. An ever-growing crowd of Italian relatives made a passage past the coffin. Angela knew most of them because she had spent much more time abroad as a child than Sophie had. Her mother had sent Angela and her nanny to the farmhouse in Italy to get her out from underfoot, her mother's words.

Tim watched as the mourners chose to kiss her forehead, touch her or just stand for a moment in silence. As he joined the back of the queue, he felt someone step in behind him and take his hand. He turned round to discover it was his wife in a flood of silent tears. Shuffling forward he bent over the coffin and kissed Olivia's forehead. He was surprised how moved he was. Sophie followed his example when kissing her mother. Releasing her husband, she stood for a moment holding her mother's hand. Tim realised he had been granted the only insight into who Mrs Vieri really was. She had allowed him to see the girl that she was meant to be, the girl she had kept hidden all of her life. This the fault of her harridan of a mother, who was vicious and cruel, and if the reports he'd had from her Italian relatives were true it appeared that her mother enjoyed putting her eldest daughter, Mrs Vieri, down. He knew that her marriage was loveless. It had been arranged by the young couple's families. Tim was sure she knew that her husband was having an affair in the later years of their marriage. Occasionally she would say something to him that hinted at her husband's infidelity.

Sophie and her family were gently guided through the funeral service. They were surprised by the number of family members from Italy who had come over. There was a small contingent of her mother's posh British friends who stayed for the food and the drink but left soon after waving at Sophie and Angela from the doorway. In years to come Sophie found she could remember virtually nothing of the service or who said what to whom.

CHAPTER 31

Mrs Simmons the solicitor handed Tim a letter, saying, 'Finally, Tim, this is for you. I advise you to open this in private.' The adult family members were sitting in her office.

Mrs Simmons was her usual immaculate self in her burgundy two-piece suit with its neat jacket, pencil skirt and black low-heeled shoes, her greying hair in a bun. Her Scottish brogue was still obvious.

Tim read the heading on the letter that said, *To Mr Timothy Cooper. Private and confidential.* There was no address, nothing. He held the letter away from him, looking as though he thought it was about to explode. 'Is this bad news, Mrs Simmons? Am I going to need your services?'

'No, Tim, it is not bad news. I think you will be surprised when you open it.'

Mr Vieri and Angela were deep in conversation.

Sophie gave Tim an enquiring look, he shook his head in response, indicating he was no wiser than her. On the drive home they were both tossing different names in the air and then discarding them, unable to guess who the letter writer may be. When they reached the boat, Sophie put the kettle on. Standing beside her Tim drew the letter from his pocket, looked at it, then returned it, saying, 'No, I will read it later.'

'No, you will read it now,' commanded Sophie. She was trying to wrestle it from his pocket.

'Stop it, woman, you'll tear my jacket. What makes you women so curious? You just have to know don't you?'

'Timothy, shut up and open the damn letter for goodness' sake,' she spat out. Realising Sophie was no longer amused he went into the main cabin and sat on the couch. Sophie plonked herself down beside him. He opened the missive. Inside there was a loose letter and a sealed envelope. The loose letter was addressed to him.

Dear Tim,

The enclosed was dictated to me by Olivia, my sister, shortly after you and Mr Graham started taking her for trips out in the Bentley. I had little to do with it. Occasionally she would ask my advice; she did not always take it. She insisted it should be lodged with her solicitor; I am happy to talk about it if you want to.

Love Angela.

Tim, now extremely puzzled, opened the other envelope.

Dear Timothy,

As you have discovered with the reading of my will I have only left you the two paintings of my home town in Italy that you admired. I do not think your personal fortune needs adding to. I have left the greater part to Sophia, as you will now know. This includes the house in Puglia.

Your care for me in the last period of my life was remarkable. Your thoughtfulness, your concern for my comfort and wellbeing when we were together was extraordinary. As I am sure Sophia has told you, my upbringing was iron hard and uncaring. I honestly believe my mother considered children to be a terrible inconvenience and an embarrassment. In her day intimacy beyond a certain age was considered inappropriate.

I know I was an enormous disappointment to her and my father. I was supposed to be a boy. The boarding school was ghastly, cold and aggressive, I cried easily in those days, this made the bullying worse. Two of the teachers could best be described as vindictive. My marriage to Victor was arranged by the families in our childhood. We had no say in the matter. We never loved each other; I am not sure we even liked each other at the end. I know his relationship with Sally, his PA, is common knowledge. I am happy for him, at least one of us has found love.

I am so pleased that Sophia is happy. Once it became apparent how much you thought of each other I was able to relax and stop worrying. I was extremely concerned at the beginning that she may suffer the same bitter experience that I have. It is clear the reverse is true; your children are delightful.

People may sneer if they learn how much value I put on our trips out, holding my hand, making me laugh, giving me a hug. No one has done this for me in decades. Your concern has meant more to me than handfuls of diamonds. Please do not show this letter to anyone except perhaps Sophia, she must be persuaded not to disclose its existence. I wish you and Sophia and your family a long and happy life. Olivia.

Sophie got up from her seat and made her way out to the rear deck and stood staring out across the river. Tim sat for a while in silence then collected two glasses and a bottle of white wine and went to join his wife. When he got there, to his surprise Sophie was dry eyed. Tim waved the wine bottle at her. She shook her head saying, 'No thank you. Can we walk?'

'Yes of course, I'll put the wine back. When will Nanny return?'

Looking at her watch Sophie said, 'About another hour, she walks them round the park.' Anticipating Tim's next question she said, 'I have given her the spare key. She did say she would knock loudly.' This was an oblique reference to the time she had caught Tim as nature had made him. This was another of his mother's expressions.

Tim returned the wine to the rack and buried the letter under all the paper in the bottom drawer of his desk.

The two of them walked hand in hand, mostly in silence. There were still no tears from Sophie and hardly any communication. She appeared absorbed by the activity on the river. Tim suspected she could not even see it.

Approaching an ice cream van Tim asked, 'Would you like an ice cream?'

'Would I what?' was the response. Tim repeated the question, Sophie simply shook her head as a refusal.

His wife was quiet for the rest of the day. Tim was doing the washing up, Nanny brought a pile of dirty crockery from the evening meal, placed them on the work surface next to him and said almost in a whisper, 'Is Sophie alright? she is very quiet.'

'It was the reading of the will, some of the disclosures that I can't talk about obviously rattled her a lot I think.'

CHAPTER 32

It was three weeks after the reading of Sophie's mother's will and the letter to Tim. His wife had been quiet and withdrawn since the funeral. The reason was the contents of the letter her mother had written to Tim. He was aware that it had hurt Sophie, mostly because it had been in its way effusive. It bore no resemblance to the usual letters from the deceased woman, which had been short, abrupt and to the point, often hovering on the edge of rudeness, overstepping even that mark on occasion

The couple left the boat to keep a dinner appointment with Angela to discuss the letter. The weather matched his wife's mood, dark and damp. Her rather ordinary dress did not display her usual joie de vivre. Mr Graham dropped the couple off at Angela's, whose greeting was quieter than the normal effusive reception. She had sensed Sophie's low mood. Taking the coats she asked, 'Would anyone like a drink?'

Responding immediately, Sophie asked, 'May I have a white wine please?' Angela poured her a drink and turned to Tim, who asked for a glass of red. Tim and Angela both noticed Sophie dispatching a good half of the glass in one long swallow. The two of them exchanged worried looks. Not saying anything, Angela topped up her glass again.

'The meal is almost ready. Give me five minutes,' Angela said as she disappeared into the kitchen.

The couple sat in silence, waiting for Angela's return. Sophie was deep in thought. Her mother's obvious affection for Tim had torn a wide rent in the fabric of her emotions. Her mother had never displayed or voiced the affection for her that had been so clearly displayed in her letter to Tim. Sophie sensed she had struggled over her decision as to whether to put, 'With all my love, Olivia'.

Her mother may as well have written the sentence. The words hung there, shouting more loudly because of their obvious omission. It was her nanny and Angela who had shown her real love and affection, even her father, who could be a cold stern fish, would sweep her into his arms and blow raspberries into her neck until she grew too big for it. Until Tim's arrival it was always her father who cuddled her when she cried, never her mother. This contrasted savagely with the cold cheek that was offered by her mother when she went to kiss her. The briefest of touches was all that was allowed.

Did her mother love her? She was racking her brains trying to remember any incident or action that would prove she did.

When Sophie first met Tim she had to admit to herself that she was a little uncomfortable with his need to hold hands. He wanted to be in constant physical contact with her. As their relationship grew so did the intimacy, his arm around her waist, or his hand on her hip or a palm on her bottom guiding her through a doorway first. In the early days she had told him that she was not always comfortable with his constant need for touching her.

When she raised the subject Tim had been quiet for some time. 'My mother was very touchy feely,' he'd said. 'When I came home from school there was always a kiss and a hug, same for Dad. He always received the same. I know that was one of the things we missed most, first of course was the loss of her presence, then it was her comfort, the kiss and the cuddle was an affirmation of the strength of family and our love for each other.'

After another period of silent thought he'd said, 'I will try not to keep grabbing you. I'm sorry, I didn't realise you didn't like it.'

Sophie, huffing with frustration, had replied firmly, 'I did not say I did not like it; it is not what I am used to is all.' She remembered Tim pulled a face and was then quiet for some time. Over the following days there were a couple of occasions when he unknowingly reached for her hand. As the contact was made he registered what he had done and dropped her hand as though it were a red hot coal. She recalled that she was not sure if she was imagining it, but it felt as though their relationship was cooling. The touching had all stopped, the good night kiss was now a brief pale example of what occurred before.

One night at Angela's her mind was made up for her. Her aunt was wearing a short, pretty, flowered dress that had two buttons undone on the top showing her not unattractive cleavage.

On arrival as usual Angela had hugged her first, then Tim. Sophie had walked on into the lounge, then turning to talk to Tim she discovered he had not followed her. Looking back into the hallway it was apparent Angela and Tim were still locked in an extremely enthusiastic hug, both laughing at something one of them had said.

Turning on her heel she had taken three long strides back into the hall and said in a cold hard voice, 'Tim will you put my aunt down please.'

'Oops, sorry, Sophie.' Her aunt had said. 'It is my fault. I was telling Tim a silly story.'.

Sophie was aware that her aunt found Tim attractive, indeed on more than one occasion she had said so, making a joke of it. Sophie was fairly sure there was a big spoonful of truth in it. When they'd reached home she had pushed Tim up against the front door then made sure there was full body contact as their tongues touched. Tim had reached down to grasp her bottom with both hands and increase the intimacy. When Tim had finally broken away he had to hold on to her to stop himself falling over. This was what Sophie had named the bedroom kiss.

Now it was often she who initiated the kiss and the hug or the reach for his hand. She recognised that this simple intimacy was what she had missed all her life.

She was still trying to recall when her mother had shown any love for her, even the arrangements for her wedding had been more about appearances and what her friends would think rather than what her daughter wanted.

Tim and Angela were sipping their soup course when Angela asked, 'Do you not want your soup?'

Sophie, dragged from her reverie, said, 'Sorry, I beg your pardon. What did you say?'

Angela repeated the question.

'Oh yes, thank you,' she replied picking up her spoon.

'Come on, Sophie love, spit it out. This letter has obviously hurt you,' continued Angela. 'We can talk and eat, my darling.'

Sophie, after a few spoonfuls of soup, reiterated most of what she had been thinking, halfway through Tim lent across and held her hand.

She finished by saying, 'Tim, her letter plainly said she loved you. She simply could not bring herself to write it.'

Angela interrupted her, 'You cannot know that, Sophie love. It was clear she had a great regard for Tim. I am inclined to believe she was not sure what she felt.'

There was a long silence. Tim was about to say something when Sophie said, 'Tim, my mother showed you more affection in that letter than she ever showed me.'

Tim could hear the catch in her voice.

'Thank God I had you, Aunty, and now you, Tim. One thing I am certain of is that we will always make sure our children know they are loved.'

Again Sophie was silent for a while, then she said. 'I know when I cut my knee badly on broken glass, she told me off for making such a fuss and called for Nanny, who said it needed stiches. Mother would have none of that. A plaster will do was her response. I remember Nanny argued with her and repeated it needed stitching. Mother told Nanny off and sent us up to the nursery. I have a scar to this day.'

There was a short silence while they digested what Sophie had said.

Angela broke it, saying, 'You know who the real culprit is in all of this? Your grandmother, my and Olivia's mother. I know she was a lot harder on Olivia than she was me. I was always silly Angela, she never expected anything of me. Nanny and I were often sent to the house in Puglia for the summer, I loved it. If it helps I can tell you some of the things she disclosed to me while she was dictating,' offered Angela.

Sophie nodded.

'She shared with me why she was so aggressive. As a girl she was nervous and shy. Mother had been so domineering. Olivia was scared of everything, nothing she did was ever good enough. At boarding school she suffered terribly from the bullies. One day she lost control and assaulted one of the bullies, knocking her to the ground. The headmistress told Mother that when the teacher arrived to stop the fighting Olivia was dragging the bully about by the hair. Olivia was warned that one more incident like that and she would be excluded from school permanently. The strange thing was, I remember, Mother never told her off. Olivia told me the incident had taught her a lesson. Attack the others before they attack you. It was the only method that appeared to work when she was growing up, drive the bullies away before they started on her. The problem was she carried it on into adulthood. Her attitude often upset people so badly they would avoid her. She came out of her malaise to dictate the letter. It was the last long conversation I had with her. I felt it was something she wanted to get off her chest. She seemed to relax once I had read it to her. She was far more compliant once the letter was written.'

Angela, standing beside her sister's grave at the funeral, had said under her breath, 'Rest easy, Olivia, your struggle is over. I loved you always.'

CHAPTER 33

Tom Cooper stepped from the tube train and was making his way towards the exit when he was grabbed from behind by both arms and pulled backwards onto the floor. He saw two hard-faced, scruffily dressed, unshaven men scowling down at him.

One said, 'Lie still, mister, and yur won't get 'urt.' The briefcase containing the wages for all the staff was chained to Tom's left wrist. Tom stopped struggling. He felt the thug who held his unencumbered arm relax the grip on his wrist. A face lowered down towards Tom, who snatched his arm free and hit the easy target with all his might, fear and a ferocious anger lending him strength. The next second something cold and metallic hit him across the forehead, rendering him unconscious. When he came to, he was surrounded by a growing group of people, including a railway guard, who was asking him questions, none of which was making any sense as far as he could work out. He felt himself drifting off, when next he surfaced the crowd had been replaced by paramedics and a policeman standing over him. He drifted off again.

The next time he was aware of what was happening he was lying on a bed, with a paramedic taking his pulse. Noticing he had come to she asked, 'Do you know where you are?'

Tom lifted his head from the pillow, that had been a mistake. 'In an ambulance,' he offered, his face screwed up because of the pain.

'Can you tell me your name please?'

'Tom Cooper,' he replied.

'We think you have had a fall.'

'No, I was robbed, I was carrying the firm's wages in a briefcase.' He pulled up his sleeve to show the steel wrist band that the chain had been attached to. 'They cut the chain; it was a set of bolt cutters. I reckon that's what he hit me with after I'd punched his mate in the face.'

'We'll get you to hospital. You will need some stitches in that cut above your eye. Now just lie back and take it easy, Mr Cooper.'

* * * * *

Tim received a phone call from Daisy at Shop Number Two, 'Hi Daisy, how can I help?'

'We're a bit worried because your dad has not turned up with our wages yet, he'd normally be here an hour ago, you can set the clock by him. Enzo's rung; he's not seen him yet neither. Harry's sayin' the same thing. I'm really worried, Tim. If he were ok, he'd have rung us.'

'I'm inclined to agree with you, Daisy. You sit tight. I will make some phone calls.' Tim was trying to decide whether he should ring the police or the hospital first when the office phone rang. A woman's firm, business-like voice said, 'May I speak to Mr Timothy Cooper, please?'

'Speaking,' he replied.

'This is the hospital here. Is Mr Thomas Cooper your father?'

He can't be dead, thought Tim, surely they wouldn't tell me over the phone. Gripped by a terrible fear he asked, 'Is he ok?'

'He is not dead, Mr Cooper, but he has been attacked and sustained a blow to the head that we are worried about. We are going to keep him in for a least one night. We will see how things go. He has asked if you can bring some things in for him, pyjamas, et cetera. We are about to run some tests. We will know more when we have those results.'

'Will he be ok?' asked Tim. Now extremely worried, he thought, tests, pyjamas, this doesn't sound like a one-night stay.

'I am sorry Mr Cooper, there is nothing more I can tell you at the moment, we will keep you informed.'

'Thank you,' he replied and rang off. He heard Bonny call out good night as she started down the stairs. Tim shouted, 'Jessica, can you get her back? We have a problem!' He walked through from his office to the girls just as Bonny reappeared.

'Come into my office please, both of you.' When they were sitting, him still standing with a white-knuckled grip on the chair top, he said, 'My father has been attacked this evening and the wages stolen. It sounds as though they were waiting for him.' Both women could hear the shake in his voice.

'Is he all right, Tim?' asked Bonny with her hand to her face and her eyes tearing up. He could see Jessica was also very moved and angry.

'Bastards!' the older woman spat out. 'What scum could attack a seventy-year-old man? I am sorry about my language, Tim, but these people must be sub-human.' This was the first time Tim or Bonny had heard her swear.

'I'm off to the hospital now; I have a big favour to ask of you. We need to pay the staff tomorrow, so all the cash and payslips need redoing, can either of you work tonight? I'll go to the hospital and find out how serious it is, then I'll come back here. Is Lynda still here?'

'No I let her go early, Tim. She has done some late nights this last week,' replied Jessica. 'I need to ring the young mum that has Polly after school and check she can look after her. She should do, I pay her quite well to look after Polly. I will ring her.' Minutes later putting the phone down she said, 'That's all fine, she is going to feed her too.'

'I can stay as long as you like,' volunteered Bonny.

'Will you cancel all the cheques then please, Jessica?'

'No problem, Tim. I can set Bonny up with the payslips. Is that ok, Bonny?'

The young woman was nodding.

'Bonny, have a word with Enzo and ask him to put a meal together for you both, and you should ring your mum,' said Tim. He was tapping the pockets of his navy trousers searching for his keys. He found them as Jessica handed him his dark overcoat. He shrugged it on over his pale blue shirt. He kept thinking he might expand his wardrobe with other coloured clothing. Then he decided not to, he felt comfortable in his blues and navies.

'Mr Graham is here, Tim,' called Bonny as Tim's driver emerged from the lift.

Jessica said, 'Can you give your dad our best?' Bonny was nodding.

Tim called out as he and Mr Graham entered the lift, saying, 'Thank you, Jessica, Bonny. I will see you later.'

Tim arrived at the hospital half an hour later. A doctor came to talk to him when he got to intensive care.

The doctor said, 'Good evening, Mr Cooper.'

Tim stopped him, saying, 'Can you call me Tim? Otherwise I am going to get confused.'

'I suggest we sit over here,' said the doctor, 'then I can explain what is going to happen.' The two men took seats facing each other.

'We thought initially he would only need stitches, but he kept drifting off, so we did some tests, an MRI scan et cetera. Now, what I am going to tell you is not as bad as it sounds, your father has a small bleed in his brain, a result of the blow. We are preparing him for an operation. This will entail going into his brain and stopping the bleeding. This is nowadays something that is quite straightforward. There is some risk, obviously, but I am confident we can put him right.' Tim's fear ratcheted up a few more notches.

'Thank you, Doctor, I don't know if you have been told but he was carrying the wages for all the staff, a lot of money. This was the reason for the attack.' Tim saw disapproval writ large on the doctor's face.

'I know what you are thinking, Doctor, he should not have been alone. I've had the conversation with him. He got incredibly angry and asked if I thought he was past it. Had I insisted he would have been deeply hurt. Now it appears I may have hurt him a lot worse.' After a long pause Tim asked, 'Could this kill him, Doctor?'

This time it was the doctor's turn to take a deep breath before answering, 'There is no surgery that is completely free of risk, but your father is fit for his age. He stands a good chance.'

Tim, now head down, his elbows on his knees staring at the floor as he gathered himself, moments later said, 'Sorry, Doctor, but I've had a tough trot lately. The people who mean a lot to me keep dying.'

'We will do the absolute best we can for him, Tim.'

As the doctor finished speaking, he noticed an attractive young woman dressed in a pale blue frock walking to join them. A gentle hand on Tim's shoulder and her perfume informed Tim that Sophie had arrived. He reached up and grasped her hand.

'My wife,' said Tim.

'Good evening, Doctor. How is he doing?'

'I have just brought your husband up to date, he can explain what's going to happen next. I will leave you together,' said the doctor. 'We will keep you informed.'

Tim shared what he had just been told. By the time he finished Sophie was in floods of tears. He was surprised how distraught she was. She was a tough positive individual usually, but this had clearly knocked her down. Standing up he wrapped his wife in his arms and held her until the tears ceased.

'Tim, you are right,' she said, pausing to blow her nose and mop up the tears. 'A lot of the people we love are either seriously ill or have died.'

Tim knew her mother's recent demise was hurting Sophie a lot.

'Don't give up, love. The medics think Dad will make it, and you know what a stubborn old beggar my father is.' The truth was that he was not as confident as he sounded, but Sophie's distress had unnerved him.

'How come you are here?'

'Bonny rang me and told Mr Graham, who came and collected me. Nanny is staying on; she will take care of the children.'

'Bonny is a smart kid, isn't she?'

'They all really do care for us, don't they?' observed Tim. 'Will you be all right here on your own? I need to get back to the office. Where is Mr Graham now?'

'In the car park. You need to go and sort this mess out, Tim.'

'Are you sure you are ok to stay?'

She nodded.

A nurse approached them, 'Your father is just going into surgery now. This may well take some time. Make yourselves comfortable, I will arrange a drink for you both.'

'I have to go back to work, the men who assaulted my father stole all the staff's wages, so we will work overnight to replace them.'

'I would like a drink please,' said Sophie. 'I am staying.'

The two women were discussing the robbery as he left.

* * * * *

The big black Bentley was standing in a pool of light in the hospital car park. Reaching the car and seeing Mr Graham was lolling back in his seat sound asleep, Tim tapped gently on the window. Mr Graham came to with a start, rubbing his hands over his eyes as he sat up. Tim climbed in beside him, knowing the older man preferred to have the family sit in the back, but he didn't want to shout information from the rear seats. He brought Mr

Graham up to date as they rode back to the office.

'I do hope he'll be all right; Mrs Graham and I have known your father since I can't remember when. It must be from when your mum and dad got married, I think. My wife will know.'

Arriving back at the office, Mr Graham said, 'Tim, tell your staff that I'll drive them around. We can't have the women wandering around in the dark. I've already told Mrs Cooper to contact me if she wants to leave the hospital.'

'No, you need your sleep, Mr Graham. I'll arrange taxis for everyone.'

'Tim, during the war I learnt to snatch every moment of sleep I could get; I can still do that. As they say I can sleep on a rail.' Tim knew this meant that Mr Graham could sleep on the most uncomfortable of resting places. 'I can be ready whenever, Tim.'

It dawned on him how lucky he was with his employees. There was not a bad apple amongst them. He needed to reward them better. He would work something out similar to Mr Well's store. His staff received a percentage of profit, something else to think about for the future.

* * * * *

As he walked in Bonny went to Enzo's kitchen and brought back a hot half of a pizza.

Jessica said, 'Hi, Tim, how is he?' Tim explained about the surgery his father was undergoing. Both women were visibly upset. Surprisingly, Jessica was the one that went to pieces. Bonny hugged her until she had regained control.

'Would you like me to make a cup of tea?' he asked.

'No, I will make it, Tim, it will give me a chance to pull myself together. Sorry, I have always had a soft spot for your father. I would like to go looking for these guys with a machete.'

'Then it will be you in jail,' said Bonny.

'The way I feel at the moment it would be worth it,' replied Jessica.

'How are you two doing?' he asked between mouthfuls.

'We are nearly there,' replied Jessica, sniffing the last of the tears away. 'I would guess there is about an hour's work left. Bonny, are you happy to stay a little longer?'

'Yeah sure, no problem.'

'You need to sign the cheques, of course, Tim. We will have to do the cash in the morning,' continued Jessica. 'All the stolen cheques are cancelled. I have not contacted the insurer; I have left that for you to sort out.'

'Ok, I will do that in the morning. I have left a message for Mr Murdoch at the bank and explained about the robbery and that we will need the money again tomorrow as soon as possible.'

Jessica said, 'One other thing, Tim. We ought to review staffing levels in here. We need at least one more body. The business is growing so fast.'

'Right, Bonny, once this problem is over can you, working with Jessica, list the upgrades we need to make please?'

'Yes, boss,' she replied.

When Mr Graham dropped Tim back at the hospital he was about to walk in when a young voice from out of an unlit corner asked, 'Is he gunna be all right, mister?'

Tim stared into the space where the voice had come from. He struggled to make out who was there, then Sammy stepped into the light.

'Come on, we'll talk inside,' said Tim, putting his arm around the boy's shoulder.

'Nah, they won't let me in, mister. I've tried earlier,' said the boy.

'They will if you're with me, Sammy.'

'Yeah right,' said the boy, ably voicing his disbelief.

As they walked through the doors and approached the reception desk one of the admin staff said, 'Excuse me one moment, Mr Cooper, but this boy tried to get in earlier this evening. Come on, you, out you go.'

Before Tim could respond Sammy said, as he turned towards the door, 'Told you so, mister, her sort 'ates the likes of me.'

Tim said, 'Come back here, Sammy. Just stand beside me.'

Now leaning forward and addressing the admin assistant very quietly he said, 'My father is the only family this child has, we think of Sammy as one of us. They are very close.'

Later Tim and Sammy were sitting in the reception area chatting.

'What have you done about the dog, Sammy?' asked Tim.

'I've fed her an' filled her water bowl, and it ain't cold so I've left her out. Yur dad has built her a real fancy kennel. It's on wheels so he can move it about like, you know, between the shops and that. It fits in the van an' all. Sometimes she sits in it while he's pushing 'er, it's a right laugh.'

Tim was feeling a real sense of guilt, with his enormous workload he had not visited his father for, how long, it must be weeks, he thought. They had not seen much of each other at work. Their paths rarely crossed now that he was mostly office based. He made a mental note to talk to Sophie about it.

* * * * *

Earlier Sophie had asked if she could sit with Tom. A nurse had explained to her that Mr Cooper was barely hanging on. 'It could all go wrong very quickly, and we don't want civilians in the way.'

Sophie looked at the nurse quizzically. 'Army?' she asked.

'Yes,' was the reply. 'Please don't tell anyone else what I have just told you, I would get into trouble.'

'I will not tell anyone else. Thank you for your honesty, it gives me a better grasp of the situation. We must pray for him.'

'Maybe that's what's needed,' said the nurse as she turned away.

Sophie had read somewhere that it was the shock of the accident that often killed the elderly. Sophie never told Tim that she had found the hospital chapel, lit a candle and offered up a prayer for the likeable old man. She was not sure why she did not tell Tim. She thought it may diminish the act itself in some way.

The man and the boy found Sophie sitting in the waiting room. 'How is he doing?' asked Tim.

'I have been told he is hanging in there,' she replied as she rose from the chair.

Sophie kissed Tim goodbye, saying, 'I must go home and relieve Nanny.' She did not disturb Sammy, who was sound asleep on a chair, wound around in a circle. He sleeps like an animal, she thought. That was how the poor boy lived, like a stray dog. She experienced a wave of sympathy for him. It gave her cause to reflect how blessed her childhood had been by comparison in spite of her mother's harsh regime. On the way out Sophie lit another votive candle for her father-in-law and offered up a prayer for him and Sammy.

* * * * *

Tim was being shaken awake. Opening his eyes he saw it was Sammy doing the shaking. The boy was crying and pointing at the activity beyond the glass in the intensive care department.

Tim could see a red light blinking on and off and there was a beeper going. There were two nurses in there now, one of whom walked out of the room and called down a far corridor. A white coated doctor walked at a good pace towards the unit followed by a big piece of machinery on wheels, pushed by a nurse. The beeping and the flashing red light persisted. The man and boy watched an injection being prepared and administered. Whatever it contained Tim could detect no difference. The doctor was holding his father's wrist and staring at his watch, he was shaking his head.

He said something neither man nor boy could hear.

This time a doctor called down the corridor. Shortly afterwards an overweight older man in a smart grey suit strode towards the sight of all the activity. As he arrived the beeping stopped and became a continuous sound. One of the nurses started doing chest compressions.

Sammy, now terrified, asked, 'Is he goin' to die, mister? I've seen on the telly when that thing ain't beepin' no more it means yur dying. Iffen he dies I'll be back on the street.' The boy was in tears, Tim had never seen him cry before.

'Sammy,' said Tim. The child ignored him; he was too far gone in his misery to make sense of anything. Shaking the boy quite hard to gain his attention, Tim said, 'Sammy, I promise you that you'll never be back on the street. We will find a job and some digs for you.' He was not sure if the boy had understood him or not.

The two of them watched the big machine being prepared. The paddles were placed on his father's chest, the loud bang that was emitted as the machine was operated made them both jump. Still the continuous whine from the monitor persisted. Three times the paddles were applied with the same result.

In desperation Tim growled aloud, 'Come on, you cantankerous old sod, breath dammit.' Seeing no change he turned his back and walked a few paces down the waiting room. He was straining every sinew in his body to will his father to breathe.

CHAPTER 34

Tom stumbled over a root on the forest path, the grip on his right hand tightened momentarily to steady him. He was not sure. Was he dreaming? He knew he had been lying in hospital very ill. A black bird flew close past his left shoulder. This made him flinch, turning his head away. Now he could see the person who had prevented his fall. Now he knew he was dreaming; it was his dead wife. Seeing recognition in his eyes she embraced him.

The couple held each other close, when they finally let go he held her away from him.

'You are so young and even more beautiful.' She was wearing the pretty pink dress that was his favourite.

There was no verbal reply but the light shining in her eyes and the squeeze of his hand said it all.

'I have waited so long for you,' she said.

'Me too,' he replied. 'I talk to you at night before I go to sleep.'

'I know you do; I always say goodnight. I know you cannot hear me, but I say it anyway.'

As they stepped from the wood Tom became aware of the smell of new mown grass and the warmth of sunshine on his head and shoulders

A long slope led down to a wide river with a centuries-old stone bridge crossing it. There were a number of paths to the bridge beside the one they were on. One exited from the wood not far from them. Tom could see another away to the left that had skirted around the trees but was now bending towards that same bridge. Another family were climbing down a steep rocky route away to his right.

'Shall we go and help them?' he asked.

'No,' she replied, 'if they have got this far they will make it.'

Looking into the distance across the river the path was broader. It climbed a gentle slope then disappeared from view as it reached the top of the low hill and started its descent down the other side. There were more people on it, even the very old seemed to be walking with more alacrity, more purpose.

As they reached the bridge Tom was overcome with a severe bout of dizziness and his vision blurred. He put out his hand to grasp the handrail on the bridge, but he lost his grip on the polished woodwork that had been smoothed by an untold number of hands since the ascent of man.

Shaking his head the sensation seemed to dissipate. As he took another step it returned with greater force. Now all he could see was a very bright light. He could no longer keep a grip of his wife's hand.

His wife called, 'I will wait for you, my love.' Seconds later he realised he was back in the hospital surrounded by doctors and nurses. Now he was crying, he reached out and grasped the doctor's arm begging him through the tears saying, 'Please, please, send me back, please, I don't want to be here.'

An injection moments later sent him to sleep while the doctors and nurses confirmed his strengthening vital signs and knew he was going to live.

Tim heard his father asking to be sent back, crying out, begging to be allowed to die. It was something he remembered all his life.

* * * * *

THE NEXT GENERATION

Tom was in hospital for some time after the operation. There were some minor problems that the doctors wanted cleared up before they would discharge him. They reassured Tim there was no risk to his father, it was just easier to sort things out with him close by. One thing they were concerned about was his depression. It was usual for patients who had been very ill to be glad to have cheated the grim reaper, as one doctor put it. Not his father. When Tim visited his father the elderly man turned his head away, he was at best monosyllabic, limiting his responses to yeses or noes.

Early one morning Sophie was woken by her husband's restlessness.

'Are you ok?' she asked.

'No not really, I am worried sick about my father. He has come back from the dead but to see and hear him you would feel he wanted to die, I don't understand. He is exactly the same as when mum passed away. He won't talk to me; he turns away and ignores me.'

'I will take Charley in this evening. The two of them are very close.'

'I can't make it tonight; I have an evening appointment.'

'I was going to say, let me take Charley. He may feel more able to talk without you there.'

'Hmm,' was the response, along with lifted eyebrows. He did not believe it, but it was worth a try. Nothing else had worked.

When they got to the ward that evening she could not see her father-in-law, then she spotted him. He was lying on his side with the covers pulled up around his ears clearly indicating he did not want to communicate with anyone.

Charley looked up at her mother, saying, 'I cannot see Grandpa, Mummy.'

'There he is, look,' she said, pointing at his bed. Charley broke into a run.

Sophie held back, hoping her daughter would do what she had done when she had visited Tim in hospital when he had suffered a mild coronary.

Charley did exactly as Sophie hoped, calling 'Grandpa, Grandpa,' as she climbed the bed side.

Tom rolled over and clasped his grandchild to him. A nurse walking by noticed his tears and pulled the curtains round, saying, 'This will give you some privacy.' Sophie thanked her.

Sophie allowed the silence to stretch out. Finally, Charley said, 'You are squashing me, Grandpa.' That made them all smile.

'We are all very worried about you, Tom,' said Sophie, reaching for his hand. 'What has upset you so?'

'If I tell you you'll think me stupid. You'll think I am going daft.'

'I promise you I will not. One thing I will say is that you are very dear to all of us, and we are extremely pleased that you did not die.' This generated a firm squeeze of her hand and a quiet thank you.

There was another long silence, then he said, 'I did die for a while. My wife Dori was waiting for me.' Then he described everything he had seen and related what they had both said. He explained how he didn't want to come back.

Sophie stood and placed her arms around him. 'Oh you poor man, that must have been so painful.' Now both adults were sniffing the tears away.

'I'm glad I was able to tell you, and thanks for bringing Tinkerbell. You can tell Tim, no one else, and tell him I don't want to discuss it.'

As Sophie and her daughter were leaving the hospital she looked back and saw Tom Cooper sitting up and talking to a nurse. One outcome of his near-death experience was his weekly attendance at church on a Sunday morning. This was another subject that was not up for debate.

* * * * *

Over time Tom began to believe his 'bash on the head', as he called it, was affecting his memory and other abilities. Historically he could read an instruction pack for a new piece of machinery or resetting the controls on the gas heater and understand it first time through. Nowadays he struggled.

THE NEXT GENERATION

He had been quite proud of himself mastering a basic understanding of how transistor radios worked, but the latest technology had him floored. His memory was slowly slipping away. On occasional visits to the local pub he discovered that many of his elderly acquaintances suffered in the same way. Gertrude, Gertie to her friends, repeated the story about the day she had walked into Sophie's Shop Number One with a pair of her husband's clean underpants draped over her shoulder. Neither Tom nor any of the regular customers had said anything to her, not wishing to upset her. But of course the story spread. Entering the pub that evening she really laid into the usual small gang in the corner that included Tom. The louder she shouted, asking why they said nothing, the harder they laughed. One big benefit was none of them would let her buy a round that evening, they all agreed it was a story they would repeat down the years, how dear old Gertie would wear her husband's underwear when she went shopping. Her husband, who was apparently teetotal, never did get to hear of it.

His memory was declining. There were three things he could no longer find. His favourite hat, a walking stick and his old comfy gardening shoes. They were his favourite shoes, made of leather that had relaxed to fit his feet perfectly. The fastening was a leather strap across the bridge of his foot secured by Velcro. He had adjusted the strap so they would slide on and off easily. He would often wear them all day, gardening or not. He was tempted to wear them to the shops but the blob of apple-green paint on the toe of his right shoe was even more obvious than the stain of engine oil on the left.

One evening in desperation he asked Sammy if he had seen the missing articles, sure that it was a waste of time. Why would Sammy know? But when the boy was asked he knew where all the missing articles were. The lad had brushed his hat and hung it up in the wardrobe, along with his walking stick. Tom had not been in the wardrobe since his wife's funeral to find his dark grey suit.

Sammy, wearing his usual apparel, black jeans, white shirt and a huge smile bent down and from the floor at the back of the wardrobe he pulled out the missing shoes. Tom hardly recognised them. The colour had changed for a start. Now they were a very dark brown, the green paint had gone, the large oil stain on the other shoe had disappeared and the soles had been repaired.

He found himself really upset, these shoes were extremely old. They were a touchstone, a reminder of all sorts of events. His wife had bought them for him decades ago. He was not, he remembered, happy with the Velcro straps. He had assumed this sort of fixing was for the elderly.

He had been right. Now he and the shoes had matured together. Now they were perfect, or they had been before Sammy spoilt them. He was angry. How did the boy think he had the right to mess with his belongings? All the little marks had had their own story to tell, some funny some sad. Now they were gone. He was about to tear the boy off a strip when he saw the boy's face. The lad was wearing a huge smile, waiting for the praise he felt sure was coming. Tom quietly examined his hat and walking stick, giving himself time for his anger to cool.

After a long pause he ruffled Sammy's hair and said, 'Thank you, lad. Do I owe you any money?'

'No Tom, I saved it from me rounds. It's just to say thanks fer looking after me. I reckons I can start paying some keep soon. Is it alright if I gets a bit more money behind me afore I starts?'

'We can talk about it come the time, Sammy.' Once he had got over the surprise and given himself a good talking to he found himself wearing the shoes all the time including to work in the shop.

CHAPTER 35

The children in the boat yard were discouraged from learning to swim. Often the currents in the river were extremely strong. Add to that the constant progress of all sizes of craft up and down the river, they may not see a child in the water. The advice from the boating fraternity was unanimous: no playing in the water.

Today was the first school swimming lesson at the local baths. All the children were lined up along the pool's edge at the shallow end. Mr Payne the PE teacher called Martyn's name. The boy was sporting a pair of bright red swimming trunks.

'When I say so, lad, you will jump in and do the following. Not yet,' was the command as the boy moved towards the water. 'When I say, you will jump in and stand up. Then you will do this,' he began demonstrating as he spoke. 'You will take a big breath in and hold it, then you will lift your left leg and grasp your left ankle with your left hand. Still holding your breath you will lift your right leg and seize it with your right hand. Do you know what will happen then?'

Another boy said, 'Yes sir, he will drown.'

The class fell apart.

Mr Payne was fighting not to laugh. It was the class clown. His nickname was Jonah. The teacher could not remember the boy's real name. What made it so difficult was Jonah's timing and delivery was perfect. Some teachers got cross, Mr Payne saw it as a gift like any other and found no reason to stifle it. He ran through the instructions again, also reminding the class that no one could breathe underwater.

'Martyn, when you are holding your ankles you will float in the water like a ball. I will shout your name when I want you to put your legs down and stand up. Do you understand, lad?'

'Yes sir.'

'Ok, off you go.'

Martyn pinched his nose shut and jumped in, he struggled for a moment to find his balance, then stood up and cleared his eyes with his palms. Taking a deep breath in and holding it he did as instructed. Suddenly he was bobbing like a cork. Opening his eyes he was surprised at how much he could see. It was a beautiful blue world under the water. He was transfixed. So much so that he did not hear the command for him to stand up. At the third time of calling he heard and obeyed. He saw a boy who had followed him in doggy paddling to the side. He watched carefully for a minute then tried it himself. He reached the side of the pool all too soon. He could never explain why he did it, but he turned so his back was to the pool side, took a deep breath and sliding down the wall sat on the bottom, watching the other boys performing. He was so comfortable down here. He saw one boy get his breathing all wrong trying to do the bobbing cork thing. Standing up in a panic he was coughing and spitting water. Martyn was trying the doggy paddling again, this time with his head underwater most of the time. All too soon he heard the extended whistle blast that signalled the end of the lesson. He was the last of the class to leave the water. He was euphoric; he had found something physical he could do.

Leaving the poolside Mr Payne said, 'Did you enjoy that, lad?' The teacher knew the answer before he'd asked the question. The amount of time Martyn had spent with his head immersed was a clear indicator of the lad's comfort in the environment. The boy was wearing a huge smile. His regular visits to the pool over the years ahead built his physique and his confidence.

At dinner that evening he told his family about his swimming. He was not sure if they believed him. He did not mind; he knew what he knew.

Later, as his mother came in to kiss him goodnight she sat on the end of his bed and asked him about his swimming. He explained about the bobbing thing and then his doggy paddling looking at the bottom. 'It's a different world under the water, everything is blue and sparkling.'

'I have an idea,' said Sophie. 'I wonder if Nanny would take you. She may enjoy it. Would you like that?' Eager nodding was the answer.

'I will ask her.'

Nanny and Martyn became regular visitors to the local indoor pool. With Nanny's guidance the doggy paddle was left far behind, replaced by the breaststroke, then as the boy's confidence grew the front crawl. The following term he and two other boys left the main body of the class and practised in deeper water with Mr Payne giving them separate training. Nanny had a hand in it as well. She still took him swimming. One evening she taught him to dive. Before they left for home Martyn had got it. At school three days later when told to get in, Martyn dived off the side. Mr Payne's whistle was blowing blast after blast. Pointing his finger at him he shouted, 'Martyn, out of the water now.' Beckoning him with his hand indicated the urgency. Martyn stood in front of the master, who was making sure he could see the rest of the class over the boy's head.

'Do you know how dangerous what you just did is? People die who dive into shallow water. How did you learn to do that?'

'One of my mum's friends brings me swimming every week, sir. She did show me to look for the depth markings.' He was not about to admit that his nanny took him swimming.

'You scared the life out of me. Can you promise me if you are going to try something new that you'll tell me first?'

'Yes, sir, sorry, sir.'

'Listen boys, before you try and copy Martyn you will ask me first. Is that understood?'

There was a loud, 'Yes sir.'

As expected the trio were ferociously competitive. They were forming friendships one with another that were to last decades.

CHAPTER 36

Tim and his father were sitting on the stern of the *Sea Maiden*, each with a beer in their hands watching the sun go down. Tom's visits to the boat after work on a Saturday had become more regular since his recent brush with, as he put it, the grim reaper. The children loved his visits because he would play with them and make them laugh and was always happy to explain things to them. Also he always brought his dog Beth, who everyone loved, especially the children.

'So, Tim, why are we sitting out here and not indoors with the family? Could it be that you want to talk business and you know if we did it inside you would get frowned at by the boss?'

'Well,' said Tim, stretching the word out, 'it might be something like that.'

'I suspect it is exactly like that,' said his father with a smile on his face. 'Come on, spit it out, lad.'

'Number One is a constant niggle, Dad, that I can't get out of my head. I had a dream the other night where Mr Woodman was telling me to get on with it. Rebuild it. When I visit it I am reminded of the Second World War bombsites we used to play in when I was a kid.'

'He would have rebuilt it ages ago, lad,' said his father, 'we all know that. I had an old customer from before the fire stop me the other day and ask me when we were going to rebuild Mr Woodman's shop. I didn't understand. It turns out he was talking about Number One. Apparently the elderly have always called it that even after we changed the name to Sophie's.'

'That's interesting. I thought initially that we could replicate the shop as it had looked before the fire. The trouble with that is it will take fifty years. It had over all those years developed a patina of its own. The surfaces polished to a high shine by thousands of hands. So I have come up with the same idea but different.' Tim noted his father's frown and the shaking of his head.

'Downstairs it will be the same layout as before but in all-new varnished, honey-coloured wood, the counters, the window frames, the floor, everything. A rebirth of the original, we could use that in the advertising. We can get Bonny on it; she's mustard at this adverting lark. We can use your carpentry guy for the counters, Charley's team obviously, Larry for the electrics, all the usual suspects. The only thing that will not be copied is all the small drawers that went up the walls. What do you think?'

Tom was quiet for a while. Tim knew not to interrupt. Then his father said, 'It will be extremely expensive, and it'll be a long time before you get your money back through the shop.'

Tim went to interrupt. His father ignored him, saying, 'But it will then have some value. I haven't a clue what a hole in the ground's worth, that's all it is now. I don't suppose it's very much.'

'I expect you're right, Dad. What I had in mind for upstairs was not to have any accommodation up there but have a café instead.'

'That should increase the footfall. You will need a fire escape,' observed his father.

Tim was nodding. 'Would you like to oversee it?'

'Do you know what, lad, I could see this coming a mile off,' said his father, shaking his head as he spoke. Tom paused for a while, thinking it through. He knew it would be a lot of work, but it would be interesting.

Finally, he said, 'Yep I will do it, provided I can bring Beth. She gets lonely if left too long.'

* * * * *

Sophie called from halfway up the ladder that led down to the lower deck. Only her head and shoulders showing above the top deck. 'If you men have finished your business discussion we would like your company down here. And there is one of Nanny's cakes to eat.'

'We will be right there,' said Tom, standing up and heading for the bow, not waiting for Tim to agree. Nanny's cakes were a work of wonder and never lasted long. Tim smiled as he followed his father towards the ladder that led down from the top deck. Like most people of his generation, if they were invited out it meant dressing up. His father's brown suit, crisp white shirt and maroon tie was very smart.

While everyone was talking over dinner Tim came up with an idea. If the local folk still called the shop Woodman's perhaps, he could put up a small plaque outside in memory of the man, referring to Mr Woodman and his family and his war service, etc. He would talk to Sophie; she was very good at this sort of thing and Tim knew she had been very fond of the generous, clever man. The businessmen in his head took notice and suggested it might be something the local paper would be interested in. It would be nice to know how long his family had lived there. Sophie had noted his silence and was wearing an accusatory look on her face. She always knew when he was working.

Sorry, he, mouthed, then said, 'Can I have another slice of cake please?'

Two weeks later, standing in the large empty space that was once Shop Number One. Tim was explaining to Charlie, the builder, what he wanted with the rebuild.

When Tim had finished relaying the information about the changes, the café, etc., Charlie said, 'So you want it all the same but new and different?'

'That's it exactly,' said Tim laughing.

* * * * *

Larry the electrician called in to the burnt-out shop the next day. Seeing Tim talking to a besuited gentleman he stood just out of range until the conversation ended. The man Tim was talking to turned out to be the architect.

After he had left Tim said, 'Hallo, Larry. He doesn't think we will have too much trouble with the planning. The council are uncomfortable having an ugly derelict site in the middle of town.' Once again Tim explained what he had in mind.

'That's fine, Tim,' said Larry, looking around. He was dressed as usual in his dark dungarees.

Tim sensed something in his voice. 'Is there a problem?' he asked.

'There is, Tim, first thanks for offering me the job, but it needs to be all-new wiring. We will get the electricity board to confirm their side is ok to the meter, then I will rip everything else out and start again.'

'Is none of it reusable, Larry?'

'Let me ask you a question, Tim, do you want to rebuild it a second time? Some of the wiring will look ok from the outside but who can tell what has happened under the insulation. I am sure you will be able to find a quote cheaper than mine because whoever it is will be looking to keep the apparently undamaged wiring.'

'Thanks for being so straight about it. You're right of course. When can you start?'

'I have about a week's work left on the job I'm doing then I'm all yours.'

The two men shook hands then Larry left.

* * * * *

THE NEXT GENERATION

Tim walked around the empty fire-blasted shop. Talking out loud he said, 'I hope you approve, Mr Woodman; I expect you would have rebuilt it a long time ago.' Tim locked the door behind him and went home.

Initially the work seemed to creep forward. As his father explained to him it was taking a long time because of the fire damage.

'Is it really that serious, Dad?' he asked.

'Charlie always shows me the problem before he tears something else out that has been damaged by the heat. The problem is that there is a lot of it. Charlie is not ripping you off, Tim.'

Shaking his head he replied, 'I know he wouldn't.'

CHAPTER 37

One evening Sophie received a phone call from Mr Lawrence.

After the hallos he said, 'Regarding your request to buy the clarinet Martyn is using, I'm sorry I'm not prepared to sell it. It's mine, it's the instrument I learnt to play on. It's not the school's. I have had it for,' there was a pause, 'forty-odd years. My mother bought it cheaply for a Christmas present for me. I had complained I had nothing to do, a note inside said, "This will give you something to do, learn to play it." A small black and white guide was included.'

'Sorry, Mr Lawrence, I did not know, I will buy him another one.'

Shaking his head and holding his hand up he said, 'Please don't do that, at the moment he thinks it is the only instrument that suits him. If you take it away he may stop playing. That would be a crime, he has a gift. I am certain of that. For instance he hears a piece of music once and knows it. How about if we agree it is on permanent loan until he finds another one that suits him.'

'That is extremely kind of you, thank you very much.' Sophie went to say goodbye.

'There is one other thing. Your son and I and two other students have been playing and singing in the lunch break, now we have been asked to play at the end of term concert. I sent a letter home asking your permission to allow Martyn to stay after school so we can practice. I have not had it back.'

'I have not seen it,' said Sophie. 'I will call him.'

It took a while for the boy to appear. He was holding a screwed-up letter. As he reached her he said, 'I can't do it, Mum. The whole idea just terrifies me.'

His mother placed the phone to her ear again, saying, 'We will get back to you.' Then she hung up.

Saying nothing, she stood up and wrapped her fearful son in her arms. Now she was certain her child had a gift. Who knew how far that could carry him? Somehow we need to find a way to overcome your nerves, she said to herself.

'Come on, we will make a cup of tea and talk about it,' she said, fluffing his hair, which received an 'Oh Mum' as he tried to rake it back in place with his fingers.

Sitting at the table a little later sipping hot tea Sophie said, 'What do you enjoying doing most in the world?'

His response was a single word, 'Sleeping.'

'Ok, smarty pants, apart from sleeping?' This was an expression her now deceased nanny used, much to her mother's disapproval.

'Playing my clarinet.'

She almost reminded him that it was not his and that if he stopped playing it would go back. She decided that this was a discussion for the future.

* * * * *

During practice one lunch time in the school hall in the middle of a song they had been practicing for the piano Martyn took off on his own, improvising with Mr Lawrence on the piano. The girl joined in, scatting, making the sounds of musical instruments in harmony with the two men.

Adam the drummer was working away holding the timing together. Martyn was transported. This was what he was born for, to make music. When they finally came back to the present there was a ripple of applause. There was a small group of students listening, now clapping. Some were sitting cross legged on the floor, others standing. Among them was the headmaster, clapping.

Later that evening he said to his wife as they sat at the dinner table, 'Today, Cathy, I watched a young man find his vocation.'

'Who was that, my dear?' she asked, not really that interested.

'Young Martyn Cooper and his clarinet. In the middle of the song he started to make up the music as they went along, then Mr Lawrence and the girl joined in, all four of them rewriting it as they played. I am glad I was there.'

'I am glad you enjoyed it, dear,' was his wife's response.

The headmaster just smiled. He knew his wife's interests were entirely classical.

* * * * *

The night of the concert arrived; Martyn could not eat anything. He had a forkful of lamb halfway to his mouth when the fork was slammed down onto the plate. Leaving the table he rushed from the room. They could all hear him dry retching in the bathroom. Awhile later he returned but would not sit at the table. To say he was pasty faced was an understatement.

Sophie asked, 'Are you going to be able to do this tonight?'

'Yes,' was his adamant response.

His mother was surprised by his obvious desire to go through with the concert. She had expected him to cry off, but he was obviously determined to do it.

Later that night backstage the group were practicing the opening number. They were all dressed in smart dark clothing. Mr Lawrence said, 'Work at getting through this first song. The rest will follow. Wait, I have had an idea, we will go on one at a time. I will go on first and introduce us, playing the piano quietly with the first number. Adam, you follow me on and when you get to your drums keep it simple and quiet.' The boy nodded. 'Martyn, you're next, playing quietly as you arrive. Agatha, you come on singing. Are we all clear?' There was general agreement,

Mr Lawrence took Agatha aside and said, 'If it looks as though Martyn has frozen and can't come on, push him on. Just don't push him over.'

Looking to see if he could see his mum and dad, Martyn spotted Mr Vieri sitting with them about three rows back. Right, he would show this rude bully exactly what he could do. He saw Nanny sitting in the audience engrossed in conversation with a man by her side. He nearly didn't recognise her; she was not dressed in the green uniform she wore to work every day. She looked really nice in a pink skirt and top. They were both laughing at something.

As Mr Lawrence walked on a small group of students began to whistle and call out as he made his way to the piano and began to quietly play the first few bars of intro to the first song, 'Cry me a river'.

Adam walked on. Now people were clapping. Quickly his drums blended in, seconds later Agatha said, 'Are you ready, Martyn?'

'I have never been more ready,' was his response.

She was surprised how vehement he was, then with his clarinet to his lips he waited to find his entry then he began playing. Not the gentle start they had discussed. No, he was punching his music out to the people in the back row. Immediately the audience were beginning to move to the music, toes tapping, bodies moving. Agatha standing in the wings was taken aback. Mr Lawrence had said gentle, this was not gentle. Oh well, she thought to herself, if I can't beat him I will have to join him. Counting herself in she let rip and walked on to the stage. With the amount of power they were putting out most people were unable to sit still. Mr Lawrence and Adam were looking at each other, unsure what was happening. This was not how they had rehearsed it. Some sixth formers were already up and dancing at the back, incapable of resisting the power and the rhythm of the music that was calling to their youth and their energy.

Sometimes Martyn and the girl were standing face to face, bouncing the music off each other. Other times Agatha roamed the stage singing to different sections of the audience. The music kept coming. The mums and grandmas were up and reliving their youth. The older men were dad dancing, much to the embarrassment of their grandchildren. Near the end of the evening Martyn and Agatha were improvising together. Mr Lawrence pointed towards Adam. They all fell silent for a few minutes except for the drums. Adam displayed a lot of skill. Mr Lawrence nodded them back in.

Sophie and the family could not believe that this was Martyn standing in the middle of the stage improvising, driving the music along with Agatha and the rest of the band joining in.

Sophie said later while they were still talking about the evening, 'Agatha is pretty, Martyn. she looks like a young Aretha Franklin.'

'Yes I suppose she does. I hadn't noticed.'

Sophie realised with a mother's instinct that Martyn might not be telling the whole truth.

CHAPTER 38

Martyn gained permission to stay behind after school for an hour once a week to practise. This soon stretched to two hours, twice a week. The caretaker lived on his own in a small house in the grounds of the school. He liked Martyn and did not mind as long as he was gone by six pm, so he could lock the school up and sit down to his dinner and relax. He was short and always dressed in a pale brown work coat with a matching brown cap and dark trousers. Quite often he would draw up a chair and sit down and listen. One constant was his tapping foot.

One morning walking into school Agatha ran to catch Martyn up. He was as usual dawdling along with his hands in his pockets.

Reducing her pace to a walk she slid her arm through his, saying, 'Have I got news for you, did I mention my uncle came to the concert and liked what he heard? He has made all the arrangements for me to sing in his café in the evenings. I have asked if you and Adam can join me. I don't know if Mr Lawrence will agree to play.' Martyn went to interrupt, she stopped him by saying, 'And, if your parents will agree and we become popular, he may be able to pay us a little each week.'

'When would we play?'

'Friday nights to start with until about nine pm. What do you think?'

Martyn felt as though all his birthdays had come at once. There was only one problem. His father. The elation disappeared. He had already had to sit through one lecture about drink and drugs in the music industry. 'I will ask, but I am not sure if I will be allowed.'

'Why ever not?' she asked.

'My father thinks music and clubs et cetera are dens of iniquity, sex, drugs and rock and roll.'

'In some places he might be right,' said Agatha, 'not in my uncle's café, with Auntie May looking on. A month ago, someone was very drunk and began swearing and then blaspheming. Aunt May was not concerned about the swearing, but taking the good lord's name in vain was the final straw. She marched around the bar, picked the man up – he wasn't big. A regular had the café door open and she threw him through it. His first bounce was in the street. This is a small exaggeration, I admit, but Aunt May definitely threw him out.'

Perhaps we will not tell my father that, thought Martyn. When he mentioned it to his parents there was not the objection he had anticipated. His mother had met Agatha's aunt at school and had realised there was not going to be anything to worry about. The two women had got along extremely well.

Tim was listening to the conversation and had an idea. He might get them to play one evening in the restaurant on one of the quiet nights.

CHAPTER 39

Sophie was surprised to learn that her father and Sally were not available.

Katherine, Mr Vieri's attractive new young secretary, whispered, 'They have gone away together, abroad! Remember, I never told you.' She obviously knew more but was not going to reveal it. It was a full week before they returned. They appeared at the *Sea Maiden* one evening unannounced.

The couple were extremely happy. Mr Vieri had a smile that appeared to be pasted on. Sophie could not remember the last time he had been this jolly, not a word she would normally apply to her father. Sally was gorgeous in pink. Sophie began to suspect something. As they removed their coats Sally's hand slid from the sleeve, then she spotted them. She was wearing an ornate gold wedding ring. This was accompanied by a platinum engagement ring with a huge diamond on it. Sophie reached out and grasped Sally's hand.

Sophie was speechless. She was opening and closing her mouth, but no words were coming out.

'We are married,' announced her father, 'I am sorry it was all a bit cloak and dagger but neither of us wanted to be in the local papers. I know it is not long since your mother passed away, but I am not a young man anymore and I want to be, sorry, we want to be happy for however long we have left. As you both know I have loved this lady for years and to use a hackneyed expression, I have made an honest woman of her.' All this time Sally had Victor's hand clasped in hers in her lap. She had never looked away from his face or lost her smile while he was talking.

After a short pause, Sally said, 'I can see, Sophie, that it is a huge shock for you. I promise not to be the wicked stepmother.'

'I know you will not be; I am sorry if I seem a bit stunned. It is something I never visualised ever happening. To be honest, I do not know how I feel. I am sure you will both be happy. Tim, will you get the drinks sorted please? I will have a large Dura.' Her father's face showed surprise that she was drinking whisky.

Minutes later they all had a glass in their hands. Mr Vieri, sensing Tim was about to make a toast, said, 'Hold on, Tim, the surprises are not over yet. We are going to retire.'

Tim's immediate thought was, I do not want run his business as well as everything else. He was coming under greater pressure from Sophie to cut his workload because of his health problems.

Sally said, 'Sophia, I realise your mother left you the house in Puglia, but we would like to have your permission to live there. It would be easy to make a small apartment at the back of the house. You would hardly know we were there.'

Mr Vieri, apparently reading Tim's mind, said, 'And I am selling the business, Tim. This was Sally's idea.' He was looking at his new wife as he spoke.

'I know it seems a little drastic,' said Sally, 'but I know every time there'd be a problem, the boss,' she was now nodding at her husband, 'would be on a plane back here. I for one do not want to live like that.'

'What about Martha?' asked Sophie.

'Knowing your father,' said Tim, 'he will throw her out, sell the house from under her. She will be homeless.'

Mr Vieri bellowed with laughter and pretended to punch Tim on the shoulder. 'You are right, Tim, that was exactly what I was going to do but Sally talked me out of it.' Still laughing, he took a long swallow of his whisky; he was an extremely happy man.

'While we are talking about Martha and the house, she will come with us to Puglia. She will be overwhelmed to be back in her native country. We will have an apartment somewhere in London, perhaps overlooking the river.'

Sophie was shaken, looking at her father she realised she did not know this man. He had never revealed this side of his nature, the fun in him. It was Sally, she realised, that had unlocked this merriment in him. Now she had a better grasp of what sacrifice he had made to her and her mother. Many men would have walked away years ago and married the woman he oh so dearly loved, but he had observed the vow he had made in his own way and seen it through.

Standing up, Sophie went and hugged them both, saying, 'I believe you will both be very happy, congratulations.'

'I have been thinking, there are two fields that surround the house. We could have horses for the children when they come for the holidays,' suggested Mr Vieri.

'And us,' chorused the adults.

CHAPTER 40

Lying in bed later that night in the crook of Tim's arm she thought back on the evening. The boat rocked gently as a vessel slid downstream, its wake gently moving the *Sea Maiden*. She was, she realised, having problems coming to terms with all the changes to their future that had been revealed this evening. She realised that she was growing less acceptable of change. One of the things that disturbed her the most was selling the family home. It would be ideal for her and Tim and the children as they got older. The downside of that was moving off the *Sea Maiden*. She loved living on the boat. She was often captured by the activity on the water. Time would drift by as she watched another scenario unfold. She enjoyed the river's different moods, even the nasty nagging and tugging when the weather was angry and the *Sea Maiden* was caught in a storm. It never bothered her; she knew this craft had been designed to survive the Channel's cruel sea and the enemies' ferocious fire as the troops fought their way ashore to liberate Europe all those years ago. Circumstances may force them to move ashore but she would need a lot of persuading. Martyn did not like the storms, unlike his sister who relished the wild weather and the sometimes crazy antics of the boat. In the severe weather when the river rose really high there were two planks required to reach the shore. One from the shore to an old metal cold water tank filled with rocks, another from there to the boat. The last plank was the most difficult because the *Sea Maiden* danced around in fierce winds, moving the plank around. Tim had rigged two ropes, one each side of the planks as handholds supported by metal posts. In the past Martyn occasionally had to be carried ashore by an adult, whereas Charley would attempt to traverse both planks without touching the ropes, her hands held out from her sides like a tightrope walker. Her parents' words of warning were ignored.

Paddy – no one knew his real name – had converted a ship's lifeboat to live in. It was big and drew a lot more water than most of the other houseboats, therefore it had to be further from the bank. There were more planks between boat and bank. On stormy nights the boat and planks were all dancing around. At its worst everything shifted under your feet. Paddy had gone in more than once.

He had a love of a glass or two, as he put it. Sometimes he came home from the pub a little the worse for wear. Tim knew Martyn often stayed awake to watch the Irishman arrive home. He had done this since one night he had seen him fall in by chance. Paddy was one of the nicest most gentle men Tim had ever met, but by golly he could drink.

* * * * *

The following morning Sophie awoke to find herself the only occupant of the bed. Sitting up and looking around she saw the top of Tim's head through the rear window. He was sitting on the small deck at the back of the boat. Scrambling into some clothes she joined him on the stern. As she reached him she saw he was dressed in a heavy coat over his pyjamas and slippers.

Sitting beside him and kissing his cheek, she asked, 'How long have you been out here?' snuggling up as close to him as she could get.

Looking at his watch he said, 'Half an hour.'

'So what woke you?'

'Your father selling up and moving,' replied Tim. 'I would have bet a lot of money he would die in harness. I am stunned that he will give it all up and move abroad. I think your father's beautiful new wife may have something to do with it. Who can blame her. The two of them have worked all the hours God sent for many years. I am surprised though that they want to sell everything and move away. He can't be short of money.'

Sophie thought for a moment, then said, 'There are two things that have influenced that decision. If he continues to have a role in the business Sally will still have to work, as she said he will expect it. I think she has put her foot down and made it clear she has no intention of working.'

Tim went to say something.

'Sorry, can I finish what I was saying?' asked Sophie. 'Remember, she is a new bride with a shiny gold ring on her finger. The power has shifted, she will insist their marriage is a partnership.'

'Why though is he selling the house?' he asked.

'He wants to leave the ghosts behind,' she replied. 'It was a loveless marriage. An apartment in London near the theatres and first-class restaurants will not be cheap. He will want something expensive overlooking the river. That is why he is selling the department store, the cash from that will fund the London address. Remember, it will have to be serviced while they are away. That will be expensive. No, this has not been done on a whim, someone has given this a lot of thought down the years.'

'You think this is Sally's doing, don't you?' said Tim.

'I do, but father is not going to object, she is making him incredibly happy. He is going to live back home in his beloved Italy with his extremely attractive young wife who adores him, he will have no money worries. What's not to like? I have never seen him so happy; he was almost euphoric.' Tim was quiet for a while, his left arm across his chest, his right hand stroking his chin.

'Tim, I can hear the wheels going round, what are you thinking about?'

'How about if we buy the house? We are going to need more space soon; Charley will want her own room in the near future and Martyn is not comfortable on board.'

'I was thinking last night I will so miss living on board, Tim. I love the moods of the river. There is an ever changing vista out there, the colours alter dependent on the weather and time of day. There are special times of day, for instance, when the sunset is reflected off the water. When the wind gets angry and the *Sea Maiden* starts dancing around, or at night when all the reflected colours on the water shift and slide. Moving ashore will mean all that will be gone. The view will be red brick and well-mown lawns and people washing their cars on Sunday mornings. Look here, Tim,' she said, pointing. 'Swans.' The three large birds had their wings half open like the spinnaker on a yacht. The following wind was gently blowing them along. Their progress was effortless, 'You do not get many sights like that in the high street.'

CHAPTER 41

Tim recognised the man walking towards him but for a moment couldn't remember his name. John, John who? For the life of him he couldn't recall his surname. He stood to welcome the man and they shook hands. As they sat Tim asked, 'Coffee, John?'

The bubbly young waitress, Maria, came to serve them, saying, 'Good morning, Tim. Good morning Mr Armstrong.'

'Maria, my name is John.' Turning to Tim, he said, 'She does this to wind me up. I will have my usual, please.'

The girl was wearing a pink smile, and her eyes were sparkling. Tim sensed there was more going on below the surface between these two than he was privy to.

'Same for me please, Maria,' added Tim. Continuing, he said, 'It sounds as though you are a regular, John?' In his mind he was thanking Maria for providing the surname.

'I have been a few times to check the footfall on different days. You are always busy. You don't open on Sundays. Can I ask is that for religious reasons or what?'

'No it's not, now we have the children Sophie and I hate working on Sundays. Many of our staff have little ones and they feel the same. Obviously we're losing some turnover, but the shops do very well on the other days.

We may be forced to change in the future, we'll see. Is this a coffee stop or what?'

'No, I hoped we could talk business. I have made up my mind, I would like to open my shop here in the food hall. My landlord at my present place has just increased the rent, a chunk more money. Can you put some numbers together so that I have some idea of what it will cost please? Who builds the shop, is that you or me?'

'We build the shop, then there can never be an argument over ownership of it if you decide to move on. You will pay a reasonable rent, that we can discuss. You do realise it will be of light construction? We don't get a lot of rain in here,' he said, smiling.

'That's all good, Tim. Oh, before I forget, the shop next to mine is a florist run by a woman called Miriam Price. It's owned by the same man as mine. I have her card here. She asked me to mention her name when I saw you.' He proffered the card.

Tim nodded, then both men were silent for a while, both wrapped in their own thoughts. Tim had his chin in his hand, a clear sign to those who knew him that he was thinking hard. Eventually he said, 'How would you feel if the shops were part of a terrace? It would reduce the cost and would fit in with the feel of the place. We could fit a back door, so you have a private space out the back, and some storage upstairs. Can I suggest that you do some sketches and measurements and come back to me? I can then put you in touch with our builder, Charlie. He will give me a price, then we can talk business. It would make sense if Mrs Price were involved from the beginning. I would like to meet her before we go too far.'

'Sounds good to me, Tim,' was the response. The two men shook hands. John Armstrong waved at Maria as he was leaving, who waved back and then blushed when she saw Tim was watching.

Tim thought about what he had seen. It was clear that Maria was carrying a torch for Mr John Armstrong. Tim was fairly sure the man in question had no idea. We men are so poor at this romance thing, Tim thought. I will mention to him what I have seen next time we talk.

The opportunity arrived a few days later, sipping an early morning hot coffee outside the café with the vintner. He asked, 'Why does Maria always call you Mr Armstrong?'

'She does it to wind me up.'

'You know she's keen on you, don't you? She lights up when she sees you come in,' said Tim.

John Armstrong laughed. 'I don't think so, Tim, I'm old enough to be her father. Mind you she is lovely. '

'You aren't old. Why not ask her out? Sometimes, John, we spectators see more of the game. I will have a little bet with you. If you ask her I am sure she will say yes.'

John sat thinking, there had not been a woman in his life for, he was counting back in his head, eight years. He had realised a while ago he was lonely; it was all work and no play. He realised it was his fault. His focus was entirely on the business. Perhaps it was time for a change.

'You're on, Tim, I will ask her out for a meal.'

'When?' asked Tim.

'Now,' said John Armstrong rising from the table, 'I must get on anyway.'

Maria was cleaning a table when John walked up to her. Tim was not privy to the conversation. He saw him writing what must have been her phone number in his diary.

Maria watched John Armstrong walk away. He stopped and turned at the store exit and waved her goodbye. She waved back, moving towards Tim's table as she did so. Reaching him still with a big smile on her face she said, 'Thank you, Tim. John told me that you had said just do it when he said he would like to ask me out.'

Smiling at her he said, 'I don't know what you are talking about. Good luck to both of you, now I must get on.'

THE NEXT GENERATION

'Thank you anyway,' was her response as her boss walked away.

His father had telephoned him earlier telling him that Shop Number One was almost finished.

* * * * *

Walking in the door of Shop Number One a little later he stopped as he saw what had been achieved. He was quite overcome. He realised this was how Mr Woodman's shop must have looked when his grandfather had started it in a now distant century. The white walls and ceiling, the heavy black supporting beams overhead, the pale honey-coloured woodwork on the counters, etc. The newly varnished wooden floorboards. He noticed a new till had been installed. He wouldn't miss the old one. For some reason as a child he had found it rather scary. He had a clear picture of his mother when she had worked for Mr Woodman, sitting on her stool in her multicoloured pinafore at the shiny monster of a till that had been there for years. It had pop-up numbers that appeared in the glass top when the keys were pressed.

His father called his son over to where he was standing. As Tim reached him Tom pointed up on the wall where there were half a dozen of the small drawers fastened to it. 'Do you remember? Before the fire this wall was covered in them.'

Tim remembered his grandfather saying he knew the content of every box, all the screws, the nuts and bolts and a vast range of other things in all the sizes. His boast was that there was at least two of everything in them.

'I found those that had been thrown out because you said you didn't want them. I cleaned them and revarnished them. if you don't want them I can take them down.'

Tim's memory snatched him back down the years to when his godfather was explaining what was in all the drawers and what the contents were used for. He could smell all the different oils and Mr Woodman's aftershave.

He took a few deep breaths and cleared his throat, saying. 'It's a nice touch, Dad, thank you.' He walked up the stairs to check on the café and the fire escape.

His father had followed him, saying, 'They've done a good job, haven't they?'

Tim was nodding.

There was a long counter to serve the tea, coffee, sandwiches and cake. There were round tables surrounded by matching chairs in the same honey-coloured varnish as the counters downstairs. All the seats sported comfortable-looking blue and white striped cushions.

'When can we start stocking?'

'Charlie reckons one more week to tidy up then it's all yours.'

'You've all done a good job, Dad, well done. Can you thank Charlie and the guys for me please?'

Tom would never admit it, but he had enjoyed the task and was extremely proud of the result.

CHAPTER 42

It had been agreed that the young people and Mr Lawrence would play their gig on a Friday evening. Martyn was surprised that he did not feel too nervous when he and the family arrived at the café. This was true until he saw the huge poster in the front window that said, 'SOUL MUSIC RETURNS TO AUNT MAY'S TONIGHT'. Entering the café and looking around he was surprised how big it was. Opposite the entrance there was a low stage, only a few inches high, with what Martyn thought were rather scruffy side curtains, in fact the place was clean but had seen the passage of time. He relaxed a little. It would have been far more daunting if it were super smart, all shiny chrome and bright lights. This, he decided, was comfy, he loved the atmosphere. Yep it would do.

Aunt May came over and smothered him in a huge hug. When she let him go she said in a warm Jamaican accent, 'I'm so looking forward to hearing you play again, child. When you're ready you get up there and enjoy yourself.' There was another all-enveloping embrace and then she let him go.

The group made their way backstage. Again, everything was a little worn, clean enough though. Martyn decided that comfy was a good description. He put his clarinet together, moistened the reed and blowing gently and quietly he began to warm the instrument up, just playing snatches of tunes then moving on, slowly trying the harder notes until, now with everything working, he started improvising. He was chasing tunes down new passageways into strange places, then skilfully somehow finding his way back to the root of the piece. Tea and cake arrived and as swiftly disappeared, then it was their time to perform.

As they gathered themselves to go on stage Mr Lawrence said, 'We have got all evening. Let's do the entrance we were going to do for the school concert. Easy, not the charge of the light brigade.' This said looking at Martyn. Mr Lawrence walked on and began playing very quietly while he explained that the rest of the group were still at school but were in his opinion very gifted.

'Joining me first, ladies and gentleman, is our drummer Adam, who keeps us all in order.'

The lad sauntered on and waved at the large crowd, who responded by clapping. Gentle drumming began. A minute later it was Martyn's turn. As he walked on he saw Charley, his sister, helping behind the café counter preparing sandwiches and his father supplying chairs for an elderly couple who had come in late. It took a moment for him to recognise Nanny. She looked different in pink instead of her everyday green uniform. She and the man with her were deep in conversation. Aunt May was sitting with his mum in the front row.

Mr Lawrence mouthed 'gently' at him. Standing just to the right of the piano he began to play, two or three people began clapping. He recognised some school friends.

Then it was Agatha's turn to appear, now there was shouting and loud clapping. It went quiet as she began to sing.

Martyn's nerves fled away. Now there was sheer enjoyment. This, he realised, was who he was. During a passage that was just piano and Agatha, Martyn recognised that no matter what anyone else might say, his mum or dad, school teachers, anyone, this was what he was meant to do with the rest of his life. When he came back in after Agatha's piece he recognised a subtle variation in his music. Now there was contentment, a lot of his angst had flown away. He recognised while he was playing that this choice might well mean he would never be wealthy like his father, he may even be hungry often, but so be it. He was certain it was the only way he would be happy. The improvisation came from deep inside him. He was elsewhere, the music was playing him rather than the other way round. His heart was full, he did not believe he would ever be happier than this. He was aware of Agatha coming to stand beside him while she sang. There was now a sympathy between them. A give and take, a sharing of things unspoken, perhaps even things there were no words for, a meeting of minds maybe. At the end of their stint the audience would not let them leave the stage. The crowd were shouting for Agatha to sing something on her own.

Mr Lawrence put his finger to his lips to indicate they should all be quiet and leave her to sing on her own. The song was about a mother who had lost her baby son. Martyn was very moved, the pain in the song was tangible, there were a flurry of handkerchiefs and a long silence when it was over. Eventually there was sustained applause. The two boys and the man bowed and left the stage, leaving Agatha to take her rightful applause.

Backstage Aunt May congratulated everybody but took Martyn to one side, and grasping both his hands in hers said, 'I have been around music and musicians all my life. You are an old soul.'

'I'm sorry I don't understand,' he replied.

'It's an expression that means you have been here before, in another time. To play like you do should not be possible. You are too young to have learnt all that. You knew it before. The problem is most musicians spend their lives penniless, although you play so well it is no guarantee you won't be broke most of the time. Perhaps you need to think about a proper occupation and play your clarinet on the side.'

Martyn was shaking his head. 'Aunt May, all I want to do is this,' he said as he ran the brush through the dissembled parts of the instrument. He began polishing the black wood and metal work of the exterior to a high shine. The clarinet's appearance had changed since he had been loaned it by his music teacher, Mr Lawrence. Before it looked uncared for. Now it was obviously treasured. He sensed that the tone of the instrument had mellowed. He was unsure. Maybe he had improved.

Mr Lawrence was ready to leave but before he did, he took Martyn to one side, saying, 'That was amazing tonight. I would like you to accept my clarinet, I will never be able to play like that. I am just delighted that my mother's present to me has ended up in such capable hands.'

Sophie had joined them and had overheard. 'We must pay you, Mr Lawrence,' she said, obviously adamant.

'No thanks. You miss the point, Mrs Cooper, it has to be a gift. I can't sell my mother's present, but I can give it to this young man with his incredible skills.' Now addressing Martyn, he said, 'When you are playing in those big concerts at home and abroad in the future can you just remember at the end to say thank you to my mother.'

Martyn was completely overcome by Mr Lawrence's generosity and his belief in someone so young. Martyn decided there and then that music would dictate his life's path.

CHAPTER 43

Tim reached for the ringing phone, glad to have a distraction from the litter of paperwork that covered his desk. It was John Armstrong on the other end.

After the introductions were over, Tim said, 'How can I help you?'

'Tim, I have the drawing you wanted for the shop I had in mind, also Miriam my next door neighbour has jotted down some details of a possible building for her. We would like to see you if you have time.'

'Erm, I can't do it today, let me have a word with Jessica.'

John heard Tim call his PA, and the click of heels as she entered his office. Then there was indiscernible mumbling, then Tim's voice saying, 'Hi, John, are you still there? How about an extended lunch on me at the food hall tomorrow?'

Now it was Tim's turn to listen to only one end of a conversation while John questioned Miriam Price. They all finally settled on a time and rang off.

* * * * *

Tim was sitting outside the café sipping a flat white when he spotted the two people he was expecting walking towards him. The conversation appeared animated. Putting his cup down and standing up Tim greeted his visitors.

Miriam Price was well dressed, well-spoken and attractive. Tim guessed she was in her mid-forties. She had clearly taken trouble with her appearance. The mid-grey suit fitted her perfectly. Her dark hair was cut in an attractive short style. He sensed she was accustomed to getting her own way. In some ways she reminded him of a younger version of Sophie's mother. She did more listening than talking. When she did speak Tim felt she was a little abrupt. He decided one word that described her was prickly. She treated him as though he were not to be trusted. Some of the things she had said bordered on rude. It became obvious they were never going to become close friends; It was clear she had been mistreated by a landlord in the past, but he said to himself, we are not all the same.

Miriam Price picked at her salad. She seemed unable to relax. To Tim's eye she appeared overwound like a child's toy. One touch would set her off. She had little to say. She made her excuses and left on her own before the men had finished their food.

'It would appear she is not interested,' observed John.

Tim simply shook his head. The men enjoyed a chat, the atmosphere was vastly improved after Mrs Price's had left.

On the way out Tim watched as John Armstrong popped into the café, coming out soon after with Maria following him. The couple stood together talking with Maria's hand on his arm. Would there be a kiss, wondered Tim? John did lean in and hug her before he strode away. He looked back before he walked out into the street. She lifted a hand, he waved in reply.

* * * * *

Charlie the builder had given Tim the estimate for the shop build earlier. In conversation with Charlie, Tim was adamant the building had to look as good as the café. Sophie, looking at the build costs, worked out a figure for the annual rent, then she added a percentage for unseen future costs.

THE NEXT GENERATION

The building was completed long before Tim had expected it to be ready. Charlie explained that with normal buildings that were outside a great deal of the work happened underground with foundations, pipe work, electrics, sewage et cetera. Here it was all done on the surface. The café took longer because it had to have all the cooking facilities added.

Tim loved the design; it looked like the small privately owned shops he had seen in Italy. John the vintner had specified the orange pantiles on the pitched roof of the single-storey building. It had smooth white walls punctured by the large shop windows on each side and in the middle a pair of honey-coloured oak doors, that would usually be open. The interior had rows of dark varnished bottle racks with a long matching counter at the far end. Behind it there was a door that allowed staff access to the office at the back.

* * * * *

When John saw what Charlie and his son had achieved the new tenant hugged the builder, who was clearly uncomfortable with this and struggled out of the embrace and moved out of reach.

Tommy, Charlie's now nearly full-grown son had to turn away, he was in hysterics. He whispered to Tim, 'He can't abide being cuddled by men.'

The vintner strode over to Tim, grasped his hand and started pounding Tim's shoulder saying, 'It looks perfect, Tim. It's a little piece of Italy. When can I move in?'

'Erm, have you paid the deposit?'

'No not yet, I will see Sophie.' Looking at his watch he pulled a face. 'It will have to be tomorrow now; the banks will be closed.'

'John, I would let you in tonight but ...'

'I do understand, Tim, I know you would get a wire brushing when you went home. She's right, you know; we need to do it properly. Can you tell Sophie I will sort it out in the morning?'

'Will do,' replied Tim. 'Goodnight, Charlie, Tommy,' he shouted, watching Charlie in full retreat determined not to be cuddled again. Tommy turned round to face Tim with a huge smile on his face as he waved goodbye.

In the morning a barrow was ferrying cases of wine between the new shop and a small new maroon van with the company name in smart gold italics. *John Armstrong, Vintner.*

* * * * *

Tim thought he had seen the back of Mrs Miriam Price. She seemed to be permanently bad tempered. Now here she was again standing in his office berating him. John Armstrong had finally given in and told her what his monthly rent was and the size of the deposit.

'That's nearly as much as my new rent will be where I am now, it's a rip off,' she barked at Tim.

'Mrs Price, no one is forcing you to pay it. I am quite confident you could find a shop round a side street a lot cheaper, however, you will not have a quarter of the footfall that we have here.' Tim flipped open his diary, found the phone number for George Wainwright the estate agent and his address. He wrote it down and slid it across his desk towards the woman.

She read the details, then shouted at him, 'I don't want to go to an estate agent, he will rip me off even worse than you are trying to.'

Tim, recognising that he was about to lose his temper, rose from his desk, opened his office door and said, 'Please find your own way out.' Ushering her through and locking the door behind her he retook his seat. There was some rattling of the door handle, then some shouting. Now he could hear his father trying to calm her down. The shouting slowly died away.

Tim vowed to himself that even if *that women* got down on her knees he would never let her have a stall in the food hall.

THE NEXT GENERATION

* * * * *

Tim and his team had become accustomed to meeting in the restaurant for a drink

at six o'clock before the restaurant opened at seven. Tim had his first drink in his hand already. Jessica plonked herself down opposite him across the table emitting an audible sigh as she did so.

'It sounds as though you've had one of those days,' said Tim.

'No, not really, the problems were a fiddle. You had to do X before you could complete Y, it was all bitty. I do not feel I have achieved anything. Enough of me, what was all that shouting about?'

Tim was shaking his head. 'That woman who wanted a florist shop expected me to rent her a stall for the price of an ice cream.'

'Oh dear, how unpleasant,' said Jessica, struggling unsuccessfully to smother her laughter.

'Yes it was, and it's not funny.'

She could hear the anger in his voice for the woman and a rebuke aimed at her for thinking it was funny.

Tim continued, 'I am beginning to wonder if having private shops installed in the food hall is a good idea.'

While he was talking Oliver had arrived and sat down holding a pint of bitter. He leant over and kissed Jessica's cheek and asked, 'Why do you think that, Tim?'

'Jessica, can you explain please?' She brought her partner up to date, adding that Tim was still angry about it.

Tim leant forward, brushing his hair off his forehead as he did so. 'When you look at the income from John Armstrong's shop it's miniscule against what we take off any of our own stalls, and there is a lot of work and cost setting it up, and if I am truthful I don't have time to do it.'

Oliver sat thinking, then he said, 'You will not believe this, Tim. Jessica and I have discussed my hours.'

Tim's face was creased into a frown, clearly unsure of where this conversation was going and what if any was its relevance to the current discussion.

Oliver's response surprised him. 'Tim I do not have enough to do, I could cram my week's work into about four days easily, sometimes less. I have to admit, on occasion I am bored. I seem to be the only one who is not working flat out. These peripheral tasks that you and Sophie have, if you explained them I am sure I could do a lot of them.'

Tim, obviously extremely surprised, said, 'I have never had anyone tell me that they don't have enough to do. Are you saying you would be happy to take on other tasks outside of your normal remit?'

'Tim, at uni I achieved a first-class business degree that I am barely using. I would be happy to help in other areas.'

Tim was silent for some while, thinking. He recognised that the company could make better use of this young man and his skills. He noticed that Jessica was holding her partner's hand. Tim had a flash of intuition. These two had been talking about leaving Sophie's so that Oliver or perhaps both of them could have more interesting jobs, he was sure of it. What to do about it was the question. They certainly could not afford to lose Jessica, and Oliver was being underused. He was one of the few members of the company with a major business qualification. Sophie had shared with her husband the enormous salary Oliver had been receiving at his previous employment.

Two other members of staff had joined the group. As they made themselves comfortable Enzo arrived, carrying his own bottle of an extremely good red. Uncorking it he offered it around.

Speaking quietly to the young couple, Tim said, 'Do you have time for a chat in my office?'

They both nodded and carrying their drinks followed Tim down the hall.

CHAPTER 44

'Can I say what's on my mind first, please?' asked Tim. Both nodded. 'Jessica, what I am going to say is not flannel. The truth is you are an essential limb of this company, your organisational skills are extraordinary. If we lost you it would cripple us for a long time. If Sophie were here now she would be giving me a verbal good hiding. She would say I am trying to blackmail you into staying. I promise you there is no truth in that. But to repeat myself you need to know how important you are to this business. So, if ever you have a problem don't let it fester, come and talk to me. I will always listen, and I will do all I can to fix it.' Jessica, looking very moved, said quietly, 'Thank you, Tim, that means a lot.'

There was a short pause while the two men looked at each other, then Tim with his head on one side took a long breath in and held it. He was nodding almost imperceptibly.

Then he said, 'Thank you for being honest with me … I do appreciate it. Tell me, would you be prepared to take on a lot more responsibility, maybe longer hours, more money of course?'

Oliver was nodding vigorously. 'I certainly would.'

'Right, I'll call a board meeting and sort something out. It's ridiculous to have Sophie and me working all hours and you with all your skills twiddling your thumbs.'

* * * * *

After the young couple left Tim sat staring out of his office window, not seeing the trees, the flower beds and the close mown lawns in the park outside. He was mulling over his options, rearranging in his mind how he, Sophie and the young couple might work together in the future.

Two evenings later, Tim, Sophie, Tom, Harry and Sara were sitting in the Italian couple's house, Sara had agreed to take the minutes. It had been Harry who pointed out that it couldn't be Jessica, who was the usual minute taker.

Tim regaled them with the details of the conversation he'd had with the young couple.

'What made you think he may have been discussing leaving the company?' asked his father.

'It was mostly a feeling,' said Tim. 'What I did notice was that Jessica had a firm grip of his hand. I think she was giving him a kind of physical support. She wouldn't do that if it were a minor problem.'

Sara said, 'Can I speak please?' This was very unusual for Sara to say anything in any meeting. She sat twiddling a button on her pink blouse.

Tim nodded.

She continued, 'Tim, I think it is bigger than you believe. Oliver is not scared of anyone. This was a bombshell they were going to deliver. The hand holding was mutual support. I am sure two resignations were on the table.'

Tim, having heard Sara repeat his own belief in what was happening, found himself nodding at her in agreement.

The group were silent while they tried to take in the enormity of Sara's words.

Sophie was the first to speak. 'If this was to happen it would cripple the company for a long time to come. Bonny is good, but she could not do two jobs, not in the long term.'

THE NEXT GENERATION

'We could give him a good rise,' said Harry.

'That's not the problem, he's bored. He's a clever man. There's nothing worse than sitting staring at the walls for hours with nothing to do,' said Sophie.

'What are your thoughts, Tim?' asked his father.

'This has been keeping me awake,' he admitted.

Sophie rolled her eyes and nodded.

'Initially I thought we could give him a salary increase and hand over some of the work Sophie and I don't have time for, but this is,' he paused and took a deep breath, 'I believe an opportunity to make much more use of him. He has a first-class business degree that we are not using. He says he needs more to do; we can fix that by making him the business manager, all the team leaders report to him. That's everybody, me included. If we have a problem we put it on his desk to sort out. Obviously some things will be decided at board level, so I suggest we make him a board member, then we are using all his skills.'

'Tim, when you say everything goes through him, does that make him my boss?' asked his father. 'I can tell you here and now, son, I am not going to agree to that. I have been in this business forever, I don't need anybody telling me how to do it. If you make him my boss I'll walk away. I'm not ...'

'Dad,' said Tim interrupting, knowing his father was losing his temper, 'that's not what I envisage. You're working alright with him now aren't you, with that staffing problem?'

His father said, 'Yeah there were one or two problems. He's sorted them out ok.' His grudging tone of voice was an indicator that he was still not in full agreement.

'I promise you he will be a Mr Fixit. He will certainly not be telling you what to do, he will be there to help if you ask him to. I shall use him a lot, especially when I have to sit on the telephone for hours to resolve a problem. In future that sort of thing will be his job.'

'What will his job on the board be?' asked Harry.

'I'm hoping that he will be able to advise us on strategies to relieve Sophie and me, and or carry out my and Sophie's instructions.'

Sophie said, 'It will make my job a lot easier with him on board. When I suggest a business plan he should be able to go away and set it up, then report back to us for the go-ahead.'

'What about the ordering and all that, will that be his job or mine still?' asked his father.

'Yes and no, you will work with him to plan a normal order. All you will have to do is keep him advised of any changes. I expect he will need a lot of help from you at the beginning while he learns his way around his new job.'

'Hmmm,' was his father's response.

The team spent twenty minutes discussing Oliver's new salary. They finally agreed a substantial increase for him and a significant upgrade for Jessica.

'Right,' said Tim, 'I'm going to ask you all separately if you are ok with this, starting with you, Dad. Are you in agreement with what we've discussed?'

Tom was silent for some time. His son was about to speak when his father said, 'It's obvious we have to do something. If we lost Jessica as you say we would have a serious problem, losing the young man as well would put the tin lid on it. I can think of no alternative,' he continued. 'I realise I have a problem with change.' He paused again, Tim looked towards his father. This prompted Tom to sit up straight in his chair and say, 'There is another reason to do this, and we have overlooked it. We have to accept this change … your health, Tim. Sophie tells me you are both working Sundays again. What did that doctor ask you?'

Sophie said, 'She asked you, Tim, if you had set out to kill yourself.'

Tim grimaced. He was always uncomfortable when someone reminded him of his mild coronary and the fact that he was now on daily medication.

THE NEXT GENERATION

'We have no choice but to agree to the proposal,' confirmed his father. Everyone was nodding.

'So that's carried then?' asked Tim. There was a chorus of affirmation.

After a short chat people were exchanging goodbyes.

Sophie said, 'Bye, Tim. I must move on. I have a meeting with Alan Wells in half an hour.' She kissed his cheek on the way to the door. Tim was lost in thought as he made his way back to his office.

He was once again enthralled by his wife's skills in the debates. She gave a little push here, a nudge there, an opinion when required. She was rarely confrontational. But it was usually Sophie's clear vision and her experience, skills and training that won the day. More importantly still of course was that she was his wife, his beloved, and a wonderful mother to their children. Tim made a wry smile. Sophie would have reprimanded him for appearing to rate her business skills above her other gifts.

Tim reflected back on how close he had come to losing her in the early days. He remembered the female staff member who had lied to Sophie about her and Tim's relationship, hinting that they were a couple, the terrible row, and the awful words that he and Sophie had exchanged in the street that should have been the end of their understanding.

Tim remembered the elderly alcoholic on the river bridge the night he believed the terrible words he and Sophie had exchanged meant he had lost her forever. Tim was standing in the dark and the cold rain was only broken by a solitary dim yellow street lamp. His forearms were resting on the metal handrail while staring down at the river rushing under the bridge. He was staring into a future without purpose. He must have looked like a desperate man, a possible suicide. The old boy had promised him it would all look better in the morning. Taking his own life had not occurred to him and never would. It was clear that the old man who had spoken to him had seen it as a possibility. Tim had been extremely depressed, he remembered. He had been unable to envisage a life without her.

Perhaps he mused, angels don't always appear be-winged and clothed in a white robe.

* * * * *

The following morning Tim was sat in his office with the young couple sitting opposite him. He relayed what had been said at the board meeting. He was pleased to see both of them were smiling when he finished.

'Now,' he said, 'I need to give you a word of warning, Oliver, your role is advisory. You will be unwise to order the staff around. Some of them have been doing the job since the end of the Second World War.'

'That's not a problem, Tim. I always discuss everything and make sure they have a sense of ownership. It works better that way.'

Tim stood and shook their hands and saw them out. A sense of ownership, aye. I must remember that, he thought.

CHAPTER 45

Tim was busy going through the Saturday figures that Oliver had sent him earlier when there was a knock at the door.

'Come in,' he called.

John Armstrong, the vintner, walked in. The two men shook hands, Tim pointed at a chair as they exchanged greetings. 'What can I do for you, John?' asked Tim.

'Well, Tim, I need to ask you a big favour.' There was a long pause.

'Spit it out, John, it can't be that bad.'

'Can I ask you to listen before you decide please?'

Tim, though puzzled, agreed, he could think of no reason for the vintner to ask him to do this.

'It's about Mrs Price.'

'Now wait! I have had more than enough of that woman to last me a lifetime. She's rude, she's—' Tim was standing, now propelled to his feet by his anger.

'Tim, you agreed to listen,' said John, interrupting him. With a pained expression on his face and taking a long breath in, Tim said, 'Go on then,' sitting down as he spoke. His demeanour clearly indicated that he was not happy with Mr John flipping Armstrong.

'She has been honest with me, Tim, and has agreed that I can tell you what she has told me. She is bankrupt. Her trade went downhill when the out-of-town supermarket opened. She took out a bank loan to tide her over and was just managing when her landlord put her rent up as he had mine. She is on her knees, Tim, both financially and emotionally. She shared with me that two years ago her husband had disappeared. I believe it's desperation that makes her so ill tempered. She was not like that when first met her three years ago. I wondered, Tim, if she could rent a stall here in the food hall?'

'John, I have to say that my first instinct is to say no. Should she be rude to our customers it could damage our reputation. People may start going elsewhere. It is not my decision; it is the board's. I have to warn you, I can't predict their response. I tell you what, John, I'll call a board meeting and let them decide. I will keep quiet.'

John thanked him. 'I'll tell her,' he said as he left the room.

* * * * *

Three nights later the board members were sitting in Tim's office with a hot drink in their hands. Tim explained the reason for the meeting, sharing with them everything he had been told about Mrs Price's situation. There were a few questions. Tim explained it would be a stall, not an indoor shop like the café and the wine store.

'I thought you didn't like her?' said Oliver.

'What I think is immaterial,' said Tim. 'It's just business. A stall is cheap and easy to provide. We could put up some tables and throw a green cover over it to start with to keep the costs down for her.'

What am I doing selling this? I can't stand the woman, thought Tim.

His father said, 'I think we should help her out. Your mother and I, Tim, had to live on bread and baked beans so that you had proper food after the war because we were extremely poor and rationing was terrible.'

THE NEXT GENERATION

'Sara and I were the same, except we had no little ones to feed, more's the pity,' added Harry.

'What do we think then, folks?' asked Tim.

It was agreed that the company would offer space in the food hall at a nominal rent to start with to be reviewed in six months.

'I would like to be the one to make the offer, Tim. I suspect she will be more open with me,' said Sophie.

Tim and his wife were sitting in Tim's office awaiting Mrs Price's arrival. He had received a lecture from Sophie about his treatment of Mrs Price during the forthcoming meeting. 'Be nice,' she had commanded him. There was a tapping on the door, Sophie jumped up to answer it. She was waving at her husband to indicate that she would open the door as he started to rise.

Tim was thinking, if this woman is as rude as last time we spoke this is going to end extremely abruptly, no matter what Sophie says.

Tim and Sophie welcomed the woman. They all shook hands and Sophie indicated they would sit in the armchairs that surrounded the four sides of a low coffee table. They each chose a chair that afforded them a view of the park, the trees and the children playing.

'This is Sophie, my wife and the company finance director. She is also the finance director for a large local business.'

'Mrs Price,' said Tim, 'the board has decided to make you an offer.' He noticed the woman sit a little straighter in her chair. 'It's not a building like the café or John's wine shop. Sophie will explain what we can do for you.' Mrs Price pulled a face.

Sophie said, 'I can see you are disappointed but let me explain what we are offering. You will have noticed the costermongers' barrows in the food hall.' There was a nodded reply. 'We are proposing we supply one of those eventually once we get one built for you.'

Both Tim and Sophie watched the women behave like a leaking balloon as she slowly collapsed into her chair, shaking her head as she did so.

Speaking for the first time she said, 'Sorry, that won't work. If I have no income this month the bank will foreclose on my loan. My house may have to be sold to pay off the loan.'

The young couple could see she was fighting to keep the flood gates closed.

'Do you have stock in your shop now?'

'Yes but I have to empty the shop by tomorrow night, or I have to pay another month. I can't do that.' Now the tears came in floods, betraying a terrible, painful surrender to what appeared to be the inevitable. She could see everything collapsing around her and no way out.

'What can we do, Tim?' asked Sophie, very moved by the woman's plight. She knelt down and put her arms around the desperate woman.

Tim was holding his chin in his hand, thinking hard, finally saying, 'How would you like to be back in business tomorrow night, here in the food hall?'

Speaking through her sobs she said, 'I can't afford it, I can't afford anything.'

'Can you sit tight? Sophie and I are going to step outside for a few minutes and see what we can do.'

As they closed the door behind them Jessica came out of her office next door and asked, 'Did I hear tears?'

'Yes,' said Sophie, filling Jessica in with the detail.

'Poor woman. what can we do?'

'A good question, Jessica. Tim, what can we do?'

'Will you get your pad please, Jessica, and be ready to come in with us in a minute.'

It took seconds for her to accomplish what he had asked.

'I think we can offer the following,' he said, 'two tables with a green cloth thrown over them in one of the corners. If we get that right that will allow her to have some storage behind it. If you remember, this was proposed at the board meeting.' Both women agreed it should work.

'Sophie, what can we charge?' asked Tim. 'Nothing perhaps?'

'We cannot do that, Tim,' she replied. 'It has to be on a business footing.'

'Why not ask her what she can afford?' suggested Jessica.

'Ok, that's a good plan. Can you come back in with us, Jessica, and make some notes please?' They walked back into the room.

'Does your husband work?' asked Sophie, noticing the wedding ring on Mrs Price's finger as she sat back down. Tim stayed silent, knowing her husband had left her.

Becoming emotional again, she said, 'I may as well tell you everything. My husband just walked out one day and disappeared. He took his rucksack, hiking boots, outdoor clothing. That was three years ago. I haven't seen or heard from him since. The police told me that thousands of people disappear every year. They tried to find him for a while with no success. I wear my ring because who knows, he may walk back in.' Again she wiped the tears away with a by now soggy handkerchief.

'Jessica is here to make some notes,' said Sophie. She went on to explain what they had come up with. 'Do you think the tables would work? There are other stalls the same in the hall, as I expect you have noticed.'

Mrs Price confirmed that she had seen them, and that they should be ok. 'How much could you afford each week?' asked Sophie.

There was a long pause while she did the sums in her head then she said, 'Basing it on my present turnover, not very much. The supermarket opening up and selling bunches of flowers at the prices I have to pay for them has crippled my business.'

'The benefit here is that the nearest big store is some way away,' offered Tim.

Mrs Price finally came up with a figure, Tim asked, 'How much does that leave left over in an ordinary week?'

'Nothing,' she responded. Tim shook his head.

Sophie said, 'How about half of that?'

Mrs Price, clearly surprised, said, 'That should be manageable, you are extremely kind.'

Tim offered his hand, saying, 'Do we have a deal?'

'Yes,' was her reply, shaking his hand enthusiastically.

'Ok,' he responded. 'Jessica do you have the time to take Mrs Price's details? Then we can draw up a contract, for how long?' he asked, turning to Sophie.

'Six months,' she replied. Mrs Price was now smiling for the first time. Jessica guided the much happier woman into her office to sort the paperwork out.

'We need to move her stock tomorrow, Tim, as promised,' said Sophie.

'I'll ring Charlie. Hopefully he can give us some time in his big van,' replied Tim.

* * * * *

Late the following evening saw Mrs Price all set up and almost ready to go for the next day.

Sophie and Tim walked over to her stall where the florist was putting the final touches to the centrepiece, a large, fluted glass vase containing an abundance of yellow roses and a fan of bright green ferns to the rear as a backdrop. As they arrived she stepped away to look at it, then much to their surprise she put both hands to her face and burst into tears.

Sophie took three quick paces forward and wrapped her in her arms, saying, 'Whatever is wrong?'

Fighting to control her emotions she said through her sobs, 'Yesterday my business was doomed, I was about to lose my home. God knows what I would have done. Now thanks to you two I have a future.'

While she was speaking she had reached out to take Tim's hand and squeeze it. 'I am sorry I was so rude.' Sniffing, she said, 'I haven't cried in years.'

Sophie handed her a clean hanky, saying as she did so, 'Let's go and have a cup of tea.'

CHAPTER 46

Oliver came home one evening and said, 'I had a phone call from my mother at work today. She asked how we all were and then said would we like to go for tea on Sunday. It's her birthday and she would love to meet you both. She thinks it's time to see this woman and child who have lured her son away.'

Jessica, smiling, said, 'I would love to meet her. You would have to brief me. What is her name?'

'Mrs Adams,' replied Oliver, laughing.

'Oh ha, ha,' responded Jessica.

'Isabell,' said Oliver, 'her friends call her Izzy. You'll love her. She is such fun; she is always laughing. Father's name is George, he is quiet, not surprising really with Mother around. They are lovely. I am lucky, they are nice people.'

Jessica was thoughtful for a moment. If this relationship is going anywhere, I will have to meet them sometime. It might as well be now, she decided. 'Yes, that would be nice, I will ask Sophie if I can leave Polly with her for a while.'

'No, no,' said Oliver, shaking his head and smiling. 'I think she wants to meet Polly most of all. She loves children, I'm often asked when am I going to settle down and provide her with grandchildren. Shall we make it this

Sunday? I will ring Mother this afternoon and find out what time she wants us there.'

The following Sunday afternoon found them seated on the train heading for Pinner. Oliver was wearing his usual blue denim, Jessica a full-length white cotton dress with puff sleeves. Polly was clothed in white like her mother. It was a short walk to Oliver's parent's home from the station. The road was open to fields on one side with a row of attractive bungalows on the other. They all had names; they seemed to be named mostly after trees and flowers. Oliver stopped outside The Dell and held the gate open for them. As they walked down the path to the front door it flew open and an attractive older women strode down the path towards them. Her pretty chiffon yellow flowered dress swirled around her as she walked.

She reached Jessica and wrapped her in a huge hug and kissed her cheek, saying, 'You are just as lovely as Oliver said you were.' Releasing her and crouching down, she said, 'And you must be Polly.'

Wide eyed, the child nodded.

A tall, well-dressed man stood in the doorway watching them, then eventually called out saying, 'Let them come in, Izzy. I expect they would like a cup of tea and a sit down after the journey.'

Oliver's mother shepherded them all inside. She took their coats and hung them up, then showed them the toilet. Polly was standing at the patio doors looking out at the most beautiful garden she had ever seen. She knew none of the names, but she was enthralled by the colours.

Her mother came and crouched down beside her. Knowing what her daughter was looking at she said, 'It is beautiful. Which is your favourite flower?'

The child was quiet for some time. Jessica was about to prompt her when Polly said, 'They are all lovely, Mummy, especially the big yellow bush,' pointing at a yellow climbing rose as she spoke.

'It's called good as gold,' said Mr Adams from behind them. Mother and daughter turned to face him as they stood up.

'Would you like me to show you round, Polly?' he asked, holding out his hand. Polly looked up at her mother for permission.

'May I come with you?' asked Jessica.

'Of course,' he replied. Jessica looked around for Oliver. She saw him talking to his mother in the kitchen. The trio stepped through the conservatory door into the garden. Mr Adams senior knew most of the names.

'Izzy knows all of them,' he said, 'she is a great gardener. There's not much she doesn't know.'

Becoming aware how long the garden was, and the multiplicity of flower beds and the large swathes of lawn, Jessica said, 'This is obviously a lot of work.'

'Yes we have help. A young man comes in to do the lawns and Israel carries out Izzy's instruction regarding the flower beds. Talk of the devil here he is now.' This was said pointing out an elderly man bent double in a flower, bed trimming a rose that had gone over.

'Good morning, Israel,' called Mr Adams as they approached.

The elderly gardener winced as he straightened up holding his back and said, 'Good morning, sir. How are you?'

'Is your back still giving you grief?'

'It comes and goes,' the elderly man replied.

'Old age is not all it's cracked up to be is it? Have you been here all night? I saw you tidying up in the gloaming last evening.'

'I can't abide leaving a job unfinished,' was the reply. 'There was a good moon last night to help me wrap it up.'

'I am going to show our visitors the field,' said Mr Adams.

'I've got the youngster to mow some paths through it.'

'That's a good idea, Israel, thank you.'

As they walked towards the tall hedge at the bottom of the garden, Mr Adams was explaining that Israel came with the property years ago when they first bought it.

THE NEXT GENERATION

'We have grown old together,' he added.

'Oliver tells me you used to sail, but you sold the boat?'

'Yes I did sell her. I am not as nimble as I once was. I realised that she was just sitting there. Boats need a lot of looking after or they rot away.'

Approaching a tall laurel hedge Jessica thought initially there was no way through it, then she noticed that further away but parallel with the first hedge was another blocking the view of whatever lay beyond it. Reaching the first hedge and turning right and left the field was revealed. It was a riot of colour, wildflowers in amazing profusion waved gently in the warm wind.

All three stopped. 'Oh WOW!' said Jessica. When she looked down her daughter was staring up at her with tears running down her face. 'Why are you crying, you silly goose?' asked her mother.

'It's like fairyland,' was the response. 'Can I run?' she asked.

'Yes, but stay on the paths please,' said Mr Adams.

The child raced away from them, her arms widespread; the joy in her laughter was audible to both the grownups. They walked on in silence for a while, following the curving pathways.

'My son is always talking about you; he will get extremely cross with me if he finds out what I am about to tell you. He has disclosed that you have had a tough few years with your ex-husband's assaults on you. Your divorce, and then your ex-husband's death.' Jessica was fumbling for a handkerchief, Mr Adams reached into his top pocket and handed her an immaculately folded navy handkerchief that matched his brass buttoned blazer, saying as he did so, 'I am so sorry I have made you cry. I apologise. He asked me months back if when I met his mother, Izzy, did I know she was "the one". I said yes. He confided in me and said he knew you were his one. Please don't tell him we have had this conversation, I just wanted you to know.'

They were both quiet for a while, just walking the path when their reverie was shattered by Polly shouting, 'Mummy, Mummy, horses!' The child was standing on the bottom rung of a fence with two horses trotting towards her.

Hurrying to her daughter's side she arrived just as the two horses did. George Adams fished in his jacket pockets and fetched out two carrots, giving one to Polly and one to Jessica. He could see the child was unsure.

'Break it in half and put one piece on your palm with your hand flat like this,' he said, giving her a practical demonstration. At the same time he was making sure the horse could not reach it yet.

The child did as instructed, wiggling and laughing as the horses muzzle tickled her palm. She was braver with the second horse.

'That's very thoughtful of you, Mr Adams,' said Jessica.

'It's George, Jessica. I have a feeling you and Polly are going to become very precious to this family.'

'Can we have horses please, Mummy?'

'Perhaps at some time in the future when we are more settled.'

'How long would I have to save my pocket money to have a horse?'

'A long time I'm afraid, darling.'

Polly was quiet on the walk back. Unknown to everyone she had made a vow to herself that one day she was going to own a horse of her own.

Oliver met them halfway. 'Mother has sent me to tell you tea is served.'

* * * * *

Looking at the range of food on the table it was obvious tea had become a banquet. There was a wide range of small sandwiches with the crusts removed. Izzy explained that the bread came from a local baker who baked them overnight.

'George goes early. The bread is still warm when he gets it home.'

The fillings of the sandwiches were amongst Jessica's favourites. There was coronation chicken, egg and cress, crab and cucumber, then her most favourite, smoked salmon with crushed avocado. There were crackers for those who may want to enjoy the selection of cheeses. Amongst them she spotted a square of English oak-smoked mature cheddar. She was definitely going to leave room for that. The cake was the lightest Victoria sponge Jessica had ever tasted. There was a superb fruit base on the trifle that had just a hint of a liqueur, this covered with the best custard she had ever had, the whole topped with Chantilly cream.

'I normally have Earl Grey with this meal,' said Izzy. 'Would you like to join me?'

'Oh yes please I am extremely fond of it. My father always prefers it,' said Jessica.

The two women were to form a close bond in the future.

Going home in the taxi to the station that night with Polly asleep in the corner and the two of them holding hands, Oliver said, 'You have won my mother over. She said that if I ever let you go I would have her to answer to.'

Jessica squeezed his hand but said nothing. She knew she loved him and that he loved her, but Gerald had said he loved her at the beginning. That ended with him scarring her face and putting Polly at risk of being run over. She was not sure if she would ever completely trust a man again.

* * * * *

Opening his post one morning, Tim found a bill for the year's rental on the premises he kept his beautiful old Rover car in. It was superb with its long sloping front wings and roof in a deep black. The sides and the rest of it was bottle green. It was new in 1935. One novelty that had always amused him was that you could wind the windscreen open. It had hinges.

The amount was significantly more than last year. He realised it was always going to be expensive. It was housed in a heated storage unit with other beautiful cars, most of them worth a lot of money. When he had opened the food hall he remembered he considered putting it on display in there on a plinth, but he had never followed through on it. He rang Charlie, their builder. He did not recognise the voice on the other end of the phone immediately.

He said, 'Hallo, Tim here. Who's that?'

'It's Tommy, Mr Cooper. How can we help you?'

'Hi Tommy, sorry, I didn't recognise your voice. I want to put my old vintage Rover in the food hall on a plinth with park railings around it, you know, the black ones with small gold spikes on top. And by the way Tommy, it's Tim, ok?'

'Yes, Mr Cooper, Tim. I will pass the message on.'

'Thank you,' said Tim as he rang off.

A little later Charlie returned Tim's call. 'Hi Tim, I got your message. You do realise you are going to have to get permission to put it in the food store?'

'We are going to take the advice of an American general who said, "It is easier to apologise than to ask permission."'

'That bit is down to you, Tim. How high do you want the car off the floor?'

'About a foot,' was Tim's response.

Charlie said, 'I'll do a drawing, then come and see you.' While Charlie and his son were building the plinth Tim had the car prepared. All the fluids were drained off and the parts that required it were protected. The company that did the work issued a certificate that Tim displayed in the back window of the Rover. It described the work that had been done and guaranteed that the vehicle was safe for display. He noticed a lot of men spent a considerable period of time peering in the windows. Some wives he noticed used it as a distraction, parking their husbands there while they went off to do the shopping. One regular customer spoke to Tim one day while he was polishing the car.

'How much did it cost you when you bought it, Tim?'

'Well it was going to cost me nothing because it was a non-runner. Then my friend got it started and the wife of the owner came out and said he was to charge for it. She was ushered back inside, and the owner gave me the logbook and said give me a fiver to keep her quiet.'

Tim occasionally heard older men and some women explaining the intricacies of double declutching to their youngsters, which was necessary on that age of car to change gear. Few of them were really interested and even less of them understood.

'It has rod-operated drum brakes. It required you to virtually stand on the brake pedal to stop it,' said an elderly women to her young relative.

CHAPTER 47
THREE YEARS LATER

Tim's daughter Charley walked into the local hardware store one morning to speak to Mr Rodgers. He had previously been the store manager at her grandfather's multifloored department store for at least two decades. She was unsure how long it had been exactly; she just knew that he had worked for her grandfather for as long as she could recall. The customer he was serving took his change and left the shop.

Charley noticed Mr Rodgers had retained his military posture, straight backed and stomach in. He was wearing his inevitable black suit, white shirt, his greying hair close cut as usual. As a career soldier he had done well rising from raw recruit to regimental sergeant major. His manner indicated that he expected to be obeyed.

'Good morning, Mr Rodgers.'

'Rodgers will do, miss; I was deeply sorry to hear of your grandfather's demise. I still cannot believe he has gone. He was a real force of nature. I always thought he was indestructible. I held him in great regard. Please accept my deepest sympathy. What can I do for you?'

'Thank you, Rodgers, he was one of a kind. I have something I need to discuss with you. Can you spare me a few minutes today, please?'

A tall, good-looking, middle-aged woman with short dark hair, white blouse and pepper coloured skirt appeared from the back of the shop and asked, 'Is this important?'

Charley, responding immediately, said, 'Yes, it's extremely important.'

'Take some time off now, Rodgers, we won't be busy today.'

Holding the door open for Charley he followed her from the shop. Minutes later they were sitting in the warm sunshine in the local park watching the sparrows searching the ground around the old wooden seats for crumbs. Charley often walked in this park when she needed to think something through. The well-mown lawns with their perfect stripes, the pale green leaves on the numerous trees and the distant rose beds offered a tranquillity that was not always possible to find in the hubbub that was the streets of London.

Rogers glanced at Charley. She looked barely old enough to be at work let alone being in the position of being able to offer him a top job. He kept quiet, he was still in touch with one or two of the old staff members and he had been told that this attractive young lady was a force to be reckoned with. He noted that she was wearing the Victor Vieri uniform, straight black skirt and jacket and white blouse.

Charley opened the conversation by saying, 'Before I tell you what our offer is I insist you allow me to call you Mr Rodgers.'

'No, miss, I cannot have that; I have always been just Rodgers.'

'Supposing I offer you your old job back?'

'Which old job?'

'Shop manager at Victor Vieri's.'

'I hear it's being closed down, made into flats.'

'It's not now, we have just bought it.'

'Who's just bought it?' he asked, now extremely attentive.

'Me, Mummy and Daddy. I am the major shareholder, I have reinvested the money Grandfather left me back into the shop.'

Rodgers, struggling to get his head around what this extremely young woman was telling him, said, 'Sorry I need to clarify this, so your mother and father, Tim and Sophie, and you have bought Victor Vieri's, the store?' He was holding her face in close scrutiny as he spoke.

'Yes.'

'And you want me to manage it?'

'Yes.'

He rose and walked away a few yards, then stood with his back to her. She saw the proud man's use of his hanky and heard the serious blowing of his nose. Then his shoulders straightened, and his posture improved as he marched back to her.

He asked, 'This is for real isn't it, Charley?' His tone of voice indicated that he was worried it was some kind of ghastly joke.

'It certainly is for real, Mr Rodgers. When can you start?'

'I have to give two weeks' notice, which I will do when I get back to the shop. But I'm happy to work evenings in the meantime.'

'We can only pay you a basic wage in the interim until the shop goes into profit. Is that a problem?'

'No, I will manage.'

'Will the store be called Victor Vieri's or Sophie's?' he asked.

'We have discussed it at length,' she replied. 'We finally settled on keeping Victor Vieri's.'

'Good, that should draw a lot of our old customers back.'

Charley was pleased to hear him say our old customers. It was a good indicator that he was back in the saddle already.

'One thing I need to tell you is that I am going to lean very heavily on you for your knowledge and expertise. You and I will be doing extremely long hours while we pull the store back into shape. When we have a problem I will always turn to you. Are you happy with that?' she asked.

'Oh yes, lass,' he replied, obviously delighted by the whole idea.

'We will pay you overtime for any extra hours,' Charley noticed he was about to argue.

Continuing, she said, 'It's not up for discussion.' Now there was a strength in her voice that denied any argument. Charley stuck out her hand and said, 'Can we shake on it, Mr Rodgers?'

'We certainly can, Charley.'

The big smile and his enthusiastic shaking of her hand was another indicator of his delight at this turn of events.

There was a short discussion on what to prioritise, then Charley said, 'Onward and upwards.' They shook hands again and made their goodbyes.

Watching Charley walking away he thought to himself, Victor Vieri hasn't left; he has been reincarnated in that child. Just twenty-one and as tough as steel. Thank you lass, he said to himself. You don't know what you have done for me today. With a massive smile on his face he sprang from the bench and marched back to the hardware store, dreaming of the incredible change in his future.

* * * * *

Later that evening Charley and her mother were talking, discussing the make-up of the management team.

'There is you, me and Daddy,' said Charley.

'Your father and I will only be in an overseeing role. I do not anticipate we will have day-to-day involvement in the business, that is yours and Mr Rodgers' task.'

'I wondered if Sally would come back to work,' said Charley.

'In what role?' queried her mother.

'I am not sure,' said her daughter. 'I am aware that she must know more about the business than anyone else. Yes, we have Mr Rodgers on board to run the shop, thank goodness, but Sally knows everything about the business side. The people who we need to know. The suppliers, the manufacturers, the foreign contacts, how to deal with them, the history and so on.'

'You can but ask her, I have no idea what she will say,' replied her mother. 'Where is she now, do we know?'

'I am sorry, Charley, I have lost track of Sally's comings and goings of late. I suggest you ring her.'

Charley tried to call her a number of times that day without success. Later that evening Sally rang her back, apologising for missing Charley's calls. 'I have been busy.' Charley was aware that there was no explanation offered of what busy meant.

'Sally, have you been told we are buying Grandfather's store back?'

'You mean Victor's department store, and who is we? And no, I have not.'

'Sally, I have reinvested the money Grandpa left me, and Mummy and Daddy are going to sit on the board as partners and shareholders. We wondered if you fancied helping us run it?'

There was a long silence.

'Sally are you still there?' asked Charley, thinking that perhaps the connection had failed.

'Yes I am here, I have to say this has come as quite a shock. I will need some time to think about it. I will not want to do nine to five again. I am thoroughly enjoying my current lifestyle.'

'Sally, at university I heard an expression which fits these circumstances perfectly. We need your knowledge not your sweat.' Charley could hear Sally laughing.

'Your grandmother would have reminded you that ladies do not sweat, they glow. I am not sure, Charley. All those years Victor and I spent working from dawn to dusk. Now when I wake up in the morning I can lie there sipping my coffee and decide what I would like to do today. Charley, I am tempted to say no but let me think about it. I will …'

Charley interrupted, sensing that this conversation was moving towards a no from Sally, 'We have no intention of asking you to come back to work as such. You are the only one who knows all the suppliers, et cetera. The truth is, Sally, without you on board the business will never get off the floor. I think your main role will be as an adviser. Obviously we will work out some kind of remuneration for you, a seat on the board, or whatever. By the way, Mr Rodgers, is on board.'

'Oh wow, that helps. He is a massive asset. I will give you an answer in a few days.'

Charley hung up and sat nibbling at her thumbnail. Without Sally on board, contacting all the suppliers would be a much larger task. On reflection, she realised it would be much larger than that. Sally would know all the pricing and quantities to order. The longer she sat there the more problems occurred to her. One thing she did realise was that she had allowed her enthusiasm to run away with her. There should have been far more careful analysis of the problems they would face, like all the details about their suppliers, who they were, who did what and why.

* * * * *

One evening a week later Charley and Mr Rodgers were walking through the large empty store. At his suggestion they had taken the lift to the top floor and were intending to walk down. As they proceeded through the store Charley's new store manager was stopping regularly to examine the goods on offer, looking at the labels, where applicable rubbing the material through his thumb and fingers, nearly always shaking his head.

They reached the ground floor more than an hour later. Pulling two chairs out from behind a counter he said, 'Shall we sit?' They both did so. He went to say more but then stopped himself.

Finally Charley asked, 'So what do you think?'

He was silent for some time, then said, 'The recent owners completely misunderstood the ethos of this store, they tried to turn it into a version of

Woolworth's. There is nothing wrong with Woolworth's, but you can't buy a Cartier watch or top-quality cut glass there. Here you could. I suspect your grandfather's customers came, had a walk round and left never to return,'

'Now I am really worried. Have we made a massive mistake?' asked Charley.

'No, I don't think so, you will need a lot of advertising in national newspapers and so on. Those people who used to shop here are still out there and were extremely loyal in the past. I believe that if we bang a big drum loudly enough and long enough they will return.'

'Father wants to put a Sophie's Delicatessen in here.'

'I'm not surprised. It will fit in well.'

'What do we do with all the stock that does not fit in, the cheap stuff?' she asked.

'First of all we deal with the good stuff. Everything that is of a standard that Mr Vieri would stock goes up in the store cupboards out of the way, then we can sell off the other stuff to stall holders and so on before we open,' he explained.

'It is going to cost a fortune to restock, isn't it?'

'Yes,' responded Mr Rogers, 'but we do not have do it all at once. Initially you only open the ground and first floor. Then over the next year to eighteen months we all take minimum wages and build up the stock so we can open another floor. This gives us the opportunity to have low staffing levels at first and build up as we go along. I suspect old staff members will come tapping on the door.' This proved to be the case once the reopening adverts began to appear.

Mr Rodgers could tell Charley was becoming ever more worried. Looking to reassure the young woman he said, 'If I thought that this wouldn't work I would tell you, and I would not be sitting here now.' His last few words were extremely emphatic.

THE NEXT GENERATION

One thing Tim, Sophie and Charley were sure about was that Mr Rodgers receive a decent wage. As Charley pointed out, 'We cannot know, and we certainly cannot ask him, but I doubt he has our level of financial security.'

* * * * *

'Style and high fashion for women of all ages, the young to the young at heart returns to the high street. Victor Vieri's is back with many of the old team in control. Come and see for yourselves, ladies,' was what the street advertising said. Once again Bonny had come up with the words, and it was in the papers. It was a little lost because of the news that Prince Charles and Princess Diana were to get divorced.

CHAPTER 48

Martyn was eating his evening meal on the boat, looking forward to his evening at Aunt Mays, playing his clarinet with the band. He had changed into a pair of pale blue chinos and a crisp white shirt. His mother insisted if he was going to play in public he had to look smart.

On stage was the only place where he did not feel like a failure. A teacher in class today had been really cruel. Laughing as he placed last night's homework in front of Martyn, he said as he did so,

'It's interesting the way you continue to modify the spelling of the English language, Martyn. Mind you, it is no surprise when even your name is misspelt. You're not Welsh are you, boy?'

'No, sir.'

The teacher raised his eyebrows and moved on.

Walking into the café that evening his heart lifted as he saw Aunt May bustling towards him. He was enveloped in the usual wonderful cuddle. He had no idea what her perfume was, but it spoke to him of hot sand, blue seas and the aroma of exotic flowers. She was Afro-Caribbean and usually wore a smile. She had told Martyn she was his biggest fan. Recently he had begun to confide in her. She was always supportive and happy to listen.

Mr Lawrence was already there, seated at the piano and quietly playing a Satchmo number.

'He's early,' said Martyn.

Aunt May said, 'When he arrived a guy at the back had called out give us a tune then. He has been playing ever since.'

'Do you know why he is keen to play here?' Martyn asked. Aunt May shook her head.

'There is not a piano at home. His wife is adamant there is no room for one.'

As Martyn spoke, Mr Lawrence, dressed in a quiet suit that Martyn had seen him wearing at school, now only playing with one hand, waved at Martyn to join him. Heads turned to see who his teacher was waving at. Somebody called out, 'You're late, lad.'

'No he's not, I'm early,' responded Mr Lawrence.

Martyn walked to the back of the stage and began to assemble his clarinet on a shelf. Slowly the café filled up and became noisier. The boy used the loud chatter, laughter and the clink of cups and glasses to hide his warm up. Now ready he walked to the piano and stood within touching distance as he began to play. Adam the drummer walked from the bar and began a gentle accompaniment. Many people were still talking when the sound of a woman singing in full voice drowned out the noise of the crowd. As she walked towards the low stage the clapping broke out. It was Agatha giving it her all. Martyn had no doubt that it was her most of the crowd had come to see and listen to. Still singing she walked to the back of the stage to put her coat down near where Martyn had assembled his clarinet earlier. She took her place, stage front and centre. Martyn had spoken to Mr Lawrence during the week and said he had a new tune he would like to try out.

After a few songs Mr Lawrence stopped playing, then said, 'Martyn has a new tune he would like to play for you. I haven't heard it so who knows,' he said, laughing at Martyn, who smiled back. One of the things Martyn loved about the group was that when it came to the music there was no seniority. They all recognised each other's skills.

The boy began to play the tune that had made his mother cry when she discovered him playing on the boat. Once again the clarinet sang the boy's pain, his loneliness, his fears, his belief that once he put the instrument down he would become a total incompetent, no good at anything else.

Mr Lawrence joined in; he was playing a very deep, almost silent minimalist accompaniment. Adam the drummer, now one handed, was playing the skiffle drum with the brush, keeping the rhythm.

Agatha was silent for some time, listening hard, then she walked across the stage, taking her mike with her. Standing beside Martyn she put her spare hand in the small of his back and made her voice cry in harmony with the clarinet. After a couple of minutes he nodded at her to take over. Her input was slightly different. Although wordless it spoke of the problems she faced. Martyn sensed it was because of her ethnicity, her gender, it also spoke of pain that he could know nothing of. The tune finished in a great outpouring of emotion, all four of them playing their determination to overcome. One thing he was aware of was that he was becoming increasingly fond of this young girl and her amazing voice.

There was a long silence after the music stopped. Eventually Mr Lawrence said, 'Ladies and gentlemen we don't normally do this, but we are going to take a break. Don't go away, we will be back.'

The crowd appeared to be trapped in a reverie or to have just woken from a deep sleep. There was no clapping. A few hankies were in use. The four of them were in the room behind the stage. They were joined by Aunt May, who was still dabbing her eyes with a sodden hanky. 'We have recorded that; Uncle wants to know if you would be happy if he takes it to a couple of the people in the music business that he knows.' Aunt May was talking to Mr Lawrence.

'It's not me you should be talking to, it's Martyn's work.'

'I think we all have to agree,' said Martyn.

'There's nothing lost is there?' voiced Mr Lawrence. 'Agatha, what do

THE NEXT GENERATION

think?' She shrugged her shoulders. 'Adam?' he asked.

'I'm with Agatha, I don't mind, I think there's next to no chance of it doing anything anyway.'

Martyn lay awake a long time that night while he dreamt of stardom.

Two days later the group were playing Martyn's music in practice after school in the hall. The usual group of youngsters were present, maybe a few more than there had been before. Agatha began to sing some words in with her wordless expressions of pain that she had sung at the café. The young onlookers soon learnt the words.

The following morning walking into school he heard someone singing Agatha's words to his tune.

A boy who never had spoken to him before came up and clapped him on the shoulder saying, 'That song was great man, love the words.'

'The words are Agatha's, she added them to my …'

Interrupting, the boy said, 'She's great, isn't she? Tell her I loved it.'

After lunch he was sitting behind a girl who was talking to her friend. 'Did you hear Agatha's new song?'

'No, not yet,' was the response.

'It's great, you wait and see. I was crying like a baby.'

Martyn, making sure nothing showed on his face, was breaking up inside. This was his best composition yet and someone else was taking the applause and apparently claiming it as their own. It was so personal to him, dealing as it did with his own shy young man's fears and pain. He didn't know what to do about it. If he questioned her it would appear to be petty jealousy. Surely she should have asked him? Deep down it felt as though she had stolen it.

His mother noticed the change in her boy. When she asked him what was wrong, his reply was always the same, 'I'm fine, ta.'

Nanny arrived and congratulated him on his music, saying how much she had enjoyed the evening. She never mentioned anything about the man she was with.

The third morning he said it she replied, 'No you're not. We are going for a walk, and you are going to tell me what is upsetting you so.' Mother and son stepped ashore and turned left along the hard standing, passing a number of moored boats as they did so. Nothing was said until they reached the small wood at the far end of the boat yard. A narrow gravel path continued in under the trees. The family had named it Fox's Wood. Early every morning the town fox stared out at the boatyard and barked before he moved away.

A few paces in they reached a small seat and sat down. Eventually Sophie said, 'I can sit here all day, Martyn, until you come clean with me and tell me what is so wrong.'

Obviously emotional he told her about his tune. 'The one I played for you, we played it at the café the other night. There are no words, I didn't think it needed it. The next night at rehearsals Agatha started singing some words she had put together. The people who were there are spreading the word that it's Agatha's work and saying how marvellous it is. It's the best thing I have ever written, Mum. It's extremely personal. She has changed it and stolen it. I may never write anything like that again.'

'I am sure we can resolve it, Martyn. I will have a word with Mr Lawrence.'

Her son thought about it for a while and then said, 'No Mother, I need to sort this out myself. I would never live it down if Mummy went running to teacher. I will write my part down, name it and sign it.'

'You need to get it copyrighted,' added Sophie.

'I will,' he agreed. 'I need to own it. I will ask Agatha if she would like to write the words for it on the understanding that I may change it. We can discuss it.'

A week later, music sheet in hand, he sat beside Agatha while they waited for Mr Lawrence and Adam to arrive for practice.

'Agatha,' said Martyn, 'can we talk about my song?'

Turning towards him she smiled and nodded.

'I don't want to upset you but it's about the words.'

'Sorry,' she said, 'I don't understand.'

'People are saying it's your song, and that it's really good.'

Agatha had been complimented on it a number of times; she had not admitted that most of it was Martyn's work. That had been worrying her ever since.

Mr Lawrence and Adam had arrived and after the hallos the schoolteacher, looking at Martyn's and Agatha's faces, asked, 'Is there a problem?'

The young couple looked at each other, Agatha nodded at Martyn and said, 'You go first.'

The boy said, 'This is going to sound really petty but … this is about my song. It may be the best thing I will ever write but people are congratulating Agatha for writing it because she put some words to it.'

Agatha reached out and held Martyn's hand. 'Can I apologise? I should have told people it was your work, Martyn, I'm sorry.'

'I like some of your words, but I would want to change others,' he replied.

There was a short silence, then Mr Lawrence said, 'Martyn, would you be prepared to work with Agatha on the words? You have just said some of them are a good fit.'

The boy nodded.

'How about this? Music by Martyn Cooper, words by Martyn and Agatha, so you work on the rest of the words together. By the way, lad, you must get it copyrighted, otherwise it will definitely be stolen.' After the practice was over the young people made plans to meet at Aunt Mays and finalise the words.

As they were leaving the building Mr Lawrence said, 'If you like I am happy to help with the copyrighting.'

They both agreed.

The next practice Mr Lawrence told the usual gathering of students that the music was Martyn's work and that he and Agatha are working on the words. He had started to gain some self-confidence since he had confided in Aunt May one evening about how he always felt incompetent. She had, unusually for her, became cross with him.

'Martyn, who else in this room could play your clarinet as you have just done and have the audience in the palm of their hand, for two and a half hours? No one is the answer. You must believe in yourself; you have a unique talent. Just enjoy it.' She had kissed his cheek and walked away.

CHAPTER 49

Looking for a pair of gloves in the hall cupboard he found Sophie's riding boots. Tim remembered one of the very few times he had ridden a horse. Charley as a child had wanted to ride. Sophie had been concerned about her going alone so she was going to take her. It was all booked when on the arranged morning Sophie had a problem come up at her other job as finance director at Mr Well's company that she had to fix. She had persuaded him to take Charley. Looking at his child's tears he had agreed. He had never ridden in his life and had no desire to learn. Turning up at the stables he'd discovered the session was being run by an officious eighteen-year-old who for no apparent reason had seemed to take an instant dislike to him. He wondered if it was because he had arrived in the Bentley. There were other parents there he remembered but they were all mummies. He was the only daddy.

The young woman looked at him and had said, 'The only horse left is Satan. Is that ok?'

'Yes that's fine,' he'd said. Tim felt sure that she had altered the name in the hope of frightening him off. When he saw the giant black beast that she led from the stable he almost changed his mind.

When everyone was mounted, Miss Bossy Boots, as he had christened her, manoeuvred her horse so that she was looking at him on the end of the line.

'These are the rules that must be observed,' she'd said, 'you must not overtake the horse in front, you may not let the horse stop and eat the vegetation, you may not let the horse run, you will not let the horse turn round. Is that clear?' She had conducted the entire monologue staring at him. He was tempted, he remembered, to stick his tongue out at her, but he hadn't.

Satan, he recalled, had no intention of going anywhere. The girl had moved her horse closer to him and had begun shouting at him, 'Kick it, kick it.' He'd wiped a spot of her spittle from his cheek. When this had achieved nothing she'd started thrashing the horse's rump with her whip.

Eventually Satan had started out of the gate, turning right up a gravel path flanked with grass and weeds. Fifty yards on the horse in front had stopped. Tim's horse went to overtake. Remembering the rules he said, 'Whoa.' Satan obeyed immediately and moved in beside the other horse and began to eat the pathside undergrowth. Tim began kicking Satan's flank, gently at first, then harder as it had no effect.

Moments later Miss Bossy Boots arrived. 'Kick it, kick it,' she'd shouted again. She had left off the 'you stupid man' that hung in the air unsaid. His kicking had no effect. Seconds later she was slashing at the horse's rear end with her whip. Satan had finally capitulated and sauntered on up the hill, following the horse in front. By then Tim remembered he was finding the whole business extremely unpleasant and cruel, and his daughter was out of sight and most of the time unchaperoned. The line of horses reached the top of the hill and as the horse in front disappeared over the rim Satan spun on his heals and started running back down the hill towards the stables. Tim recalled wrapping his hands around the reins and at the same time grabbing handfuls of mane, meanwhile getting a strong grip with his legs. As the horse approached the low stone wall that surrounded the yard Tim felt the horse alter its gait. He had assumed the animal was going to stop. It had become clear at the last minute that Satan was going to jump the wall, letting go of the reins with one hand he'd established a solid grip on the part of the saddle that was between his knees as the brute of a horse took off. Horse and man flew through the air and then landed on the other side, sliding to a halt. He recalled it took all his strength to hang on. Satan had then turned left and had begun to make his way to the stable block. Checking the height of the lintel it was clear there was not enough space to allow him to slide under it if he was still on the horse. He remembered how frightened he was as he'd begun kicking his feet frantically to loosen the stirrups. The horse ducked its head as it walked in. Tim's left foot had become free but not his right. He could taste the fear he had experienced that day as he had realised there was no way he would fit under it. It had been obvious that unless he could get off he would be badly hurt. His mind took him back to that moment so strongly that now he was reliving it. The low wooden lintel was only inches away, grasping it with both hands he slid his bottom over the saddle, frantically kicking his right leg. As his body reached the horizontal the horse had stopped. One more kick and the stirrup had flown off. He let his body swing down over the horse's rump. Letting go with his hands he dropped the short distance to the ground. He had been more than a little wobbly. His new driver Neville parked a short distance away in a layby, had walked up to Tim and asked, 'Are you alright, Tim? That looked bloody dangerous.' It was clear it had frightened him as well. An hour later the cavalcade had returned. Charley was crying.

The witch in charge had scowled at him as she passed him, went to the gate, leant down and flipped the catch over to allow the riders to enter. Dismounting, she strode over to him and had barked, 'HOW DID YOU GET THE HORSE IN ITS STALL?'

'The horse jumped the wall, I hung on,' he'd explained.

The other riders, now dismounted, gathered round them.

A well-spoken woman holding a child's hand had asked him, 'Are you alright? That could have been my Hannah. My God, she might have died.'

Someone else had asked, 'Did you stay on?'

'Yes,' he'd said, 'but then when he went in the stall I couldn't stop him or get my feet out of the stirrups. It would have been a very tight fit had I still been on his back. I managed to release my feet at the last minute.' Recalling it now Tim felt shivers run down his spine that made him shrug his shoulders.

The crowd were now moving away, talking it over. The common theme was that they would not be back.

The well-spoken lady handed Tim a card. Scanning it he saw she was a solicitor called Helen Oakes. 'Can I contact you?' she had asked. 'This place needs shutting down before someone gets hurt, or worse,' she'd observed.

'Yes,' he'd replied, 'you can contact me at Sophie's.' He'd reeled off the number. 'I'm Tim Cooper. By the way, my driver here saw it all.' They'd shaken hands and left.

The girl in charge had been leaning against the wall, legs and arms crossed, scowling at the departing customers. She was obviously aware of the ill feeling displayed by the group.

'Good riddance,' she had shouted.

He remembered the RSPCA had become involved and had closed the stables down.

CHAPTER 50

Late one afternoon Tim and Jessica were dealing with her workload, which had become unsustainable. There was a tap on Tim's office door. 'Come in,' he called. He waited expectantly. Nothing happened. Not wanting to shout any louder he rose, walked over and opened the door. To his complete surprise Mr and Mrs Graham stood there, the elderly couple who had worked for his Great Aunt Victoria Longstaff as cook, cleaner, driver, gardener for somewhere in excess of forty years prior to Tim inheriting it.

Tim got them seated then asked, 'What can I do for you?'

Mrs Graham started to say, 'Our daughter, our daughter has …' Now the tears were falling so fast she could no longer speak. Mr Graham reached across and took her hand.

Mr Graham, obviously very moved himself, said, 'As Mrs Graham has just tried to explain, our daughter has cancer. Our son-in-law is a lovely guy, but he is away a lot. He's a long-distance lorry driver. With the four girls, she has two sets of twins. He has to work. There is a spare bedroom, we will be ok.'

There was another tap on the door. Tim stepped across and opened it, Bonny stood there. Seeing the tears and feeling the tension, she asked, 'Whatever's wrong?' Jessica explained to her what was happening, having risen and knelt beside the stricken woman, holding her hand.

Bonny said, 'But I thought you would always be here. You have always been so kind looking after us when we needed help. For instance, when Jessica's husband beat her up and damaged her eye, you took over looking after her and Polly.'

'Grace,' corrected Mrs Graham curtly, 'you know I don't agree with nicknames.' There was some discussion about when they would move, then the elderly couple stood up to leave.

On their way out Tim shook both their hands, Mrs Graham's first. Mr Graham didn't release Tim's hand immediately as he had a final look around the office.

Then he said, 'You've come a long way, lad. I can still see that young boy who had nothing, who had even been thrown out of his home. I remember Mrs Longstaff sorting it all out and her taking you in until you found some digs. You should be extremely proud of yourself, lad, well done.' As he showed them out Tim thanked the elderly couple for all they had done for him and those around him down the years.

After the elderly couple had left, Tim organised a round table discussion regarding Jessica's workload. With their agreement a substantial amount of work was taken on by Lynda and Bonny. Some technical stuff was moved onto Oliver's desk. It was clear that Jessica was extremely relieved and thanked Tim profusely.

* * * * *

It was going to take a long time for Tim to get used to having a stranger driving his big, black, beautiful old Bentley. He had more than once called Neville 'Mr Graham'. He had explained politely that conversation was usually not required.

The Grahams' house stood empty for a while. Tim had asked Charlie the builder to quote him for decorating throughout. The price was fine,

THE NEXT GENERATION

but the builder and his son Tommy were busy elsewhere. When the house was ready an American couple with two children, both girls, rented it for two years. It was explained to Tim that then they would go home back to America. Tim was hoping for a longer term let but at least it solved the problem for now.

CHAPTER 51

Charley and Mr Rodgers were sipping a hot cup of tea late one evening, sitting in the Victor Vieri store prior to going home. They were sharing some memories. They had worked hard all day preparing the ground floor ready for the future opening.

'We have done well today, Charley,' observed Mr Rodgers. 'I think we're about ready to reopen. We will need some advertising.'

'We will get Bonny to do it, it is her forte. She is excellent at it.'

'That's good. I know it is not any of my business, but you need to find a nice young man to take you out instead of working from sun up to sun down.'

'I have not found a nice young man yet to take me anywhere. The two I have gone out with were mad keen on football. They did not seem to have any other topic of conversation. I found it all extremely boring. If I tried to talk about what we do here they lost interest extremely quickly. Anyway, I love what we are doing with the store. Enough about me, have you been married? You never talk about it if you have.'

Mr Rodgers was silent for some while, then he said, 'I have not talked about this in years,' then he was silent again.

'Go on,' prompted Charley.

Taking a deep breath in, he said, 'I was engaged once, to a girl called

THE NEXT GENERATION

Veronica.' There was yet another silence. Charley could tell in his mind he was elsewhere.

Eventually he said, 'We were very young. She was beautiful. Her dream was to be a film star. She had been offered small parts in plays and so on. On my eighteenth birthday I received what the Americans call a Dear John letter telling me she was moving to America. She apologised for not loving me enough. She had decided to follow her dream. She hoped I would find someone else and be happy. My heart was broken. I walked through the park to our seat. It was under an enormous elderly oak tree, the foliage so dense in the summer little or no rain found its way through the leaves. We had sat there every week holding hands and sharing our dreams and planning our wedding, where we would live, how many children we would have. She always blushed a little at that. I found that very appealing.'

There was another silence. Charley reached out and held his hand. He gave her a painful smile. 'Did you ever hear from her?'

He shook his head.

'What did you do?'

'After a long time sitting where we are now I got up, went down the town and joined the army.'

'Oh my goodness. What did your family say?'

'My mother just cried and left the room. My father, who had done national service, walked across the room, shook my hand and hugged me, saying, "Well done, son, I am very proud of you." A few weeks later I was in the army, the rawest recruit you could ever meet. After I got over the initial shock I loved it. I worked hard, took advantage of every opportunity for promotion and ended up the regimental sergeant major. When I eventually came out I met your grandfather, who offered me a rather lowly job, but once again I worked hard and as you know ended up as store manager.'

'Now here you are once again store manager. In fact you are much more than that, you are also my adviser. I will include you in every decision.'

After a pause Charley said, 'Can I ask you one more question?'

'Is it why did I not find someone else?'

'Yes,' she replied.

'Because I think of her nearly every day. I didn't think it fair to marry someone else when I still love her.' He stood up and before he walked away he said, 'I have never told anyone that. Please keep it to yourself.'

Charley watched him march away, his back ramrod straight, his head held high, his arms swinging in perfect synchrony. To her surprise a small tear escaped from the corner of her eye. Perhaps, she thought, I am not the tough cookie everyone thinks I am.

* * * * *

Some weeks later at the next board meeting Mr Rodgers was offered a non-executive director's position and a place on the board. Charley could tell how moved he was when later he squeezed her hand and fighting back his emotions said quietly, 'My father would have been proud. A raw recruit rising to be a director on the board of a company like Victor Vieri's. Thank you, Charley. I know it was you who proposed me.'

'You are very welcome. It feels right to me, all your years of work helping to make Victor Vieri's the success it was and will be again.'

CHAPTER 52

Three riders, silhouetted against the remaining third of the Italian setting sun, came into view over the crest of the hill in front of him. Even at his range he could recognise each one. The one on the left as he looked at them was his beautiful wife, Sophie. She always looked so at home in the saddle, there was no tension in her posture at all. She and her horse were always in perfect harmony, the slightest touch of a knee, the merest movement of the reins was enough for the horse to obey. Tim was on occasion frightened for his wife. A gentle kick on the chestnut mare's flank and Conker would take off. Sophie then lifted into the crouch adopted by the racing jockeys. Woman and horse were ecstatic as they flew over the ground. In the past he had heard his wife's excited laughter ringing out in her wake. He was not sure, but he thought this encouraged the horse to run faster still. The only problem she experienced occasionally was getting Conker to stop. The horse was obviously intoxicated by the speed, the rush of air over its body and its mistress's pure joy in the headlong flight over the ground, horse and owner in perfect synchrony.

The middle rider, his daughter Charley, was now a major force within the company. He had lost track of how many things within the organisation were now under her direct control. The best way of describing her riding style was to say, like the rest of her life, she was very much in charge.

Charley's close friend was on her right. She was riding with one leg hooked around the pommel, the reigns loose in her hands. As she had explained after the first ride out, when questioned she had replied, 'The horse knows where it's going. Why should I interfere?'

* * * * *

When they had moved into the house in Puglia Sophie had spoken to the staff, saying, 'Tim and I are very keen that everyone who works here will see themselves as part of our family and therefore entitled to eat here for free. This is a benefit that comes with the job. This applies to all the staff.'

Late one evening Sophie and two of the live-in house staff were sitting in the garden watching the last of the light from the setting sun, now below the horizon reflected on the bottom of the distant clouds.

The cook asked, 'Why does Tim never talk about his mother or family?'

'There is a reason for this. Tim's mother died when he was thirteen years old. He was very poor when he was growing up and often hungry. His father became very ill, so Tim became the wage earner, out in the open air in rain or shine twelve hours a day, sometimes longer. In the beginning there was little money coming in. Then he was made homeless. On his way home at night he would read the menus outside the expensive restaurants, then with his nose pressed to the glass he would watch the wealthy sit and eat. Often he has said the plate would be pushed away half eaten. Most of the well to do were unaware that the waitresses and other restaurant staff serving them probably could not have afforded the meals on the table. He was often chased away by the maître d'. Now on a slightly different topic I would like to say if you have a problem of any kind please feel free to bring it to us. We may be able to help. One thing I can guarantee is that we will not discuss it with anyone else.'

Most of the women had relaxed and joined them for lunch, and some for an evening meal. Sophie had asked the men if they would like to join them. They had declined, explaining that their wives or mothers furnished them with a packed lunch. They would eat their main meal at home with their families in the evening.

Initially the women intended to sit at a small table they had set up in a corner. He saw immediately there was not enough room for all of them. Tim, on entering the spacious dining room and seeing the separate table, began shaking his head.

'No, no, no, we have to sit together,' he said. Walking into a room that was off the kitchen he saw the long wooden folding table that he had seen previously was still there propped against the wall. He and Sophie, with help from the girls, moved it into the dining room and placed it against the end of the original. Now there was one long table stretching down the length of the room. He made it clear that this was how it was to remain. However, the women insisted that the family sit at the original table and the staff sat at the extension.

Seeing her husband's frustration Sophie walked across the room and said quietly, 'Tim, let them make some decisions, I believe they will be happier with their own space.'

During the meal the laughter and the banter flowed up and down the long room, from one end to the other.

CHAPTER 53

It was late when Charley's phone rang. Pushing aside the paperwork she was ploughing through she picked up the phone and said, 'Hallo.'

'Hallo, Charley, how are you?' Sally asked. The pleasantries were quickly dealt with.

'Charley, I have given your request a lot of thought. Really you only need me for the names and addresses et cetera, don't you?'

'Yes,' was the response.

'Good, I still have all my notes in the Thames-ide apartment in London. I keep meaning to throw them away, but it is the one real link I have with Victor.'

'You must miss him so much.'

Charley heard Sally take a long breath in, then after a pause she said, 'Yes I do, but life moves on … Now about your request. How about you pay me an hourly rate to compile it into alphabetical order?'

'Can you put it into a card system so that I can add to it?'

'Yes I can, Charley, but you need to know I am not going to do this for nothing.' She suggested a substantial amount per hour.

Ouch! thought Charley, this could mount up and become expensive.

Sally allowed Charley's silence to continue while the young woman thought about it. Then she said, 'Charley, this may sound expensive but in the long run it will save the company a fortune. I will go so far as to say that I believe the future of the company may depend on it. At the moment all you have is a building with a small amount of saleable stock. When I have finished, every individual company and supplier will be at your fingertips. Their names, their addresses, who to contact. Think how your father Tim would have struggled opening the shops without his father's intimate knowledge of everything. How will you get information otherwise? It will take you years, and I could charge you a great deal more. The alternative is for me to bag it up and give you the lot as is. Much of it will not make sense. It is my system, it will take you a long time to unravel it all, and I don't want to do that anyway. When I was looking at the names and addresses et cetera all kinds of memories returned. Trips abroad to visit suppliers, Victor and I having time together without having to hide how we felt about each other. The restaurants we have visited, the incredible food, the special people who Victor introduced me to. Back home in Italy he was an important person, held in extremely high regard by those who knew him. He was a different man once we were married. It was a strange feeling for a while though. In the beginning he felt guilty because Mrs Vieri's death freed him from the prison of his first marriage. His words not mine. Both of them, Victor and Olivia, admitted they did not like each other in the end. They were thrown together by the two families. It was made clear to them that divorce was not an option.

'I fell in love with him as soon as I saw him, and I am sure he with me. It was the briefest interview I have ever known. He asked my name and address and my typing and shorthand speed and then asked me when could I start. We became lovers a month later. Sorry, have I been too specific? I did not mean to embarrass you. I have never loved anyone like I loved your grandfather, and I never will again.'

* * * * *

A month later Sally and Charley were sitting in the office that had been Victor's. The small suitcase sitting on the desk between the two women contained the completed index.

Opening the case and examining the first few entries Charley was very impressed with the detail and how well organised it was.

Sally said, 'I ought to charge you extra for the times it made me cry, as I said last time we met there are so many memories in there. Victor appeared as a hard man but now and then he would leave me a note tucked in there, thanking me for being so diligent. He loved that word, because it sounded very English. He would sign off by saying how much he loved me. I have not included any little notes. I have stored them carefully in a beautiful, carved, antique wooden box.'

'I never knew how he …' Charley choked off the question she was about to ask as she realised how insensitive and cruel it was.

'You were going to ask how he died. I haven't been able to discuss it until now.' She took a long breath in then said, 'You know we were in the farmhouse in Italy?'

Charley nodded.

'It was late Sunday morning. The staff were at mass, I was in the kitchen preparing a salad for lunch when I heard a strange noise, a clang and then breaking glass. I rushed out onto the patio …'

Sally's voice was breaking and there were a number of breaths taken before she could speak again.

'He was lying on the patio tangled in the garden furniture. He was bleeding from a cut on his head. Kneeling down, I asked, "Are you ok?" His reply was garbled. I asked him again. He just shook his head. Using my hanky I dabbed at the cuts on his fingers. He grasped my hand and would not let go. I said, "Victor, please let me go, I can help you up." Again there was a slight shake of his head and then he said something else. I asked him to say it again. I leant closer, he whispered, "I will always love you."

Moments later his face screwed up in agony, his body curled up into a ball, his free hand clutching his chest'.

Sally's tears were falling freely as she relived the moment that the person she loved with all her heart and soul died in her arms.

'I could not believe it. I kept saying, "Wake up, Victor, wake up, please wake up." I had no idea how long I lay there talking to him, stroking his face and kissing him. I thanked him for all the years we had enjoyed together. I reminisced over the funny bits in our relationship. There was one occasion when he got shut in the shower and I called the locksmith in the next village. Victor was very embarrassed because he had gone in there naked. I found myself laughing and crying at the same time.

'Eventually the girls came back from church to begin to prepare the evening meal. They were inconsolable. They cried nonstop. In the end I had to pull myself together and take over. The police and the doctor were kind. They both thought Victor had suffered a heart attack. The postmortem confirmed it. You will remember the funeral; it was thoroughly Italian. I console myself by recognising that he and I shared a love for each other many people never get to experience.'

CHAPTER 54

This morning Charley and Mr Rodgers had started to sort the stock on the first floor of the Vieri store. They were upstairs in one of the stock rooms hanging up a lift full of ladies' quality coats, pulling dust covers over to protect them. They had started two hours ago at 7 am. As they were leaving the stock room they heard someone calling from downstairs.

Mr Rodgers said, 'I know the voice, that's Carol.' He leant over the bannisters and called down, 'Sorry, ladies, we are not open.'

'Oh ha, ha,' responded Carol.

'Hang on, we are coming down,' he replied.

Reaching the ground floor he said, 'Good morning, ladies, what can we do for you?'

'We've come to see if you're hiring yet. We heard on the grapevine that Vieri's is going to reopen. Jo passed by earlier and saw the someone was in here. She rang us, so we came to see if there are any jobs. We've bought our overalls,' she said, patting her shopping bag. She turned to Charley and said, 'Hallo, are you here for a visit?'

Mr Rodgers said, 'No she is the part owner, along with her mother and father. I am the store manager and Charley is my boss.'

Charley jumped in and said, shaking her head as she spoke, 'That's not how it's going to be. It will be Mr Rodgers running the store and I will work beside him, learning as I go, and as an aside it is Mr Rodgers from now on. Not just Rodgers.' The man in question rolled his eyes but said nothing. Charley continued, 'What we want to do is to recreate Victor Vieri the quality store, with one change. When the store was sold it was really only catering for the wealthy older woman in terms of the fashion side of things. There are beautiful modern clothes out there for the younger woman. I want us to end up selling high fashion for all ages.'

'Will that not be right expensive?' asked Carol.

'Yes, and one more thing, Mr Rodgers is now a company director as well as the store manager.'

He was clearly rather embarrassed when the women congratulated him. Then he asked, 'Have you really brought your overalls?'

All three women nodded and began pulling the articles in question from their shopping bags. 'Will we get our jobs back?' asked Carol, pausing before she received the affirmation.

'Yes,' replied Charley.

Carol, checking that the other two women were nodding in agreement, asked, 'What do you want us to do?'

Everyone looked at the newly promoted company director, who said, 'Right, ladies, I know you can recognise Vieri quality at a glance, so here is the plan. I want all the quality stock taken from elsewhere in the building to the first floor and carefully stored away for now. The other stuff to go up on the second floor, Charley will show you where. As you can see we have done a lot of the work here on the ground floor. Our intention is to get the first floor open at the same time if we can. Charley, do you have anything?'

'Ladies, can you keep a check on the hours you do, please, and let me have the list. We will pay you as soon as possible. One thing I want to share with you is the measure of my commitment to this project. If this fails most of my inheritance will go down with it, I will be poor. But that is not going to happen. We will succeed. Now let me show what needs doing. If you will follow me, please.'

* * * * *

Two months later they opened the ground floor to the general public. Charley had worked out there was not enough stock to open the first floor. Many of the original staff had come looking for their jobs back. Everyone had poured their hearts and souls into the preparations for the reopening. Charley realised it was not just a job for the majority of the older staff. It was their personal pride in the business. They and their colleagues had built it with the sweat of their brow for years, ensuring it was the best of the best.

The first day had been quieter than they had hoped. A good number of their old customers had come to look; regrettably not many of them bought in any major way. A number of obviously well-off younger women had visited and had spoken to Charley, emphasising their disappointment that there were no dresses or coats or anything in fact for their age group, in spite of it being advertised.

Charley was apologising profusely and working hard to reassure these women that her next priority was to open the first floor, where clothes for their age group would be stocked. She promised to discount the younger women's range of clothes for one day. The day itself would be advertised in the local papers. That pacified some of them.

CHAPTER 55

Just before closing a young women walked in and asked a member of staff who was in charge. She was directed to Mr Rodgers.

'Mr Rodgers?' she enquired to the man who she had been directed to.

As he turned and said, 'Yes,' he saw what he thought was a teenager. It turned out she was in her late twenties but looked considerably younger.

Holding out a strong-looking hand, she said, 'My name is Molly Page, I am a milliner. I wonder If I could show you some of my ideas. I never saw any young women's hats before in here when …'

Mr Rodgers had put his hand out to stop her. Immediately her face had fallen to display deep disappointment.

'Don't panic yet,' he said, 'you are talking to the wrong person. Our boss Charley Cooper does most of the buying,' as he spoke he was leading her to a counter with a phone on it.

Before they got there he asked, 'Could I take look?'

'Of course,' she replied.

He flicked through the first few pages, then, holding the phone to his ear, said, 'Hallo, Charley, I have got a young milliner down here who would like to show you her portfolio for the younger woman. I have looked through it. I think you would be interested. Our customers certainly are. Come down and have a look if you're free.'

Two women were now looking over Molly's shoulder, obviously extremely interested, displaying that by firing questions at her. Young Molly was explaining how she did a part of the construction. They were now joined by a third.

'Will you be displaying them here?' asked one of the original women.

'I hope to,' was the reply.

The woman handed Molly a card, saying, 'When you are ready give me a ring. I think your designs are beautiful.'

Charley had just arrived and overheard what had been said. Shaking the young woman's hand, she said, 'Hallo I am Charley. You have something to show me? Let's go behind the counter.' She realised that possibly the women who were interested would have a better view. She was right. A growing group of women were gathering on the other side of the counter asking questions. Charley realised there could not be a better recommendation than this group of wealthy fashion-conscious women's opinion. Charley loved the way the young milliner looked in her full-length, bright yellow dress printed with branches of trees complete with green leaves and red apples. Her long, dark auburn hair was tied in a ponytail down her back.

Later up in the office Molly explained that one drawback she faced was that she could not afford to rent a workshop.

'I will not need much. A large cutting table, power, light and heat, and then somewhere adjacent to display my hats.'

'I anticipate your hats will be adorning some of the manikins, so they will be displayed throughout the younger women's department. They will be marketed under your trade name, that is?'

'I don't have one yet.'

'That is now fairly urgent. We need it for the young woman's advert. Regarding your workshop, I think we can sort that out here. I will have to ask my father and see what he recommends.'

'He is who I thought I would be dealing with,' she said.

'No, Daddy and Mummy are shareholders, most of the time they leave it to me. There are others that you will meet over time. Sometimes I feel I have been involved with the company ever since I was born. It's not that long, but almost. Mr Rodgers is a company director and store manager, we work in tandem. He will tell you he has worked here ever since the dinosaurs disappeared.' The two women both laughed.

'The way we usually work is to charge rent for the stall, or in your case the workshop. In the old days that was all the costs but in today's financial climate we have had to make some changes. Now we want a five percent return on everything you sell. I am sorry about that. If not we will go under.'

Molly was scribbling in the back of her folder.

'Ok,' said Charley. 'I suggest you go away and think about it and let me know one way or the other.'

'No, no,' was the reply. 'Can I confide in you? Perhaps I shouldn't tell you this but you're not the first company I have approached. They were all disinterested. So why are you different?'

'Because accidently we have carried out a customer survey and they loved your hats. I think it would make sense for both of us to take notice of that. Now I will draft something out, so we have an understanding, and it will indicate that it is all negotiable. Is that acceptable?'

Molly nodded. Minutes later, now in Charley's office, the young woman was handed a copy of the agreement.

'If you will read it and add your address and phone number and sign it we are good to go.' The young redhead, after a short pause while she read the document, then did as asked. 'Molly, this is your copy. Oh, can you also supply a colour A4 copy of your favourite hat, and a picture of you, just face and shoulders please. I will put it with the advertising for the younger women. Your millinery may be just what we need to separate us from the herd. Do not price your hats too cheaply, they need to appear expensive. If they are too cheap our clientele will turn away. Your hats will be included in the top of the range clothing, everything of which will be extremely expensive. So include a good mark up for yourself, the profit margin always gets gnawed away at.'

Molly was panicking now; it was obvious the name for the advertising was needed today. She said, 'How about "Molly Page, a milliner for the young and young at heart, in store now".'

Charley said, 'That's ok for now, you can always change it later if you want.'

Molly said her goodbyes. As she passed Mr Rodgers he asked, 'All ok?'

'Very much so, thank you, Mr Rodgers.' Her huge smile said it all. She was walking on air, at the exit she turned around and looked back into the store. Then she remembered one of her father's sayings, at the start of any knew venture he would say, "So it begins." After a short pause she spun on her heel, making her full-length dress flare and her ponytail spin out. Looking down she realised the effect of her spin was rather diminished by exposing a pair of grubby trainers.

Striding out towards the street she vowed to do whatever it took to make her dream come true.

Charley asked Bonny about the street advertising and the newspapers etc. The young woman agreed to have it ready in the near future.

When Charley questioned her father about a workshop for the young milliner he thought for a moment, then said, 'I've got it, she can use what was Mr Vieri's office as a work room. It's not being used at the moment, the light's good. If necessary her customers can be directed upstairs for fittings, or whatever happens if you're a milliner. The lift stops right opposite what will be her workshop. Can you give her a ring and ask her to come and have a look?'

'There will need to be some advertising spread around the store indicating where she can be found,' said Charley.

'Good idea, let it be so, Number One,' said Tim.

THE NEXT GENERATION

Charley watched him walk away. I hope he is not going to be Captain Kirk all day long, she thought. The TV series Star Trek was one of her father's special favourites.

A month later, Tim, blowing hard having walked up three flights of stairs, tapped on the young milliner's door. Molly answered it and said, 'Good morning, Mr Cooper.' Seeing his frown she said, 'Sorry, I mean Tim, please come in.'

Stepping into the workshop he looked around and was blown away. The sunshine from all the windows illuminating the wonderful colours of the materials spread around the workshop forced an involuntary 'Wow!' from him. He was also fascinated by the range of fabrics. There were rolls of soft filmy stuff in bright colours, a roll of deep burgundy that looked like velvet, a rack of different ribbons. A pretty apple-green hat on a stand was obviously being worked on. A row of pins and a needle with matching green thread stuck in it was the clue. Tim realised this would make a wonderful photo for the company's advertising. While he was talking to Bonny that afternoon about the advertising she had agreed with to him to launch Molly the milliner along with the discount day. He had realised that the discount had to apply throughout the store for that one day. He knew young Molly, seen in her workshop with all the wonderful colours, as the main focus of the advert underlined by the discount offer would pull people in. On his way downstairs he mentally compared the look of the room when it had been his father-in-law's very grand office and now that it was this display of beautiful colours. It reminded him of a beautiful display of flowers he had seen at the Chelsea Flower Show years ago with his mum and dad.

CHAPTER 56

Martyn was returning from his part-time job at Aunt May's café late one evening in filthy
weather. When he reached the *Sea Maiden*, the family's houseboat, it was dancing around in the gale force winds. There were two planks in place, one from the bank to a disused metal cold water tank filled with rocks, the other from the tank to the boat. The *Sea Maiden*'s erratic motion caused the second plank to move unpredictably. Screwing up his courage he seized the rope that acted as a handrail from ship to shore. Sliding his feet one at a time up the first plank he made it to the water tank. This was stable with all the rocks in it. Half way, he thought. Looking at the action of the next plank that was moving around because of the waves he realised he had done the easy bit. Putting one foot on the second plank and holding the rope with both hands he struggled to stay upright. Letting go of the rope with one hand he knelt down and grasped the edge of the plank. Now sliding both his hands alternately along the plank and the rope he started to make progress towards the bow of the boat. He was doing well, nearly there, when the boat made a particularly malevolent lurch and threw him off the plank. A sheer sense of survival made him reach up and grasp the rope with his second hand as he fell in. Much to his surprise he could stand up. However, without the rope's support he might have been swept away in the strong

tidal current that was running. Now talking to himself as he moved further out he could feel the waves moving further up his chest as the water got deeper nearer the boat.

Now he was talking out loud, 'You can do this.' Moving closer, a wave broke against his chest, the spray hitting him in the face. There was still a yard to go, he would be swimming then, the rope too high to hold on to.

Now in his panic he shouted, 'Dad, help me I'm drowning.'

Tim did not hear him over the storm's noise, his mother did. Jumping from the bed and dragging the bedclothes from Tim, she shouted at him, 'Tim, wake up. Martyn is in the water.' Coming awake in a flash Tim moved his wife aside, raced the length of the boat and burst onto the foredeck. He could see nothing at first, then he saw his son's head appear from a wave that had just broken over him. The force of the wave had torn one of Martyn's hands free of the rope and had knocked his feet from under him. Tim landed next to his son and grabbed his clothing, pulling him close. Martyn did not need telling to hang onto his dad. Both hands had a savage grip on his father's pyjama top. Turning round he lifted the boy so that he could grab the hand rail and haul himself aboard. Tim followed suit. Half an hour later Tim and Martyn had bathed and changed and were now dry and warm. All were sipping hot chocolate.

'Are you alright now, son?' asked his mother, struggling to disguise her own distress.

'That bloody river is trying to kill me,' was his response. Neither parent tried to correct him. This was the third time he could have drowned. Tim lay in bed that night planning some safety measures for the boat. A set of metal steps welded on each side was the first decision. At the moment there was no way for a short adult or child to climb out safely when the river flooded. Later that night he came up with the idea of a wide plank on large wheels with its own handrails and adjustable steps at the boat end. It would be far safer and easier to move around. It would not bounce around like the present arrangement. He would talk to Tabby the boat yard owner in the morning. In the meantime he left the bed, making sure he did not wake his wife, and scribbled some notes on the pad for the shopping list. Martyn was very quiet while working at Aunt May's the next evening. She became more concerned as his shift wore on and his mood had not improved. When he went for his break she joined him at his table, carrying her own coffee.

Taking an appreciative sip she put her cup down and then asked him, 'Spit it out. What has got you so worried, lad?' Martyn sat and looked back at her, saying nothing.

'Do you want me to tell your mother you have been stealing from the till?'

The boy burst out laughing.

'Well that's an improvement anyway. Come on, tell me what's wrong.'

Looking around to make sure no one could overhear him, he said. 'I fell in the river again last night, the waves were breaking over my head and pulling at me. I thought I was going to get swept away and drowned; I've had no sleep. Every time I closed my eyes I was underwater drowning. I kept waking up soaked in sweat and panting.'

Aunt May reached out and held his hand, saying, 'You must have been terrified.'

'I still am.'

She pulled a face. 'You can swim though, can't you.'

'Yes in a nice calm swimming pool, not in freezing cold water with the river tugging at me trying to drag me away and the waves breaking over my head, hanging on by only one hand. The river kills someone every year. It wasn't long ago that a little girl was drowned from a boat in the yard. The family moved away. The general opinion was that the mother would never get over it. I would be happy if I never had to step aboard the *Sea Maiden* ever again.'

'Would you like to stay here tonight?' she asked.

Martyn nodded, saying, 'Oh yes, please.'

'Jot down your phone number. I will ring your mother and get her permission.' She was pushing a serviette and a pen towards him as she spoke. Martyn did as he was asked. Aunt May disappeared through the door into the private rooms. There was a long delay before she returned.

'Your mother has agreed. Your driver is bringing your school stuff for tomorrow.' Martyn was trying to interrupt. 'Yes, she has included your clarinet.'

Martyn gave her a double thumbs up.

His mother arrived later carrying a rucksack and his clarinet case. The two women hugged and Aunt May asked if Sophie would like a coffee. 'Oh yes please,' was the response.

'Martyn, would you get us some coffee and then you can get back to work please.' She was nodding at the queue by the counter.

The two women were in conversation for a considerable period of time. Later when the last customer had left Aunt May rose and walked over to the door, flipping the sign to closed. She indicated Martyn should join them. Before sitting down she called through the door marked private, saying, 'Uncle, we need you.'

Uncle walked into the café, nodded at all of them and sat down, saying hallo to Sophie. He was in his usual multicoloured jumper and dark brown corduroy trousers. Aunt May explained that Martyn had almost drowned last night because he had fallen in.

'Uncle, I thought my child was going to die,' said Sophie. 'I do not know what would have happened if Tim had not been there. It is no wonder Martyn was so scared.'

Uncle said, 'Thank the good lord that it didn't happen.'

Martyn was nodding vigorously.

'Aunt May has been extremely generous and offered you a room here from now on if you want it.'

'You will have to work for it,' said Aunt May. 'Your mother has insisted on it, so what we have arranged is that the first two hours you work every day will pay for your keep, after that it will be wages. What do you think? We will also pay you when you play.'

Martyn was shaking his head. 'I don't want to be paid to play.'

Uncle broke into the conversation, his tone of voice was firm. 'Listen to me, boy, the path you have chosen is a hard one. Some days you are going to be hungry with nothing in your pocket to pay for food. If you are offered money to play, take it, are you hearing me?'

'Yes, Uncle.'

Martyn often remembered Uncle's words on days in the future when he was striving to make a name for himself. More than once his main meal was a coffee and a plain roll.

Martyn was early to bed; he only woke up once and smiled when he realised he was on dry land. Seconds later he fell back to sleep.

CHAPTER 57

Bonny was on her way for a regular check-up on her shortened leg that her attack of polio had caused. Her mother used to accompany her but some time ago she had assured her mother that she was more than capable of attending on her own. This was part of Bonny's plan to become entirely self-reliant. There was another reason. Of late she had to admit to herself that the young specialist she saw, Michael Cardew, was becoming more and more attractive to her. Him examining her foot and lower leg was becoming an extremely pleasant experience. Today his examination of her limb caused her to display a deep blush that he noticed.

He completed the examination, and putting her special shoe on he said, 'I would like you to stay here, please, while I sort something out.' Once he had left the room Bonny had time to look at the charts etc. on the walls. In the corner was a small print by Lowry, one of her favourite artists. The fact that the crowds of characters were stick figures made no difference. They were all dynamic, intent upon their various purposes and destinations. Besides that the grim factories and small terraced houses were silent witnesses to the poverty prevalent when he was making his art. Standing now in front of the picture she jumped when the medic returned. For some reason she found herself embarrassed.

'I'm sorry,' she said sitting back down. 'He's one of my favourite artists.'

'And mine,' he responded. 'I have rearranged who you will see when you visit for your check-ups in future. It will be Dr Meredith, he's extremely good. Long term care is his speciality. I have done as much as I can for you.' He was holding the door open as he spoke.

She found herself walking away from the now closed door completely confused by what had just happened. Her mind was making it clear how deep her feelings were for him. Dabbing the tears from her eyes with a small white lace hanky she strode on. He was never going to find her attractive. He was examining damaged limbs all day long. Obviously all her silly dreams about him had been just childish nonsense. A growing depression gripped her. Surely she was not doomed to a solitary lonely existence for the rest of her life?

Reaching home she explained to her mother that she would see a different man next time. Her mother frowned at her then asked, 'Are you ok?' sensing that something was amiss.

'I'm just tired, it's been a long day. I'm going to watch some television.'

'Dinner will not be long; I will call you.'

She did not want anything to eat but if she refused her mother would badger her till she disclosed her sense of loss. Sitting with her mother that evening she could remember nothing of what they watched. Eventually she made her apologies and went to bed.

At work the next day she was extremely quiet, so much so that Jessica asked her what was wrong.

'Nothing. I'm fine, ta.'

'We both know that's not true.'

Bonny burst into tears, Jessica slipped the catch on the office door, then pulled the crying girl into an embrace, saying, 'Come on, tell me what is wrong. I cannot help you if you don't confide in me.'

'No one can help me. I am a cripple, no man will look at me. I will never have my babies. I will die a sad old spinster.'

'Whatever has brought this on? You normally cope so well with your leg.'

'If I tell you must promise not to share it with anyone else.'

'Of course I won't, what is said in the office stays in the office.'

'The doctor I see for my leg is very young and attractive. Lately I have found myself looking forwards to the visits. Yesterday when he was examining my foot I realised I was enjoying it and started blushing. In embarrassment I suppose. He noticed, excused himself and left the room. When he returned he said that he had done as much as he could for me and had handed me on to another doctor who was more experienced with adults. I can't even remember the new doctor's name.'

Jessica held her until she finished crying. Not knowing what to say that would not sound facile, in the end she said, 'If ever you want to talk, I will always listen.'

Bonny, sniffing, thanked her and went back to work.

Jessica was aware that the young woman was not the happy-go-lucky girl of old. There was a sadness there. Most of the time Bonny was able to hide it. Jessica noticed it because she was more aware, knowing the reason behind it. The easy happy laughter that was Bonny's gift to the office was a great loss.

CHAPTER 58

Tim sat in his office on the top floor gazing out at the park watching the parents walking and the children playing. One young boy was running toward the flock of sparrows that were feeding on the crumbs being scattered by the other children. As he got near the birds lifted into the air then settled back down behind him. Eventually realising he was never going to win he gave up.

A soft tapping on his office door broke his reverie. 'Hallo,' he called, 'come in.'

Jessica walked in holding the inevitable thick file. The normal polite exchanges were made, then she said, 'It's the Longstaff Trust time again, and by the way JJ has a display of his artwork in Edinburgh next week.'

Tim remembered the young lad. He was one of the first beneficiaries of the charitable trust that he had started with the substantial amount his aunt Victoria Longstaff had gifted him in her will.

'How do you know that?' asked Tim.

'We got quite close while he was receiving our cash support so that he could go to art school. I get the occasional phone call from him. He is sharing a flat with a friend, he did not say what gender the friend was. I know some of the girls at art school were quite keen on him.'

'How is that so-and-so of a father these days?' asked Tim, frowning, remembering how unpleasant JJ's father had been over the trust fund money.

'JJ never sees him. He meets his mother downtown and he treats her to a meal and the pictures.'

'That's nice, next time he contacts you say hallo from me please. Do you ever hear from Tiana Marshall, the mathematician?'

'Yes, but not for some time, she has a good job. It's all a bit hush hush, she cannot tell anyone what she does or who for.'

'Have we given birth to a spook?' he asked.

Jessica laughed and shrugged her shoulders, saying, 'I doubt we will ever know.'

'So who have we got this year?'

'There are very few really, five in total. I am always surprised that there are not greater numbers. I think we would get more if we advertised nationally. You do not want to do that, do you?'

'No, I think there is a good chance it would get out of hand, and we can only spend the interest the capital makes. I think most of the young people just want to get out there and earn some money. We must also recognise college does not suit everybody,' reasoned Tim.

'It may not be many, Tim, but it is an interesting mix. The two girls want to start nursing. One young man wants to go to college to learn how to manufacture modern furniture using natural materials, wood, wool, glass, cane etc. He brought some of his designs in. They really are extremely good. The other two young men want to go to uni. I will leave this file with you if you like.' She knew Tim would not want to wade through the detail.

This time he surprised her by asking, 'Are the furniture designs in here?'

'Yes.' Standing over him and leaning over his shoulder she leafed through the pages, finally saying, 'Found some of them.' She continued looking.

Tim was now benefitting in full from her perfume and warmth and the proximity of her attractive body. His mind went back to that day when she had kissed him. It had never been discussed or repeated. In his head he could hear Sophie berating him. Grumbling to himself he thought, it wasn't me that initiated the kiss. And it wasn't you that broke it either, his conscience replied.

His thoughts were interrupted when she said, 'Found them,' as she pulled a separate small file from the folder. 'Would you like me to leave the rest of the folder, Tim?' she asked with a smile in her voice.

He turned to look at her, shaking his head in denial with one eyebrow raised and a quizzical expression on his face.

'Just that then,' she said, nodding at the furniture file that he was already reading.

'Yes please,' he replied.

Laughing she went back to her own office carrying the rest of the folder with her. She was secretly pleased that he trusted her enough to run his Longstaff charity that supported gifted young people to achieve their goals.

When he walked back into the girl's office a little later he handed the file back to Jessica, saying, 'When you next speak to him can you say I would like to have a chat, please.'

The women were silent until they heard Tim's office door shut. 'He's spotted something in that young man's work, hasn't he?' said Bonny. Jessica nodded.

'I'm sorry, I don't understand,' said Lynda.

'JJ,' said Bonny. Lynda was still shaking her head.

'Our boss,' said Jessica, 'has a gift for recognising people with a special talent. He has obviously noticed something about this young man's work. As he did for the young artist JJ, who is now doing very well thanks to Tim's support.'

CHAPTER 59

Tim waved at his wife as she walked her horse in through the five-bar gate that was the entrance to the Italian farm that was now their home away from home. He was sitting upstairs in a large, comfortable leather armchair on his bedroom balcony from where he could see the road. He would love to join her in a ride. However, his experience with an ill-trained riding school brute of a horse rightly called Satan had put him off riding forever. Everyone agreed he could have been badly injured or worse.

Later a local farmer trotted by with his pony and trap. 'I wonder if I could learn to use one of those?' he said quietly to himself.

'Drive one of them is the expression,' said his wife as she entered the room. She stood behind him eased her arms around his neck and kissed the top of his head. 'I think you would be fine; If you got a decent sized one you could carry three or four people at a time. We could go shopping in it, take it for picnics.'

'Take it when we go to the pub,' added Tim.

'I think the no drinking rules still apply,' added Sophie.

'You wouldn't think that if you watched the locals on a Saturday night. They are as drunk as who knows what by ten o'clock,' countered Tim.

'It is the horses that get them home,' she agreed.

'Hmm, you may be right,' said Tim, quite happy to concede the point.

Sophie said, 'There is plenty of room for both the trap and the horse around the back. There are at least two unused stables there and I expect one of Mother's relatives will know who to talk to. Ciro will know what to do with the horse and trap.'

'He does seem very young though, Sophie.'

'He may appear young, but his father Fabio worked here with the horses from leaving school to retirement. When he started it was all horses here, no tractors in those days, Tim. His father is still alive and what he doesn't know about their care is not important. I am sure that the young man is the place to start. I am really excited, Tim; I think it will be great fun.'

'I will want to learn to look after it myself. It will be useful as a tool to stop me working while I'm here.'

'Can we do it together please, Tim? I love horses.'

'Hmm,' was his response again. He knew how expert Sophie was with any horse. I'm behaving like a spoilt child, he thought to himself. 'It will be our horse, the family's horse,' he said out loud. 'We will all learn to care for it. What do you think?'

'It sounds like a wonderful idea,' she replied. 'We can go on picnics; we will see more of the countryside.'

Tim, frowning, asked, 'Why is that? I don't understand.'

'There is time to take in the scenery, and some green lanes are not suitable for cars. I will have a word with Ciro,' she finished.

It was a week before Tim had any spare time, There had been a problem in the office back home and it had taken some time for him to unravel it. Jessica and Oliver were also on holiday.

When he spoke to them over the phone in their hotel Jessica said, 'Tim, we have to make sure this doesn't happen again.'

'I doubt it will, Mrs Simmons the solicitor seems to have it in hand. I think it was a one off, certainly not one we could have foreseen.'

'I do agree with that, Tim, but it is not what I meant. We have to liaise so a senior staff member is always in the office, I know you like to just get up and go but the rest of us will have to work around that.'

'Jessica, we will do that the other way round. You and Oliver have to book your holidays, we don't. If you tell me at the beginning of the year when you want to go away we will work around it.'

'That's extremely kind, Tim, thank you.'

'You're very welcome. I apologise for having to involve you both. Enjoy the rest of your holiday.'

* * * * *

Later that night Tim and Sophie were a tangle of legs and bedclothes, both struggling to get their breath back, when Sophie said, 'I am so excited about the horse and trap suggestion of yours. Have you had any more thoughts?'

Tim lifted his head from between her breasts, saying, 'Yes, I have spoken to Ciro the stable lad …'

'I think he is a bit more than that but never mind,' said Sophie, interrupting. 'Hold on a moment, I need to untangle my legs, one has gone to sleep.'

Moments later she was now comfortable. 'What did he have to say?'

'He was very keen on the idea; he told me that in the past there were all sorts of carts for different jobs. The ladies of the family had smart black two-wheel traps. Is that the right word? To tell the truth I didn't have a clue what he was talking about.'

'Tim, Tim, hold on, I do not want to ride around looking like lord and lady muck. We only want something in good condition and ordinary looking. The horse's nature is more important than its appearance. It needs to be fit and well, obviously, and up to the job, but that is about it I think. I don't really know much about it. Ciro and his father will know, now I must go to sleep. Goodnight, my darling. Thank you for just now.' Turning on her side and pulling his arm around her waist she wiggled her bottom into contact with him and promptly fell asleep.

The following morning Ciro spoke to Sophie as she arrived for her early morning ride, telling her that his father Fabio had let it be known that she was looking for a pony and trap. She briefed the youngster on what they were looking for.

'It needs to carry about four or five people for when the family are here. Nothing very smart, it just needs to be sound.' Ciro shook his head. 'Strong, well made,' she explained.

Now the lad was nodding saying 'Sí, sí.'

Tim and Sophie heard nothing for ten days. then one afternoon someone was tapping on the back door.

Sophie was making cakes in the large kitchen. 'Come in,' she called, not knowing who it was. She was rinsing her hands under the tap as Ciro peered around the door. 'Please come in,' she said. 'What can we do for you?' she asked.

'My father has a horse,' he replied. 'In the front.'

'How exciting. Let me shout at Tim, he is asleep upstairs. He always denies he has a nap in the afternoon.' She was making her way through the kitchen door and into the hall towards the front door. She sensed that Ciro was not following her, turning round she saw he was still standing in the middle of the kitchen looking uncomfortable. Sophie was uncomfortable herself, realising that the young man had never been in the front of the house before.

Waving Ciro towards her she shouted up the stairs, 'Tim, Ciro and Fabio are here with a horse.'

There was a lot of noises from upstairs, then Tim appeared from the bedroom saying, 'How exciting.' Now he was hopping on one leg on the landing trying to pull his left shoe on properly.

Sophie, now concerned that her husband was going to break his neck in a fall down the stairs, said, 'For goodness' sake, sit down and put your shoe on properly. You are going to fall and hurt yourself.' Minutes later they were walking down the front path towards where Fabio and a stranger were standing next to a horse and four-wheeled cart. Everyone shook hands and the introductions made.

Fabio with Ciro standing beside him began a very thorough examination of the horse, running his hands and eyes over the horse's body and legs. Feet were inspected, its mouth was peered into. Tim had no idea what Fabio was looking for because the elderly man gave no indication of what if anything he had found. Eventually the attention was turned to the cart. Now it was Ciro's turn to slide under the vehicle. Another careful inspection ensued, then coming out from underneath the lad checked the rest of the cart. When he had finished, the father and son moved some distance away and began an indistinct conversation. There was some head wagging, some shoulders shrugged, finally some nodding, then the two of them came back to join the group. Tim heard the owner say something but finished by saying, 'Molto robusto.' Even with his almost complete lack of Italian he understood that. The price was asked and the response in lira caused Fabio to burst out laughing. He suggested another figure, this time it was the owner's turn to laugh. The haggling went on for some time. A long silence descended, then Ciro's father raised his hands, shrugged his shoulders again and began to usher them all away towards the house. Sophie was extremely disappointed, the horse and trap looked exactly as she had envisioned. She went to say something, but Fabio whispered, 'Silencio.' They were almost at the front door when the owner called out another figure. Fabio turned around and walked nonchalantly back to the horse and trap. Reaching the man he thrust out his hand, the owner shook it. There was a lot of back slapping, laughter and rapid Italian, none of which Tim understood. He had been asked to have a certain amount of lira to hand spread around his pockets so it would not look as though he had been prepared to pay a lot more. By the time the transaction was completed both the buyer and the seller seemed content. All but one of Tim's pockets was empty.

'What is the horse's name?' asked Sophie.

'Sleepy,' replied Ciro. 'It sounds the same in English and Italian,' explained the young man. 'If he is left standing too long he sleeps.'

'I'm surprised we didn't take him for a test drive or whatever,' said Tim. The young man laughed and translated for his father, who joined in the merriment.

Fabio spoke to his son, who then said to Tim, 'My father says he watched them arrive from a long way off. The horse is, how you say, sound and the cart is good.'

Sophie moved to the front of the horse to stroke Sleepy's neck. He seemed to enjoy it. She was talking quietly to the horse while she patted him.

'How will you get back home?' asked Tim.

There was more Italian, then Ciro said, 'He will get the train. We can give him a lift to the station if you agree.'

Unsure which of them he was talking to, both Tim and Sophie nodded. Fabio made it clear that he would not be coming. Before he left he shook the man's hand and said, 'Arrivederci,' as he walked away. Tim was a little surprised the man had nothing to say to the horse.

The man, Tim, Sophie and Ciro climbed aboard the cart with Ciro driving and the man sitting beside him. Tim and his wife never did learn the man's name.

The road past the house was in good repair and the outfit moved smoothly over the surface. They soon reached the railway, and seeing the train ready to depart the man vaulted from the cart as it was stopping and ran towards the station entrance, waving over his shoulder as he went. The occupants of the cart waved the train away but saw no returned goodbye.

'Ciro, before we start for home can Sophie join you in the front and you can explain to her what you are doing, please?' The lad agreed.

THE NEXT GENERATION

'Do you not want to do that?' she asked him.

'No, you will learn more quickly than me, then you can share it.'

Tim picked it up faster than he thought he would. He admitted to Sophie one evening, 'The truth of the matter is the horse is the clever one, a lot of the time he is teaching me.'

Tim was returning from a shopping trip to the village. He sank back into the dark brown leather upholstery, his left arm spread along the top of the seat, his legs crossed. His other hand had a casual grip on the reins as he admired the view. He had discovered that Sleepy knew where they were going dependent upon the direction of travel. Most of his journeys were to the village and back. Sophie was right, he thought, you can see more from up here. He spent the rest of the journey taking in the view of the groves of olive trees. Some of them were so old and gnarled they looked as though they had been planted at the beginning of time itself. He knew that from now on this was his preferred mode of transport, at least locally.

CHAPTER 60

Tim sat in a comfortable beige armchair on his first-floor bedroom balcony as he often did when here in Italy watching the world go by. He waved at a local farmer as the elderly man trotted by in his horse and trap. This was a regular occurrence. There was a difference: on this occasion, a sandy-coloured, short-furred, medium-sized dog was padding along behind the trap.

Later that evening he mentioned it to the local girls who worked for him, and they provided the explanation.

The younger girl said, 'The village has named the dog Solo. He is a tramp, very independent. Last year he was away for months. How long we are unsure, the village cannot agree,' as she spoke her head was rocking, 'I think it was about six months, maybe a little more. No one knows for certain. He comes and goes as he pleases.'

'He looks well enough on it,' said Tim.

'Sí,' said the girl, nodding her head as she made her way back to the kitchen.

The following morning Solo was sitting at the front door as Tim, an early riser, came down to make the tea. He had crept out of bed so as not to wake Sophie. Should she wake and want tea she would call down from their bedroom window above his chair and he would walk a cup upstairs, complete with two biscuits. As he took his first tentative sip of his extremely hot tea – he could not abide what he called cold tea – others would still be sipping it, he breathed a contented sigh. The sun was creeping up into the sky behind the stand of olive trees. Small, irregular chinks of golden light made their way through the tiny gaps in the foliage. He could feel the growing warmth in the air. This was for him the best of times here in Italy. He loved the sunshine, the people, the food, the wine, the scents of the blossom, their relaxed way of life. Some of their arguments were not relaxed. However, he could forgive them that. He had found them in the main to be a kind and generous people.

'Would you like a drink?' he asked as he stood up. The dog moved away a few paces in response to Tim standing. He realised the animal could not always be sure of man's intentions towards him.

'You have nothing to fear from me, old son,' he said quietly as he moved towards the door. 'I will get you some water, Solo.'

When he returned he was carrying a large water bowl and the bone from last night's beef dinner, there was still some meat on it. The dog drank deeply from the bowl then carried the bone away under a tree to chew on it. Tim purchased a bag of dog biscuits and on those mornings when Solo graced Tim with his presence the bowl was filled, and the biscuits provided. He became ever more trustful and would eat his food at Tim's side. However, the occasional bone was always carried away. On the now rare occasions when the family were not home the girls who looked after the house were asked to feed and water him.

When Solo did one of his disappearing acts Tim was always concerned and would ask in the village if anyone had seen him. The tradespeople who travelled between the villages would often stop at the house to tell Tim they had seen the dog, and where and when. Tim spent a considerable amount of time building a kennel that Solo refused to use. The villagers pulled Tim's leg remorselessly.

When Solo was in the area he followed Tim on his trips into town. He occupied his normal position trotting behind the cart. Early one morning Tim came downstairs and made his way out into the garden. As he passed the dog he bent down to pat him. For the first time ever Solo did not shy away.

* * * * *

Tim and Sophie were lunching in a small vineyard with the owner, his wife, and their grown-up children, a boy and a girl. The couple had a pleasant journey there with Sleepy pulling the cart through the lanes. Now he was standing in the shade of a large tree with his nose bag on.

It quickly became clear to Sophie this was not a leisure visit, it was business. Tim was talking prices and quantities. If it were not such a beautiful day with the sunshine, the incredible food, dishes she had never tried before, the wine and the excellent company she would have been really angry.

The owner and his wife were lovely people, the son and daughter were pleasant. The technical side of the business, the theory, had been taken over by the daughter, who had attended college. The son worked alongside his father tending the vines, organising the picking etc. Their mother oversaw the financial side. She admitted that some time back she had to take on a part-time member of staff because the exporting side had grown substantially.

Sophie said nothing but she noticed how bent and distorted the owner's fingers were.

He saw her looking, and now examining his hands he said, 'These show the thousands of hours I have spent picking grapes and tending the vines.' He turned to his wife and asked her something in Italian.

She replied, 'Sixty years. Your father told me before he died, you were out picking before your tenth birthday.' Continuing, she said, 'our son,' she turned to him while she was speaking, 'you were out picking after school.' He nodded.

'I got stopped from helping,' said the girl.

'She ate half of everything she picked,' added her father.

'There is a grape, Primitivo, that we pick early in the year,' the girl said, 'I could eat the whole crop, they are delicious.' Again her father said something in Italian. This was not explained. His daughter pulled a face.

Tim and Sophie spent a pleasant two hours tasting the wine and eating the wonderful food. He wanted some wine for the farmhouse here in Italy and also for John Armstrong the vintner in the food hall and the restaurant and shops back home. There was a discussion in Italian amongst the family about the price. Tim kept himself abreast of the relationship between sterling and the lira.

This was not an inconsiderable order, a sum was mentioned, then Tim said, 'Ok, but what about the discount. If this works out we could be ordering a lot more in the future.' There was a discussion, eventually a price was agreed on that would include a further discount if the order became larger in the future.

As the horse trotted out of the vineyard, Sophie said, 'You didn't tell me you were working this morning, and why did you bring me along?'

'It never hurts to have a beautiful woman on the team.'

'So I am only here as decoration?' she said, sounding angry.

'No, you are here because you are extremely clever and stunningly attractive.' Turning her head away she smiled her woman's smile.

On the way home Tim turned down a green lane he had found when out exercising the horse. There was a slow climb to the top of the hill. The road stopped at the edge of a vast grove of olive trees that sloped away into the valley below. Tim made sure the horse could reach the grass at the side of the lane.

The trees near them were extremely old, the branches gnarled and twisted. It looked to Tim as though someone had set out to grow the ugliest trees possible. Sophie in the meantime had gone to the back of the trap and was withdrawing a large heavy woollen blanket from the box.

Tim was sitting on the comfortable seats at the rear of the cart as Sophie climbed in beside him, she arranged the rug over their knees. They spent the next hour reminiscing, laughing at some of the silly things that had happened to them. They were quiet when they remembered those who were still close in memory but had passed on. The sunset was amazing. The sky was streaked with lines of gold that lit the underside of the now navy blue clouds. The going down of the sun prompted them to make their way home.

CHAPTER 61

A month later Tim and Sophie were trotting home in the pony and trap in the late summer sun when a mile outside the village Tim's eye was caught by the flash of pale brown in the ditch on their side of the road.

'Whoa,' he said, as he slowed the horse down. Stopping, he put the brake on. He was already aware what the body in the ditch was. In an extremely distressed voice he was saying, 'Oh no, no, no, please God, it's not Solo.' Reaching the edge of the ditch and looking down his fears were confirmed. It was Solo and he was dead, there was no sign of life, and anyway there was so much damage to his upper body. Scrambling down into the ditch it was obvious he could not have survived his injuries. Tim put his hand on the dog's side. The body was cold, the blood had dried and there were flies.

Sophie had stepped down from the trap and was looking down at her husband in the ditch. In a small voice she asked, 'Is he …?' she was unable to say the word.

Tim nodded; Sophie realised Tim was fighting to hold back the tears. He could be hard with humans, but he was extremely soft with animals. He climbed from the ditch and pulled his wife to him, they stood locked in each other's arms. Tim with his chin on the top of her head. He was extremely upset. Eventually he sniffed hard, apologised and lifted his head. Sophie's hand reached around his neck and pulled his head down so she could kiss him. She loved this gentleness about him, she knew he would not show this side of himself to anyone but her.

They had not known Solo long, but they had got close to him. He was often found in the entrance to the barn fast asleep on the straw. The horses seemed completely disinterested.

He found a black plastic sack in the box at the rear of the cart. With extreme care he slipped Solo into it. Sophie was moved that although the animal was dead Tim showed the poor dog great respect. He was muttering to Solo; Sophie was unable to hear what he was saying. He placed the bag on the floor of the trap at the back. The horse started to fidget; Tim thought it may have been because the smell of blood. Sophie moved to the horse's head and with quiet words soothed the creature.

They trotted into town slowly, Sophie guessed it was to give her husband time to get his head together.

* * * * *

The following morning one of the women who helped in the house stopped Sophie, saying, 'The children know who killed Solo.' Apparently the whole village knew the dog was dead. Later that day Sophie was relaying what she had been told to Tim. 'The children are upset; they saw him moving down the middle of the road dragging one leg behind him, obviously in great pain. They went out into the road to try and help him. No sooner had they reached him than that filthy old lorry drove towards them blowing his horn.'

Tim interrupted her, 'Is that the rusty green one?'

She nodded, then continued, 'The children had to run to get out of the way. They tried to wave him down but apparently he just kept coming and blowing his horn as he ran over Solo. The children were in a terrible state. One of the boys moved him to the side of the road even though they knew he was dead. Then they decided to move him into the ditch. I understand the girls cried themselves to sleep last night. The women are really angry, not just because of Solo's death, but it sounds as though he put the children's lives at risk. If he goes in the pub I think he will run into trouble.'

* * * * *

Two days later Sophie found Tim wheeling a barrow around the property collecting flat stones.

With a frown of enquiry on her face she asked, 'What are you doing?'

'I'm going to bury Solo properly. I'm building him a cairn, so we remember him.'

Sophie could look out the front window and watch her husband work, he had shown her a strong wooden box that was to be the dog's coffin. He'd dug a deep hole and checked with her that it was deep enough. A day later he lowered the box and dog into its grave. Filling in the hole he laid some substantial stones across it to prevent it being dug up. Two days later he began carefully placing flat stones in a circle, then using small stones to fill in the middle, the diameter slowly decreasing as the cairn rose. He stopped building at about knee high. Sophie saw him rise, step back and stand looking at it. She went out to discover what he was thinking.

Hearing her footsteps he turned to her and asked, 'Do you think this is high enough?'

Sophie looked carefully at it, then said, 'I think the proportions are good, it's certainly substantial. Yes, it is good, are you happy with it?'

'Yes I think so.'

'It needs a plaque,' observed Sophie.

'Really?'

'Yes it needs to say words like, intrepid, independent, self-reliant. It is what he was.'

'Ok I'll sort it out.' Tim had a brass plate made as his wife had suggested and fixed it on large flat stone that topped the cairn. The plaque said, *'Here lies Solo the intrepid, the most noble of animals. You are much missed'.*

* * * * *

Down in the village a few days later a woman he didn't know came to talk to him.

'Mr Cooper?' she asked.

'Yes,' he replied, 'I prefer Tim. You're English, aren't you? That sounds like a midlands accent?'

'No, I was born in Italy but when I was still young my father got a job in the UK in Birmingham. I had no children and my husband died incredibly young, so I decided to come home. I was a headmistress in England. My mother and father kept our native tongue alive at home when I was growing up. I have no regrets. I love it here.'

'How can I help you?'

'I am the headmistress at the school. The children would like to come and visit Solo's grave. He was much loved; would that be possible?' She was looking into his eyes. The power of her questioning gaze and the raised eyebrow was helping to strengthen the request.

'When would you like to come?'

'That's the problem, they don't want to come on an arranged visit. They want to visit him in the same way as if he was in a graveyard.'

Tim thought for a moment, then said, 'I have no problem with that. They must not touch his grave. I have built a cairn, a tower of rocks.'

'I know, a lot of people have remarked on its progress. I can guarantee no one will damage it. You may be surprised who your visitors may be.'

Tim, unclear as to what she meant, asked, 'What do you mean?'

'Wait and see,' was her response.

On the following Sunday Sophie asked, 'Have you looked at the cairn lately?'

THE NEXT GENERATION

'No,' responded Tim.

'Come with me,' she said, reaching out for his hand and leading him to the graveside.

When they were standing beside the cairn Tim was silent, unsure what he was seeing. There were flowers tucked carefully into the small gaps in the stones and here and there little screws of paper rolled into a tight tube and placed in the same way as the flowers. Sophie teased one such out of its gap and rolled it open.

Tim said, 'I don't know why but I'm uncomfortable with you doing that.'

Sophie, surprised, said, 'Why would you say that? I don't understand.'

'I think the words are private, is that silly?'

It was obvious to her that the cairn and people's response to it was affecting her husband far more than it affected her.

Three days later in the small hours of the morning she heard a car stop outside the house. Stepping from her bed to the window she moved them just an inch so she could peer out. She saw a well-dressed middle-aged woman place flowers on top of the stones and slide a scrap of paper into a crack. She did all this on her knees. Finally she reached up and briefly rested her fingers on the brass nameplate. As the woman rose Sophie moved slowly away from the window so as not to be seen. After a pause she heard the car door close, the engine start and the car drive away. When she told her husband later that morning he was clearly moved.

Tim noted a week later that the number of flowers and notes on and around the stones were growing in number.

Speaking to Sophie about it she said, 'The staff have told me that he was often talked of. It was agreed that he was more than just a dog. They stressed his self-reliance, his independence. There is a growing belief that in the village that it is lucky to touch the cairn. Had you decided to build the usual flat grave I doubt any of this would have happened.'

'Stone monuments have always had a mystique about them. I don't know why but cairns are powerful symbols,' said Tim.

'Do you think it is similar to throwing coins into a well?' she asked.

'Similar I guess,' said Tim, not really agreeing. 'I remember years ago someone built a cairn on a beach. It appeared overnight. Lots of people stopped to take photographs but once they had done that many of them remained. They sat, knelt, or simply stood and looked in silence or spoke quietly. One thing I noticed when they were doing this was that they were very still. A number of them were there for a considerable period of time. They were mostly adults of all ages. We know that cairns are some of the earliest structures made by man, they go back to the dawn of time.'

'I am not sure of that,' said Sophie.

'It seems to be attracting a growing number of people,' he responded, 'and all the flowers and little messages. I have noticed people touch it, for luck I guess. I don't really understand what is going on,' said Tim. 'That one I mentioned got knocked down on the beach one night. It became a pile of stones, but the strange thing was people still stopped to take pictures of it and stand awhile.'

* * * * *

Later that evening Tim was standing on the doorstep when a lady with two young girls in white and pink gingham dresses hand in hand went to open the gate. One of the children spotted Tim and said, 'Mummy,' pointing at him.

The mother said, 'Sorry,' and started ushering her children out through the gate.

'Wait, wait,' called Tim making his way quickly to the gate and saying, 'please, come in.' He swung the gate open again. 'I will go inside and leave you some privacy.'

'Are you sure?' asked the woman. The oldest child was looking at her mother for guidance.

THE NEXT GENERATION

Now looking at the children, Tim said, 'Please come in.'

The mother nodded at the two girls. Indicating they were to continue. As she walked past him she said, 'The village is so pleased you have done this, he was a special dog.' She paused for a moment, then said, 'He belonged to no one, he belonged to everyone.'

'Thank you,' said Tim as he went inside. Then realised he knew her; she was a schoolteacher. Tim decided to make a second gate in the perimeter fence that gave access to an enclosure that surrounded the cairn. People would not then have to roam in the garden.

Over supper one night Sophie said, 'There's been a real set to in the village. Did you know some of the children saw the lorry driver run Solo over? They are saying he did it on purpose. They saw him swerve and drive over him.'

'The lorry driver went in the pub last night and they would not serve him. He started shouting and swearing. The landlady came out from behind the bar then she and some angry mothers threw him out. He was getting slapped, punched and kicked and having drinks thrown over him. I am glad I was not there,' she added.

Tim let it be known in the village that he was going to burn the flowers as they died, and the paper notes and the ashes would be scattered around the garden. He assured everyone none of the notes would be read. The locals made it clear his decision was the right one, he was often thanked for what he had done.

One warm afternoon there was a woman in a navy suit standing at the open front door calling Tim's name. Walking around the side of the house he said hallo and was met by a stream of rapid fire Italian.

'I'm sorry, I don't speak Italian.'

The woman apologised in English and said, 'My newspaper has heard of the dog's grave, and we would like to run an article on it.'

Sophie joined them and said, 'I don't think so, Tim, a story like this will catch on and we will have coachloads of people at the gate. There will be noise and people trampling on the flower beds and throwing their litter everywhere.'

Turning to the woman, she said, 'Thank you for your interest but no thanks. I am certain that the people of the village would be very offended. I expect the sales of your newspaper will fall through the floor locally if you print the story.' She leant in and read the woman's name from the badge on her lapel and made a mental note. 'Thank you for your interest, but it is not appropriate.'

The women turned and made her way to the car. 'I will tell my editor that you are not prepared to agree to the article.'

'Thank you,' responded Sophie.

Down the years people of all ages came to the grave. Never in vast groups, usually people on their own or couples, sometimes in tears. They were all afforded absolute privacy.

CHAPTER 62

Tim and Sophie had recently returned from Italy. Sitting down to tea one evening on the boat with the rest of the family. Nanny had produced a celebratory meal to welcome them home. The whole deal, roast beef and potatoes with a range of vegetables. This was topped by a thick gravy with finely chopped red onions and a good splosh of red wine. Desert was a wonderful trifle blessed with a splosh of sherry. This was Nanny's description.

Martyn disclosed he had something to discuss. Sophie realised this must be important. His dislike of the boat normally kept him away unless it was very calm on the river. As a youngster he believed the boat hated him and the river wanted to drown him. Now he was just uncomfortable aboard. His memory of falling in and having the waves breaking over his head still woke him in the night sometimes. He relived the fear his father and Paddy from the boat next door experienced struggling in the water to save the three of them being crushed between the boats. A motorboat travelling much too quickly had triggered the violent waves.

Charley arrived on board with her girlfriend. Apparently this had become a regular occurrence. This was the first he had known of it. He realised that this may make his revelation harder to discuss. Tim arrived, kissed his wife, slapped his son on the back, hugged his daughter and welcomed her girlfriend.

Sophie stood up from the couch, tapped Martyn on the shoulder, pointed at the kitchen door and said quietly, 'Follow me.'

Martyn followed his mother into the kitchen. They entered, and Sophie closed the door behind them. Turning to her son she could see how excited he was. Parking themselves on the two kitchen stools, Sophie said, 'Come on then, what has got you so animated?'

The shine in his eyes and his huge smile gave his mother some idea of her son's level of excitement, although she would never have guessed the enormity of the size of the secret he was holding inside himself.

Now unable to sit still any longer he stood up, grasped his mother's arms and gently shaking her said, 'I have been asked to play with a group in New York. The leader is a relative of Uncle's, and, and …' he said, cutting off his mother's unasked question. 'The group is mostly older men, apparently they play at religious events as well as nighttime gigs. They are quite well known; this is their third trip to New York. Uncle sent them a copy of my tune and they have told Uncle they would like me to go to New York and play with them.'

'When would you go?' asked his mother, dumbfounded, unable to take in the enormity of what her son was telling her.

'At the beginning of the summer holidays, oh and Uncle says he will come with me and stay till I come home.'

'How will you pay for it?' she asked.

'Uncle says he will pay. If I earn any money over there I will use it to pay him back.'

Sophie was almost incapable of believing the change in her son. Also, she knew Tim would never agree to anyone but him financing the trip if he allowed the lad to go.

'Are you ready to tell the rest of the tribe?'

'Yep,' was his extremely positive response.

As she followed her son into the lounge she realised he was two people. In ordinary everyday life he was often nervous and unsure; when it came to his music he knew exactly what he was doing. Considering the fact that Uncle was in charge and that it was with Aunt May's blessing she was not that worried. Who was she kidding?

Reaching the lounge, Sophie said, 'Can we have some quiet please? Martyn has something to tell you.' Charley's girlfriend was still talking when Martyn began speaking over the top of her. Something he would never have done normally.

'You will not believe what I am going to tell you. I have been asked to play with a blues band in New York.'

Charley's girlfriend burst out laughing and said, 'Of course you have, and Father Christmas does exist.'

Charley gathered up the woman's coat and hand bag, took her arm and led her to the front door. Seconds later the door slammed shut and Charley returned to the lounge alone. She heard her name called twice then nothing.

Sitting down, she said, 'Sorry, Martyn, please carry on.' There were some raised eyebrows, then he repeated what he had said earlier. Then he added, 'Uncle will be taking me. I have Aunt May's approval, now I just need yours.'

Everyone began talking at once, then Tim broke in and said, 'Hold on, everyone let Martyn tell us.' The young man repeated what he had told his mother earlier.

Charley was the first to speak. 'What a marvellous opportunity. Any musician would give everything to have this chance.'

Sophie was extremely unsure. In her mind Martyn was not much more than a child. If it was Charley going she would not have worried, her daughter she was sure could look after herself in almost any circumstances. The truth was she realised she did not want her boy to go. There was a tap on the front door, Charley answered it. Their neighbour Paddy, who lived on the converted ship's lifeboat moored alongside the *Sea Maiden*, was standing in the rain. He said nothing. He just pointed to the girl sitting on the deck now soaking wet.

Charley rolled her eyes and said, 'Come in, Paddy, go on through.' Charley stepped out onto the front deck, grabbed her girlfriend and dragged her into the kitchen, closing both the front door and the lounge door. Then, being extremely blunt, she explained that she had spent most of her life protecting her little brother.

Then she said, 'Thank God I have, because as it turns out he has an incredible gift, he is a musician and songwriter.' On the way to Charley's bedroom to change the young woman apologised to Martyn, who just shrugged it off.

'What is this song then, Martyn?' asked his father.

'Give me a moment. I will get the CD.'

'How come you have a CD?'

'Uncle sorted it out,' the lad replied.

When he returned he had the disc in one hand, his clarinet in the other. 'I thought I would play along so you know that it's me.' The music started, initially he only added little bits. As it went on he added more. Now he was gone, he was following different paths in the music, occasionally fetching it back to the source. When he stopped there was a silence. The pain and the sorrow in the music was tangible, a living thing. Martyn's additions simply added to the suffering contained in the music. Agatha's singing was astounding, singing her and Martyn's words took the music to another level.

Charley's girlfriend stepped out of the bedroom in floods of tears and hugged the boy, apologising again she said, 'I have never been more wrong. That is amazing. Can you play something else, please?' Martyn started playing a well-known song by Aka Bilk, 'Strangers on the Shore'. That evening Paddy revealed that his singing voice was a pleasant Irish tenor. A few days later Charley brought home a present from work that was a knitted Father Christmas. He was carrying a sign that said, 'There is a Father Christmas, with love from big mouth'. Sophie was in bed before her husband that night, she had stopped watching the film on the TV before the end. When he entered the bedroom the lights were out, and Sophie had turned her face to the wall. She didn't roll over towards him when he slid into bed. He was going to sleep as his head hit the pillow. It was the muted sniffles that made him aware that something was wrong. He put his hand on her back. This triggered an audible cascade of tears and sorrow.

'Whatever's wrong?' he asked.

Rolling towards him, she said 'My baby boy is leaving home. Who knows if he will come back? You have said yourself the music industry is rife with drugs and alcohol. I cannot look after him all that distance away.' All this was said through a veil of tears.

'Two things,' said Tim calmly. 'Firstly, Martyn is no longer a child. Secondly, to cause our boy any harm they have to get past Uncle. The third that I did not mention is Aunt May, who would be on a plane faster than Jack Robinson, whoever he was.' He noticed the tears had stopped but the sniffing continued. 'And' he added, 'we would be right behind her.' He cuddled her to him. Eventually her tears dried on his chest as they slept.

Late one evening Sophie answered the phone on the boat. 'Mum, Mum,' said her son, shouting down the phone, 'you'll never guess what's happened.'

'Good evening, Martyn how are you? I am well by the way.'

'Oh sorry, yes I'm good, they want us to do a going-away concert.'

'Who is they?'

'The band, the school. The headmaster, he has always been interested.'

'Why?' she asked.

'To raise a little bit of money to help with our expense.'

'But we do not need it,' said his mother.

'Mr Lawrence explained that the people were doing it so they could feel they were involved in something special.'

Because the boy's departure was imminent it was arranged very rapidly for the last day of term, just a few days hence. There were no tickets, just a collection tin. It was a lot more relaxed than usual; the audience were invited to make requests. Some the band knew some they did not. There was a lot of laughter. Eventually the evening drew to a close. One of the last things that happened was when Martyn's mum walked on stage and handed Mr Lawrence a slip of paper. There were raised eyebrows and muttering. Mr Lawrence stood up and said, 'Your generosity has been amazing this evening.' He read out the sum. The crowd started clapping. Martyn walked to the front edge of the stage and waited for the storm of applause to die down. When it did he thanked everyone and said how moved he was. Then Mr Lawrence began the first few bars of Martyn's song that they had not played until then. Agatha put more emotion into it than usual. She had not disclosed that she was going home to the West Indies at the end of term and did not expect to return. Halfway through she and Martyn had the house in tears. Backstage after the crowds had begun to depart the elderly caretaker waiting to close up came across to Martyn and shook his hand.

'I knew youse was good lad. I hopes you have a good time over there, all that practice you'll be fine.'

'Thank you, Mr …' Martyn did not know the man's name, he began to apologise.

'Don't you worry, lad. Perkins the name, Samuel Perkins. I enjoyed listening to yur music. In years to come when you're on the telly and that, I will tell people that I knew yur afore you was famous like.'

'I am really grateful to you for allowing me to practice long after you could have gone home.'

'Don't you fret, lad, I thoroughly enjoyed it. You knock 'em dead out there.'

'Thank you, Mr Perkins,' said Martyn, shaking the old man's hand.

'You're welcome, lad.' With that the caretaker walked away.

* * * * *

THE NEXT GENERATION

On the day of his departure Sophie had said a tremulous goodbye to her son on the boat. When the Bentley had disappeared she stepped inside, shut the door and cried her eyes out.

CHAPTER 63

The car arrived at the airport. Uncle, Martyn and Tim stepped out. A porter arrived and loaded the baggage onto a trolley and asked them to follow him. Tim shook Uncle's hand and thanked him once again for looking after his lad.

Uncle laughed and said, 'A free holiday with everything paid. What's not to like? Thank you very much.' Tim shook his son's hand then pulled him into a hug. 'You will be great, lad; you are very good at what you do. Ring us now and then eh?'

'Thank you, Dad,' said the boy as he stepped away.

Tim watched as Uncle and Martyn both looked back and waved before disappearing out of site through departures. Tim took a long breath in and said quietly, 'Go safely, you two.' As he started for home he knew Sophie was going to need a lot of comforting. She was extremely close to her young, timid boy.

* * * * *

One of the hostesses asked what was in the case as they boarded. Martyn explained it was his clarinet. Uncle revealed the lad had been asked to play with a band in New York. The staff looked suitably impressed and offered to lock it away up forward.

'No thank you, I must keep it by me. It's over fifty years old. It was a gift

THE NEXT GENERATION

from a lady who has passed on. No two instruments are the same, so I will look after it.'

The two of them slept most of the way, only waking when the food arrived. In first class the food was good.

Stepping through arrivals, Uncle spotted a man holding a card with his name on it. The driver led them out of the airport to the taxi. They were soon on their way. Their hotel overlooked Central Park; Martyn remembered that the area was made famous by the Beatles music.

Once they had unpacked, Martyn explained he would love to see Times Square now in the dark. He was studying a map spread out on the bed that the concierge had given him. 'It's not far, Uncle.' He was using his fingers to measure the distance.

'No one walks in New York, especially not when your dad is paying.' In the taxi the lad's nose was jammed against the window. The ride to Times Square was over too soon for the youngster. Uncle was out first, paying the cabby. Martyn joined him on the pavement, his mouth open, his eyes huge, staring upwards. The height of the buildings was unbelievable, the advertising often went up the sides into the sky. The yellow cabs were busy, backwards and forwards through the square. Occasionally the braying of car horns signalled a disagreement of some kind between the drivers, accompanied by some shouting. Martyn loved the feel of the place. It was so busy everybody seemed to have somewhere to go, now, quickly.

Uncle said, 'There is an amazing energy, Martyn. I have been here before, it's always like this, it never stops. I would like a coffee; will you join me?' They found a café with seats in the window.

'I had cheesecake last time I was here. It's super.' They sat sipping the hot coffee and eating an enormous slice of cheesecake each.

At almost the same time they both started yawning. They both laughed. 'Bed?' asked Uncle. He had chosen the bed nearest the toilet so he would not disturb Martyn.

A very tired young man nodded. Just before he slept Martyn reviewed how much his life had changed in just twenty-four hours.

This time tomorrow night he would hopefully be playing with the band. Before he and Uncle had left home he was worried that he may be too nervous to play. In reality the reverse was true. He couldn't wait for tomorrow.

Much to Martyn's surprise sleep claimed him more quickly than he had anticipated. He was dragged awake in the night by Uncle's snoring. He soon went back to sleep after the older man had turned over. The following morning the boy was woken by the sound of a teacup being placed on his small bedside table. Yawning his head off he said, 'Thank you, Uncle, good morning. Did you sleep well?'

'Yes thank you. Do you need the loo? I am going to have a shower.'

'No thanks, I will stay here a while longer. What time is breakfast?'

'Whenever you decide to get up.'

Eventually the two of them were seated in the hotel restaurant ordering breakfast. Uncle had decided on scrambled egg, bacon and pancakes. Martyn found it easier to follow suit. The waitress clearly took a shine to Martyn. She said, 'Gee, aren't you cute. Are you English? Are you on holiday?'

'No, he's a clarinettist. He's here to play with a blues band. I have some cards here.' With that he pulled three postcards from his pocket advertising the band's appearances.

'What sort of music did you say you play?'

'Blues.'

'Oh wow, I'll tell my friends.'

After breakfast the two of them on Uncle's advice walked to Central Park and ambled slowly under the trees, watching the runners and the strollers. The man and boy were both well dressed in pale grey suits and ties. Uncle explained that the group were always smart on stage. There was laughter in a group of girls, serious discussions between three besuited men sitting on a park bench, their briefcases on their knees, A4 sheets of paper being passed between them. In one case there was a heated argument underway between a young couple. She was pushing her baby in a buggy, her facial expression and her loud angry voice defining her mood. The baby, picking up on the tension, was crying hysterically. Her partner was walking silently beside her with his fists clenched. He was dressed in blue jeans and a matching shirt, she in a pretty yellow knee-length dress.

Martyn, keen to meet the band members, asked, 'Will they be there yet?'

'No, we will meet them after lunch. Remember, they were performing until about midnight. I guess some of them may still be in bed.'

Martyn nodding, walked on.

Later they stopped at a café, Martyn discovered that now he was nervous. A cup of coffee was all he could stomach.

Uncle devoured his pancake and swallowed his coffee, then said, 'I can tell you're nervous. That's a good thing, it puts you on your metal. You have no need to worry. Just remember you are very good at what you do. I believe in you. If you continue to work at this gift you have been given I believe you have the chance to be outstanding. I would not say this if I did not think it was true. But you will still have to work so, so hard. There will be days when you want to give it away, do something else, get an easy job. With your songwriting, sometimes nothing will come. You still have to try; it's easy to stop, much harder to start again. Write rubbish if necessary, keep the rubbish, there may be a kernel of something in there that you cannot yet see.'

Seeing how much what he had said had moved the boy he wrapped an arm round him and hugged him hard. 'One last thing, Martyn, don't be afraid to improvise. That's where your gift lies. Most people can't do that. Do it early on this afternoon, they'll be blown away.'

Martyn was surprised when later on Uncle turned down a scruffy alley with rubbish piled against the left-hand wall. As they walked past the piled cardboard it moved. Instinctively he leapt to the other side of the alley. An old man's grimy face looked up at him before he pulled the cardboard back over him. The boy could not hear what the down-and-out was muttering. Further on Uncle was tapping on an old green door. The majority of the paint had peeled off, exposing the pale bare wood underneath.

The door was opened by an enormous white guy who said. 'Round the front, mate, we are not open yet.'

Uncle was laughing as he was pushing the giant man aside. 'Just shut up and let us in, Shamus.'

'Uncle, Uncle, stop bullying the hired staff.' This was said by a short West Indian man who was grinning from ear to ear. The two men shook hands. Uncle shook hands with Shamus, saying, 'Good afternoon. how are you?'

'Uncle, it's been long time. I didn't recognise you. I'm sorry.'

'That's too many blows to the head, Shamus,' said Uncle.

'You may be right at that,' agreed Shamus, smiling.

Years before the giant man had been very successful in the illegal bare-knuckle fights that took place in secret in the backs of pubs and clubs. He rarely lost.

Aaden, Uncle's relative, was the leader of the band. The other members of the group were introduced as follows, Carlo, Bartram, and Lance. Grace was the girl singer.

Aaden said, 'Have you had lunch?' Uncle shook his head. 'Come in, we have just started,' he said, leading the way. Everybody was introduced to everyone else. Martyn was unsure if he would remember the names. Uncle leant towards him and said, 'I will remind you.'

Lunch was spread out over a large table. There was a lot of laughing while the bandmembers caught up. Martyn and the girl were checking each other out. In many ways she reminded him of Agatha. Martyn nibbled some cheese and biscuits, desperate to make a start, to see if he could do it with these experienced long-time professionals. It was mid-afternoon before the plates were pushed aside and they moved out onto the small stage in the hall. There was no sense of urgency. He was surprised how similar to Aunt May's it looked with the low stage, the rows of comfortable green-cushioned seating and in the far corner a small bar.

Martyn decided to do his own thing exactly as he would do it at Aunt May's, warm up with the easy notes then stretch himself as it all began to come together. As the instrument in his hands slowly came alive he relaxed. It didn't matter that he was in New York miles away from everything he knew. With his clarinet in his hands he was home. His heart and the instrument were singing in harmony. He was making it up as he went along. He would later develop it and name it after this incredible city that he realised he had fallen in love with. Now he was improvising on the first few bars, eyes tight shut, lost who knew where. The clarinet was singing about the tall buildings that went up into the sky. Some of the adverts climbed up so high on their walls they could only be seen from the skyscrapers opposite them. The ceaseless patterns woven by the yellow cabs in the street below were all involved in some fascinating dance. From on high they mimicked a disturbed ant's nest. There was an ever-restless crowd of people, each apparently with a purpose. There were knots of folk, some of them alive with laughter. Others obviously more serious. These tended to be the suits and briefcase brigade.

Now there was a piano accompaniment. Where had that come from? Now the two instruments were sharing a conversation. He heard the drum come in and a guitar, then the girl was scatting, using her voice as another instrument. He opened his eyes to check that it was not Agatha singing, her voice was so similar. He felt a pang of regret that she had gone home. He missed her. He saw everyone was playing along, like him they slowly stopped.

Aaden, sitting at his piano, said, 'Good afternoon, Martyn, I think you passed the interview. What is that called?'

'I think I will call it "New York". That's what triggered it.'

'Did you just make that up?' he asked. The boy nodded.

'What did I tell you, Aaden?' said Uncle. For the young man the rest of the afternoon passed in a haze of pleasure.

It was clear that the session was winding down when Uncle asked, 'Can Martyn play his song, his first one?'

'Yeh go for it, Martyn.'

'One thing I have to apologise for is that it's never the same twice,' said the young man.

'I have some copies of it,' said Uncle offering one to Grace for the words.

'Never you mind,' said Aaden. 'You get started, we'll jump in when we're ready.' Martyn began to play; it took him a while to make the transition from the euphoria of the afternoon to go back to what his life was before his music. His incompetence. He was sure his only real ability was this, his music. Having fallen into the river and endured waves breaking over his head and having to be rescued forced him to move ashore to live with Aunt May and Uncle. There was a plus to that. Aunt May was his biggest fan and spoilt him rotten.

Martyn was aware that there was a short silence when the music ended. The evening passed by in a blur. The audience were generous in their appreciation of the band's performance, Aaden was generous in his praise of Martyn's skill in one so young. The group sat into the small hours swapping stories and laughing. Martyn did not feel excluded, a band member often broke off to explain to him why what was being talked about was funny. For the first time in his life he felt part of something. It was an environment he was comfortable in. As the evening was winding down the band leader came and sat down next to Uncle and said, 'We are here for the rest of this week. Can you and Martyn stay that long?'

'Yes,' said Martyn, not waiting for Uncle to answer.

Everyone laughed. Uncle said, 'I will need to check with Aunt May, but unless there is a calamity back home I see no reason why not.'

Martyn was wearing the biggest smile ever. Going to bed that night he found that for some time sleep evaded him as he strolled through his memories of the day. Eventually in the small hours of the morning he slept. That first week with the band was to set the pattern. He would spend his formative years playing with small groups both in America and at home. He could never have imagined the course his later years would take.

CHAPTER 64

It was Sunday afternoon, a crowd of laughing smiling people were in the garden of the large house that Sophie grew up in and now owned in partnership with Tim. The couple had invited all the staff and their families to the party to celebrate the reopening of Victor Vieri's, Sophie's father's store. As an only child the large garden had been a sanctuary she could get lost in. A wide long lawn with perfectly mown grass stretching halfway down the garden, with a large white tent sat in the middle. At the end of the lawn a rustic arch enticed people to explore further through the centre of a rose-draped terrace. Her favourite rose, Albertine, was in full flower and filling the garden with its scent. This was almost universally true except for the area around the patio where a hog roast was coming to cooked perfection. The aroma was prompting people to ask if it was ready yet. Tim had been up since first light to set the process in motion. He was following the instructions he had been given the night before by Enzo, the company chef. Tim was hot and sweaty and had vowed to himself he would never do it again.

A little later Enzo, in his chef's uniform, walked over and asked, 'Tim would you like a shower and a sit down? I'm happy to take over if you want.'

Tim thought hard, he really didn't want to give up so close to the finish. But Enzo would be much better at the carving and serving. The thought of leaning over the heat and the smoke while he served everyone for the next hour made his mind up for him.

Pulling his apron off and handing it to Enzo, he said, 'Thanks, you will make a better job of the carving than I will.'

'You've done a good job of the cooking, Tim; you can come and help us with the barbeques in the restaurant any time.'

'No thanks,' said Tim, walking away.

The chef laughed. 'It's harder than it looks, isn't it?' he called after him. Tim nodded and walked on.

Tim intended to walk around the tables saying hallo to all the staff. He showered and changed out of his smoky clothing. Looking around he noticed that unsurprisingly the men and women who worked together were seated together.

Minutes later he felt someone take his hand. Recognising his wife's scent he moved her closer and kissed her cheek. He noticed a large group of people sitting at a long table away to his right. The men were all smartly dressed, and the women looked pretty in their party frocks. A selection of bottles, most of them open, occupied the centre of the table indicating the diversity of taste. The couple moved across to join the group that contained a number of the senior people in the organisation. Harry had apparently named the group the old originals. Tim and his wife Sophie were included in this group. They both objected strongly to being considered old.

Harry said, 'Here we are, you two, we have kept seats for you.'

Tim thanked him and said, 'We are going to walk round and say hallo to everyone in a bit.' He looked around the group. There was Tim's father, Tom, whose dog Beth was asleep under the table with her chin on his foot. Daisy and her badly burnt husband Declan were sitting there. He was doing remarkably well considering the extent of his injuries. Jessica and her partner Oliver were also present. Harry was sitting with his wife, Sara, who was berating him for telling a rather risqué joke, it didn't help that the rest of the men, that included Tom, Declan, Mr Rogers and Ben the Barbadian IT expert, were doubled up with laughter. Ben's wife had not come.

He explained to Tom that she was extremely shy. 'You must get her to come, she will be made very welcome, I can guarantee it.'

'I will tell her,' said Ben.

Sophie, who had overheard Ben and Tom's conversation, put her hand on Ben's shoulder and speaking quietly said, 'Next time make sure you introduce her to me, and I will introduce her to the other women.' Ben thanked her.

Tim saw Nanny through the kitchen window standing at the sink washing up. He waved, she, smiling, waved back.

Tim heard Ben ask his father when he had started his delicatessen stall. Tom regaled the group with his stories of travelling in Europe and some of the terrible destruction he had seen after the war and how poor and shattered the people were. They could not believe what had happened to them. They had been told they were the master race and now here they were crushed under the Allies' heel.

John the vintner asked Ben what had brought him to London and the horrid English weather. Ben, continuing, said, 'When I was growing up as a boy I had been besotted by the sights of London in the newspapers and the magazines, the pictures of St Paul's Cathedral, Buckingham Palace, Big Ben. When I was quite young I decided to work hard and earn enough money to come here to live. I came here on my own to start with. First off I shared a room with two other men, then I met my wife and we saved to get married. Our first home was a room on the second floor of an elderly building. It had a bed and a gas stove; we shared a bathroom down the hall with three other families. When my first winter arrived I thought I was going die of the cold. I could not believe how bitter it was. The wind hitting my face was really painful. My strongest memory of that time was the amazing shapes the ice made on the inside of the windows. I remember I stepped out of the front door on my way to work and slid five yards down the slope to the lamp post. I was clinging on just to stay upright. Someone walking past me out in the road said, "Copy me, they have gritted it." I did not understand but I followed their advice and managed to get to work. I wore newspaper inside my shirt most of that winter. The first thing I bought was a pair of long johns and to this day I rarely take them off. It has to be in the thirties before I am warm enough.'

Putting his hand on Ben's shoulder Tim said, 'Thank you for all your work with the IT, it is a lot more understandable now you have written out that crib for me. I have to admit I do still ask the girls for help occasionally.' Turning to face his wife he said, 'Sophie is good at it.'

'Ben, can you make sure your wife comes next time? We would love to see her,' said Sophie.

Afterwards everyone agreed the get-together had been a great success and they hoped it could happen every year.

CHAPTER 65

Bonny was a little late arriving at Aunt May's café where Martyn and the group were playing that Friday night. She had chosen her favourite clothes, a dark red trouser suit. She had felt the need to get out of her formal office attire.

She had not known how popular the band had become locally. She was searching to find somewhere to sit. Having had a long day she had no desire stand up all evening. Standing on tiptoe she spotted an end seat halfway back from the stage. An attractive young man was sitting alongside the vacant chair. Making her way towards it. She saw that the people on the other side of him were elderly. Doubtless he was waiting for his girlfriend or some such who was just about to arrive.

Pointing at the seat she asked, 'Is anyone sitting ...?'

The young man interrupted her, saying, 'No, no, please.' Once she was seated he opened a large box of Maltesers and offered her one.

'Oh that's kind, thank you.' Taking one she said, 'I have a terrible chocolate habit.'

'You had better take more than one then,' he said laughing. 'Cup your hands.' When she had complied he shook a good number into her palm.

'Oh no, that's plenty,' said Bonny, rather embarrassed at this stranger's generosity.

'I'm Joshua,' he said, holding out his hand. He looked extremely relaxed in his dark grey trousers that were offset by a colourful Caribbean shirt.

'Bonny,' she said as she shook his hand, trying not to drop any sweets.

'Have you heard them before?' he asked, pointing at the stage.

Putting her hand to her mouth, she said, 'No,' trying not to spit chocolate all over him.

'Nor me,' he added.

He laughed, realising her problem, 'Would you like some more Maltesers?' he asked.

She responded by shaking her head. The mouthful of chocolate prohibited her from answering. Eventually she said, 'No, thank you. I know the clarinettist. He is the son of my boss, Tim Cooper, who owns Sophie's.' She gave him the once over from the corner of her eyes. She guessed he was Caribbean. He was obviously extremely fit given the spread of his chest and the muscles showing under his shirt. She felt a strong physical attraction towards this man. Bonny became aware that her trouser leg had risen up and was showing her boot. She knew he had seen it. Now he will change seats or ignore me all evening, she thought. She could not have been more wrong.

'Polio?' he asked in a calm, questioning voice.

She flushed bright red. No one had ever asked her about her leg. They had become embarrassed; one young woman had shuddered when she saw it. Some had moved away from her as though she was contagious. She was sure she had failed to get jobs because of it. She had become hardened to all this, what had stunned her was him apparently wanting to discuss it.

'Yes,' she said, 'I contracted it as a child. Why do you ask?'

'I am a nurse in a specialist unit. It's my job. I have found it easier if we get the nasty facts out in the open straight away. How old were you?'

'About five, I spent a long time in hospital, then I had to learn to walk again.'

'That's tough?'

'Yes.'

Then the clapping broke out as the group's leader Mr Lawrence walked onto the stage, sat at the piano and started to play the first few bars of Mack the Knife. Then Adam the drummer walked on and began to lay down the rhythm. Both of them were playing extremely quietly. Mr Lawrence spoke, saying, 'Tonight, ladies and gentlemen, just back from playing in NEW YORK,' he shouted out the name, 'with a professional band it's our very own Martyn Cooper with his clarinet.' His school pals and the locals who knew him clapped and hollered. Agatha followed him on singing, her wonderful voice fitting the music perfectly.

* * * * *

'Will you have a meal with me afterwards?' he asked. 'I would like to talk some more.'

His breathing into her ear as he spoke made her spine go all squiggly. This was a word from her childhood, whatever, she enjoyed the sensation. She was rendered speechless; she remembered a word her mother sometimes used was fast. This described someone with all the chat up lines. Searching his face and his eyes she could see no mischief there, another of her mother's words. She recalled a conversation where her mother explained about the birds and the bees and then warned her that some men only wanted sex and did not care whether you got pregnant or not. If you did they would be gone, never to be seen again. Then she added, 'You can get pregnant the first time, run from any man who tells you otherwise.'

'I can understand why you are thinking about whether to accept my invitation,' he said, breaking her train of thought. 'If I tell you that Aunt May is my real aunt and we will be eating here, is that ok?'

Now she was puzzled. Was this a date? If so it was the first one she had been on, ever. Should she ask him? No she was not going to do that; she was going to go carefully and see what happened. 'Yes please,' she mouthed.

'I have to go to the loo,' whispered Bonny as she was getting to her feet.

Aunt May took the opportunity while Bonny was gone to talk quietly in Joshua's ear. 'Be gentle with her, she is much younger than her years. If you hurt her you will have me to answer to.' Aunt May was the only person he was afraid of. He had seen her fire a member of staff who had been caught stealing. It would have been less painful if she had flayed him alive.

He nodded and then said, 'Can I book a table for when this is over?'

'You can, but remember what I have said.' She knew that some of his girlfriends had not lasted long. Everybody liked Bonny, you could not help yourself. Physically she was extremely attractive. Her happy personality and her ready laugh were wonderfully unique. He watched Bonny dancing back towards him, her body moving with the music. She looked as though each part of her was doing its own thing. Men could not do this, or not many of them anyway. In his opinion it was an entirely female thing, something he could watch all day long. Her vitality and happiness bubbled out of her. This was amazing when you consider at five years old because of the polio she was forced to learn to stand and walk again. It was not difficult for him to admit she was a special woman. The music ended all too soon, they were both on their feet clapping like mad. Slowly the café began to empty. A few diners had like them booked tables. Joshua spotted Aunt May beckoning them.

'Dinner's ready,' he said pointing to a corner of the café. Bonny felt extremely special when he pulled out her chair. The food looked amazing and tasted better still. She didn't recognise all of the ingredients but that was unimportant, she loved Caribbean food. She would talk to Aunt May. After the first few mouthfuls and a sip of the squash they had ordered, Joshua said, 'Tell me about the leg.'

Bonny frowned and asked, 'Are you usually this blunt?'

'I'm sorry, I was back in work mode, but I'm genuinely interested. How did you learn to walk again?'

'By falling on the floor and then working out how to get up again.'

'That is obviously painful,' he said.

'Especially when your mother refuses to help you up,' added Bonny.

'By golly that's hard. So she stood there and watched you struggle?'

'Yes and cry,' said Bonny, palming a tear away. 'Sometimes she cried as well.'

'That could be considered cruel,' he observed. 'But it wasn't, was it? It's called tough love. Am I right?'

Bonny was nodding and brushing more tears away. 'When I could get up on my own I threw the stick away.'

Joshua was silent. He was sitting very still, his arms across his chest, thinking hard. With his job he had met some remarkable people. It was impossible to know by their appearance which were the brave vessels that contained an almost inexhaustible supply of strength and courage and who refused to accept defeat. They could be children or the really old or anywhere in between. You never knew. This young women was one of that extraordinary group.

He leant forward and reached for her hand and enclosed it in both of his, saying as he did so. 'You are a remarkable woman, Bonny.'

She could feel her face flaming scarlet, she had never been called a woman before by anyone, especially an extremely attractive young man. That squiggly feeling was back.

'You would not think that if you had seen me in the early days, fighting a battle with my leg and my balance, muttering swear words under my breath. More than once the stick was hurled across the room. When it got out of hand Mother would stop my pocket money then buy me the sweets anyway. There was one incident when I fell down coming out of Sainsbury's. It was one of the few times I recognised that Mother was embarrassed. I was blocking the doorway, she went to help me. "Don't touch me," I'd growled loudly. I struggled to stand, eventually using the door handle and the wall I got up. I had a cracking bruise on my elbow, that must have hit the floor first. I do remember a middle-aged man and his wife pushed past me quite roughly. I nearly fell again.'

Shaking his head he asked, 'How did you get on at school?'

Bonny thought for a moment then said, 'Once I sorted the school bully out it was fine.' 'What do you mean, sorted out?' asked Joshua.

'If I tell you, you must promise not to laugh.'

He nodded agreement.

'I would walk around the garden at home pretending I was Princess Bonny defending my kingdom from the dragons, swishing my stick like a sword.'

'What has this to do with the bully?' he asked.

'It was playtime, sometimes I was still using my stick when I got tired. She kicked my stick away and down I went. One of her henchmen kicked it further away, laughing as she did so. One of my friends called my name and kicked it back again. I was quickly up on my feet and became Princess Bonny. I remember a quotation from somewhere, I don't know where, but I "smote them hip and thigh" as hard as I could. They never bothered me or my friends again.'

'Did you get into trouble?'

'No, the headmaster asked me if I needed the nurse to look at anything. I shook my head and said no. He finished by saying, as long as you are ok, right, well done, carry on, and that was that.'

Recalling the conversation later Joshua believed the quote was Shakespearean.

* * * * *

They leant back in their chairs having eaten every mouthful of the amazing meal. It did not matter that she was unable to recognise some of the ingredients. She would ask later. Aunt May and Uncle appeared, each carrying a drink.

'Can we join you?' they asked. Joshua knew this was his aunt's determination to chaperone Bonny. He had to admit to himself that he had established a reputation as a lothario with young women. To his utter surprise he felt extremely defensive of this young lady sitting opposite him. As Aunt May sat down beside him he gave her a hard stare. She smiled then looked away, pretending that she had no idea why he had done that. Bonny was quizzed about her job. Her enthusiasm was obvious, as was her respect for Tim and Sophie. She explained how well she worked with her immediate boss, Jessica, and how she was trusted to do really complicated tasks and research. After a few minutes of eulogising about it she suddenly blushed, then apologised for hogging the conversation.

Shaking his head, Uncle said, 'It's good to see a youngster so keen on what they do.' From then on Bonny stayed quiet, listening to the conversation about the friends and relatives back home in the West Indies. It was apparent that in spite of the vast distances that separated the families they remained extremely close.

After some time had elapsed Uncle said, 'I'm going to find a comfy chair, who will join me?' The four of them made their way into the back room, 'You youngsters take that couch, we will sit over here,' Uncle said while waving his arms to add emphasis to his instruction.

Bonny had to smother a smile; Aunt May was trying to keep them apart while Uncle was trying to achieve the reverse.

Bonny sat and listened to the conversations around her. She was very aware of the young man sitting beside her. When he lent forward to make a point their knees touched. She pretended to examine her hands in her lap to hide the blush that had suffused her face. When she next looked up Aunt

May had fixed her with critical eyes. Bonny ignored her. Eventually the evening drew to a close. Bonny wished it would go on forever.

Joshua turned to her and asked, 'How are you getting home?'

'By bus,' was the reply.

'I can give you a lift,' he responded.

'Are you on your motorbike?' asked Aunt May, in a voice that clearly indicated disapproval.

'Yes,' was the response, 'and Bonny is wearing trousers,' he continued. 'She will be safer with me rather than a bus load of drunks.'

'I have never been on a motorbike. It sounds like fun,' said Bonny.

'There you go then. That decides it, I will take you home.'

The goodbyes were said and Aunt May promised to write down the ingredients for the dinner.

Outside Joshua helped her into his heavy mid-brown leather jacket and placed a spare helmet on her head.

Bonny thought the jacket smelt exciting. It was an admixture of leather and the slightly intoxicating warm man smell of him and his deodorant. She waited while he mounted the bike, then he was looking down and indicating where she should put her foot. Following his instruction she lifted herself onto the bike, threw her leg over the back of the seat, found the other footrest and held his waist. He jumped on the kick starter and the bike roared into life. Even inside her helmet the noise was loud. She felt him lift the bike upright and push the stand away with his foot. There was an audible snick as he engaged first gear and the bike moved smoothly away.

Bonny was so excited; she had never done anything like this before. She could feel the enormous power of the machine through her body.

Approaching a corner he turned his head towards her and shouted, 'Hold tight.' As he leant the bike over.

Bonny's heart was in her mouth, she was experiencing a mixture of fear and an all-consuming adrenaline rush. Searching for a better grip she slid her hands around his waist and clamped her knees onto his legs, pressing her body into close contact with his back. It was not only the speed, it was the intimacy. She'd never had this level of human contact with a man before. Especially not one who was a complete stranger. She moved her head to rest on his shoulder out of the wind. Her body was undergoing a range of emotions, not least of which was a growing arousal. She quickly became accustomed to the motions of the bike and learnt to move with him. This was the most exciting thing she had ever done.

Joshua was very aware of the close contact of this extraordinary woman who had broken down all his defences. In all his numerous affairs he had never felt this level of attraction. He had made a total commitment of his heart, body and soul to this woman.

Stationary at a set of red traffic lights he closed the throttle so that the engine noise was a low burble. Turning his head he asked, 'Are you ok?'

Bonny's smile said it all. 'It's so exciting,' she replied. As the green light appeared, allowing them to proceed, she replaced her cheek on his back.

As Joshua swung the bike into the next bend she used it as an excuse to hug him harder.

Joshua mistakenly assumed that she was frightened so slowed down. Bonny was about to ask him to speed up again when she changed her mind, realising it meant that the journey would last longer.

He was experiencing a range of conflicting emotions. Because she was so innocent in many ways he felt extremely protective of her. Now with her breasts and her inner thighs pressed hard against him he was experiencing a wholly different range of emotions, mostly predatory. He could hear Aunt May's stern warning not to hurt her. He wouldn't do that, but he could imagine doing a number of other things to her, gently.

* * * * *

The rest of the journey was over far too soon. Getting off the bike she was unsure what, if anything, was about to happen. He was still sat on the bike, the engine died. She removed her helmet and handed it to him, then slipped off the jacket. Stowing the spare helmet and donning his jacket he said, 'I will wait until you are safe indoors.'

Bonny stood for a moment, unsure if the evening was going to end as coldly as this. On the last part of the ride she had visualised a scenario where he asked her for her phone number then kissed her cheek. She would stand watching as he rode away, him waving as he cranked the bike over into the bend and disappeared from sight.

Instead he had not even got off the bike. It was clear he was uninterested in her in any way except clinically.

She lay in bed that night realising what a colossal impact meeting him had made on her. She buried her face in the pillow so that her mother would not hear her sobbing. It was obvious that once again her leg had prohibited any form of romantic relationship. She was now sure she would die a lonely, unfulfilled old woman. In the grey light of dawn she finally found some sleep.

* * * * *

Unbeknown to Bonny, Joshua was having similar problems. His brain kept sending mini scenarios of her that had occurred during the evening. Pictures of her laughing, her cornflower blue eyes that carried a wonderful sparkle that came from deep within her. He was aware that she was the most beautiful woman, girl, child he had ever met. He had watched her switch between all of these ages in the course of the evening. He was sure this was completely artless. She did not know she was doing it.

Neither of them could know that they were both experience the same internal tug, a need to be each with the other.

Bonny's mother noticed a change in her daughter. When she enquired Bonny said, 'I think the second glass of wine was a mistake.'

'Did you get a meal?' asked her mother.

'Yes, Aunt May and Uncle invited me to dine with them. Don't ask me what we ate but it was very tasty.'

'That was kind of them.'

'Yes it was,' Bonny replied.

'Did I hear a motor bike when you came in?'

'Yes a nephew of theirs gave me a lift home. He rode very carefully, I would have liked him to go faster, it is extremely exciting.'

'I'm not sure if I am happy with you riding motorbikes.'

'Mother you don't need to worry. he gave me his leather jacket and a crash helmet.'

* * * * *

The next day Jessica noticed she was quiet, she decided it was a continuation of the new Bonny who was a lot less effusive. Jessica was aware that her own relationship with Oliver had highlighted Bonny's solitary status. She was also aware that the young woman blamed her shortened leg for driving the boys away.

A week went by. Bonny was becoming ever quieter. On Friday she decided she would go back to Aunt May's. She would use it to end this silly malaise. She tried to convince herself that he would not be there. Bonny suspected that was a load of toffee, she would go anyway. If he did speak to her she would be polite and walk away.

She had dressed early in her usual plain clothing, smart black trousers and jacket but had sat watching the television, taking none of it in. There was a moment when the decision to go was rescinded. Then her mind was changed yet again. She was angry with herself for behaving like a silly teenager. Bonny had walked out of the house banging the door behind her. She'd heard her mother's loud complaint from the kitchen as she strode away. She arrived later than the previous week so joined a shorter queue at the door. As she was about to enter her arm was held just firmly enough to stop her walking in. Looking around she discovered it was him. He was smiling at her.

'Will you sit with me?' he asked. Forgetting all the promises she had made to herself she nodded. He was dressed similarly to the week before, smart trousers and a colourful shirt, his leather jacket hung over his shoulder. They both enjoyed the music and the food. Again she was not sure what it was, but it was tasty. This time they had sat together at a small side table. Aunt May was busy elsewhere, Uncle waved from behind the counter.

'Can we talk?' he asked, as they stood up from their seats. It was obvious from his expression that he was unsure of her reply.

After a moment's hesitation she nodded. Holding her arm he led her out of the building and turned towards his motorbike that she had noticed earlier.

Arriving beside the bike he opened the carrier on the back and reached inside for the spare helmet, but did not lift it out.

'Are you ok with this?' he asked. 'I thought we could go somewhere quiet and talk.'

She banished her mother's voice in her head shouting about stranger danger and not going with men she didn't know.

'Are you sure?' he asked.

She nodded.

Now the engine was burbling with him sitting astride. Buckling on the helmet and zipping up the leather jacket she swung her leg over the saddle. She adopted the same stance as the week before, clamping herself to his back with her arms and legs. She thought sod what may happen, I am so unhappy and lonely I don't care. I don't want to spend the rest of my life a virgin. spinster

Joshua rode down a narrow track to the riverside, stopping the bike near an old wooden seat.

He hasn't just discovered this, she thought, she ignored the warning bells that were once again ringing in her head. They settled themselves on the bench. Looking out at the river she was surprised how beautiful it was in spite of the fact it was dark. The myriad coloured lights moved as though alive on the shifting surface of the black water. A tug slid by, jumbling the colours into broken shards. All you could see of the tug was a nearly invisible dark silhouette with three riding lights.

They removed their helmets and he started to talk. 'I hoped I might see you tonight, I have missed you this week.'

She had no response. Was this a chat up line? she asked herself. With no previous experience with men she had no idea. They talked for two hours, sharing childhood memories and some of the memorable things about their families and their jobs. He talked about back home on the island, the sun and the sand and the interesting people he knew. Her shiver broke the spell.

'I must take you home,' he said rising from the seat.

'Can we go somewhere for a cup of tea?' she asked.

Looking at his watch he said, 'I think everywhere will be closed.' He paused and then said, 'I can make you a cup of tea at home if you trust me.'

'Of course I trust you,' was the response. A beatific smile on her face. Can you trust me is the question, she thought. And no is the answer. This was the perfect scenario to lose her virginity. She would address any problems that arose later. This was the only man who had ever shown any interest in her. She remembered how rude the boys at school had been about her leg. The ride to his flat was soon over, once again she had cuddled him all the way there. She trotted up the stairs behind him to his first-floor flat. Much to her surprise it was remarkable tidy. There were numerous paintings with a clear African heritage. Pride of place was held by a larger than life-size warrior's carved wooden head and headdress. This was beautifully painted. She was

THE NEXT GENERATION

a little unnerved by how lifelike it was, the piercing dark eyes seemed to follow her wherever she went. The couple continued their chat while Joshua prepared their tea. She asked where the toilet was, he showed her. Again it was clean and tidy. She did what she had to do then undid another button on her blouse to give him a better view of her not unattractive cleavage. When she returned to the lounge he was sitting at one end of a small red settee set back a little from a low, small, black lacquered wood coffee table. The two cups of tea were placed on round cork mats. She purposely sat close enough so that they brushed knees whenever either of them leant forwards to reach or replace the teacup. When her cup was almost empty she left her knee touching. Now uncomfortable, he moved away a little.

She said, 'Can we cuddle? I got really cold out there.' She moved so that there was much more contact between them.

Now really unsure he put a tentative arm around her. He felt her lean into him. Suddenly he heard Aunt May's stern warning not to hurt her. Removing his arm, he said. 'This isn't you, what's going on?'

Bonny looked at him and burst into tears. Like most men he had no idea what to do with a crying women, so he put his arm back around her and asked, 'Whatever is wrong?' handing her his hanky as he spoke.

Fighting back the tears she decided to tell him the truth. 'You are the only man who has ever shown any interest in me.' She had emphasised the ever. 'I have a real fear of never being a mum, never having a child to cuddle, never knowing the love of a man and dying a spinster. You are a very attractive man; I had hoped to seduce you. I have no idea how to do that and I have obviously failed.' This was said with a crumpled brow and more tears.

Joshua held her for some time while she regained her composure. Then he said, 'This must be the most peculiar seduction scene ever. If you saw it at the pictures it would have no credibility at all, far too much conversation, not enough sex. I have been controlling my baser instincts all evening,' he said, laughing.

Now Bonny was laughing as well.

He was still laughing as he asked, 'Would you like to accompany me to the bedroom, miss, where if we are careful I can address some of your problems.'

'I will need a shower,' she said.

'That will be our pleasure, madam.'

Did he mean they would shower together, was that a step too far? Also she realised she would see him naked as well. Minutes later they were standing outside the warming shower while they undressed each other. He was stunned by her body. He realised that she dressed plainly so as not to draw attention to herself. She was extremely beautiful under this rather severe clothing.

She was thinking similarly. She loved his colour that was a gift from the Caribbean sun. He was the first to start soaping her. It was the most pleasurable thing anyone had done for her. Spotting another bar of soap she began soaping him. His hands were everywhere, gently soaping her body. Both of them were spreading the soap ever more intimately, his hands dropped below her waist, and she was gone. Now she had both hands on his shoulders to help her remain standing as the sensations shook her body.

Joshua quickly scrubbed himself clean with a large white flannel while Bonny dried herself in a large colourful towel, watching his progress as he rinsed himself under the shower. When he had finished she helped dry him. Now rather nervous she followed him into the bedroom. Sensing that she was unsure he reached into the drawer on his side of the bed and withdrew a pot of Nivea skin cream for women.

Showing her the pot he asked, 'Would you like me to …?'

Snatching it away from him she said, 'Perhaps another day. Now I just want you to get on with it, please.' Her voice betrayed her uncertainty.

He opened the same drawer and withdrew a packet of condoms. She felt she should look away as he fitted it, but she was unable to. Lifting himself above her he found her and pushed gently in. There was a little resistance, then it was fine.

'Put more weight on me,' she commanded. He obliged. The couple were quickly carried away. He was surprised by how enthusiastic her participation was. She became ever more voluble. It sounded as though she was crying but she was not trying to push him off, she was if anything holding him tighter. She was lifting her hips to meet his thrusts. Seconds later his senses flew apart. Realising she had not joined him in the climax he continued. Moments later her breathing became more ragged and uneven, there were words he could not understand, her crying out got louder. With a loud shout she reached the top of her mountain.

She was still crying. He went to roll off. She wrapped her arms and legs more tightly around him to keep him there.

'Please stay, I don't want you to leave me yet.' The sentence was broken up by her need to breathe.

'Why are you crying?' he asked. 'Did I hurt you?'

'No,' she replied, 'it was just so much more than I thought it would be. Can we do it again in a bit?'

'Yes we can but you need to ring your mother,' he said, kissing her nose before he rolled away.

Standing up she asked, 'What am I going to say?' She was unaware that in her concern for the upcoming phone call she had not thought to cover herself, thereby giving Joshua a wonderful view of her naked body.

His response was, 'My God, you're beautiful.'

She went bright red and pulled a thin cover off the bed to drape around herself. Although embarrassed she was thrilled at the compliment.

'Tell her you are staying with a relative of Aunt May's,' suggested Joshua.

On the way to the phone she had an idea. Speaking to her mother she whispered, 'Mum, I'm ok. I am staying with a relative of Aunt May's.'

'Who?' asked her mother.

'A relative of Aunt May's,' she repeated, still whispering. 'I can't shout, other people are sleeping here. Love you, Mum, I will see you in the morning, bye.'

On the way back to bed she thought about how well he knew his way around a woman's body and how skilled he was. Returning to bed she found Joshua sleeping. Getting into bed as carefully as possible so as not to wake him she began stroking his body. She loved the colour of him. He was a gorgeous honey brown. Now he was naked she was more aware that he was in really good shape with a six pack and muscled arms, she was beginning to move the cover further down when he came awake and grabbed her wrist, making her jump. He began to tickle her, with all the thrashing about, they were both naked, both hysterical with joyous laughter. Moments later they were once again making love. This time it was slow as he explored her entire body. Him sucking her toes drove her crazy, his kisses became ever more intimate as he slowly moved up her body. When he reached the centre of her she tried to hold him in place. His stay was brief, denying her the closure she was desperate for. Later the two of them were locked together as they reached the pinnacle. She didn't cry this time. They slept in each other's arms.

CHAPTER 66

He woke first and lay there thinking hard. He realised that for the first time in his life he was in love. He turned to look at her. She appeared so young, so fragile, so extraordinarily beautiful, so innocent. Not as innocent as she was last night though. His laugh was a quiet, deep rumble that woke her. He was aware that something within him had changed fundamentally. It was no longer just all about him. He was experiencing a complex range of emotions. He realised that this woman was who he was supposed to spend the rest of his days with. He could not imagine journeying through life without her. He wanted her to have his babies, their babies. He needed to get her commitment today. A counterpoint to these emotions swept through him. It was a deep fear of losing her. He had, as she knew, known a lot of women. He had to prove she was not just another conquest. He would buy her an engagement ring this morning and see her mum afterwards.

'Tea?' he asked, as he was leaving the bed. She nodded, barely awake.

Bonny had woken confused, not knowing where she was, then her memories of last night returned. A bright red flush suffused her face. Lifting the edge of the blanket her greatest fear was realised, she was stark naked.

'I will get you a dressing gown in a moment, but first I have something I need to ask you.' As he was saying this he had knelt beside the bed. She noticed he was down on one knee wearing only a pair of black cotton shorts.

'I understand I have only known you for a week, but you are all I have thought about ever since that first day. This may seem too fast and crazy, but I want to marry you, I want to have babies with you. Bonny Atkins, will you marry me? I haven't got a ring, but I will buy one today, then we will go and tell your mum.'

Bonny looked at him, then the tears began to flow. 'That's not funny, you are being even crueller than the boys at school.' She began to struggle to get out of bed. She was past caring whether she was naked or not.

Holding her in place gently with one hand he said, 'Listen, I am not joking, honestly I have thought of nothing else since I met you. I know you are the one. I fell in love with you at first sight. I am a good bet; I have a good job. I am not a drunkard. I own this flat.' He did in fact own the whole building, all three flats, but he thought she may not believe him if he said three.

'I want us to get engaged today, married in the near future. I am really frightened I may lose you now I have found you. Please, please, say you will at least get engaged today.'

She thought for a moment, then started trying to get out of bed again, saying, 'No, no, this is nonsense, I'm going home.' There was one thing that gave her pause for thought. She remembered a girl at college who had spent a night with a man and never left. They were married a year later. Could he be telling the truth, she wondered?

Now he was desperately racking his brains to find a way of convincing her that he was in earnest. 'Will you come with me to Aunt May's? She can read me like a book, she will be able to tell you if I am telling the truth.' The look on his face revealed the desperate frightened child in him. She didn't believe he could fake that. Just to be sure they would go and see Aunt May and call his bluff if that was what it was.

'I will ring Aunt May now and get you a dressing gown,' he said as he left the room.

Bonny ceased her efforts to leave the bed and began to think this bizarre offer through. His aunt would definitely know if he was lying. If he wasn't then maybe? Did she want to get married so she could have babies? That was a given. Did she love this man? She could not tell, he was extremely attractive and highly skilled in the bedroom. This was an assumption, she had no yardstick to judge him by. Also she recognised she may not get many more offers. Who was she kidding? It was likely to be no more offers.

Right, we would see his aunt. If he meant what he said it would be better than the bitter cold of a solitary existence. Did she love him? There was an attraction. Was it love? Maybe it would grow. Should she wait for the emotional fireworks going off, the brass bands playing?

She was intelligent enough to realise that from past experience it was highly unlikely. Yes, Aunt May was a good idea. She was very down to earth, she would countenance no chicanery on his part.

Joshua returned to the bedroom carrying a cup of tea and a dressing gown slung over his arm. 'I have spoken to my aunt, and she has invited us to breakfast in about an hour's time.'

Standing in the shower she realised if she was going to walk away now was the time. She stood with the warm water falling on her while she kicked the options around in her head. Whatever she decided she would never forget last night. Until then she had never understood the real meaning of the word ecstasy. She felt her heart move in her chest as she recalled how he had made her feel and she could hear again his shouting her name as he joined her at the top of the mountain. She could not be certain but on at least one occasion she believed she had seen moisture in the corners of his eyes. Fifty minutes later they were tapping on the side door of the café. Aunt May took them through to the private rooms at the back of the building, sat them down, poured cups of tea, then said, 'So why are you here?'

Joshua and Bonny looked at each other, waiting for the other to speak. Finally Joshua said, 'I have asked her to marry me.'

The older woman jolted back in her chair and then said, 'You have only known each other for five minutes. Have you slept together?' Turning to Bonny, she asked, 'Are you worried you may be pregnant?' Now turning to Joshua she barked at him, her growing anger all too apparent. 'I warned you, didn't I?'

Bonny jumped in and said, 'Can I explain to you in private, please?'

'Follow me, girl,' was the response. Bonny was led through to a small office. 'Sit,' was the command. 'Now talk to me,' she said.

Bonny, now red in the face, explained that she had never had a boyfriend. She had only been ridiculed and hurt by boys because of her foot. She explained briefly what had happened between her and Joshua, including her pathetic attempt to seduce him.

There was a long silence while Aunt May considered all she had been told. She felt desperately sorry for the girl. She recognised that for men the woman's appearance was the first trigger. The boot would not work in her favour in that first glance.

'Do you love him, Bonny?'

There was a long silence then the girl replied, 'I don't know, he is extremely attractive, and very caring, and my foot does not seem to freak him out. It really upsets some people.'

'Could you live with him?'

'I cannot know, can I? He wants us to get engaged.'

As she said this they both heard a man's firm deliberate footsteps walking down the passage towards them.

Stepping into the room, he said, 'I couldn't sit out there any longer while the rest of my life was decided in here. I have a proposition. Supposing I buy you an engagement ring today and a necklace, and you wear the ring around your neck and put it on your finger when you decide you are ready?'

Both the women noticed he had not said if. Plonking himself down onto a chair he said, 'Aunt May, I promise you I fell in love with this one as soon as I clapped eyes on her. I have known other men who have said that you always know when you meet the one.'

Aunt May knew this young man very well and recognised he was in love with this beautiful young women, who in many ways was still a child.

Now addressing Bonny, she said, 'I believe my nephew is telling the truth. It's now up to you to decide what you want to do. Just don't get pregnant.'

There was a silence, waiting for her to speak. The multicoloured fireworks she had experienced last night threw her previous existence into a collection of pale grey images. To have a man desire her was something she had not thought would ever happen.

Now speaking out loud almost to herself, she said, 'Arranged marriages seem to work sometimes, maybe this could.'

Joshua was growing ever more hopeful but said nothing because he didn't want to break the spell. He felt as though she were coming around to his way of thinking.

Bonny was thinking, I could do a lot worse, he loves me, he's kind and clever, he's not poor. I may wait forever for someone else. Finally, she said, 'Can we spend time together and see how it goes? I will let you know my decision when I have decided.' Joshua leapt from his chair and crushed her in a bear hug.

Laughing, she said, 'I can't breathe.'

'So what's your next step?' asked Aunt May.

'I want to do this out in the open,' said Josh, 'there will be no creeping about in the shrubbery. For all the women I have known it was never love. When I met you, Bonny, I knew you were the one. You sat down beside me, and my world stood on its head. I will marry you when you say yes, and we will have lots of beautiful children.'

Aunt May went to reprimand him but then changed her mind. Bonny would never be able to say that he had not been forthright in his declaration of his love for her or his determination to have her for his wife.

Uncle walked in, greeting everyone; he could feel an atmosphere in the room but was unable to determine what had generated it. 'So what's going on?' he asked.

Joshua looked at Bonny, who nodded. 'I have asked Bonny to marry me.'

'Good on you.'

Aunt May jumped in before he could say more. 'Bonny has not said yes yet.'

'Surely you will though, girl. Anyone who looks at you together can see you are a perfect match, each a half of the whole.'

Aunt May, now cross, said, 'Shut up, you silly old man. It's not a decision to be taken lightly.'

'Well let's wait and see,' said Uncle. 'Bonny I will say this, if you do become a member of our family I for one will be delighted.' Somehow Bonny felt sure that if this marriage did go ahead Uncle would always be there to fight her corner.

Turning to Joshua, he said, 'Don't you mess this one up, boy, can you hear me?'

Joshua nodded his head. Bonny thanked the kindly old man, smiling as she did so.

Aunt May tutted and shook her head. 'This is one of the most important decisions she will ever have to make. The girl has to make her own mind up, leave her be.'

'I know what I know,' was his response, saying this as he settled into his favourite armchair near the fire.

'Don't listen, Bonny, he thinks he can predict the future,' grumbled Aunt May. Once again she was shaking her head. After a quick breakfast the couple made their excuses, saying that Joshua was keen to get the necklace and the ring and speak to Bonny's mum.

The young couple were in a quaint jeweller's shop. This one was owned by a short, round, jovial elderly man in a conker-brown corduroy suit. It would appear that his ruddy features wore a permanent smile. He was thoroughly bald; indeed, his pate was polished to a high shine.

The shop was wonderfully old fashioned, Bonny thought for a moment and decided the shop and the owner felt friendly. A small sign above the door said Horace G Goodey, Jeweller.

Bonny, after checking that they were the only customers in the shop, explained to the jeweller what they were looking for, the ring and a necklace. Then she explained that they had known each other for only a few days when Joshua had proposed.

'I have never known anybody to do this, but it is extremely romantic,' he said. 'Let me see what I can suggest.' He walked around his shop, picking up a ring. He looked at it for a moment then put it back into the display, mumbling to himself under his breath.

After a few minutes they heard the owner say, 'Oh yes this is superb.' Returning to the counter, he said, 'Try this on please.'

'I don't want to put it on my ring finger. Can I put it on my right hand?'

'Of course,' was the response.

The ring was white gold with a tiny rose made up of small diamonds that sparkled on her finger, exhibiting the full range of the colours of a rainbow. Now Bonny was reaching for her hanky. Even if this romance came to nothing she had at least known what it was like to be made love to. She would not die a virgin. A spinster maybe. What a horrid word. Maiden was a far kinder term, although now no longer applicable.

The young couple were both delighted with the ring.

'Do you want to look at any others?' he asked.

'No thanks,' said Bonny, looking at Joshua, who was nodding. 'This is beautiful.'

'You will think me strange,' said the proprietor, 'but I believe the ring chooses the wearer. If it is the wrong ring it doesn't matter how much it costs, it will never look good. Is this ok?' he asked, showing Joshua the price. The young man nodded.

'Now we want a necklace, a fine one. Nothing heavy I assume?' asked the owner. This question was addressed to Bonny.

'Yes please,' she replied.

The jeweller resumed pulling open small shallow drawers, umming and ahhing to himself as before.

Bonny took the opportunity to ask him how long the shop had been in existence.

After a momentary pause he said, 'Sixty-two years. I worked here with my father, who started it as soon as I left school. My wife and I have no children, so who knows.' There was an obvious note of regret in his voice.

Turning back to the counter, he said, 'I cannot choose between them, it has to be your decision.' As he was speaking he was arranging the two necklaces on a black velvet covered display board laid on the counter.

Joshua, who had said almost nothing so far, now pointed at the heavier chain, saying, 'This looks stronger.' She picked up the one he had chosen and nodded her head in agreement.

'I am so moved by your story I will gift you the necklace,' said Mr Goodey.

For one mad moment as she was sliding the ring from her finger she was strongly tempted to give Joshua the ring and ask him to put it on her ring finger. Then the jeweller picked up the ring and reached towards her for the chain. Wrapping them nicely he placed them carefully in their respective pretty boxes. These were made of a white card with a finely drawn gold motif. She was unsure how she felt. For just a few seconds she had teetered on the edge of becoming engaged. The two men were sorting out the finances. She turned her back on them to them to dab away the tears unseen. She had a dreadful premonition that because she had not acted on her feelings in that moment her chance of marriage was snatched away. On top of that she had now to go and tell her mum, who may well think she had gone insane.

Arriving home Bonny knocked on her front door. She didn't feel able to march in without introducing Joshua first.

After a short delay her mother opened the door and said, 'Have you forgotten your key?' then seeing Joshua said, 'Have you brought a friend home?'

'Sort of, Mum, we will explain. This is Joshua, he's a nurse.'

'Nice to meet you, Joshua, please come in. Tea?' she asked.

'Mum, can we talk first, please?'

'I will put the kettle on, I won't be a moment.'

As her mum left the room Bonny rolled her eyes and mouthed sorry at Joshua, and he said quietly, 'No problem.' He was obviously far more relaxed than she was.

Returning to the room her mother said, 'There is obviously something very important you want to tell me.'

Joshua said, 'Can I tell you about myself? As you can see I was born in the Caribbean, my father is a doctor, and my mother is a senior nurse. I am in charge of the nursing side of a department that deals with damage to limbs et cetera. Bonny would be in my department if there was a problem. I own my own house outright; I have no debts and I am comfortably well off.'

'You want to marry my daughter?'

'I am going to just come out with it. I met your daughter about a week ago and fell in love. I knew she was the one. My father said he met my mother across a hospital bed when he was on ward rounds and knew she was the one. I want to spend the rest of my life with her. I don't know what Bonny thinks.' The kettle's whistle was ill timed or well-timed depending on your point of view.

'Come with me, Bonny, while I pour the tea. Will you be alright, Joshua, for ten minutes while I talk to my daughter.'

He nodded. Moments later he could hear the muted voices from the kitchen and the ring of bone china as the tea things were assembled.

'Have you slept together?' asked her mother in a flat, business-like manner.

'We have, but we've been extremely careful, taken all the usual precautions.'

'I get the impression that he has been a bit of a ladies' man?' said her mother.

'Yes, he has admitted that, but Aunt May has interrogated him, and he was effusive about how he felt about me, apparently insisting that he loved me. Aunt May told me he had never said that about any of the women he had known previously. She believes him.'

'What did he say to get you into bed?'

'He didn't, I tried to seduce him. I made a terrible job of it, he thought it was hilarious when I admitted what I was doing. Afterwards he quizzed me and took me gently to bed. It was amazing. Whatever happens I will never regret what I did.' All through this conversation Bonny had been bright red in the face with embarrassment.

Later that night Bonny's mother was woken in the small hours by she knew not what. Listening hard she heard the noise again. It was coming from Bonny's room. Swinging her legs from the bed and slipping her feet into her pale pink slippers she was pulling on a pretty lilac cotton dressing gown with a print of large matching pink fluffy roses as she made her way to her daughter's bedroom. Bonny had always been uncomfortable in the dark. A small red riding hood figurine lamp cast enough light to banish the shadows.

Sitting on the bed and tidying the hair from Bonny's face she said, 'Whatever's wrong?'

Bonny, brushing aside her tears and her runny nose with her hand, said, 'Mum, I realise I made a terrible mistake today, while I was looking at the ring in the shop I had a strong premonition that I should ask Joshua to put it on my finger there and then, but the man took it from me and packed it and the moment was gone. Now I am really scared that I will continue to live my life as a lonely, ugly-footed spinster.' Her mother passed her a hanky.

'Bonny, my darling, you are not ugly. You are a beautiful women. I know I have only just met him, but he seems to me to be a decent sort.' She pushed away the thought that entered her head saying, apart from his philandering. 'Aunt May has said he is straight and that he does love you. Would you like to come into the big bed so we can snuggle up and sleep?'

'Yes please,' was the response.

'Will you see him tomorrow?' asked her mother.

'No,' was the reply. 'There are staff off sick so he's doing a double shift. He will ring me early Monday morning.'

Settling down lying back to back as she had done since she was tiny, a sleepy, 'Goodnight, Mum,' was followed minutes later by the sound of her daughter in a deep sleep. Sunday was spent daydreaming and working through various future scenarios in her mind. Going to bed that Sunday night she was on the brink of deciding she would marry him.

* * * * *

Bonny, waking late on Monday morning, rushed into the kitchen, finding her mother eating her second boiled egg still wearing her dressing gown. The debris from the first egg lay on a small white side plate.

'Has Joshua rung, Mother? He said he would ring first thing.'

'I was up early as usual; I have heard nothing.'

'He has changed his mind about marrying me. He said he would ring when he came off duty. My premonition was correct, I have missed my chance, he's, he's, changed his mind. Why ever did I not take the ring back off the jeweller as I was being urged to do and ask Joshua to put it on my finger?'

Her mother rose from the table and wrapped her daughter in a comforting hug, saying as she did so, 'I am sure he will ring.'

'I have to get dressed and go to work.'

'What about breakfast?' asked her mother.

'Sorry, Mum, I'm late and I'm not hungry. I will get something at work.

* * * * *

It was late morning. Bonny was sat at her desk; Jessica was in with Tim in his office. The tears had swept over her. There were no messages of any kind as she sat sipping her hot coffee, not even a scribbled note left for her. She was disappointed in him. She thought he would be bigger than that. He could at least ring her. It was obvious that this was the way he had operated with all the women before her. Take what he wanted and then dump them. My God, she was naïve to believe the rubbish he had told her.

She was special, she was the one, he wanted to marry her. Now angry and pacing around her office and speaking out loud she said, 'Yeah right.' Regaining her desk she plonked herself down and using her hanky she began to mop up her tears.

A gentle tapping lifted her up off her chair and took her the three paces to the door. Opening it he was standing there, his face a grey mask.

'Why are you here?' she barked at him. 'You were supposed to ring me hours ago,' this said as she was looking at her watch. 'I spent most of the night coming to terms with the realisation that you had dumped me like all of those women in your past.' Her anger was a physical entity, fuelled by the solitary years of the past and the ache of her loneliness that once more threatened in the years ahead.

There was a short silence, then in a flat monotone he said, 'I and the team spent sixteen hours trying to save the lives of eight drunken teenagers who had crashed the van they were in on the motorway. One girl died; we did everything we could, but it was all in vain. She was conscious, I was holding her hand, she looked up at me, smiled, shut her eyes and died.' His voice was breaking up, distorted by his pain.

She could tell he was no longer standing in her office; he was back in the theatre watching the girl die, knowing that everybody in the room had done everything they could to save her.

'A boy has lost a leg.' Joshua's face was a blank sheet devoid of any expression. He paused, then said, 'I've come straight from the hospital.'

Bonny stepped forward, saying nothing and wrapped him in her arms. His silent sobbing shook them both. They were unaware that Jessica was standing outside to the right of the door and had heard every word. Walking in, she squeezed his arm and said, 'You need to take him home, Bonny,' fishing in her handbag she pulled out some notes and said, 'Take a taxi. He needs a warm bed and a hot drink. I will get one of the men to make sure the motorbike is safe. I will ring for a taxi now.'

The taxi was waiting outside. Joshua gave the driver the address. Starting to shiver he said, 'I'm cold.' Bonny put her arm round him and held him close, rubbing his hands with hers.

Reaching his home she paid and tipped the cabby. Entering the flat she was aware it was warm and welcoming.

'We are going to get you into bed with a hot water bottle and a hot drink. Tea or coffee?'

'Tea, please.' Was the quiet reply. Joshua began to get undressed as she made her way towards the kitchen. Ten minutes later she walked back into the bedroom carrying a tray with teapot mugs and a milk jug. The hot water bottle was tucked under her arm. Reaching up, Joshua took it from her and held it to his chest. Bonny noticed he was shivering hard. Placing the tea things on the bedside table. She removed her blouse and trousers and climbed into bed beside him. He pulled her to him, trapping the hot water bottle between them. The tears when they came were again silent. Bonny waited until he had got himself back together before she poured the tea.

Hours later she awoke to find him almost nose to nose. He said, 'Thank you for sorting me out. Our team hasn't lost anyone for a long time. it was a terrible shock. I want to talk about us,' he continued, 'I hope you are going to agree to us marrying in the near future, as soon as we can arrange it. The death of that young woman reminded me how tenuous our grip on life can be. I love you, why should we wait? I have never felt like this before. I am only happy when I am with you.'

For years she had watched her friends pairing up, finding boyfriends and girlfriends. Everywhere she looked there were couples holding hands, walking and talking and laughing at shared jokes. Her life by comparison was mundane and often lonely. Joshua offered her an escape from that. She was sure he loved her. This most recent indicator, his falling apart in front of her. Most men's pride would have insisted they remove themselves to somewhere private. The myth dictates that men don't cry.

Bonny could feel herself becoming ever more nervous, she took a long breath in and metaphorically jumped off the cliff by saying, 'Ask me again.'

'Ask you what again?' he queried, looking thoroughly confused.

'I thought there was only one question you wanted an answer to.'

She watched as he realised what the question was. A huge smile lit his face up. He rolled from the bed and knelt down beside it on one knee and said, 'Bonny Atkins, will you marry me?'

'I need to say some things before I answer your question. Firstly, I have grown fond of you in the short time I have known you. You make me laugh, you are extremely practised in bed.' Her face was now bright pink. 'You are kind and caring and you are comfortably off. You want children. My manky leg does not seem to bother you. But I have only known you for five minutes, I cannot know whether I love you, can I?'

Joshua's face was a picture, changing every time Bonny made a new observation, from a smile, to a frown and back again repeatedly.

The young man was silent for some time. Bonny was beginning to think she had scuppered her chances when Joshua replied, 'Will you marry me, Bonny Atkins?'

'Have you heard anything I have said?' she asked.

'I have. I think it's a reasonable statement of where we are now. I am content with this as a contract. So for the third time, woman, will you marry me, please?'

Now smiling she said, 'Yes.'

She held out her left hand so he could slide the ring on her finger.

The young couple napped the day away, recalling their childhoods in the intervals where they were awake at the same time. Joshua's upbringing sounded wonderful to Bonny, the sea, the sand, the perpetual warmth. She did not talk about her own childhood that was a round of doctors and hospital visits.

When they were awake Bonny was aware he was often silent and staring at the ceiling.

Although she felt sure she knew the answer, eventually she asked, 'What are you thinking about?'

'I have been going through everything we did for that young woman; I can't find anything wrong. I am not looking for an excuse, I just need to know if there is anything we could have done better for her. Hopefully the postmortem will clarify why she died.'

The two of them were sitting at the kitchen table eating an evening meal that Joshua had cooked, having declared himself hungry. It was his favourite, bangers and mash with a thick red wine beef gravy. Bonny was pleased to see his colour had returned and he was now more like his usual self. The meal was just what was required. She made a mental note to find out how he did the gravy and the mash, it was the best ever.

Pushing his now empty dinner plate away from him he said, 'We need to tell your mother tonight, before someone else does.'

Bonny nodded her agreement, piling the plates up and walking them to the kitchen she said, 'I'm ready now. We can't leave it too late, she will be in bed.'

Returning to the lounge he handed her his warm leather jacket and pulled on an anorak, 'We need to kit you out for the bike, if you are ok riding it?'

Bonnies face lit up with a big smile. 'I love it,' she said.

Joshua now and in the future rode more carefully when he had such a precious cargo on board.

The couple stood on Mrs Atkins' doorstep waiting for her to respond to Joshua's ringing of the doorbell. Much to her daughter's surprise her mother was still fully dressed when she opened the door. The truth was her mother never got ready for bed until she knew her daughter was safe.

Mrs Atkins sensed the young couple's excitement. 'To what do I owe the pleasure of this visit?' she asked, as they followed her down the hall and into the warmth of the kitchen. The Aga as usual was warming the whole house. Bonny's mum busied herself filling the kettle and placing it on the stove. Joshua had a speech prepared about how much he loved her daughter and that he could afford to look after her. Bonny sensed that he was about to say something. Putting her finger to her lips she motioned him to be quiet. Reaching around her mother, who was standing at the sink, Bonny started assembling the cups. Her left hand passed across her mother's line of sight. It was impossible to miss the sparkles of light given off by the diamonds on her ring. Mrs Atkins' right hand flew to cover her mouth, her left hand grasped the edge of the white enamelled draining board to steady herself.

'Can I look?' asked her mother.

Bonny held her fingers so that the ring was in a good light.

'Oh that's beautiful. It's a rose. You were nearly called Rose, but your father didn't like it. Apparently a distant relative had the same name, and she was rather horrible. It turned out right in the end, you are well named.' Her mother wrapped her arms around her daughter and said, 'I wish you both every happiness.' Both of the women were tearful.

The tea and custard cream biscuits were carried through into the lounge.

Raking the coal fire into life and throwing more fuel on the three of them settled back into the armchairs.

Turning to Joshua, Mrs Atkins asked, 'When did you propose?'

Bonny interrupted his reply and said, 'I made him ask me again this evening.'

'Would you like to know a bit about me?' asked Joshua.

'I have spent a couple of hours with Aunt May and Uncle. They have filled me in with most of your shenanigans, all the women for instance.' She gave the young man a hard look, displaying her disapproval without words. 'She also told me how hard you work and how serious you are about your job. How important it is to you, and that you own your house that you have divided into flats. So you are quite well off. What else should I know?' asked Bonny's mother.

Joshua, looking extremely embarrassed and shaking his head, said, 'That's pretty much it, apart from the fact that I love your daughter and always will.'

Turning to her daughter she asked, 'Where are you going to live?'

Joshua turned to Bonny with a raised questioning eyebrow.

Bonny thought for a moment then said, 'I don't think I would like to sleep on my own at yours, Joshua, when you are on a night shift. I have always shared a room or a house. At first can I move between the two homes, please?'

He nodded his agreement. Her mother agreed. She was pleased that she would see more of her daughter than she thought she would. It would have been nice, she decided, if they had resisted sleeping with each other until they were married but at least they were engaged. Many young people today just leapt into bed with no real commitment or forethought. The young couple went on to discussing some of the basic arrangements. Her mother was quiet watching the interplay between the two of them. It was obvious the two young people were completely committed to each other. Bonny's previously permanent smile that she had lost had returned. Joshua was gentle in his conversation with her. There was a strong comparison between the couple's treatment of each other and her relationship with her deceased husband. There was the usual stab of pain when she remembered him.

Shaking herself, she said, 'When will you want it to happen?'

'This afternoon,' was Joshua's apparently serious response.

Mrs Atkins, now looking totally confused, said, 'Pardon?'

'Take no notice, Mother. He can see no reason why we shouldn't marry now.'

'Mrs Atkins, as you discovered I have known a number of women. Not one of them had any real effect on me. Your daughter, however, asked me if she could sit next to me at the gig in the café, and suddenly there were fireworks going off in my head. My world stood on end.' Reaching for his fiancé's hand and grasping it, he looked into her eyes and said, 'I am so sure you are the one. I'm scared of losing you.' She blew him a kiss.

* * * * *

'I have been thinking about the wedding,' said Joshua. 'I would like to have it in St Lucia so my family can attend. The plane fare would be a big ask for them and anyway it would be more fun in the sun with the white sand and the blue sea.'

'I cannot afford it, but don't let me stop you, it sounds wonderful,' said her mother.

'It is obviously essential that you are at the wedding, Mrs Atkins. I would like you to accept my offer of paying for all your expenses. As you have discovered, I can afford it.'

The older woman was about to refuse his offer when Bonny said, 'Mum, if you are not going nor will I. We will get married in a registry office.'

'Can I call you Mum?' he asked. 'Mum Atkins,' he had said it out loud to see how it sounded and felt on his tongue. His normal certainty had deserted him. 'I can't call you Mrs Atkins, that's very formal. And I am uncomfortable calling you by your first name.'

She thought for a moment. She was warming to this young man. 'Yes,' she replied, 'that would be nice, and I will take you up on your offer. I have never been abroad. We always took our holidays in Brighton.'

'Do you remember the landlady, Mum?' asked her daughter. 'She was a tough old stick.'

'She had to be; her husband was one of the thousands who never came home from the war,' said her mother.

The following morning in the office everyone was so pleased for Bonny. There were lots of hugs and kisses. Jessica and Lynda were delighted. Tim and Sophie phoned her to congratulate her. Joshua never said anything at work the following day. There will be time enough he decided.

CHAPTER 67

Bonny was sitting on a reclining chair on a white sand beach under a large multicoloured sunshade. She was now Mrs Joshua Jones, Mrs Bonny Jones. She loved the sound of the name and the feel of it on her lips. Never in a million years did she ever believe she would be Mrs anything because of her maimed leg. Thinking back, the wedding had been incredible. It had taken place on the beach not far from the where she was sitting now under the palm trees. The sun had shone down out of a clear blue sky. A succession of small lazy waves whispered to the sand as they slid up the beach.

Joshua's family and friends had all dressed in island party dress. There must have been every colour under the sun on show.

She had asked her mother if she would walk her down the aisle, her mother had agreed.

She and Joshua had elected to wear traditional wedding attire, him in a smart three-piece light grey suit and bow tie, her looking stunning in a full-length white bridal gown with a white satin train.

When she had reached the front, Joshua leant towards her and whispered, 'You look amazing.' She could tell he was extremely emotional.

'Thank you,' she replied. Afterwards she remembered little of the service. The vicar had been extremely supportive and had shepherded them both through it. On reflection there were bits she recalled. The giving and receiving of rings moved her, 'With this ring I thee wed.' These were words she had become certain she would never utter let alone to someone like the gorgeous man that had been standing beside her. Then at the end of the service when her husband had been told he could kiss the bride it had been his turn to be overcome. She had seen the tears in the corner of his eyes, their presence underlining how much this ceremony meant to him.

Swivelling round in her chair and looking behind her she could see the lush green of the rainforest and beyond that the twin mountain peaks of this beautiful island of St Lucia.

Since the wedding it had been one long party with some incredible trips dotted through it. The most noteworthy was the helicopter ride that flew them on a sightseeing tour across the island. Flying between the twin peaks was a bit scary. The helicopter was thrown around by the conflicting air currents.

The island music was wonderful, Bob Marley was her favourite. One morning she had come down the steps from their beach house, which she had fallen in love with as soon as she saw it. The round wooden building stood on four heavy stilts above the sand reached by strong wooden steps. A circular pointed wooden roof clad with palm leaves topped it off. Bob Marley was playing on the hotel music system. She was dancing to it as she descended to her favourite song, 'No Woman No Cry'. The staff manning the small beech side café and bar were watching her and smiling at her while they joined in and danced on the spot. The weather was superb, warm sunshine every day. The night skies were amazing. They were ablaze with stars, far more than she would see back home. The nights were short, the parties went on long into the night. Usually Joshua took her to bed at about midnight and continued his appreciation of her beautiful body, his words. When she had questioned his appetite, she smiled to herself. Her fear of being a virgin spinster was being thoroughly put to bed, she laughed at her choice of words.

Most of their guests from the UK had returned home by now but Joshua's family were still entertaining friends from all over the Caribbean.

One thing the young couple were extremely pleased with was that their mothers had become firm friends and had promised to write regularly. While he had said nothing to Bonny, he was hoping she would agree to make St Lucia, his family's home, an annual holiday destination. There were occasions of late when he had really missed his parents and the extended family. Especially recently when the team had not been able to save that beautiful young girl's life. When he had told his mother the details in private she had said nothing, she had just held him allowing him to unload.

When he was silent she said, 'Thank God there are people like you in the world who are prepared to do these demanding jobs. I am very proud of you, my son.' Changing the subject her mother continued, 'Bonny is a beautiful soul. I hope you realise how lucky you are. You could have searched for a lifetime and not found another like her. No sacrifice is too great for you to make to keep her, do you understand?'

He nodded.

His mother jumped on him verbally. 'Nodding is no good, do you understand how important she is now, not just to you but to the rest of the family? We have all fallen in love with her and I can promise you if you discard her like you did those other women you will find it is you that is discarded, Bonny is now part of this family and that will not change.'

'Mother, I didn't mean to be glib just now. She is everything to me, I love her and always will.'

'Good,' was his mother's response before she walked away.

CHAPTER 68

Daisy was taking her evening stroll around the food store; this had become a habit. The purpose was to ensure that everyone had tidied up their stalls, that the floors were swept, the counters were clear and that there were no problems to worry about for the morning.

For some reason her mind leapt back to her start in life growing up with her drunken, abusive father, she recalled him beating her mother, who never cried. She had told Daisy she would not give him the pleasure. She recalled her mother knocking her husband unconscious with a fire iron when she rescued Daisy when he was trying to rape her. Daisy had done everything in her power to stop him. She was kicking him, punching and biting him. Her mother wielding the heavy metal poker had saved Daisy. She had warned her brute of a husband that if he did something like that again she would use the poker and beat him to death. The implement in question stood in pride of place in the kitchen. He didn't attack either of them again.

She remembered the disgusting stench of the last digs. A nearby sewer had cracked and was now leaking into the road outside their window. The walls were old and covered with damp peeling wallpaper. The fungus growing in patterns on it. Their accommodation was so poor because her father drank his wages. He had often beaten her mother for her wages from the office cleaning jobs she and her mother did into the small hours. More than once she had to help her mother stand after her father had finished with her. She recalled that her mother had insisted that she apply for a job here at Sophie's. She could still feel the shock when Sophie had told her she had been successful, the job was hers. Now she was in charge of all this. Who would have believed it? Her mother was proud of her but there seemed to be a distance between them. Recently when she had visited her aunt's house where her mother also lived Daisy asked her why she was treating her differently. She recalled her mother saying, 'We don't really know yur now you've gone up so high. Nobody in the family has never amounted to nuffin'. Now you can afford to send us money to help with the bills. I knows you can afford it cause yur told us how much you earn.' Daisy didn't tell her that she had recently been given a substantial rise. Daisy could see no way of fixing it. Her mother had obviously decided Daisy was no longer a member of the lower working class. Her aunt had summed it up when she said, 'Do you think you are getting above yourself, Daisy?'

The young woman knew her aunt had a sharp side to her and was jealous of anyone who managed to climb out of poverty. What Daisy did not understand was why she was like it. Her husband did two jobs, he was a milkman in the morning and worked an evening shift in a café at night, so they had the money to keep up appearances.

Daisy decided to call it a day. Everything seemed to be as it should be. Taking off her blue and white striped apron that she had suggested for the staff instead of them wearing ordinary clothing, she made her way home.

The next day Daisy was sitting over an early morning cuppa at home. Again she was mulling over the baby decision, yes or no. Yes meant giving up her job and everything she had achieved. While she would not discuss it with anyone she was extremely proud of how far she had come. From living in filthy, disgusting accommodation to one day hopefully owning her own house. She didn't mind if it was a two-bedroom flat. She would, though, prefer a small, terraced house like her aunt's. One thing she was adamant about was that it had to be hers. She was unsure how Declan would feel about that, but he would almost certainly inherit his father's shop back in Ireland.

Did she want babies more than she wanted to be successful? No she didn't. The other thing that had to be faced was that Declan would need some care. She had been warned there would be further hospital visits in the future. Nursing him and a baby would be a full-time job.

Declan, still in his pyjamas, wandered into the room rubbing the sleep from his eyes.

Daisy said, 'Tea?' as she got up and he sat down.

'Yes please,' he replied.

'I've been thinking,' she said, 'about babies. We keep pushing this around and we never decides anythin'. Do you want a baby? We have to be honest about it. I'm going to make your tea.'

Declan sat for some time. How did he really feel about it? There was one thing he was sure of: he didn't want to look after a baby all day long for years and years. He felt sure that he could contribute to their income if he found the right job, even if it was part time. He had noticed that Daisy often slowed down as she passed an estate agent. If he said anything she brushed it off by saying, 'Just looking.' She wanted her own home, understandable considering the sewers she grew up in. There was something else he was going to pursue. There was an advert for a job at their local library. He knew nothing about it, but he was keen on books and reading. He would enquire. So no he didn't want a baby, and didn't want to become a child minder twenty-four seven.

Daisy returned to the room and passed him his tea. 'Have you decided?' she asked.

'I have,' he replied. 'I expect I'm the bad guy here, but I don't want to be changing nappies for years to come and pushing a pram and so on and being a house husband. I'm sorry, but that's the truth.' Declan's Irish accent had come to the fore.

Daisy looked at him for a few seconds trying to calculate whether he meant it or not, she decided that it was a definite no. 'I don't want babies either, I want to see how far I can get in my job. I would be very upset if I had to give it up.'

'So,' responded Declan, 'we're of the same mind. There is one other benefit, we should be able to afford that house you want.'

'Has it become that obvious?' she asked.

'Yes,' he said. He decided not to say anything about the library until he had got the job. Two weeks later he announced that in future he would be working part time as a trainee librarian. Daisy was so pleased for him. She was not sure but she thought he stood taller.

After another eighteen months they were able to put a deposit down on a small two-bed terrace down a cul-de-sac that George Wainwright, the estate agent, had found for them.

Opening the door to her own home Daisy stepped inside, closed the door behind them and burst into tears. Hugging her to him Declan asked, 'Why are you crying?'

'I'm so happy; I've never had a home of my own before. Harry, Sara and your aunt were ever so kind putting me up for so long. As a child we lived one step ahead of the bailiffs, making moonlight flits when my B of a father had drunk the rent again. If you had kept dogs in some of the places we lived in the RSPCA would have had my father in court. This house is mine. No more depending on other people.'

The couple slept on a new mattress on the floor for a while. Their workmates and family gifted them pillows, sheets and blankets, insisting they accepted them. The first morning she awoke in her new home she shut her eyes and thanked God for rescuing her from the hell that had been her previous existence as a child.

CHAPTER 69

Charley and Sally were sitting in the food store café after closing time. The two of them were finishing a short business meeting. Sally had arrived that morning from her flat in the farmhouse in Puglia that Charley now owned since Mrs Vieri's demise. The two women had always got along well so there was no friction.

The younger women had wanted to ask her grandfather's wife a delicate question. Sally was too young to be a grandmother.

Sally, always intuitive said, 'Come on then, what is it you want to say? Do you want me to leave the flat in Puglia?'

'No, no, it's nothing like that, it's about Grandfather. Why did he never visit the shop after we had reopened it?'

Sally stared into the distance for a few seconds before answering, then said, 'I did ask him once if he wanted to visit the shop after you had bought it and reopened it. He did not say anything. He just shook his head and changed the subject. Later on he did admit that he was pleased you had not changed the name.'

'I was always surprised and disappointed that he did not want to see what we had done,' admitted Charley.

'I think he always regretted selling it. I do know he was pleased when you took it on with Tim and Sophie. He always quizzed me when you and I had met to discuss the business. I will be honest with you, Charley, I'd had more than enough of it when he suggested we sell it and move to Italy. I jumped at the idea. I had got bored with the whole thing, the long hours, the repetitiveness of it. Having said all that,' she continued, 'I love what you've done, modernising it and making it relate to the younger fashion-conscious woman. It was Olivia who would not allow us to modernise. She was horrid to me, saying I had no taste or style. She berated Victor at every opportunity. In the end they really disliked each other, they hardly ever spoke.'

'I knew there was a problem,' said Charley, 'they tried to hide it from me.'

'Changing the subject slightly, isn't your new young milliner a treasure, and so gifted. I am seriously thinking of getting something made. I am unsure of what yet, but I will come up with something.'

'She has certainly made a difference to the young women's department,' replied Charley. 'Did you notice most of our mannikins have one of her hats on?'

'Yes I did, she was telling me a number of the older women had asked for a more up-to-date style.'

'We have noticed that. We are starting to look for a younger look for that age group, I know it's a bit of a gamble but it's quite exciting to see if we can influence the styles for the older women,' confirmed Charley. 'So far it is being surprisingly well received.'

'One thing I am sure of, Olivia would never have allowed it,' observed Sally. 'I think her old-fashioned ideas would have killed the business eventually. The older women would have gone elsewhere.'

'And the younger,' confirmed Charley.

'She always ignored me. That's understandable I suppose given my relationship with your grandfather. The only person who got along with her was your father, Tim. She was extremely fond of him.'

'Not in the beginning,' said Charley, 'little bits of information have slipped out down the years from Mummy or Daddy. Apparently there was a battle royale when Daddy told Grandfather he was going to marry Mummy no matter what anyone said.'

'That did come as quite a shock to Victor. There were not many people who stood up to him,' said Sally. 'They did have a good relationship in the end though. Victor often said how highly he thought of him. He was the son he'd never had.'

'One little piece of gossip that you may not have heard, there was a fight in the food hall.'

Sally sat up straight with open mouth and wide eyes. 'You are joking.'

Charley, shaking her head, said, 'No, I'm telling you the truth. Apparently Mrs Price's husband showed up at the food hall, completely out of the blue. They were shouting at each other. Mrs Price had changed the door locks, he couldn't get into the house, and she had emptied their joint account. All this was disclosed at the top of their voices. She has got herself a dog that was barking its head off and jumping at the door trying to get at him. At one stage he lost his footing, she was on him in a flash wielding one of those heavy wooden brooms. She caught him full in the face. He was then bleeding like a stuck pig. The staff had to haul her of him. She threatened him with the police if he ever came back. Apparently he looked very unkempt.'

'How long had he been away?'

'I am not sure; it is years, though.'

Sally, looking at her watch, said, 'Goodness is that the time? I must go,' this said as she was gathering her handbag and shopping bags, then kissing Charley she left.

CHAPTER 70

While this conversation was going on in the UK, Tim and Sophie were sitting in the garden at the rear of the farmhouse in Puglia. Tim had been silent for some time, Sophie assumed he was asleep in the early afternoon sunlight. He had enjoyed two large glasses of the local red wine. Sophie had made a mental note to check up on how many empty bottles were being thrown in the bin each week. She enjoyed a single glass of wine with her evening meal, but that was it. Tim was drinking a lot more.

Tim stirred in his chair, then interrupting his line of thought said, 'I don't want to fly home tomorrow.'

Sophie, surprised, said, 'We can leave it for one day if they can alter the flight.'

'No I mean I don't want to go home at all.'

Now Sophie was beyond surprised. Stunned was a better description. Her workaholic husband was saying … she did not know what he was saying.

'I am sorry, I do not understand. What do you mean?'

'I have been thinking, what else is there to achieve? We have more than enough money, the shops are all in profit and running well. The staff seem happy. Even if we expand it would just be more of the same.'

'What would you find to do, for goodness' sake?'

'Paint.'

'Sorry, I do not understand.'

'I want to paint. Art. Paint people, the countryside, you.'

There was a long silence then Sophie said, 'Would you have lessons?'

'No, I used to be able to paint. I believe it would all come back once I started.'

'Who said you could paint?'

'The art master. I know this is bragging but some of my paintings were hung in the school corridor, I drew a friend of mine and when that was hung in the corridor people recognised who it was. I picture myself with an easel, a fold up chair, a rucksack for all the kit that will include a bottle of wine and an old felt hat.'

'Do you mean it?' she asked.

'Yes, I do.'

'Do you want me to stand away as well?'

'That's up to you. Although I had hoped you would stay on, perhaps working at long range.'

'We would have to look at how we set it all up,' she added.

Tim said, 'We could promote Adam to vice chair, give him a lot more responsibility and more money of course. He is a clever man. I bet he would jump at the chance to run it day to day. I'm sure you and Adam could sort it out.'

Sophie nodded and then said, 'Who would chair it?'

'You, I hope, I am adamant it has to be a Vieri or a Cooper at the helm. You tick both boxes.'

'It would mean we will be apart more,' she added.

'Not if I come with you on the longer visits. I hope we can hand over to Charley before too long.'

* * * * *

Flying back to the UK in first class Sophie revealed the list of the chair and vice chair, directors and shareholders and the changes in their roles to Tim.

Tim was silent for some time after he had read it. He was gazing out of the window unseeing. After a moment's reflection he said, 'That seems pretty good to me.'

'Do you agree with it?' she asked.

There was another pause while he read through it again, then nodding he said, 'Yes that's fine.'

'Are you sure you want to step down as chairman?' she asked.

'Yes,' was his response. 'You are the obvious choice for the role. Will you stay on at Mr Wells as finance director?'

Shaking her head, she said, 'No. For Sophie's, with a bit of luck, all I will have to do is make a few phone calls and the monthly trip home. Adam and I should be able to handle the business side together. If there is a major problem I will get on a plane.'

'I will always help if you need me,' said Tim.

'I will always need you, my darling,' said Sophie, leaning in and kissing his cheek. 'One of my major jobs will be to train Charley to take over from me.'

'I worry the job seems to be her whole focus,' said Tim. 'I wonder who she takes after?'

Sophie burst out laughing. 'You,' she said, 'she is her father's daughter. I am sure that like you one part of her brain is always working on some part of the business.'

* * * * *

The following week back in Britain in Tim's office there were a number of surprises. When Tim had asked Oliver to come to his office the young man had arrived unsure why he was there.

When both men were seated Tim explained that he intended to retire and that Sophie would be taking over the chairmanship. 'But,' he said, 'most of the time she will be working at long range from Italy, so we need someone in charge here full time. To that end I would like to offer you the vice chairman's job.'

Oliver looked as though someone had hit him. Struggling to control his emotions he said, 'I don't know what to say, Tim. I never dreamt I would get to that level.'

'You haven't agreed to do it yet.'

'I will do it. Thank you so much. I am lost for words.'

'We will have to get the board's approval, but I don't anticipate any problems with that. Now the other part of your job is to help my daughter Charley to get ready to take over in the future. Is that a problem? I envisage at that point you will work hand in hand. Obviously that is still some time in the future.'

Oliver was shaking his head then said, 'I see no problem. We get along well now, why should it be different then? Tim, I need to say a massive thank you for having the confidence in me to offer the job.'

Tim said, 'Sophie and I have every confidence in you.'

* * * * *

Tim had no sooner informed the board of his intention to resign the chairmanship than his father revealed his intention to also retire. Harry said, 'I'm also going to retire as of now.'

After some chatter, Tim said, 'Can I bring us back to order please? I propose Sophie to take over my role.' There was universal agreement, the vote clinched it.

Tim rose from his seat behind his beautiful honey-coloured oak desk and took a seat facing it with his back to the windows. Moments later his father and Harry joined him.

Sophie, who had moved to Tim's former chair at the desk, said, 'There is one other piece of business we need your approval for. I shall be working from Italy most of the time, so we need someone here to run the business day to day. Given the circumstances we have asked Oliver to take over the role of vice chair assuming there is a majority agreement here today. Can we vote please? Those for the proposal.' There was a universal show of hands for Oliver's promotion. 'I declare that Oliver has been voted into the post of vice chair.'

Jessica, who had been doing her usual task of minute taking, put her pad down and moved to kiss her husband. When she stood up to retake her seat it became apparent that she was wearing a huge smile and crying her eyes out. 'Please ignore me,' she said, mopping up the tears.

Now everyone was laughing and clapping and shaking Oliver's hand. When it all calmed down Sophie noticed that Oliver had his hand raised.

Sophie said, 'Yes, Oliver,' firmly enough to silence the conversations.

Oliver sat forward in his seat and said, 'Thank you everyone for your confidence in me. I promise to do the job to the best of my ability. However, I am extremely concerned that the three people who have the greatest knowledge and the experience of the business have all resigned. I know you have a lot of experience, Madam Chair, but I am worried.'

Tim stayed quiet; this was now down to his wife.

'All the retirees are shareholder and therefore are eligible to vote and attend meetings. Tim has already assured me that if we need his advice he will be happy to give it. I assume the two older men will also agree to do so.' Looking at Harry and Tom, they were both nodding.

*

Earlier that morning, sitting with Sophie in Mrs Oakes, the solicitor's office poised to sign all the documents placed in front of him. Tim hesitated and stared out of the window, not seeing the stream of traffic that crawled by outside. Suddenly the enormity of what he was about to do hit him.

All the thousands of hours he had worked down the years reaching this moment in time. For a moment he was unable to remember when he had started work. He was only thirteen at the time of his mother's death.

His father had become more and more incapable because of the loss of his wife. At fifteen Tim had left school and taken over the family delicatessen stall. It was then he decided to build an empire. Looking back he believed he had made a pretty good stab at it. There were six houses rented out. The two shops, the food hall, the restaurant, the cafés. The Vieri's home and his and Sophie's family home the *Sea Maiden*. He was aware that one of the reasons for his success was the extremely generous sum his aunt had gifted him in her will.

It was Sophie speaking his name that jerked him back to the here and now. He leant forward and signed the papers.

THE END

Bill Carmen's book are available from his website www.billcarmen.com or on billcarmen@btinternet.com or contact him direct for a signed copy on 0770 380 9619.

LOVE IN STORE, book one, the paperback is only available directly. Post and packing within the UK is £3.50. His books are also available from the usual outlets and amazon etc.

Bill Carmen spent the first 10 years of his life afloat in a house boat on the river Thames Near Kingston. He was taught to row at five years of age. He still retains a love of the water. His other interests apart from writing is growing orchids and travelling. *THE NEXT GENERATION* is the third book in the LOVE IN STORE saga.

Books in this series:

Love in Store

Tim's Progress

Next Generation